D1518331

Cover designed by Lisa Messegee, TheWriteDesigner.com

This book is a work of fiction. Names, characters, places, and incidents either are products of the author's imagination or are used fictitiously. Any resemblance to actual persons, living or dead, events, or locales is entirely coincidental.

Celeste Barclay
Visit my website at www.celestebarclay.com

Printed in the United States of America

First Printing: Nov 2018
Celeste Barclay

ISBN-13 9781790782611

His Highland Pledge

The Clan Sinclair Book 4

Celeste Barclay

This is novel is dedicated to the hopeless romantics who still believe in happily ever after, even if only in a book. Let this be one more tale where the girl gets her guy.

~Happy Reading~
Celeste

The Clan Sinclair

Book 0 *Their Highland Beginning, Prequel Novella*
    Liam Sinclair and Kyla Sutherland
    FREE
    Book Funnel
    MyBookCave
    Prolific Works

Book 1 *His Highland Lass*
    Mairghread Sinclair and Tristan Mackay

Book 2 *His Bonnie Highland Temptation*
    Callum Sinclair and Siùsan Mackenzie

Book 3 *His Highland Prize*
    Alexander Sinclair and Brighde Kerr

Book 4   *His Highland Pledge*- Magnus Sinclair and Deirdre Fraser

Book 5   TBD-Tavish Sinclair and Ceit Comyn

The Clan Sinclair

Liam Sinclair m. Kyla Sutherland

    b. Callum Sinclair m. Siùsan Mackenzie (SH-IY-oo-san)
        b. Thormud Seamus Magnus Sinclair (TOR-mood SHAY-mus)
        b. Rose Kyla Sinclair

    b. Alexander Sinclair m. Brighde Kerr (BREE-ju KAIR)
    b. Saoirse Sinead Sinclair (SEER-sha shi-NAYD)

    b. Tavish Sinclair m. Ceit Comyn (KAIT-ch CUM-in)

    b. Magnus Sinclair m. Deirdre Fraser (DEER-dreh FRA-zer)

    b. Mairghread Sinclair m. Tristan Mackay (Mah-GAID)
        b. "Wee" Liam Brodie Mackay

Chapter One

Magnus Sinclair detested being at the royal court. There was nothing redeemable in his eyes, and his face ensured everyone knew the Highland giant was not there to exchange pleasantries. Standing at six and a half feet tall, he towered over almost every man in the king's household and all the men who sought the monarch's attention. Only a few visiting Highlanders mirrored him in height and physique. As though sticking out like a sore thumb from his height and his insistence upon wearing his plaid was not enough, he felt naked without his claymore. Locked away in his chamber, his two-handed broadsword was as much a part of him as either hand. For the safety of the king and his family, they allowed no one to wear or carry a sword into the main gathering hall. Magnus's sword forged to accommodate his size, and even though custom designed, the enormous sword looked like little more than a young lad's wooden practice sword when Magnus held it. Needless to say, it was not a welcome sight strapped to his back. When he arrived the day before, he resigned himself to just carrying his dirks, of which he had at least eight on various parts of his body.

Arriving early the previous morning, Magnus spent all of the day and much of the evening in a passageway, standing, awaiting an audience with the king. This day came and went, just as the previous one had, with no indicator of when the king would meet with him. This only aggravated Magnus more as a representative from the Sinclair clan summoned rather than volunteered to attend court.

The royal court's opulence was lost on Magnus as he saw no need for the ornate decorations, the expensive fabric, the great expenditures on excessive food, or the waste on such things as hundreds of candles. He understood the king's significant birthright and could rationalize the necessity for the king to maintain an aura of wealth, but the material items held no importance to him. He was much more concerned with whether the king would continue to be a fair and judicious leader.

Magnus craned his neck to look over the crowd and catch sight of the king and queen entering the massive gathering hall from the far side. Resolved not to be ignored any longer, Magnus weaved his way through the crowd. He knew this was not the time for a private audience, but he determined to make his presence known to the king. As his father's, Laird Liam Sinclair, representative, he was in the wretched smelling, overcrowded, viper's nest to settle the ongoing dispute between the Sinclairs and the Gunns complicated by a potential feud with the Kerrs and de Soules. He was not there to make the pretty and hobnob with the grasping aristocrats with whom he was peers. His impatience to return to his home in the Highlands overlooking the North Sea rolled off him like the waves that crashed along the rocks he could see from his chamber in Castle Dunbeath.

Couldnae ma bluidy brothers manage to marry without killing anyone? First, it was Callum killing Laird Gunn's brother for kidnapping and molesting Siùsan, which I didna blame him for since I was ready to run him through too. Then it was Alexander's hiding Brighde away that brought not only the Gunns but the Kerrs and de Soules along for the fun too. I dinna blame him for that either, as I was the one who laid waste to the Gunn maself. But now the Gunn laird is dead and buried alongside the Kerr laird and Randolph de Soules. It wouldnae surprise me if the grass died over their rotting souls. And I'm stuck here making nice with these Lowland fops and trying to appease a king who's worried he looks incapable of controlling the Highlands. The sooner he, and everyone else who isnae a Highlander, realizes we canna be controlled nor manipulated, the better off Scotland would be.

Magnus forced his scowl to relax into the most neutral face he could muster. He only looked to be grimacing now instead of ready to take someone's head off. He did not have to worry about the crowds of people who thronged about as they parted for him like he was Moses brought back from the dead. Magnus attempted to move about without bumping into people, but there were far too many bodies for even such a large room. He neared the dais when he heard a sound that froze him in his tracks and thrust him back in time seven years.

He would recognize that peal of laughter anywhere. It was a sound that was so etched into his every nerve and fiber he could never forget it. He could feel his pulse speed up, his brow broke out in dots of perspiration, and his hands felt clammy. The hammering of his heart in his ears almost drowned out the offending sound but not quite. Slowly, he turned to face the table where the owner of the throaty laugh sat. He knew exactly who would be seated there but seeing Deirdre Fraser for the first time in seven years felt like a poleax just swung into his gut. His visceral reaction to seeing the lady for the first time in so many years made him feel so physically ill he wanted to run and hide for the first time since he was a wean. He forced himself to take several deep and calming breaths as he managed to put one foot in front of the other and continue his path to the dais. Accustomed to the whispers that followed him about everywhere he went, Magnus paid little attention to them now, especially those coming from women. Coupled with his impressive height, his dark chestnut hair gleamed with threads of gold in the light from the hundreds of candles in the chandeliers, and women frequently complimented his dark chocolate eyes that had an amber starburst around the pupils. His arms were as wide around as a blacksmith's and his legs were as sturdy as two oak tree trunks. His chest and shoulders were so broad he had to turn sideways to make his way through doors in this castle. That was yet another thing he missed about home; in the Highlands, they made doors for men, not boys, to pass through. Women began chasing Magnus when he was barely over four and ten. He began paying them attention when he was five and ten, and by seven and ten, he was ready to swear them all off. All but one, Deirdre Fraser. He moved past court ladies who tried to gain his attention. He never had an interest in their provocative stares and glancing touches, and he was in even less of a mood to tolerate them.

Deirdre Fraser forced herself to laugh at another incomprehensible joke her cousin Elizabeth yet again mistold. She stopped listening quite some time ago but at least knew when she had to give an expected response. Her mind was drifting off to Alpin, her newest eyasses. The young falcon was only a few weeks old and had a deformed claw that worried her. She was mulling over how she might make her escape to check on him when Mary Kerr elbowed her in the ribs.

"Look at that heathen! Why he's gigantic and hardly clothed. I do not understand why those Highlanders believe walking around in a blanket is an appropriate means of attire for His Grace's court. That man is larger than any other I have ever seen, and I am sure I see knives on him. Zounds! Are we safe? What if he turns beserker and attacks the king or worse tries to steal us, ladies, away?"

Deirdre forced herself to bite her tongue. She and her family had lived at court long enough that most of the queen's ladies-in-waiting forgot that she, too, was a Highlander. Her brogue had softened over the past half a score of years to a light burr, but in her heart, she was still a Highlander and would not change that for all the gowns and courtly graces foisted upon her.

Elizabeth leaned around her to see for herself what had caused Mary to become so agitated. She gasped and turned to Deirdre, but before she could whisper a warning to her cousin, Mary was speaking again.

"I believe he's one of those barbarian Sinclairs. Did you hear what they did to my father? I cannot believe he has the audacity to show his face in here. He should be chained up and dropped into the oubliette."

Deirdre froze.

Ever so slowly, she turned on the bench where she sat and scanned the crowd. It took only the length of a breath to find Magnus Sinclair. He was walking parallel to her table with his head held high and his eyes focused forwards, and as he came even with her, his eyes could not help but shift and lock onto hers. Only a heartbeat later he refocused on making his way to the king, and Deirdre was attempting to maneuver herself out of her seat without tripping over all of her skirts.

3

What in the name of St. Columbo's bones is he doing here? And why the devil canna I get over this bench without putting ma slipper through ma hem? Dammit! I need out now and not fall on ma bluidy face in the process. I canna stay here.

Deirdre righted her kirtle and step back from the table.

"Dee, where are you going," Elizabeth hissed.

"Ye ken I canna stay here. I canna breathe," Deirdre whispered back.

"Lady Deirdre, what did you say? Why in heavens do you suddenly sound like some peasant? You sound like one of *those* people," and she gestured toward Magnus.

"I beg your pardon, Lady Mary, but I am suddenly not feeling well. I believe I should not have had that last cup of wine until after I ate. Please excuse me."

Without waiting for a response from Mary or her cousin, Deirdre made her way as inconspicuously as she could to the wall that would lead to doors to the passageway to her private chamber. Her eyes swung between where Magnus now stood and where she knew her parents, or specifically her father, sat.

Dear God in Heaven, please dinna let Da see him. Not yet at least. I dinna want to be here for that reunion. I dinna want any reunions.

Bah, ye little liar. Ye ken that isnae true. Ye've craved seeing him again every day for the past seven years.

Now he is here, and I'm running away. Just like I did seven years ago. I canna see him now or talk to him here. But I must find a way. I canna ken he is here and not be near him. If I could just touch him once. Just once to ken, he is real. God how I miss him.

Deirdre swallowed the sob that tried to escape. Her eyes were becoming glassy, and she felt unsteady on her feet. She tried to move faster towards the exit, but even with servants about to serve the meal, there were still a substantial amount of people milling about and standing between her and escape.

She made it to the door when she felt a body press against her from behind. She recognized it thanks to the perfume saturated satin clothes used to hide a suffocating odor. A bony hand gripped her arm, and a whiny voice came from just behind her ear.

"Just where do you think you are sneaking off to, my dove?" Archibald Hay sneered. He pinched the skin on the back of her arm, and it stung even though she had thick fabric between her skin and his. She could not fathom the disgust she would feel if and when his skin contacted hers.

"I am feeling a little peaked and thought to retire early. I hope I have not caught the ague, but if so, I would not want to give it to you, my lord. It would be best if I was not to close to anyone."

"I have a very healthy constitution. Once we wed, we shall be together quite a bit. At least until you birth me my two sons. I suppose I shall have to get used to your sickly nature if you turn out prone to illness. As long as you can survive the

4

birth, we shall get along quite nicely." Hay tugged at her arm and dragged her from the hall.

Deirdre looked over her shoulder and scanned the room for her father. A man she had purposely just avoided, her father was the one man she most needed to find. She attempted to push her heels into the floor and slow their progress, but even though he was a thin man, Hay was still stronger than her.

"Come along," she could not miss the note of warning as they passed through the doorway and he yanked her down the passageway.

Chapter Two

Magnus faced the king but his eyes had not left Deirdre since he walked past. He forced himself to look forward after catching her eye, but once he could angle himself to see her again, he watched like one of her prized falcons.

Why do I have to remember every little detail as though it were just a day ago? It's been seven long, miserable years, and it's as though it was yesterday we were last together.

"Magnus, I believe you wanted an audience with me and now your mind is clearly elsewhere," the king sounded annoyed by the lack of attention he received from the youngest son of one of his favorite lairds. The Sinclairs were one of the most loyal clans he had in the Highlands, even across all of Scotland. The king was amenable to supporting the Sinclairs in resolving their current feuds but not if Magnus could not remember his manners.

"Aye, sire. But just a wee moment ago, I saw Lady Deirdre Fraser leaving with a mon who didna seem vera gentle with her person. Who might he be?"

"That would most likely have been Archibald Hay, the younger nephew of Lord Hay. Fraser is in the process of arranging a betrothal between Hay and his daughter. I rather like the lass and her father dotes upon her, so I cannot understand why he would even remotely consider marrying her off to him."

Magnus thought his head would explode. The ringing in his ears was back, and anger he reserved for the battlefield coursed through him. He leaned forward into a step before he realized from whom he was about to walk away.

"Begging yer pardon, Yer Grace, but I wanted to greet ye and thank ye for the accommodations ye've provided during ma stay. I dinna want to keep ye from yer supper or yer advisors who seem to grow anxious. If ye will excuse me, I shall find ma way to a table."

Magnus bowed and backed away before the king could do more than nod. As he took another two steps back, the crowd filled in around him, so he could swing around and make his way to the door. He did not attempt subtlety while leaving.

If she thinks she is marrying that mon or any other, then she will explain herself to nae just me but the bluidy pope.

Magnus's angry stride made it obvious to the guards he intended to leave, so the two men opened wide both doors. He passed through and scanned the passageway, spotting two figures just as the larger one pushed the smaller one into an alcove.

Magnus began to run.

"Lord Archibald, you will ruin my gown if you are not careful. My maid will surely tell my parents if I arrive with a ruined gown. They will not appreciate the wasted expense."

"I will buy you all the pretty gowns you will need, which will not be many since I intend to take you back to Slains Castle where you will not have to worry since it is remote, and no one shall visit." He spun Deirdre around and pulled her to him. His hands grasped the front of the gown and pulled. The sturdy silk and embroidered satin of her court gown were strong enough to withstand his manhandling.

"Lord Archibald, stop. Ye canna be doing this. This isnae right nor proper. Stop now." A hand whipped through the air and a whistle followed just before Hay's palm contacted Deirdre's cheek.

"I never want to hear that barbaric brogue come out from between your lips, or I will be shoving something between them to keep them quiet. Do you understand my meaning?"

Deirdre was too scared and now too angry to think about her accent. She knew she had precious few minutes left to make her escape before Hay ensured there would be a wedding without question. She struggled against him and tried to push him away. She shoved him back a few steps, but his inability to stand his ground against a woman only infuriated him.

"Good to know you like it rough. We shall get along quite well in the bedchamber or any other chamber I desire. Someone needs to teach you obedience. Your weak-willed father has spoiled you entirely too much. You're in need of someone who will break that stubborn streak."

Deirdre respected her father, and while she would admit to herself that he had numerous and significant flaws, she would not stand for anyone disparaging him even if done in private. She tried to push her way past the odious man, but he wrapped his arm around her waist and practically carried her all the way into the back of the alcove until her back hit a wall.

"Dinna! Stop!" Deirdre screamed as loud as she could, hoping at least one guard would realize that she had not agreed to this tryst or someone passing by might inquire why a young woman was calling out for rescue.

As Hay struggled to pin her against the wall while fumbling with his breeks, Deirdre struggled to reach her own dirk. She began wearing dirks the summer she turned three and ten. It was Magnus who had insisted that she carry protection against unwanted attention. Her only problem now was that she could not reach either dirk strapped to her thigh without lifting her skirts, and she had no intention of offering anything Hay might consider an invitation.

Suddenly, the hand that was unfastening his pants was pulling her hand forward. Her fingers brushed against something small and hard. She knew what it was, and she let forth the most blood-curdling scream she could muster as Hay forced her to wrap her fingers around his manhood.

She screamed yet again just as Magnus grabbed a lit torch from a wall sconce before pushing the curtain aside. He dropped it in the bracket inside the entrance.

Before she could attempt to pull her hand away, someone flung the curtain open and the frame of a very large and very irate man filled the opening and blocked out any light that might have slid in. Lord Archibald was lifted off his feet and thrown back towards the passageway.

Deirdre knew within an instant who came to rescue her. She shrank back into the shadows to avoid anyone seeing her. The last thing she needed was for a witness to identify her as being the woman caught in a dark and secluded area with Lord Archibald Hay. She would have happily stayed hidden until both men left, but when she saw the gleam of metal in Magnus's hand, she knew only one man would walk away if she did not step forward.

"Ye thought ye could rape yer way to making her yer wife. Ye thought ye would overpower her, harm her, then claim her. I saw ye pushing her into here, and I heard all of her screams. The lass didna want ye, and I would venture ma last fourthling she never will want ye. I wouldnae set yer heart on a betrothal." Magnus raised his arm and drew it back in preparation to castrate the man. Even in his anger, he knew he could not kill the man in the king's castle. Regardless of whether or not he was defending a woman, killing anyone, especially a border lord, would see him locked away and that would only leave Deirdre more defenseless. He would have to content himself with making sure Archibald Hay would never impose himself upon another woman.

"Magnus," Deirdre whispered, "please dinna. Nae here. Dinna kill him. Nae over me. Dinna forfeit yer life with his."

"I amnae going to kill the bastard only geld him." He pulled his arm back further and was ready to strike when two small hands rested on his back, and he felt her lean around him.

"He's too well connected. He has ties to the de Soules, Magnus." Deirdre's voice was barely audible but the name de Soules was enough to make him pause. "Just make him go away, please. Magnus, just make him leave."

Magnus chanced a glance over his shoulder and quickly took in her disheveled hair and the mangled front of her gown. His desire to kill Hay rose again, but he also saw the apprehension in her eyes. He nodded once and turned back to Hay.

"Ye live to see another day. But come near her again, threaten her again, and ye willna see another sunset." He pulled Hay back to his feet and pulled him by the collar to the doorway. He nudged him out and stood in his most intimidating stance with his feet hip-width apart and arms crossed. He, his father, and brothers all stood this way so often that it was second nature to them, but it had the desired effect of frightening most people away.

"You may think you've won, Highlander, but she will be my wife soon enough. Then you will not be able to touch me, but I will certainly touch her. Any and every way I want."

Magnus flexed his chest, and Hayscrambled to his feet. Seeing Magnus's arms flex, Hay hastily retreated down the passageway. Once he was out of sight, Magnus pulled the curtain closed before turning to face the one woman who was the bane of his existence, the torment of his life, and the keeper of his heart.

Deirdre took in the man who stood in front of her. In so many ways he was a complete stranger. He had filled out and seemingly doubled in size since she last saw him. He was barely more than a young man then. The person in front of her was a battle-seasoned warrior. She worried her bottom lip as she breathed in the scent that wafted through her mind just as she fell asleep. The pine and bergamot scent along with something uniquely his. Her eyes slid closed as the pad of his thumb pried her lip loose.

This was the gesture of a lover, not a stranger. Her senses filled with memories from what felt like a lifetime ago, what was a lifetime ago. His hand cupped her cheek, and his long fingers massaged tension from the base of her scalp.

"Ye remember."

"How could I ever forget?"

Deirdre opened her eyes to look into his smoky brown ones just as she had done so many times over the years before being forced apart.

"Magnus, ye ken I didna choose to be in here, right? I didna choose any of it." Her voice trailed off as the lump in her throat felt as though it would strangle her.

"I ken ye didna want to come in here. I saw him with ye before ye even left the gathering hall, then I saw him bring ye in here, and I heard yer screams. Would that I never have to hear them again." He used his other hand to brush her honey-colored spiral curls back over her shoulder. "I also ken that neither of us had any say in how things stand. I took a long time to accept that, but I have."

"Ye accept it? Deirdre shrank back and looked around wildy, suddenly needing to escape Magnus almost as badly as she did Hay.

"Wheesht, eun beag."

9

Little bird. Zounds. How I have missed hearing that. I canna stand Archibald calling me his dove, but to hear Magnus call me his little bird makes everything feel right again. But it isnae right. It maynae ever be right again.

A soft sob escaped her as she tried to squeeze past the monolith that stood between her and the exit.

Magnus pulled her in and wrapped his arms around her. At a foot shorter than Magnus, Deirdre's head rested squarely in the center of his chest. She could hear the steady, albeit fast, rhythm of his heart. The cadence calmed her as it always had; however, that only made her remember it had been years since she had heard it or felt it. She tried to pull back, but while he did not force her to stay in place, he did not let go. Deirdre knew if she stepped back again, he would release her. She did not want that after all.

"Ye accept it?" She repeated.

"Aye, I accepted that ye werenae responsible for yer father's decisions. Ye made yer choice, and I have accepted it."

Deirdre's sigh of relief was audible, and Magnus looked down at her raising one brow.

"I thought ye accepted that we canna be together."

"Canna? Is that what ye've accepted?"

"Nay. The heavens ken I would be better off if I could, but I dinna think I will ever accept losing ye."

"Deir, what are ye talking aboot losing me? I dinna think ye mean just the time apart. Ye chose to follow yer father instead."

"I dinna want to talk aboot this. Nae here and nae now."

"Then when? When exactly do ye think we will have a chance to be alone again? Once yer father kens I'm here, if he hasnae already heard from Hay or someone else, he willna let ye in spitting distance of me. If ye dinna want me near ye, if ye dinna want me anymore, then say as much, lass. But dinna think it will be enough to end things or to allow ye to marry someone else."

Deirdre heard the hard edge creeping into his voice and the unbending steel that laced each of his final words. She shook her head and once again felt tears pricking behind her eyelids, but after years of crying herself to sleep every night, she seemed to have none left to fall.

"How could ye think I dinna want ye anymore? It's ye who's moved on. It's ye who ignored every attempt I made."

"Moved on? Attempts? I havenae moved a barleycorn on, and ye are the one who turned away every attempt I made to contact ye."

"What attempts? Ye barely waited for me to leave the last gathering before ye had another lass on yer lap. Ye forgot aboot me and carried on yer merry way."

Deirdre watched as a stone mask slipped down over Magnus's face. A hardness entered his eyes she never saw before. A shiver ran down her spine, and when he spoke again, the void of emotion made the hair on her arms stand up.

"Dinna think to pass off on me what ye are guilty of yerself. Ye left that gathering without saying goodbye. Ye didnae even look back over yer shoulder. Since then, ye sent back every single one of ma letters. Do ye have any idea just how many pieces of folded vellum I have tucked away in ma chamber? Let us see. There are fifty-two sennights in a year, and it's been seven years. That would be three hundred and sixty-four letters carried by one of ma clan's messengers only to be brought back to me. Aye, ye heard me. One for each sennight. In the beginning, I sent them off the first day of each sennight. Then it became every fortnight, and eventually every moon. Even to this day, one of our messengers travels with four letters to either Castle Dounie or wherever yer clan says ye are in residence."

"Three hundred and sixty-four?" Deirdre emphatically shook her head. "That canna be. How could I nae have received a single one of those? I have never received a letter or missive of any kind from ye once we separated."

"We didna separate. Ye were taken from me," Magnus growled. "And wait just a wee moment. I'd like to go back to the part where ye claimed I've been unfaithful. Just which lass was on ma lap and when?"

"Ma sisters told me they saw ye in the mead tent after ma father told ye that we couldnae wed. They said they saw ye with some wench sprawled across ye with her tits half hanging out." Deirdre could feel her cheeks heating from anger and embarrassment. She knew she may swear from time to time, but she usually was not vulgar.

Magnus pulled his arms in and crossed them. He looked down at her with a sneer that almost rivaled Hay's.

"Did ye sisters tell ye that before or after they heard yer father malign me? Ye do remember that I have three older brothers, and we're three peas in a pod. Did it cross yer mind that mayhap it wasnae me but one of them? Or more likely, yer sisters saw naught because there was naught to see. Just what were those fine young ladies doing near a mead tent, to begin with? How did they come to be near such a place to have witnessed such a thing?"

It forced Deirdre to consider what her family had told her so long ago. She had rebelled against the very notion, but her sisters and then father and mother had been so adamant that Magnus had barely batted an eye when her family forced her to leave without saying goodbye.

"I have heard the tales though. Even all the way at court, ye Sinclair brothers are well renowned for yer charm and appeal to the ladies. I have heard what ye have become."

Magnus leaned all the way forward so that their noses were nearly touching.

"And just what have I become? Ye seem to ken a great deal aboot me when we havenae seen each other in seven years, and ye definitely havenae heard any of the news I've tried to share with ye."

Deirdre licked her lips and pushed her hair off her shoulder before wiping her hands on her kirtle. She felt ill thinking about and now having to say what they forced her to hear repeatedly throughout the past seven years.

"I ken that ye are popular with the ladies. Ye go gallivanting with yer randy brothers and are often found with a wench on yer lap. Ye tup willing lasses whenever one catches yer eye, and ye have quite the reputation as a lover."

There. She had said it, and now she wanted to be violently ill all over his calf-skin boots. Black spots danced around the corners of her eyes, and her body swayed. Strong but gentle hands grasped her arms as she felt herself being walked over to a bench she had not noticed before. She expected to feel the cold firmness of stone beneath her; however, her backside met the warm firmness of his lap.

"Deirdre, hear me now for I willnae have ye gainsaying me on this. Ye kenned that I had been with a few other women before I met ye that first summer. I remember exactly what ye were wearing and what ye were doing the vera first time I ever laid eyes on ye, but ye were barely three and ten, and I was a lusty and curious six and ten. I told ye from the vera start I bedded ma first barmaid when I was barely five and ten. I can thank Callum for that saint's day gift, and I can thank Mairghread for interrupting the only other time I tried tupping a barmaid. I was interested in ye, but ye were far too young that first summer. Ye ken already that I wasna celibate between that summer and the next, but neither was I some man whore. I was simply healthy and curious. That following summer though, when I started courting ye, everything changed. I havenae been with any woman but ye since I was seven and ten, Deirdre. Did ye nae believe me when I told ye that I would wait for ye? Did ye nae believe me when I said I hadnae been with anyone else during our entire courtship? How could ye believe I would be with another woman once we were wed?"

"Magnus, we handfasted, and it has certainly been far more than a year and a day."

"And I told ye before we pledged ourselves, a handfast was as good as a kirking. That never once changed, Deir. Ye are still ma wife, and I am still yer husband." Deirdre heard him swallow. "Unless ye believed it was only for a year and a day, and ye dinna want to be bound to me. Mayhap ye have already moved on, or ye dinna want to be stuck with me now that ye have an opportunity to marry again."

Deirdre needed space. She scooted off Magnus's lap, and he let her go. She put her hands on her hips and looked down at him, then dropped her arms before turning away, but just as quickly, she spun back around. With her hands on her hips again, she looked almost squarely into his eyes even though he sat and she stood.

"I didna think it was just for a year and a day, but what was I supposed to think when I heard all these stories aboot ye with other women. Do ye have any idea how that pained me? How it still pains me? I dinna want to marry anyone else, certainly nae Archibald. To me, ye have always been ma husband, but I didna think ye still considered me yer wife." She dropped her arms and seemed to wilt before Magnus's eyes.

He guided her back onto his lap and tucked her head below his chin.

"Eun beag, there is much that we need to talk aboot, and much we need to resolve that we canna do now. But if naught else, I need ye to ken one thing. I havenae been with any other woman, nae touched, kissed, nor bedded any, since before I began courting ye. That was half a score of years ago. I have three older brothers who enjoy drinking and carousing as much as any other mon our ages. I do go with them, I do drink, but it was Callum and still is Tavish who chases the ladies. Alex was known to bed a lass here and there, but he was naught like Callum and Tavish. More often than nae, Alex and I shared a chamber and retired early while Callum and Tavish did whatever it was they did. Deir, I canna say this without sounding conceited, but it is the truth. Women chase me, but I dinna want aught to do with them. They see ma size and wonder if the auld wives' tales are true. Then when they canna catch ma eye or gain ma attention, they want the chase. I admit I have used this to ma advantage to gain information, save a coin or two, or to distract someone, but I havenae ever done aught considered unfaithful. Ye ken what fidelity means to the Sinclairs, especially the men of the laird's family. Ye must remember. Dinna ye?"

Chapter Three

*M*agnus's question transported Deirdre back in time. She recalled so vividly the first time she saw Magnus. She was a young lass of only three and ten, but at five and ten, he was already the most gorgeous man she had ever seen. In her mind, she was no longer in the king's castle, but a Highland gathering hosted by her own clan.

~~~

"Coming, Mama!" Deirdre scrambled to collect all of her books and sheets of vellum along with her inkwell and quill. Her mother was rarely a patient woman and with the main feast about to start, Deirdre was dreadfully late preparing for the meal. As the only daughter of Laird Donald Fraser, there was an expectation she not only attended the feast but be properly turned out.

Deirdre attempted to stack all her books neatly and then place the parchment on the top of the pile, but not all the sheets were dry yet. If she let them touch, they would smear, and it would waste her hours of work. She had worn a smock over her kirtle that had large pockets, already stained numerous times from her ink, in which she dropped her inkwell and used quills. She bent to lift the stack of books but realized that her hands were no longer free to gather the vellum. She tried to tuck half the stack under each arm, which seemed to be working. She stuck the corner of one sheet between her lips, and divided the other four between her two hands and sets of fingers. She began to straighten her legs but felt the left stack of books slip. When she tried to adjust her arm, she succeeded in dropping all of them.

"Zounds," she groaned. When she spoke, the sheet from between her lips sailed away. Instinctively, she reached for the page, but that only resulted in her dropping two more sheets. Shaking her head, she set down the remaining books and the last two sheets of parchment just as a breeze picked up her writing and thought to carry it away.

"Nay! Ma work. Nae ma work."

Deirdre halted when a large shadow fell over her and her jumble of belongings. Barely looking up, she tried to sidestep the hulk, but he reached out a hand that held the first sheet that took flight.

"Lass, I think ye're wanting this back."

Deirdre raised her eyes and caught her breath when she saw a face not much older than hers but resembled Adonis or Apollo from her books. The only difference in her mind was that she readily preferred the head of dark waves to the golden curls in the illustrations. She gulped before she could respond.

"Thank ye. I was most distraught." She could not bring herself to look him in the eye. Her stomach suddenly felt like a flock of sparrows was flying about. However, when she heard a soft chuckle, her eyes darted up to glare at the owner of the offensive sound.

"Ye dinna seem that distraught, lass. Put out, perhaps. Even peeved, but definitely nae distraught. It isnae some great catastrophe."

"Says ye," she bit out between clenched teeth. "I have been working on this since sunrise. Vellum is vera expensive, and these books belong to ma father. He willna be pleased if they come back dirty and marred." She bent to begin restacking the books.

"I didna mean to say they werenae important. I simply meant that ye didna overreact as some lasses might. Please let me help ye. Ma arms are longer."

Everything is longer. He canna be that much older than me, but he's gigantic. Does he have to be so braw? How is he so large? Fie! Why am I standing here gauping at him?

"I would vera much appreciate yer help. Everything was much easier to carry out this morning when the parchment didna have wet ink on them. Now I canna stack them and dinna have enough hands to hold it all."

Magnus simply nodded as he squatted to gather all the books. He tucked the entire pile under one arm, and Deirdre's eyes widened to see the ease with which he lifted something that was a burden for her.

Magnus bent down again and picked up two sheets of parchment that looked to be mostly dry. He turned them back to back and held them up.

"Ye have a vera fine script."

"Ye're kind to notice. It's in Latin," she finished quietly. She did not want to insult the young man, but she doubted he would know what the marks meant.

"Aye, and the one by yer feet is in Greek and the first one I picked up was in French. Two of these books are in Italian, one in Spanish, another two in Aramaic. I must admit that the two in Aramaic were the hardest ones for me to learn. I didna care for them overly much."

Magnus turned to walk towards the keep. He could not keep from grinning when he knew the girl stood staring at his retreating back. He had known from the start she would assume he was illiterate. His size meant that most people took him to be lumbering and dimwitted at worst and a farm laborer at best. Most did not know he was the fourth son of a powerful laird.

Deirdre dashed to keep up with the long strides of this strange young man who had not bothered to introduce himself and now possessed her hard work and treasured resources.

"Ye're familiar with some of these texts? The ones in Aramaic are rather rare."

"Aye, there are only five known copies of that set anywhere in the Christian world. One is in England, one is in Spain, and two are in Scotland. Who do ye suppose owns the other set if ye have one of them?"

"Ye?" She asked in disbelief.

"Well, ma da does. We were all made to study them, but they technically belong to him."

"Who is yer da? Ye havenae even introduced yerself."

"Neither have ye."

"I shouldnae even be talking to ye without a fromal introduction by a chaperone."

"But ye are. We can walk back in silence if ye prefer."

"That isnae what I meant, I ken ye ken that."

"I am simply trying to come to yer aid. Ye seemed in need of an extra set of hands. I dinna think ye were too picky, nor do I think ye believed me to be worth much company before this moment."

His accurate assessment of her first impression and her desire to make it back to the keep with any available help stunned Deirdre. She did not realize that she had stopped dead in her tracks until he looked back over his shoulder and nodded his head towards the keep. Once again, she found herself jogging to catch up.

"Deirdre. Deirdre Fraser."

"Och, ye're the lass Laird Fraser was going on aboot. I'm Magnus Sinclair."

"Ye ken ma father? He was talking aboot me?"

"Aye. Only good things mind ye, but he said yer head was in the clouds and that yer mother had her work cut out for her."

Deirdre jerked her chin back and narrowed her eyes. She was not sure who annoyed her most: her father for insulting her, her mother for always seeming inconvenienced by her, or this Magnus Sinclair who dared to repeat such an insult."

"Is now when ye're going to actually become distraught? He said it lovingly before one and all. There isnae a doubt in anyone's mind that yer father dotes on ye."

"One and all? Anyone's mind? Just how many people were there when he said this."

Magnus could hear the change in her voice and knew she was on the edge of actually being distraught. If his hands were not full, he could have slapped himself for being so insensitive as to repeat what he now realized was an exceedingly backhanded compliment.

"Deirdre, I am sorry. I realize I shouldnae repeated what I heard. Out of context, it doesnae seem vera kind, and ye father wasnae trying to speak ill of ye. I apologize for upsetting ye." Magnus stopped and turned to face her.

He had already taken in her wild and curly hair that blew about in the breeze and showed she had run her hands through it numerous times. He had already counted the ink smears on her nose, cheeks, forehead, and chin. There were seven. He noticed her petite and slight frame as only an adolescent boy moving into manhood would. But he had not taken in the brilliance of her blue hazel eyes. They were the North Sea on a bright and clear day. He had seen the sea almost every day of his life whenever he looked from his chamber window. The blues and greens of her eyes matched the water on a calm day. As he looked at her longer, he felt himself slipping into their depths just as he did when he and his siblings went swimming in the chilly waters. He nearly shook his head when he realized how close he was to letting go of the parchment to wipe the ink from her face.

She is the bonniest lass I have seen here. I thought I would always prefer them buxom like the lass last eve, but she far exceeds the likes of any woman I have met before. I rather liked our banter too. She might be someone intelligent enough to talk with. Mairghread is off again with that lass she met from who kens which clan. Strange that the lass never wears a plaid.

Magnus found his mind wandering. He looked down again at Deirdre.

I dinna care what ma sister is up to. She can occupy herself with her friend, and I willnae have to babysit her. I can talk to Deirdre instead.

Magnus pulled himself back to the moment and smiled down at Deirdre.

"If ye will forgive me, perhaps we could meet on the morrow to discuss why ye've been scribbling away like a monk. I wouldnae mind learning what ye consider to be yer life's work."

"How do ye ken I consider it that?"

"It's clear it holds tremendous importance to ye beyond the cost of the vellum and books."

"Aye. Well, perhaps. I intend to work under the tree again."

"Ye dinna plan to attend the games?"

"Nay. I ken what happens. The running, the archery, the caber. Naught new," dismissive of the purpose of the Highland Gathering.

"Och, but ye havenae ever seen me compete before."

Why did I just say that? Haud yer wheesht, mon, before ye're inviting her to watch.

"I'm competing in the foot race, the caber toss, and dirk toss. Mayhap I could interest ye in taking a break for a wee moment."

Didna I say mum's the word? Now I've done it.

Deirdre tilted her head to one side as she examined Magnus to the point where he wanted to shuffle his feet. Suddenly, the collar of his leine felt too tight.

"Nay. But thank ye all the same. I can already tell ye will win them all. I havenae the time to watch others compete when the winner is a foregone conclusion. Even if it's ye." Deirdre felt her cheeks heat as the last sentence slipped out as more of a murmur.

"Thank ye for yer vote of confidence. I willna pester ye any longer."

They reached the doors to the keep, and Magnus checked the ink. It was dry, so he handed the books back to Deirdre and put the sheets on top. He bowed from the waist and walked away. He left Deirdre standing alone staring after his retreating form. She could have kicked herself all the way up the stairs to her chamber where she changed to prepare for the feast.

He's the only one near ma age who's been nice. And I turned down his offer when he was just trying to be friendly. Fool!

Magnus stood around the Fraser's Great Hall with his three older brothers and several other older lads and young men. Bored and hungry, which was his usual state of being, Magnus's encounter with Deirdre Fraser still weighed on his mind.

"Are ye going to the mead tent again this evening? Or shall we try the tavern in the village? The wench I tupped last eve offered me another go. I plan to take her up on it." Tavish asked Magnus quietly.

"Aye, I'll go, but I dinna ken if I'm in the mood for tupping any barmaids. Mairghread catching me at home has soured ma taste on them. Mayhap there's a servant aboot who might be interested." Magnus knew as he spoke, he was not telling the truth. He was not particularly interested in bedding anyone who did not have blue hazel eyes. He felt a wave of guilt and disgust roll over him when he remembered that the girl he met that afternoon had to be at least a few years younger than him.

Ye're too young to be a lecher. And she's far too young, and she's the laird's daughter. She isnae some whore I can bed for a copper.

"I like ma women to have a wee more substance to them. Aye, one set of tits is usually as good as another as long as they're big enough for me to find them." Magnus heard one of the other young men comment as he forced himself to bring his mind back to the group.

"Aye, an arse and tits are all a mon really needs if it isnae food or time in the lists," another lad said as he adjusted his crotch.

Magnus looked at his other brothers. They might talk about women among themselves, but not in such crass terms. Magnus saw Alex cock his head and nod for them to go. Magnus was just about to agree, but the next comment had him pause.

"The laird's daughter might come with a healthy dowry, but who would want to bed her? She's thinner than a maypole. Ye wouldnae ken if ye were holding her from the front or the back." Magnus bristled as he heard the others laugh.

"Och, as long as each hole works, it doesnae matter which is the front or the back."

Magnus opened his mouth to chastise the lads, but his height afforded him the ability to see past their shoulders to a face that was stark white with shock and humiliation. Deirdre's face was set in a mask, but the color came rushing back as her face turned crimson. She spun on her heels and ran towards a darkened passageway.

"Ye *arse!* She heard ye."

Magnus drew his fist back and slammed it in the young man's stomach who just spoke. He threw a fist into the mouth of the other lad who began the rude comments about Deirdre. Magnus pushed past his brothers and ran to catch up with her. He saw a brief gleam of moonlight as a door opened and shut with enough force to echo. He sprinted to the end and pushed open the door which led him to a small orchard. He scanned the area, but the setting sun made it difficult for him to see anyone. A soft rustling of leaves drew his attention, and he glimpsed feet being pulled up. He tiptoed to the trunk of the tree and turned to rest his back against it. He looked up and saw her arrange her skirts about her. He smiled to himself then realized she might think he was laughing at her.

"Lass, ye canna stay up there all night. If naught else, they will miss ye on the dais."

"True, but I would rather deal with Mama after the feast than return and be humiliated all over again."

"Ye never did tell me how old ye are. I dinna think ye're as old as ma six and ten or even ma sister's five and ten."

"I'm three and ten," she whispered.

"Will ye come down so we might talk and I dinna have to keep ma eyes averted?"

"Nay. Ye dinna need to stand there if ye dinna want to."

"Vera well. I accept yer invitation to come up." Magnus hoisted himself up and perched on the branch across from hers.

"I didna invite ye up," she spluttered.

"Och, I thought yer refusal to come down was just another way of asking me to come up. Ye ken I canna be vera bright on account of ma size. All brawn and nay brains."

Magnus winked at her. Surprised that he would joke at his own expense, it took Deirdre a moment before she burst out laughing.

Magnus knew in that moment he was lost. The sound of her laughter soaked into his mind and his heart, if not even his soul. He forced himself to remember that she said she was only three and ten. There was nothing he could do at this gathering, but he resolved to wait until she was four and ten. He would begin courting her then.

"Deir, I ken ye heard what they said, and I'm sorry for it. I wish I could take it all back so ye wouldnae be hurt or embarrassed. But do ye see how ridiculous it is that those two lads, who are older than me, are even commenting on a lass as young as ye and how it makes them look like naught more than lechers."

Ye're nae far off either, but at least she doesnae ken that.

"I'm old enough to marry, but I amnae what any mon wants. I dinna look more than a child." Deirdre pulled her knees to her chest and laid her cheek upon them as she wrapped her arms around them.

Magnus recognized the position as protective. She wanted to shrink away to nothing. His heart ached for her. She had been vibrant and wild that afternoon and full of spirit. Now, she seemed to be retreating into a shell.

"Mayhap ye are old enough to wed, but ye dina have to. Ma sister, Mairghread, is less than a year younger than I am. She's only five and ten, and I ken ma da wouldnae ever consider marrying her off so young.   I dinna think ye father would either. From his tone this afternoon, I think he might try to keep ye forever." Magnus beamed hoping to coax her out.

"That's only because ma brother is still too young to hunt with him. Once he is old enough to ride and hunt and train in the lists, ma father willna be so keen to keep me around."

Magnus would not argue with her, but something told him he would have an uphill battle ahead of him when he requested permission to court Deirdre.

How am I so sure already?

"Magnus, do ye think I'll ever become a woman that a mon might want?"

The question was asked so softly that he almost did not hear her. He looked into the eyes that reminded him so much of home and reached out to cup her cheek.

"Ye already have," Magnus swept his lips over hers.

~~~

It took a moment before Deirdre realized Magnus was waiting for an answer. She was so lost to her memories she almost forgot what he was saying.

"Aye, I remember ye explained what fidelity means to the Sinclairs, but after a year and a day, after seven years, I didna ken if ye would feel bound to that pledge anymore. I could understand if ye wouldnae."

Mangus shook his head and scowled. Absentmindedly, Deirdre reached out and smoothed the crease between his eyebrows.

"Where were ye a moment ago? Ye seemed so far away."

"I was remembering the day we met."

Magnus stood and took a step towards her, and when she did not back up or shift away, he cupped her cheek and whisked his lips against hers.

"The day I knew I would be yers for a lifetime, Deir."

She lifted her chin to meet his lips and pressed back against them. Her mewl was enough to have them wrapping their arms around one another. Magnus brushed his tongue against her lips, and she instantly parted them. She opened her mouth wide, inviting his thrusting tongue in, so she could softly suck on it. Magnus wrapped her hair around his hand as he pinned her against his chest. Deirdre did not think twice about melting into his hold. She spent almost every night of the past seven years falling asleep to thoughts about this exact moment when she could kiss him again for the first time, when they could touch each other again, when they could reunite. Her hands traveled over his chest and back then over his shoulders and up and down his arms. Her frustration grew as material kept her from the heat emanating through every inch of him. Magnus's mouth meandered from hers and kissed a line along her jaw to the hollow at the base of her throat. He followed her collarbone to her shoulder and up her neck until he caught her between a laugh and a moan before nipping her earlobe.

"Ye remembered that I'm ticklish there."

"Aye. I remember a great many things aboot yer body. I remember that we learned them together."

Deirdre's hands slid to his belt and tugged him forward then moved to his outer hips. She found the grooves that fascinated her when she first discovered them all those years ago. She marveled then and now at how different his body was from her own. The nooks and crannies he had that did not exist on her own body felt familiar but different all at once. There was so much that she wanted to become reacquainted with and so much she wanted to learn.

"I remember that ye liked it when I sucked yer tongue. Seems that hasnae changed." She grinned up at him.

"Nay, that certainly hasnae changed. Ye had me almost spilling when ye did that."

Voices from the passageway that were entirely too close for either of their comfort cut Magnus's comment short. They stood still and held their breath as they waited for whoever was in the passageway to move on. When there was silence once again, he kissed the tip of her nose.

"Deir, we canna stay in here forever. Someone will miss yer presence, and ye dinna need yer mother and father searching for ye."

A soul-deep sigh passed Deirdre's lips.

"I ken ye're right, but I dinna want to return to the Great Hall, I dinna feel safe walking the passageways alone," she looked into Magnus's eyes and melted into him. "Dinna make me leave ye," she finished in little more than a whisper.

Magnus held her tightly, breathing in the soft scent of apples. She had always been the only lass he knew who favored a fruit scent to floral. He wanted nothing more than to hold her for every moment until forever, but he knew that was not an option. At least not yet.

I amnae a lad anymore who will have his future dictated by a social climber. I amnae letting Deirdre go again. She was mine, is mine, and will always be mine.

Magnus did not realize how he tightened his grip until he felt a light tapping on his chest.

"Magnus, I canna breathe."

"Sorry, love," he kissed the crown of her head. "I dinna want to let you go either, but it still doesnae change that we canna stay here much longer. Why were ye fleeing in the first place? It was because of me." He finished with a statement.

He felt Deirdre shudder before he felt her nod.

"It was just too much seeing ye so suddenly, and ye seemed so angry and cold when ye did look at me. I felt like I was suffocating or drowning, mayhap both at once. I wanted to cry in private."

"Deirdre, I was angry. I didna expect to hear yer laugh. God how that hurt since I didna even ken ye were at court, then to see ye there laughing and merry. Ye seem to have made a happy life for yerself here. It made ma letters' rejection hurt all over again. It's bad enough once a moon, but to see ye." He shook his head.

Tears slid down Deirdre's cheeks in a current too fast for her to wipe away. Magnus pulled the end of his plaid that lay over his shoulder to blot away the fat droplets.

"It's like losing ye all over again to hear ye've been trying for so long, and I had nay idea. I tried to write to ye, but ma father and mother kept telling me that ye didna want me. They forbid me and told me to stop embarrassing the family by mooning over a lad who was tupping another lass before we even left the gathering."

"And ye believed them." Magnus's voice had an edge to it that sliced through Deirdre like a hot knife through butter.

"Nae at first. It hurt me to hear ye had some wench on yer lap. Merciful heavens, how that nearly drove me mad. But then ma family kept insisting that ye had moved on. They shared stories of ye that infuriated me. I wanted to murder ye. Then it was just numbness. I couldnae resolve what I kenned of ye after so many years with what they told me. I may make merry here, but that's only because they expect it of me. My duties to the queen are much more tolerable when ma family thinks I am being biddable. It doesnae mean I feel any less hollow."

22

Once again, Deirdre looked up at Magnus. She noticed at some point, she grabbed handfuls of his leine now bunched into her closed fists. She held onto the only lifeline thrown to her in years.

"Please, Magnus, dinna make me go back. Dinna make me leave ye," she caught her breath as she felt her heart race, this time out of fear rather than pleasure, "Dinna leave me. I canna survive that again. Aught but that."

"Just what are ye asking for, eun beag? A night? One more tryst before ye marry another mon?"

"Nay!" Her sobs became uncontrollable. They rattled through her whole body but were silent. Years of crying herself to sleep or escaping into secluded gardens taught her the value of keeping quiet.

Magnus was at a loss for what to do now. He comforted her as best he could, moving back to sit down and cradling her in his arms.

"Take me away. Find us a kirk, so we can be wed. Make me yer wife. Again. For this night and every one after. I canna go back. Magnus, I willna."

Magnus heard the determination he had admired in her from the moment he picked up her first perfectly scribed piece of vellum.

"Deirdre, there is naught more in this life or the next that I want more than to do just that. Every part of me screams to run with ye, but we arenae children anymore. I dinna need a king's bounty on ma head nor our marriage overturned. Besides, I came here to seek the king's support in the ongoing feuds that endanger ma clan and ma family. I canna desert them or ma duty. They dinna deserve that. Could ye respect me if I did? If I was that selfish and irresponsible? I wouldnae want ye to. We must at least try to gain the king's approval of our union. First, I must resolve ma family's disputes then I can petition for yer hand."

Once again, a bone-weary sigh seeped from her.

"And if ye dinna succeed? If ma father has too much sway with the king? He has already petitioned the king for permission to marry me to Lord Archibald."

Magnus's teeth ground together with such force that Deirdre thought they might crack. She ran her hand along his jaw, and he turned his cheek into her palm, relaxing immediately.

"I amnae above bride stealing."

With that, Magnus rose to his feet and once more set Deirdre on hers. Holding her hand, he peered out of the alcove, looking both ways. He stepped out but blocked Deirdre from following. He took his time counting to twenty before being convinced Deirdre was safe to reappear.

"Take me to yer chamber."

They said nothing else once in the passageway, and they continued to her lady-in-waiting chamber.

Chapter Four

D eirdre slid a key from a secret pocket in her gown before unlocking the door. Magnus could see clearly over the top of her head. There was only one bed within the chamber. He looked down at her curiously and a little suspiciously.

"Ma mother has enough influence to arrange a private chamber, and in turn, ma father uses this common knowledge to prove his own significant influence. It's naught more than a power play. It has naught to do with me."

Magnus could not miss the bitterness in her voice and it did not match the affection she once held for her father.

"I think there's a great deal we need to share between us aboot our time apart. I ken there is a chance ye willna like or love the mon I have become."

"Ye told me ye have been faithful for the past seven summers. Ye havenae given me an ultimatum aboot the future. Ye havenae tried to force me nor have ye even blamed me. Magnus, it's clear to anyone's eyes that ye are a warrior. I have heard of yer family's recent battles," her voice hiccupped as the image of him in danger crept into her mind, "I kenned ye must have fought in them. I ken ye've had to kill other men. I ken ye've had to do what ye must to survive. I dinna fault ye that at all. To me, ye have already proven ye are the same lad as ye once were. Just in a much bigger package."

She ran her eyes appreciatively over him, and Magnus knew she was not aware that she licked her lips. He pressed her inside the door and kicked it shut. Grabbing her waist, he spun her so her back was against it, and he turned the lock.

It's like nay time has passed. I ken much has changed, yet it feels like naught has changed. How can it feel so right so soon? She is like the air ma lungs crave, and I can finally breathe again.

Deirdre had no time to catch her breath before his mouth was devouring hers once more. Her arms shot up to wrap around his neck. Magnus bunched her skirts within his hands lifting them to her waist before running his palms over the backs of her shapely thighs. They ventured up to capture her round bottom. He could not suppress the groan that came from deep within his chest. He let go long enough to push his sporran out of the way, and he was quick to refill his hands with her perfectly rounded backside. She had been lithe as a young woman and not much had changed. His hot hands kneaded the supple flesh.

I kenned I missed the feel of him, but dear God in heaven, this is better than any of ma dreams, any of ma memories. I dinna care that this is going too fast. Heaven kens we're owed this.

He let out a fierce growl when he felt her hands slip below his plaid, and one hand gripped his cock as the other palmed his bullocks. Her hands explored him as she tried to wrap her petite hands around him and found her fingers barely met. She pulled back to free her mouth.

"Ye're bigger. Everywhere."

"And ye are just as perfect as I remembered."

"Lift me up just as ye used to. I want to feel ye. It's been so damn long. I thought I didna ever want a mon's touch again, and I ken I dinna if it's nae ye. But it is, and we can. I need ye, mo ghaol."

Magnus rested his forehead against hers for a moment before looking into her eyes.

"Ye ken the moment I realized ye were here, I had every intention of leaving with ye. If we do this, I willna pull out like in the past. I will spill inside ye because ye are ma wife, and this time naught will keep me from ye. I amnae a lad of nine and ten anymore. I canna be intimidated or coerced. I warn ye now, that if we join, it's as good as marriage by consent. I will kill anyone who stands between us, Deirdre. I mean that. Anyone."

"Aye, I want to join with ye, and marry ye, and be yer wife. I never stopped wanting that."

Deirdre held his gaze without blinking once. Her pronouncement was the acknowledgment given three times to wed them by consent. She also knew he meant he would not let her father interfere again. Much had changed in her relationship with her father ever since he refused Magnus, and now she knew her family lied to her over and over. The rift was now irreparable, and her father's increasingly manipulative decisions robbed her of her father's love. In turn, she had little left to give him.

"Magnus, there hasnae been a day in over seven summers that ye havenae been ma husband. I've missed ye, and I thought at times that the loneliness would kill me. I ken ye have yer responsibilities here, but I would run away with ye right this minute if I could. But we canna, nae yet at least, so we can at least have this together. This is our new start nae our end.

Magnus thrust inside her without any further hesitation. Her back arched off the wall as her legs squeezed him. He instantly regretted his force. He had never taken her so quickly, not even when they first made love. He tried to pull back, but a sharp yank on his hair made him pause.

"Dinna even think aboot stopping. It wasna pain, nae like the first time. It's tight, and ye are most definitely bigger, but sweet Mother Mary, *naught* has ever felt better than when ye are inside me. Keep going." She clenched her inner muscles as tightly around him as she could. She could feel her body was on the precipice. "I'm almost there already."

"Ye and me both, mo chridhe." He thrust twice more, and they both shattered. His hips twitched forward as the hardest, most intense climax he ever experienced pulsed through him.

Deirdre felt lightheaded as her muscles continued to spasm and tremble. She dropped her head to his shoulder as she tried to calm her breathing.

"Lass, I wish I had lasted longer. To make it better for ye."

She raised her head and gave him a solemn look before bursting into laughter.

"I dinna. I wanted that, and I vera well may have expired if it took any longer. Next time." She stroked a lock of hair back from his forehead and rubbed noses with him. It was how they had finished the few times they had made love all those years ago.

Magnus stepped back, prepared to carry her to the bed when a sharp knock came at the door. Deirdre's eyes opened wide as she pointed to the ground and then placed her finger over her lips. When she was once more on her own feet, she turned to the door.

"Who is it?"

"Una, my lady."

Deirdre looked over her shoulder and pointed to the wall beside the door hinges and once again placed her finger to her lips. She ran her hands over her hair to smoothen it to a point where it would not be too questionable. Taking a deep breath, she turned the lock and opened the door wide enough for only part of her to show.

"Una, I am not in need of you tonight." Listening to her maid, Deirdre realized how quickly she reverted to her burr. She made an effort to once again use her court diction. "I have a horrid headache which had me leaving the Great Hall early. I care to be on my own for the eve."

"How will you manage your laces, my lady," the skepticism on the older woman's face was clear.

She tried to peer around Deirdre, but fortunately for them both, the bed was untouched. Deirdre showed Una her back and pointed to the end of her laces.

"Please just pull the knot loose. I will be fine with the rest."

"My lady, I cannot be doing that out in the hall. That simply is not proper."

"And I cannot tolerate the lights from the passageway much longer nor do I want any more lit in here. Just undo the knot, and that shall suffice for this eve." Deirdre injected a haughtiness she seldom used, but Una was already her least favorite and least trustworthy maid.

"As you say, my lady." Magnus did not miss the snideness and bristled from behind the door. Deirdre did not dare look in his direction. Once she felt her laces loosen even a breath, she stepped from Una and turned around.

"Thank you for your help. I shall see you in the morn. Please let it be known that I retired feeling unwell and expect to be asleep very soon."

Deirdre knew Una would go immediately to tell her parents what happened. It was Una who told her mother all those years ago that Deirdre was writing missives to Magnus. Deirdre learned from another maid that Una took her private letters to her father when she found them while tidying. Deirdre had never forgiven that invasion of privacy, but now she saw it for even more. It dawned on Deirdre that her parents used Una to spy on her. She quickly closed the door before Una could say or do anything more. She turned the lock in the key and pulled it from the door. She took it and withdrew the key already in her pocket. With both in her hand, she looked at Magnus and tilted her head towards the interior of the chamber and went to the small table that held her combs and fragrances. She laid the keys on the table before reaching for the back of her gown.

Magnus appeared behind Deirdre in the looking glass the table and the wall supported. His hands slid from her shoulders down to her hands and entwined their fingers. He feathered kisses from her shoulder up to her neck to the sensitive skin behind her ears. He brushed his lips across the shell of her ear.

"I have loved ye since the vera first. I have continued to love only ye nay matter the time or the distance. There is nay body I will love but ye. It's only ever been ye," he whispered softly.

His hands pulled the laces loose, and he slid the gown off her arms. Once it reached her waist, Deirdre pushed it to the ground and let it well around her feet.

"So incredibly beautiful," Magnus murmured, enraptured by the sight reflected in the mirror. He could make out the dusky nipples that sat high upon her chest and the thatch of honey curls that rested between her thighs. He longed to plunge into her as he had moments ago, but he determined to go slowly. This time was not about slaking a long-dormant lust or the need to bind their bodies. This time was about rebinding their souls and minds just as they had been so many years ago.

His hands slid up her ribs and around to cup her firm breasts. His hands as much as his mind remembered exactly how they fit into his palms. He liked that he could hold them perfectly within the center of his hands. It sparked a possessiveness he had not even felt when they first fell in love.

"Ye dinna think them too small?" she queried.

"Nae at all. They fit as though they were always made just for me, that they are mine," Magnus wondered briefly if she would rebel against the very possessiveness that brought him calm.

When she melted into his chest, she reassured him she was where she wanted to be.

"They have always been yers. There has been nay one but ye. Nae a brush of the lips. Nae even a kiss on the cheek."

Magnus shuddered in relief. A small part of him had wondered if she had maintained the same degree of fidelity as he had. No longer a maiden for so many years, he admitted he feared she sought pleasure elsewhere.

"Ye worried that I didna stay true to ye, just as I worried the same. I suppose it is only natural, but I want ye to ken that naught short of being forced would ever make me stray."

The reference to Archibald Hay made Magnus wrap his arm around her middle and press her further into his chest.

"Mine," he repeated.

Deirdre snaked her arms around his and pressed her hip back.

"Mine," she answered.

Magnus could no longer wait to reveal what was stolen from him. Deirdre pulled the ribbon loose at the neck of her chemise, and Magnus lifted it over her head. Magnus's breath audibly caught in the back of his throat as his eyes gorged on the long lines of her slim figure. She had always been on the thin side when she was younger, but she had filled out to give her more womanly curves. However, there was no escaping the drastic size difference between the two of them. Magnus towered over and around her. When he embraced her, she felt like he cocooned her. Now, his hands rested over her belly as though he was protecting a new life that might grow inside her. She noticed that his thumb and fingers formed a heart, and she traced her forefinger over them.

"I think ye are a wee overdressed for the occasion," she did not realize how seductive her smile appeared, but it was enough to have Magnus reaching for the brooch that pinned the extra length of his breacan feile, or great plaid, to his shoulder. She pulled at the belt prongs that held his plaid and sporran in place. He caught up the material as it fell and laid it on the chair in front of her. She tugged impatiently on his leine, and he chuckled as he pulled it over his head.

"Patience, mo ghaol."

"Ye ken I had none when it came to ye."

Deirdre could not stop herself from running her hands over and around his smooth chest. She inhaled his scent, and as it filled her nose, she kissed his chest. Magnus skimmed his hands over her lower back, finding the two small bones that had fascinated him upon discovery so long ago. He grasped her bottom and enjoyed the same sensations as when he cupped her breasts. He leaned forward to press his lips against hers. She skated the tip of her tongue sideways, and Magnus encouraged her by opening his mouth. She did not hesitate to sweep her tongue into his mouth where they dueled. Unable to reach his neck, Deirdre grasped the grooves on the sides of his hips, where she always marveled they were an exact fit for her hands. The need built, and they both pressed their mouth more firmly against the other. When they could wait no longer to take a breath, Magnus tenderly guided her to face the mirror again.

The sight they made now they were both bare entranced Deirdre. Magnus's skin glistened a golden brown from days spent training shirtless in the lists. She could just glimpse the white skin of his hips as he pressed them into her. His cock felt like an iron rod as it slid between the cheeks of her bottom, and she moaned as his hand crept between her thighs. She parted them when his finger slid across her moist seam. He tapped twice on the hidden nub before sliding one then two and finally three fingers into her. She had always insisted that he not hold back, that she craved the fullness that his cock gave her and no less than three fingers would do. Deirdre lifted her foot to rest on the seat of the chair. This not only gained Magnus easier entry, it presented them both with a clear view of Deirdre's hidden passage. While one hand worked in and out of her sheath, Magnus's other hand kneaded her breasts. Focusing on one, he circled the darker skin until her nipple puckered. He tugged on her nipple until it hardened into a dart. Magnus leaned forward as Deirdre's arm slithered up to coil around his neck. She arched her back thrusting both her top and bottom into his hands.

"I'd nearly forgotten how it feels to have yer hands on and in me. I could watch us like this forever."

"Aye. There is nay more glorious sight than watching ye find yer release and kenning it was me who brought ye there. I can still see ye when I close ma eyes, and it was that vision that carried me through."

"Did ye think of me when ye—" Deirdre was not sure how to phrase what she meant, but she desperately wanted to know who he thought of if he thought of anyone.

"Ye mean when I took maself in hand? When I thought of thrusting into ye over and over until I could barely breathe. Aye, I thought of ye. My body craved the sensations that only ye ever gave me. It is nae only ma mind that remembers ye. Ma body would ken yers anywhere, and it ached when I had to work maself to release."

"I touched maself too," she whispered and looked down embarrassed.

Magnus raised his hand from her breast to cup her chin. He lifted it and locked eyes with her in the mirror.

"I am glad that ye found pleasure. Tell me," he finished on a murmur.

"I canna do that," her cheeks pinkened.

"If ye could do it in the secrecy of yer chamber, then ye can tell me. I dinna want there ever be aught that ye canna tell me, and together, alone, what we do is nae body's concern but ours. I want to ken if ye thought of me, ached for me, just as I did ye.

"How could ye think I didna? Ye're the only mon I've ever been with."

"Is that the only reason? Cause ye havenae seen any other mon's body to fantasize aboot?"

"Och, of course, nae. I dreamed of ye nae because I didna have anyone else to picture. I did it because it was the only way I could still feel close to ye. I did it to remember the way I wanted to give maself to ye, and how ye gave just as much as ye ever got."

She twisted as best she could and raised her chin, parting her lips. The invitation was clear, and Magnus swooped in to claim it. His fingers worked her again as his long arms could wrap around her and still grasp her breasts. He tugged on her nipple until it became a dart again and then pinched until she mewled in pleasure. Deirdre pulled back first, ending the kiss just as she had started it.

Looking back into the mirror again, she took a deep breath before pressing her hand beneath Magnus's and sliding two of her own fingers into the slick skin.

"I would start by closing ma eyes and picturing us at the loch that year we gathered at the Campbells. Do ye remember how we used to slip out to the loch well after everyone else had retired? How ye bribed the guardsmen with a cask of yer family's best whisky? I would think of how it felt to wrap my body around yers as the water lapped at our shoulders and the moon hung over the water. It gave us enough light to see one another but not be seen by someone else. My body would feel weightless in the water and dreaming of it made me feel as though I could float away from it all. Other times, I would remember how we slipped away from the hunt at the Menzies. Do ye remember how ye made a bed of fallen leaves and pine needles before spreading out yer plaid for us? Ye wrapped us in it nae only to keep warm, for I never feared being too cold when I touched ye, but because ye insisted on protecting me in case they caught us."

"I didna want anyone else to catch sight of what would always only be for ma eyes and ma body," he whispered hoarsely.

"These memories were from before ye even broke ma maidenhead. Ma greatest memory was when we finally joined after pledging our handfast vows. We found that cave along the beach on MacLeod land. How the water of the Hebrides was freezing, but I have never felt a greater warmth radiate from me than when we wed."

"We swear by peace and love to stand," Magnus began.

"Heart to heart and hand to hand" Deirdre followed.

"Mark, o' Spirit, and hear us now, confirming this our Sacred vow. To thee, I pledge ma troth." Together, they finished the words they recited the day they handfasted.

"Does this mean we have handfasted again?"

"Mayhap, but I ken ye already gave yer consent thrice. We were married for the second time in that alcove. I will fight that that takes precedence over a betrothal or even a handfast. I consider us legally wed, and I would vera much like to make love to ma wife for the first time on a bed."

They both could not help chuckling as Magnus scooped Deirdre into his arms and moved to the bed. Laying her down, he fanned out her hair and drew a curly lock across her cheek. He dropped his head to kiss her, but she only pecked his lips.

"I wasna done telling ye aboot how I thought of ye when I was alone in ma chamber," she smiled, shy once again.

"By all means, do continue," Magnus urged as he captured one breast in his mouth. He could fit most, suckling until he reached the tip of her nipple and then taking all of it into his mouth again. Deirdre tried to remember what she had been saying.

"I would press ma breast together while my hand pinched ma nipples just as ye are now. My other hand would find the sensitive nub and rub it until the waves of pleasure began in ma belly and flowed through me. I would cry out yer name in silence every time I came."

Magnus switched to the other side, kneading the damp flesh of the abandoned breast.

"Magnus, dinna make me wait any longer. I ken there are other pleasures before the main course, but holy Saint Michael and all the angels, I will expire if I dinna feel ye inside me right now. I ache so much that it's near pain. I need ye to fill me."

Magnus was already pressing against her entrance, and her entreaty had him stretching her opening once again before he thrust. She grabbed his buttocks and pressed as hard as she could to keep him rooted inside her.

"Saint Columbo's bones, the first moments of feeling ye engulf ma cock is almost as good as finding ma release. And sweet Jesus, being able to finish inside ye is beyond aught I could have ever imagined."

"There is nay reason that ye should ever pull out again. I dinna want ye to. I want a life and a family with ye."

"Ye speak to the vera depths of ma soul." Magnus rocked his hips and swiveled as Deirdre lightened her hold just enough, so she could press her hips upwards. This started the rhythm that carried them closer to completion. Magnus rested on his knees and forearms, staring into her eyes. Deirdre pressed her feet into the mattress as she rose to meet him thrust for thrust.

"Mo eun beag, I am getting close. Och, this feels so good. Ye're even tighter than I remembered. Ye're milking me for all I have."

"I'm there. I can feel it, aye, there. Dinna stop. Ye're so long and hard, I almost feel like ye'll split me in half, and dear God, it feels amazing. I want ye. Harder, Magnus. Aye. Just like that. I'm—Magnus!"

"Deirdre!" Magnus felt the jets of his seed spray free from him, and his cock pulsed rapidly as he felt light headed. He had never had a release so powerful, certainly not on his own or any other time with a woman.

He brushed the damp hairs from her forehead as he felt himself sinking to the depth of her hazel eyes. Deirdre tucked a long lock of chocolate colored hair behind. The familiarity and intimacy of the movement were not lost on either of them.

They lay in one another's arms basking in the afterglow of their love making. Magnus caressed her back as she absentmindedly tapped her fingers against his chest. Deirdre could feel her body relaxing toward sleep and was drifting off when a loud rapping came from the door. Her eyes widened as she looked at Magnus. He was already climbing off the bed and dashing to gather his leine which he slid over his head. He did not bother pleating his plaid before he wrapped it around his waist and belted it. He pressed a finger to his lips before pointing to her chemise that laid crumpled on the floor next to her now wrinkled gown. She picked up both and hastily pushed her gown into the wardrobe before donning the chemise and a robe she pulled from a hook in the wardrobe.

"Deirdre, open this bloody door right this minute! I will not wait another moment before I have an ax taken to it."

"Donald, she may already be asleep. She retired quite some time ago," came a quieter voice that did not last long. More stridently they heard, "Deirdre, you must open this door now. You have much to account for."

Deirdre's anxious gaze jumped to Magnus who was scanning the chamber, spotting the pillows that were both indented. He rushed to the bed and grabbed one and flipped it over. He yanked the sheets back in place before walking to the window embrasure. The warmer weather meant the window was already open. He murmured a prayer of thanksgiving that the room did not smell of their lovemaking. He looked over his shoulder at Deirdre and nodded once before he stepped onto the ledge outside her window. With his back pressed hard against the wall, Magnus scooted far enough to be out of sight but still close enough to overhear the conversation between Deirdre and her parents.

Deirdre opened the door, and her father pushed inside. Her mother came to stand next to her but offered no support or warmth.

"He's here."

Deirdre's heart nearly stopped at her father's pronouncement.

"He's here at court to deal with his bloody family's feuds. Damn heathens." Laird Fraser conveniently forgot that he was a Highlander unless it suited him. "You are not to see him. Not even once, do you understand?"

Deirdre watched as the vein that ran along his left temple thickened and stood out. She had only seen her father this livid a few times, one of which was when he dragged her away from Magnus as they returned from the beach already handfasted. She did not dare play ignorant with her parents.

"Aye, I ken. He rescued me from Lord Archibald."

"You do not need rescuing from your future husband. And get rid of that disgusting burr in your accent," Lady Maeve Fraser stated firmly. It was not a voice of reassurance in the least. It was the judgemental tone that Deirdre had heard her entire life.

Deirdre bit her tongue hard. She had not realized how significantly her accent lapsed in the short time she had with Magnus. She was lucky Una had not heard it, but if she was not careful, it would give away the fact they had been together.

"Father, Lord Archibald accosted me in the passageway when I attempted to retire early with a headache. He pulled me into an alcove and tried to take what is not his."

"It will be his soon enough," her father barked, but when Deirdre shrank back and even his wife paled, he realized that he had just condoned his daughter being raped.

"I did not mean it that way. He should not be trying to compromise you, but you need to realize that once you marry there is little anyone will do to come to your aid. He will be your husband, and you will be his."

Deirdre bristled at her father's complete disregard for her. She noticed that he did not even name her Hay's wife but rather left her sounding like a possession. She did not find it anywhere near as desirable as when she thought about Magnus and being his anything.

"We are not married yet, and until that happens, I will not have my name besmirched among the other ladies in waiting by Lord Archibald's improprieties."

Deirdre knew by staking her reputation, one linked to her parents', she could gain traction.

"Donald, she is right. She cannot be seen as unvirtuous, though she may be, in the eyes of the court. We must tread carefully. She is a favorite of the queen's and even the king. If word gets out she is being molested, they will side with her. If Campbell and Comyn believe you cannot control a waspish man like Archibald Hay, they will not recommend you for the seat on the Privy Council. I am thinking Archibald is not the best possible alliance if you would like the king to grant you stewardship of the Hay land nearest ours. We might all fair better if we lend our attention to that Keith boy. With the Hay land sandwiched between ours and the

Keiths, it would behoove us to build a stronger alliance with them, so we might gain that stewardship *and* influence the Keiths."

Deirdre stood in stunned silence. She always knew her mother had a sharp mind because it was she who first insisted that Deirdre learn to read and write. Deirdre never realized, though, that her mother was so ambitious. As she watched her father mull over her mother's idea, she wondered if it was not Lady Maeve who was the great engineer of her parents' rising status.

"The Keith boy may do the trick though Hay already paid half of her bride price," Donald spoke as though Deirdre was not even present. She felt a wave of disgust roll over her when she remembered that Aiden Keith was barely more than a boy of twelve. Her parents would marry her to a child!

"Tell him it is the gift of his silence that the betrothal fell through. Negotiate with Hay until he comes to his own conclusion that an unchaste bride will not do."

Regret washed over Deirdre as though she stood in the ocean. She wished she had never once admitted to a single member of her family she and Magnus had not only handfasted but consummated their relationship. Her mother never got past it and took every opportunity to remind her. Her father resolved himself and continued to show his ongoing affection for her, yet ever since the opportunity to marry her to Archibald Hay developed, Donald treated her as little more than an expensive mare to trade and put out for Hay to stud. Listening to her parents argue over her future made her anger simmer. She walked to the window for fresh air and sucked in a sharp breath when she saw a bare foot out the corner of her eye. She looked up without moving her head much and found Magnus standing on the narrow ledge. She met his eyes and while her fear for him shone through, rage radiated from his.

"Come away from that window. You need no one seeing you gawking like a washerwoman gossiping to her neighbor."

"Yes, Mother," she backed away. She had to try at least once to defend herself. "Father, you cannot mean to marry me to a child. What will people say? It's unseemly that a woman of my age marries a lad who is still a page. Why I'm closer in age to being his mother than his wife."

"That is only because you whored yourself out to that Sinclair lad." Maeve bit back.

"Maeve," Donald warned. His wife knew she could only press so hard before Donald would defend Deirdre rather than support her. Especially after his earlier ignoble comment.

Deirdre once again watched the interplay between her parents and saw that her father would lean towards her if she could antagonize her mother just enough.

"You are correct that I am no longer a virgin," her mind flashed to what she and Magnus had already done twice. "Aiden Keith is but a boy. What will you do if his parents insist on an examination? Lord Archibald is aware and thought it a boon to not have to bed a virgin. The Keiths may not feel the same. Father, I don't believe Mother has thought of the fact it may take several years before Aiden Keith could ever become my husband in a true sense. We could annul the marriage without consummation. Mother may think me a *whore*, but it will not matter if the Keith lad cannot do his duty." Deirdre stressed the word that seemed to trigger her father the most, but before she could say more, her mother already had a response.

"We could not hope for better than to have you married to the child long enough to gain the Hay land and bend him to our will. He may be a page here but already a laird of his clan. We set aside the marriage once we accomplish that and we can seek another, better match."

"No, Maeve. There is too much risk in losing the Hay land. The clan needs that land, and we need to claim the influence by forcing Hay to cave to us, even if we are paying him to take Deirdre off our hands." Her father was becoming impatient with her, her mother, and the situation. His frustration with the slow progress to his coveted stewardship bubbled to the surface.

Deirdre drew back as though her father slapped her. She had never heard him refer to her in such a distant and cruel way as he had today. Her father's disregard built a brick wall inside Deirdre no one could tear down. At that moment, she no longer considered herself a Fraser. She was truly a Sinclair now, and she would allow nothing to stand in the way of that.

As though he could read her mind, her father circled back to their original intention for haranguing her.

"Dinna think I forgot that I came to tell ye to stay away from that Sinclair bastard. I amnae having a repeat of last time. Ye come within a hairsbreadth of him, and I'll lock ye in yer chamber just as I did before. Dinna think for a moment I am kidding. I'll kill him and have ye shipped off to a convent if need be. Ye willna disgrace us or jeopardize this betrothal." Donald was so irate at this point he had not noticed that he slipped back into his own burr.

At his wife's distasteful look, he pulled on the front of his doublet. They picked up their conversation between themselves and continued their machinations. Her parents were still talking, ignoring her, as they walked to the door. They passed through, and her father slammed it shut. The final reminder of his control over her.

She ran to the window, but Magnus was already gone. She wondered just how much he heard.

Chapter Five

Magnus inched along the ledge, leaving Deirdre's window just as he heard her parents walk to the door. Even from outside, he could hear the door slam. He arrived at the first window and used his fingers to search for a latch of any type. Instead, he felt the lip was slightly apart and he could pull the window open. He thanked God and all the saints he could name as he slid into the chamber, both because the window was unlocked and because the chamber was empty. He looked around the room and confirmed it was one that belonged to the ladies-in-waiting and that it was very unusual for Deirdre to have her own chamber. Magnus took in three beds with wooden frames and trundles below them. He moved to one and quickly removed his plaid. He fished around in his sporran looking for his brooch but cringed when he realized that it must lay somewhere on Deirdre's floor. He prayed she found it before anyone else. He pleated his plaid faster than he may have ever done before. Once dressed, minus the brooch, he opened the door a crack and placed his eye against the opening. He looked up and down the passageway and once again counted to twenty before he emerged.

He had not taken over ten steps when he heard his name being called. He wanted to melt into the floor. He recognized the voice and the one that followed. One, the whiny one, belonged to his brother by marriage Tristan Mackay's stepmother. The other was the voice of Tristan's former mistress, Sorcha. Both were responsible for the significant danger in which they had placed his sister. He scowled as he turned and looked at the two women. He took in Sorcha's fine gown and satin slippers peeking out below her hem. He raised an eyebrow as his lip curled in disgust. Sorcha had moved up in station and hardly resembled the servant she once was.

"Magnus," Sorcha purred. She reached out her hand expecting him to kiss it.

He broadened his feet and crossed his arms. At the same time, he heard a door creak open. It was a soft sound that most would miss, but he knew it was Deirdre's.

Sorcha stepped further forward and placed both of her hands on his arms. He pulled back like she scalded him.

"Dinna," he growled.

She pulled back and giggled coyly.

"It is so good to see ye again, Magnus. It has been such a long time since we were under the same roof. We heard ye had arrived, and I told Lady Beatris that I just had to see ye again since we were once such close acquaintances." Her purring reminded him of a cat rubbing against him, and he suddenly felt itchy.

He stood to his fullest height and breathed in deeply to expand his chest. He knew he was a veritable mountain to these women, and he planned to use it to his advantage. Scaring them a little would do them no harm, and it would ensure that they kept their distance. He knew Deirdre was still at her door, and he would leave no doubt in her mind as to the outcome of being trapped by these two women.

"Do ye remember how close we truly were?" He sneered at them both. "So close I nearly gutted ye, Sorcha, and I would have gladly done the same to ye, Lady Beatris. Ye were going to allow those guardsmen to rape ma sister, and ye planned to sell her off as a bed slave to the Norse. Ye are lucky that someone intervened and agreed to send ye both here. Ye fit well into this pit of vipers. Remind me of the past once more, and I will be only too glad to reminisce as I do away with ye both."

Magnus stalked past their huffs and puffs and 'why I never's. His eyes slid to Deirdre's door and saw just the outline of her ear pressed to the open crevice. He longed to stop and reassure her after her confrontation with her parents and what she just heard. That was not an option, not with Sorcha and Beatris still present and her parents possibly still nearby. Besides, he reminded himself, at court, the walls had eyes and ears. They would have to be more discreet.

Instead, Magnus made his way to the wing where the king's council met. He was just arriving at the last step when he once again heard his name called. This time, he was excited to recognize it. He hurried his pace and opened his arms to a bear of a man. One who nearly rivaled him in size.

"Uncle Hamish, I didna ken ye were at court now. I hadnae heard aught aboot ye."

"That would be because I arrived just this eve. The king summoned me to testify aboot the troubles ye had with the MacDonnells during Mairghread's abduction. I might also put a bug in the king's ear to side with ye on the matters with the Gunns, Kerrs, and de Soules. I may have only been in contact with ye during Mairghread's captivity, but I have seen yer da more than once since then."

"I would appreciate any help. I saw the king at supper, but I still await a formal interview."

"Aye well, I suspect he will want to see me first. Hear ma version of the story to see if it matches yers."

Hamish Sutherland, the older brother of Magnus's now deceased mother, was a close friend and ally to the Sinclairs. The two clans feuded for generations, but the marriage of Liam Sinclair to Kyla Sutherland ended it. The love that grew between his parents made the extended family an integral part of Magnus's childhood. He breathed easy to know his uncle was there to come to his aid. Hamish was also one of the few people beyond his siblings that knew of his past relationship with Deirdre. He had found them once after they snook out of a Highland gathering camp to go for a walk.

"Uncle Hamish, I've seen her." His look told Hamish exactly who he meant.

"And?"

"It was hard at first, but we have reconciled and intend to be together."

"Have ye already?" Hamish's knowing look made Magnus blush.

"Aye, and without precaution. She is ma wife. She gave her consent thrice, and we repeated our handfasting vows. There is just a wee hiccup that her father still loathes me, and most likely Da too, and he has arranged a betrothal to Archibald Hay."

At the mention of Hay, his uncle grimaced.

"Slimy fellow. I dinna ken what her parents are thinking of becoming bedfellows with him."

"Apparently, the land that borders theirs may fall to them under stewardship. It is too far away from their main seat, with the Keith land in the way. They want control over the land for their clan to use and, more importantly to them, to gain greater standing and influence here. What's worse is they considered, albeit briefly, marrying Deirdre to Aiden Keith. He's ten summers and still a page here. I never realized that Lady Maeve may very well be the mastermind for their grasping. Laird Donald is nae eejit, but his wife may be even more ambitious than him."

"I ken all too well. I vera nearly ended up with her." When Magnus looked askance at him, Hamish chuckled and continued. "I'd barely come into the lairdship, and she was a Ross before marrying Fraser. She was a social climber even then. She kenned that I have a large and prosperous clan. What's more, we have stood in many kings' good graces. She cornered me at court when I had to make ma first appearance before the king as a laird. She was a lady-in-waiting at the time and tried to claim I'd compromised her. Lucky for me, Fraser wanted her and maneuvered his way into getting her and my way out. Dinna underestimate his own ambitiousness."

Magnus nodded as he took in the story. He wanted to discuss his situation more with his uncle, but before they could talk further about Deirdre or the feuds, a page called Hamish in to meet with the king. They hugged, and Magnus resigned himself to leaning against the wall or pacing for yet another night.

~ ~ ~

Magnus's stomach rumbled. It was well into the night, and Magnus had not stayed in the Great Hall long enough to eat before he chased after Deirdre, but he did not dare abandon his position in case he missed his summons. Hamish spent close to two hours with the king before emerging looking haggard and tired. His uncle explained that he recounted his knowledge of the events with Mairghread and Tristan along with what he knew of the situation with Callum and Siùsan and then Alexander and Brighde. He mentioned that the Privy Council unwillingly drew him into a conversation about tax increases for several clans in the Highlands. When he finally broke free, Hamish needed to check on his own family to be sure they were settled in their chambers. The two men hugged, and Magnus paced the edges of the small room in which he waited.

~ ~ ~

"Ye remember me do ye, lass?"

"Of course," came the timid response. Deirdre peered out from under her lashes but could not bring herself to look directly at Magnus.

It had been a year since they last saw one another. Her mother had been ill, so her father traveled to the king's annual autumn hunt on his own. The women remained at the Fraser keep. While Deirdre enjoyed hunting, she had been more disappointed that she would not have the opportunity to see Magnus again. She hoped she would have this opportunity at this Highland gathering, and her prayers were answered; however, now she was immensely shy.

"Ye ken I reach all the way up here? My eyes arenae on ma toes?" Magnus tapped his booted toes, and a small laugh escaped Deirdre. "Och, much better. I thought mayhap ye didna want to see me. I ken I must be disturbing ye."

"Nay."

"Nay, ye didna want to see me, or nay, I amnae disturbing ye?"

She finally looked up and blew out a flustered breath that turned into more of a gasp when she looked into Magnus's eyes. He had easily grown another head taller, and his shoulders were wider. Last year, at six and ten, Magnus had looked like a young man but still had some of his boyishness in his face. This year, it was clearly a man who stood before her. His seven and ten year old face was chiseled and angular. His cheekbones defined, and his jaw pronounced. His hair was longer and sat at his collar. The tips were sun bleached to blond, but the rest of his hair was still the rich mahogany brown she remembered. As she examined him, he shifted his feet and crossed his arms. She felt like her eyes might pop out of their sockets as she watched his leine strain to contain the newly enlarged muscles.

"Deir?" Magnus almost sounded impatient, but butterflies danced in her belly when she heard the endearment that only he used. The rest of her family called her Dee.

39

"Aye. I dinna think ye are disturbing me. It is vera nice to see ye again."

All of ye. Sweet Mother Mary, he is even more gorgeous than last year. How can that possibly be?

"What are ye laboring over this time?" He smiled and reminded her of their initial meeting the year prior.

"I am attempting to make a written recitation of Beowulf, but it isnae an easy tale to write."

"Mayhap that is why it was spoken rather than read."

"That may be, but that doesnae mean it canna be done," she said with a note of defiance.

"Then ye are just the one to do it. How long have ye been working on it?"

"Nearly three moons. There are have been many crossing outs and rearranging of parts, but I am nearly ready to begin a fresh and final copy. That will take me at least another moon," she sighed in frustration.

"May I look?"

"Of course, but ye maynae be able to read ma script. It isnae an immaculate version yet."

"Dinna fash. Ye have beautiful script regardless of what ye write," Magnus murmured as he peered over her shoulder at her work.

His chest brushed against her shoulder, and they froze as a bolt of electricity surged through them both.

Magnus turned back to the parchment stretched out on the table. He could read her handwriting easily. It was far neater than she claimed, and while his body hummed with attention for Deirdre's form so near him, his mind became absorbed in her written recitation of the centuries-old tale. Magnus pointed to parts where her script was a little less clear. Neither realized the time that past as they discussed not only Deirdre's work recording the tale but the actual events of the epic poem and what life must have been like at the time of its creation. The sun had shifted, and the room was growing dim when they finally rolled up her parchment. Magnus looked as Deirdre rubbed an ink smudge from her chin. He felt bolder this year than he had the previous. He would not miss an opportunity to touch her.

"Deir, I've thought of ye many times over the past year. Have ye spared me a thought or two?"

"Aye, mayhap one or two," she breathed out.

"That is all? I must nae have made a good enough impression. Ye certainly did for me."

Deirdre turned to look over her shoulder to see Magnus but did not realize how close his head was to hers. Their noses brushed. When she started to pull back, Magnus's hand slid under her hair to cup her nape. He rubbed his nose against hers, and they both smiled. Without releasing her, Magnus guided her to stand before him.

"Do ye ken how much I have missed talking with ye? We didna have that much time last year, but it was enough to make me long for more. I ken I havenae ever missed talking to any other lass, nae even ma sister."

"I've missed ye too, Magnus. I've thought of ye quite a bit more than once or twice."

Her warm breath puffed across Magnus's lips, and he knew he could not resist. Yet he would take nothing not offered to him.

"Deirdre, has a lad ever kissed ye before?"

"Nay."

"Would ye let me be the first?"

And preferably the only and the last.

Magnus bit his tongue to keep from speaking all of his thoughts.

"Aye, Magnus. I would like that, but I dinna ken what I am doing," the shyness had returned.

"Dinna fash. I will show ye."

Magnus slowly brushed his lips against hers and gently increased the pressure as his arm embraced her. Her hands came to rest on his chest, and she could feel the pace increasing with every moment they kissed. She did not understand what he wanted her to do until his thumb grazed her jaw and pressed down ever so slightly.

"Open for me, leannan," he murmured.

Deirdre parted her lips and felt the tip of Magnus's tongue against her teeth. When he pressed, she opened wider and mewled when she felt his tongue fully stroke her own. He tasted of fresh mint and smelled of pine. Her body began to tingle.

Magnus could not believe Deirdre agreed to kiss him. He had thought of it countless times and knew he was risking much by asking. He would thank God later for his good fortune. She tasted of the strawberries he had seen on the table next to her work. The sweetness of the berries lingered on her tongue as she grew braver and swirled her tongue with his. He was not sure where a groan came from until he felt the rumble in his own chest, her soft hands pressing against it. He intended to keep the kiss to barely more than a peck, but her curiosity made her willing to explore. He itched to run his hands over her body but reminded himself that she was a maiden, not a tavern wench.

When Magnus felt his cock twitch against the back of his sporran, he knew he needed to slow things. His cock hardened the moment he walked into the solar where she escaped to within the Graham keep that hosted the spring Highland gathering. Catching a view of her more developed breasts as he approached had been enough to make him want to seek privacy to take himself in hand as he had done countless times over the past year, thinking of her as he stroked himself. That thought only made his mind jump to picturing her hands on his cock, or her mouth. It was sheer determination that allowed him to approach her, and it was sheer willpower now that made him pull away. He looked down at her swollen lips, the slight redness around the edges from his stubble, and the glazed look that still coated her eyes. He leaned forward again to rub his nose with hers before stepping back.

"Did I do aught wrong?"

"Wrong? Nay! How could ye think that? Ye did everything entirely too well. If I didnae step back, I would have truly compromised ye."

"And been forced to wed me," she said flatly as she turned back to her chair. Her heart hammered in her chest, and she became lightheaded. She sat down, but her body felt as though it floated above her. Reality came crashing down all too abruptly when she realized that Magnus would resent feeling trapped into a marriage.

"They wouldnae ever have to force me." Magnus made his statement with such forthrightness and confidence she whipped her head up to look at him. He stepped next to her and boxed her in as one arm rested on the back of her chair and the other on the table. "I am going to marry ye, dinna ever doubt that. I will court ye, woo ye, fall in love with ye and ye with me, and I will marry ye."

Magnus stood up and turned towards the door. He walked to the door, but before he could leave, he heard Deirdre push back her chair none too lightly.

"Ye expect me to wait for ye when ye dinna give me any clue as to when all of this might take place. What if I dinna want to wait for ye while ye're off nae waiting for me?" She knew her question sounded illogical as the words spewed forth, but they made perfect sense to her.

Magnus stalked back over to her and lightly grasped her shoulders in his warm hands. She felt scorched by his touch as if it lit a fire inside her.

"I dinna speak codswallop. I am telling ye the truth. We are too young to wed right now. I dinna think yer father would even consider it, but I will court ye until ye are old enough to marry, then I will."

"How will ye court me when we only see each other twice a year? Just how do ye plan to spend yer time in between?" She crossed her arms between them and offered him a mutinous glare.

Magnus scanned the room and spotted a wide backed chair. He swept Deirdre into his arms, and she squeaked. He marched to the chair and sat down, adjusting her on his lap.

"Have it out. Just what are ye asking or mayhap accusing me of?"

Deirdre had not uncrossed her arms and kept them there as a border between them. Magnus looked down at her and smiled which only made her scowl.

"Ye're as light as a sparrow but as sharp as a hawk, eun beag."

"Little bird? Ye think to insult me on top of asking me to wait for ye while ye go on yer own merry way."

"Insult? I didna insult ye. I meant it in affection just as I call ye Deir. And where is it ye think I am going? I dinna understand why ye have taken offense. If ye dinna want me to court ye, just say as much, and I will let it stand as friendship between us."

"Ye meant it as a compliment?"

"Mo eun beag. Is that better?" *My little bird.*

"Aye."

"Now, can ye explain what ye mean when ye say I willnae wait for ye? Didna I just say that was exactly what I plan to do."

"Ye didna learn to kiss that way with yer sister."

"Nay, I didna."

"Ye clearly learned somewhere. Ye seemed to enjoy it as well. It gets mighty cold as far north as ye are. Just how will ye stay warm this winter?"

Magnus broke into a wide grin.

"Jealous are ye? I dinna think ye ken too much of what happens between a woman and a mon, but there are ways that a mon can stay warm without anyone else to help." He raised one eyebrow.

"Is that how ye stayed warm this past winter?"

Magnus's smiled slipped. He looked into Deirdre's eyes and knew there was no point in lying.

"Deirdre, let us nae dither aboot anymore. Ye want to ken if I will be faithful to ye. And ye want to ken if I've been with any other women since I met ye. Well, the answer to both is aye. Aye, I have been with other women in the past year. We had nay agreement between us, and I thought I could make maself move on. That it was just infatuation, but it isnae. I kenned coming in here that I would ask ye if ye would let me court ye. I canna get ye out of ma mind or ma heart. Naught I do seems to be enough to replace ye or to sooth the ache I feel when I look and ye are nae there. I will nae ask ye to marry me as I dinna want ye trapped into a betrothal that ye may later regret, and I havenae asked yer father's permission, but I want ye to ken ye are the one, the only one, for me. Ye are still young at four and ten summers, so I hadnae even planned to ask ye to consider me, but when I saw ye yestereve, I kenned I had to. I couldnae wait. As for faithfulness, there is one thing that ye should ken aboot all the Sinclair men. We will always be faithful to our last breath. We willna ever stray from a woman to whom we pledge ourselves. I intend to marry ye and have said as much, so that is as good as making ma first pledge. There willna be anyone else from this moment forth. There doesnae need to be anyone else now I ken ye return ma feelings. Or at least I think ye do." Magnus had sounded so resolute through his entire speech until the end when uncertainty swamped him.

Deirdre unfolded her arms and rested her hands once again on his chest.

"I do return yer feelings, Magnus. I havenae stopped thinking aboot ye either. It is so lonely without ye kenning how we get along. Last year was the only gathering I ever enjoyed. I have nae one else to speak to aboot ma work or ma books. Ye didna seem to tire of listening at all during that fortnight. Ye listened to me, really listened. We clearly share much in common beyond scholarly pursuits. I hadnae been fishing in years because ma father was always too busy. Ye let me enjoy maself without the constant reminder that I am the laird's daughter and should be more proper. I havenae had anyone to race nor does anyone let me ride as ye did. I feel free and the real me when I am with ye."

"Ye have described how I have felt too."

"I would be lying though if I didna say I worry ye will change yer mind. Out of sight, out of mind."

"Has that happened in the past year?"

She raised her eyebrow at him.

"Ye were never out of ma mind. That was the problem. Deir, I dinna want anyone else. I dinna think I can touch another woman again. It's only ye, that I can pledge." He pressed his lips to hers once more, and her arms slipped around his neck. She nodded her head once before opening her mouth to him.

She said aye.

~ ~ ~

Magnus decided that he would return to his chamber for a few hours of sleep before returning to wait. The blackness of the night was lightening to a deep predawn blue when he stepped towards the door. He had not yet reached it when a guardsman finally called his name. He looked over his shoulder at the guard who nodded. Magnus sighed; he almost wanted his bed more than to meet with the king. For the sake of his family and his clan, he forced himself toward the guard, but not until after he had looked through the exit once more.

It surprised Magnus to see that the king was alone except for one young scribe. All of his councilors and advisors had left, probably to seek their own beds, and the king leaned against the arm of a heavy wooden and well-padded chair.

Magnus approached and bowed before the man who held his clan's fate.

"Sire."

"Rise, Magnus. They're all gone, and we're here alone." Magnus noticed that the scribe went unacknowledged nor did the young man raise his head. "I know I have kept you waiting, and I do recognize your patience. However, it was important to me to hear your uncle's side of the story before letting you launch into yours. I know you to be an honest man, as are the members of your family, but I wanted someone a little removed from the situation to explain your position. I have heard the ramblings and rantings of first the MacDonnells and now the Gunns, de Soules," he grimaced at that name, "and the Kerrs. The last three are claiming a wergild for their dead relatives. I do not believe they suffer their losses more than pride dictates you compensate them."

Magnus stood as the king spoke. He did not respond since he was not sure if the king finished, and no one invited him to do so.

"What say you?" At Magnus's drawn-out silence, the king added, "I have known you since you were a bairn. I was at your baptism, and you used to sit on my lap and pull my beard as a wean. Do not suddenly get shy now."

"As ye say, sire. The situation with the MacDonnells extends beyond just the Sinclairs, as ye ken. It was Laird Mackay's stepmother and his former—servant," Magnus chose his words carefully, "who conspired to have my sister abducted by Lord Alan. Lord Alan kidnapped her out of revenge and covetousness. Simply put, he did not want her until Tristan did. Lady Beatris and Sorcha threatened Mairghread that they would sell her to a Norseman. Two MacDonnell guardsmen attempted to assult her, and Laird MacDonnell hadnae any clue what was going on in his own keep. Fortunately for him, he suffered little more than some bruising to his face. His guardsmen did not fare so well. Lord Alan paid the price with his life. I dinna see how any reasonable mon would consider Lord Alan's death worthy of recompense. He stole ma sister from her husband. The MacDonnell should consider himself a fortunate mon that Lady Beatris and Sorcha were banished to here rather than face death or their own sale to the Norse. He should also count his blessings that he still wakes each morn."

Magnus could feel his blood pressure rising as he had to recount the tale of his sister's abduction in greater depth to the king. He took calming breaths and unclenched his hands which he had not realized he fisted. He must have done it early in his story because his fingers ached as he straightened them. He was then prompted to explain what transpired with his oldest brother, Callum.

"Ye may already ken the story of Laird Mackenzie's first marriage to Rose MacLeod and how she died. Before she passed, she gave birth to Siùsan. Forced into the vera marriage he was attempting to avoid with Lady Elizabeth Gunn, he abandoned his daughter to a village woman who raised her. It was her son, Robert, who conspired, here at court, with Laird Gunn's younger brother, James. The two men found a woman, another Lady Elizabeth, willing to seduce Callum before Da arranged his betrothal. He was foolish enough to bring that bluidy bitch back to Dunbeath. When Siùsan arrived, Callum became determined to make their relationship work. More than that, they fell in love, but Elizabeth was just as determined to become Lady Sinclair. She connived and created a scene to trap Callum. James Gunn attacked us when we were on our way home from tracking

Siùsan after she ran from Callum. Jumping ahead, Callum and Siùsan were traveling together with me and Tavish when Lady Elizabeth had us drugged. Gunn and Robert took Siùsan and tried to molest her. I dinna ken if Tristan or Callum will ever be quite the same after what they saw their wives endure. I ken I amnae after what I saw of ma sister. Be forewarned, that as lairds, both men will choose their wives above all else. Alex's story is a mite different. Brighde's father sold her to Randulph de Soules, the depraved bastard. Her father and de Soules conspired to have her killed so they both stood to gain a small fortune. She managed to make her way, alone, all the way to Castle Dunbeath. Alex nursed her back to health and vera nearly lost his heart when she wouldnae agree to marry him. It terrified Brighde that her past would endanger Alex and our clan. Rightly so. De Soules showed up in the Highlands and reconnected with an old friend from court, Laird Gunn. The Gunn brought de Soules and Brighde's father to us. The battle ensued. They lost, and we won. The Mackays aided us. There isnae much more than that. Sire, I dinna believe we should pay a penny of recompense to anyone. If naught else, they should reward us for doing away with a traitor, an attempted murderer, two attempted rapists, and a conspirator against the crown."

"Conspirator?"

"Aye, anyone who would ally themselves to de Soules, who we all ken lied when he swore his allegiance to ye, is a traitor too. The Gunn did just that. His brother wasnae any better. Those clans all came out nay worse for wear by having their lives purged of those festering boils."

The king looked at Magnus for a long time, and Magnus was tempted to shuffle his feet or ease into his normal stance with arms crossed.

"How fairs Lady Deirdre?" the king asked unexpectedly.

"I would imagine quite well," Magnus hedged.

"I know you have seen her. I watched as you chased her and Lord Archibald out of the Great Hall."

"I didna like the way he approached her, and he manhandled her as they were leaving."

"What is how her betrothed handles her to you?"

"He isnae her betrothed and nay lady deserves to be mistreated. I just told ye how ma sister and sister by marriage were abused. Do ye think I could stand by after what I have seen?" Magnus forced a smoothness to his voice he did not feel. He refused to rise to the king's bait, which he knew was what the king intended.

"You were once very close to Lady Deirdre. I believe you wished to marry her many moons ago. The falling out between your father and the Fraser rather spoiled that. Did you know she had become one of the queen's most favored ladies?"

"Nay. I didna ken where she was until I saw her."

"Really? You never once received word she joined the court. Gossip buzzes through the air in the Highlands like flies to dung."

"I suppose we are simply too far north, and the flies dinna like the cold."

The king barked a laugh and shook his head.

"It is most unfortunate she will marry Lord Archibald. I gave my consent to the marriage tonight. If only you met with me sooner."

Magnus felt his anger rising as heat suffused his cheeks. His ears rang, and his hands clenched again.

If I could have met with ye sooner. Ye bluidy self-important prig. Ye've kenned I was here for days, and ye purposely kept me waiting. Ye did this on purpose.

"It would seem Laird Fraser has made an advantageous match for his daughter. As a former friend, I wish her happy and that she doesnae suffer too greatly at Lord Archibald's hands."

"Too greatly? Why would she suffer at all? He is a wealthy man, and she will want for nothing."

"She may want for her safety. Did ye nae hear what happened when I encountered them after leaving the Great Hall.?"

"You mean your fit of jealousy that could have broken Lord Hay's nose."

"My Grace, that was nae jealousy. That was pure rage. He was trying to assault Lady Deirdre in an alcove. I heard her scream for him to stop and nae to touch her. Yer bluidy guards did naught to come to her rescue. They hadnae any problems ignoring a woman being molested. Lord Archibald should count himself lucky. The Sinclairs dinna stand for women being mistreated, and we certainly willna ever turn a blind eye to a woman in danger."

Magnus's voiced grew softer, and as he spoke, the resolve only grew stronger. The king once again looked at Magnus for a long time. The Sinclairs had been ever loyal, and the king relied on them to help manage the Highlands. He had also known Magnus since his birth and knew the man was difficult to anger. Easy going and jovial, the man who stood before him was all warrior. He was the very image of his father that the king remembered from when he and Liam Sinclair had been younger. Nodding his head once more, the king spoke.

"You have given me much to think about, some of which is news even to me. I will have to consider all the parties involved and what is best for all.

Magnus swallowed hard before bowing. He backed away, but before he could reach the door, the king called to him.

"Magnus, know Lady Deirdre is dear to me and my wife. We will not tolerate any harm coming to her. I pledge that at your sovereign and as a family friend."

Magnus left thinking, *a whole lot a good that empty pledge will do if she's locked away somewhere on Hay land and nae allowed to see the light of day. She'll be forgotten and replaced before the next moon.*

47

Chapter Six

The sun rose several hours before Deirdre left her chamber, but she was up with it. Her sleep was restless and fitful. She still felt weighed down by the events with her parents and the final confirmed realization that any affection her father harbored for her was gone. She had none left to give either of her parents. Awake long before any of the other ladies-in-waiting or the queen, Deirdre tried to spend the time in prayer, but her mind kept drifting. She knelt at her prie-dieu reciting the lengthy prayers instilled in her since childhood. She said them out of routine rather than devotion which caused her momentary pangs of guilt. She could not stop herself from turning back to a happier time.

~~~

"Magnus, slow down. Ma legs arenae as long as yers. I canna keep up," Deirdre panted as she tried to match Magnus's stride, but she had to take two and three steps for his one. She dug her heels into the soft ground and almost fell from the force of Magnus pulling. He stopped and looked at her before taking the step back. She thought he would slow down for her, instead, he lifted her over his shoulder like a sack of potatoes.

They were at the fall royal hunt hosted this year by Clan McKinnon. It was the fourth day, and the hunt would end tomorrow. Deirdre and Magnus spent as much time together as they could to make up for their six-month separation, and they spent several hours discussing Caedmon's Hymn and its meaning. Their banter drew attention from others at times, but they thoroughly enjoyed the intellectual parrying. They had not, however, been able to find any privacy.

"Ye ken we havenae much time, so I willna waste a minute I can spend with ye."

"I feel the same, but I canna make ma legs grow to match yers. Ye're making all the blood rush to my head."

Magnus eased her off his shoulder and cradled her in his arms. He kept his pace despite the added weight. He entered the wooded area near to the McKinnon keep, and when he was sure that no one could spy them, he put Deirdre back on her feet. He led her behind the trunk of a massive oak. They came together instantly. Magnus bent to take Deirdre's proffered lips, she tugged on his hair demanding their kiss as much as he. She opened to him as she felt his hand on one breast and the other on her backside. She gripped his biceps as she felt herself floating above the scene below. She was drunk from Magnus's kisses and touch, she moaned when the rough skin of his hand brushed against the bare skin of her leg.

"It's been six moons since I saw ye at the Grahams, Deir, and it's felt like a lifetime. Christ on the cross, ye taste so fine. I want to sweep ma tongue over every inch of ye until none of it is a mystery."

"Magnus," she panted, "what are ye doing to me? I'm floating and yet ma body is so heavy. Ye're making me ache, and I canna think aboot anything other than yer hands on me and yer mouth. Dinna stop kissing me."

"As ye wish, mo leannan."

Magnus's lips pressed with a demand she willingly accepted. His hand crept higher on her thigh until it slid to her mound. He cupped her warm core and slowly rubbed his fingers against her entrance. He knew she was still young and inexperienced at fourteen and a half summers even if other girls her age married by now.

"Deir, I'm going to place ma fingers inside ye. I amnae taking yer maidenhead, but I will bring ye pleasure. Is that what ye want?"

"Aye. Now." Deirdre barely registered that he was asking her permission rather than just taking. She dug her fingers deeper into his arms as her heart swelled. When his finger slipped between her damp folds, she moaned and thrust her hips into his hand. The dampness was an invitation to Magnus to slide another finger into her. He did not want to scare her or hurt her since this was their first time. As his fingers found the smooth skin of her inner wall and began to stroke, his thumb found the sensitive little bud that called to him. He lifted her leg to his hip and when she wrapped it around him, he used his now free hand to pull her kirtle down her shoulder. He freed her breast from the gown and lowered his head to lick the dusky nipple. Deirdre gasped as the cool air washed across her moist skin. Her nipple puckered, and Magnus dove back to capture it between his teeth. He bit it lightly before taking almost her entire breast into his mouth. He alternated suckling and nipping until she could no longer control her moans. Her hips rocked against his hand, and he added a third finger. She was so tight that Magnus could not stop imagining his cock being milked by her narrow passage. He could feel his cock leaking, and as her muscles began to spasm, he thought he would find his release without her even touching him. Suddenly, it was Magnus's turn to feel cold air against his overheated skin. Deirdre's small hand wrapped around his rod and squeezed gently.

Deirdre's eyes were closed throughout Magnus's onslaught. She could not keep them open even though she longed to see what he was doing to make her body respond. Absently, her hands ran over his chest and to his hips. She found indentations on the sides of his hip that fascinated her. She fit her hands there and then slid them around to grasp his hard buttocks. His body was so different from her own, and she marveled in his strength of physique but gentleness of touch. As her body ached more for something she did not know, her intuition told her she needed to touch him as he touched her. Searching, she found the end of his plaid and lifted it enough to slip her hand below. It was easy to find his steel length. She brushed her fingers along the ridge that jutted out and discovered a warm liquid that dripped from the top. She swirled it and then wrapped her hand around him.

"Tell me what to do," she breathed. "I want to make ye feel like I do."

"St. Columbo's bones, ye are. I will spill ma seed if ye dinna stop."

"Would that make ye feel good?"

Her naïve question had Magnus pausing from his exploration. He looked down into eyes that opened. The innocence laced with lust was his undoing.

"Aye, it would feel vera good to find ma release from ye. Stroke up and down, Deir. It willna take long, but I willna finish before I bring ye to yer own release."

His hand slid around to her backside, and he pressed her hips forward, so his thrusting fingers could go deeper while still mindful not to tear her barrier. He growled as her hand started working him.

"So hard but so smooth. Magnus, I want to see it. See ye."

He barely nodded his head, his senses consumed by the feel, smell, taste, sight, and sounds coming from his woman.

She is mine. She will be ma wife one day, and I will bask in the pleasure of her body as she does mine. I willna let her go. Dear God, how she kens how to hold me. I feel her uncertainty, and it's driving me to the brink even faster. I ken I am the only one she has ever touched. The only one she ever will. She's mine.

Magnus was racing towards his finish and was desperate to bring Deirdre pleasure before his own. He took her breast into his mouth again and suckled as hard as he could while his fingers and thumb continued to dance against her core, his free hand pressing her close.

Deirdre managed to look down. She saw Magnus's dark head bent over her breasts, her hand hidden by his plaid, and his hand which disappeared under her gown. She hesitated for a breath before lifting Magnus's plaid to his waist. She caught sight of the enormous sword that jutted from his hips and that her hand could barely enclose. She watched her hand move as a milky liquid leaked from his tip. She brushed her thumb over it and caught the dew. She had a sudden urge to taste it, to taste him. She squeezed gingerly again and picked up her pace as she felt her own body contracting around his hands.

"Oh, God. What's happening, Magnus? I ache for ye, and ma body feels like it's being licked by flames."

"We're both close to release. Dinna stop stroking me, please." He was begging by the time he finished speaking.

Deirdre felt her core tighten as a wave of pleasure and relief coursed through her. She held her breath as she trembled and could only pant from the aftershocks that rippled long after the intensity eased. She felt Magnus's entire body stiffen before the sticky liquid she had encountered earlier coated her hand.

"Good God, lass. It hasnae ever been that good before."

Magnus gulped as he realized that he admitted to one woman that he had been with others, and they had just finished their loveplay seconds earlier.

Deirdre smiled like the cat that got the cream.

"Good. Dinna forget that when other lasses are offering ye the same or more than I did."

"What other lasses? There are none." Magnus brushed his lips across hers before brushing his nose against hers.

"Deirdre, there arenae any others. There havenae been since before the gathering at the Grahams. I canna even look at any other women cause all I can think of is ye and how I want to marry ye. I want to do this every day for the rest of our lives. I want to watch as I make ye come apart around me and on me. One day it willna just be ma hand buried deep inside ye. I hope ye feel the same. I hope ye dinna want anyone else when I canna be near."

Deirdre heard the uncertainty and almost fear in Magnus's voice, and his vulnerability shocked her.

"Magnus, I dinna take what we did or how we feel for granted. I pined for ye for a year, and nay other lad or mon caught ma eye. I canna imagine letting any other mon touch me as ye do. I dinna like that idea at all. I, too, want all of ye. I want to learn from ye what making love is aboot."

"With ye."

"Huh?"

"I want to learn with ye, nae from ye. This is new to me, too. I havenae ever had feelings for a woman before. I canna get ye out of ma mind or ma heart, and I dinna want to. Our missives from the past six moons have sustained me when I couldnae see ye, touch ye, or speak to ye. I long for our discussions and yer easy laughter, but I crave this too. There isnae ever a need or want for anyone else. It's ye I dream aboot every night, and it's ye I picture when I take maself in hand. Yer name is on ma lips when I finish."

"What're you saying? Do ye—" Deirdre trailed off. She would not be the first one to say it even if she was asking him.

"Aye, mo eun beag. I love ye. Deeply."

"I love ye, too, mo fhuamhaire."

"Yer giant? I amnae that big."

"Och, ye are. All over." Deirdre's grin was far more seductive than she could have imagined. Magnus felt his cock hardening again.

"And all of it is mine. I dinna share, ever."

Her claim of possession brought Magnus fully erect. He pressed her back against the tree again. This time his kiss was savage and rough. There was no tenderness or finesse. He consumed her mouth as his tongue parried with hers. As forceful as he was, she met him and gave no quarter. She growled as she pushed his sporran aside and ground her mound against his shaft. He lifted her, and she wrapped her legs around him, rocking and creating the friction they both desired.

"I am yers. Always. And dinna think for even a moment I will ever share ye. Dinna underestimate what I will do or how far I will go to keep ye."

Deirdre exploded as he thrust against his plaid and her gown, and she felt his release as his cock beat against her core.

~ ~ ~

"Lady Deirdre, are ye awake? Dee, it's Beth. Ye must awake or we'll be late."

Deirdre came back to the present as she noticed her cousin's light rapping on her door. She rose and rubbed her sore knees before crossing the room and opening the door.

"Thank heavens, you are dressed and ready. We must hurry. You missed matins, and the queen noticed."

"I was at ma prie-dieu and lost track of the time."

There. That sounds good, and it's true. Nay body need ken I wasna preying at all, though I probably need to go to confession now.

Deirdre's skin heated again as the scene in the woods flashed once more before her eyes.

"Are you not well? You're rather flushed."

Deirdre gave her cousin a blank stare before she thought about what she heard.

"I am vera well. I just didna sleep that much."

"Because of Magnus." Her cousin stated rather than asked.

"Sshh! Dinna say his name so loudly. I dinna want any of the other lasses to hear, and these walls tell ma parents secrets."

"Dee, your voice. Your burr is back again. You have been with him."

"Aye. Yes." Deirdre was close to Elizabeth and often thought of her more as a sister than a cousin. She was her best friend and often felt she was her only friend at court, but she would not share the intimacies between her and Magnus to anyone. It was theirs only.

"When?"

"When I left the Great Hall, Lord Archibald followed me and cornered me into an alcove. Magnus saw him pushing me through the door into the passageway, so he followed. He found us right before Archibald tried to rape me."

"He rescued you? Lord Archibald tried to molest you?"

"It was more than molest, and he told me as much. He warned he would send me to his remotest keep and leave me there, only bedding me when and how he wanted until I produced the heir and spare."

"Did Magnus hear any of that?"

"He must have. I thought he would kill Archibald. I wanted to let him, to be honest, but I could nae trade Magnus's safety for mine. He would be in the oubliette now if he had. I willna risk that."

"You still love him."

Deirdre stopped and looked straight at Elizabeth.

"Ye ken I never stopped. Ye're one of the few that ken he's ma husband. I do love him and always will. I just hadnae remembered the intensity, that's all." Deirdre's voice was a hoarse whisper.

"But he isn't your husband. That ended a year and a day after your handfast. If you were honest with yourself, you would admit it ended the day you left that gathering and your father declared he was sending you to court."

"That may be what everyone else thinks, but it isnae what Magnus and I think."

"So, you would commit bigamy? Married to both Magnus and Lord Archibald?"

"I amnae ever marrying Lord Archibald Hay. I wouldnae even if Magnus hadnae shown up."

"You think you have a choice? This is the most ridiculous thing you have ever thought, and I have heard plenty of far-fetched notions from you since we were children." Elizabeth hissed as they both tried to keep their voices inaudible to anyone else who might be near.

"I didna say I would be given a choice, but I most certainly do have one. I will go to a convent and commit maself to God before I open ma mouth to say vows to anyone other than Magnus. We are still in Scotland, and a priest canna marry an unwilling bride nae matter what the arrangement may be between the father and the groom."

Elizabeth took her by the arm and walked them towards the gardens.

"You are treading dangerous grounds. Neither your father nor Lord Archibald will stand for being made a fool. Archibald has already threatened and manhandled you. What do you think he will be like if you're awkward at the wedding? And what of your father? He loves you, but he's a politician first nowadays."

"Och, I ken that all too well. He and Mother came to my chamber last night to question me aboot Archibald's claim that Magnus attacked him. I told him what Archibald did and said, and ma father practically gave him permission to accost me. I also saw that ma mother is even more grasping and ambitious than ma father. I will nae find sanctuary from them. I am on ma own with Magnus, but I swear to ye now, I willnae ever marry anyone else but Magnus. It's a convent or the cliffs."

Elizabeth stared horrified at her cousin but had no opportunity to say more as they stepped into the gardens. Other young women who looked for any chance to gossip and do harm if it would elevate their position with the queen surrounded them. Deirdre was a favorite of the king and queen because she was precisely the opposite. She sought no favors and asked for none. It was not a strategy but true indifference. There was nothing, short of marrying Magnus, that she ever wanted from the royal couple. She petitioned them when she first arrived at court but they refused her separately and jointly then informed her parents. When they denied her and told her parents of her request, she vowed to trust no one at court and to never rely on anyone else. She had stuck with that until Magnus arrived. He was the only one she put her faith in. She even kept Elizabeth at some distance.

"There ye are, ladies. We were beginning to believe you ran off with a stableboy." The queen crowed. The other ladies-in-waiting twittered at the queen's poor attempt at humor.

"I was at my prie-dieu and lost track of time, Your Grace. I thank you for sending Elizabeth to summon me." *Watch yer brogue. Watch your speech.*

"Very well. A morning spent in prayer does the soul good." The queen floated away as the older ladies followed her.

They left Deirdre and Elizabeth with a swarm that was closer to their own age. They walked through the gardens for some time. Deirdre stopped to look at various flowers and the small bird baths, but her mind was still not in the present. She tried but could not stop her reminiscences.

~ ~ ~

"Did ye see me in the foot race? Or swimming? Mayhap the caber toss?"

"How could I nae? Ye won the swimming and the caber toss, and I dinna ken how the four of ye did it, but ye and yer brothers all tied in the foot race. There wasna any chance for someone else to win. There was a Sinclair mountain in the way."

Deirdre giggled as she and Magnus walked towards the loch where his swimming event had only finished an hour ago. Water still dripped from the ends of Magnus's hair. She longed to run her fingers through it, but there were still people nearby. She contented herself in knowing they were to have a picnic together. They each convinced their families they were continuing their discussion of

"Heimskringla", the tale of Norse kings, that they had corresponded about. No one seemed to notice that for once, Deirdre had no scrolls with her. Unlike at the McKinnon hunt where they snuck off to the woods, Magnus insisted people see them walking out together while they held the gathering at the Campbells. He knew his own father's suspicions grew. He believed no one would question them if they did not appear to have anything to hide.

"Did ye see me in the archery competition? Aye, ye ken I snuck over to the women's pavilion to see ye compete. Ye are far better than any of the lads I ken. I wish ye could be a competitor against the other lads. Ye would trounce them all. Might do some of them some good to learn a little humility."

"And would that include ye when I trounce ye too?" Deirdre sprinted forward, her curls bouncing as she looked back over her shoulder at Magnus. She picked up her skirts and ran towards the loch. It took only a few strides for Magnus to catch up to her. The basket in one hand and the other arm wrapped around her middle, he carried both to a shady spot near the shore.

"When will ye ever learn that ye may run, but I will always chase? Ye may scamper, but I will always catch ma prey."

"I dinna scamper!" Deirdre looked indignant. "I amnae a squirrel."

"But ye climb trees like one." He tickled her ribs and listened to her laughter that reminded him of fairy bells.

Deirdre looked at him for a moment before her face turned beet red. She looked him up and down, and Magnus could not miss the lust that sparked there.

"I can think of one tree trunk I would like to climb."

Magnus froze. He could not believe his sprite of a sweetheart said something so risqué. He rather liked it. He pulled her in and dropped the basket to the ground. His lips stopped just short of her mouth.

"I can think of something I'd like ye to climb on."

Deirdre lifted her chin and pressed her mouth to his. She initiated the kiss, and Magnus let her control it. She darted her tongue out and licked the seam of his lips. He parted them for her, and she thrust hers into his warm mouth. She swept hers around before drawing him into her mouth. She sucked lustily on it, and Magnus growled. Both of his hands pulled at her laces. It was only when cool air hit the middle of her back that Deirdre drew back. She looked around and shook her head.

"We canna do this here, Magnus. We'll be seen."

Magnus took her hand and led her to a secluded spot that sat tucked between a large maple tree and some boulders. He pulled a plaid from the basket and laid it out. He helped Deirdre down and was prepared to set out their lunch though he was not interested in their food. He was unprepared for her to launch herself at him. He caught her as they fell back, and she stretched across his chest. She spread her hands growing accustomed to how it was yet again broader and harder than the last time she saw him. She dove in for a kiss, and his fingers knotted into her hair, turning her head slightly, so he could deepen the kiss. She pushed his sporran out of the way and wriggled into between his legs. Magnus groaned as her weight shifted onto his swollen cock.

"Did I hurt ye?"

"Nay," he ground out.

"I dinna believe ye."

Deirdre tried to lift her weight off him, but he pinned her back down.

"It will hurt far more if ye abandon me."

"I amnae going anywhere. I do want to be able to reach though."

She shifted again and slid her hand up his thigh. She felt his muscles bunch under her fingers, and a tremble passed over him as her fingertips brushed against his rod.

"Will ye ever stop growing?"

Magnus's eyes flew open, and he choked on his own laughter.

"Ye ken what I mean. I didna mean this," she stroked him, "I meant that ye are taller and broader yet again, but I havenae grown any in over a year. I'm tiny compared to ye, mo fhuamhaire."

"Are ye worried that I will crush ye?"

"Nay. I never thought of that actually. I just dinna want to look ridiculous next to ye. Ye look like a mon at eight and ten summers, and I am naught but a lass at five and ten summers"

Magnus separated her laces enough to pull the neckline down and free her breasts.

"There is definitely naught aboot ye that makes me think of ye as a lass anymore. Ye are a woman, and I like every *wee* bit of it."

Magnus did not understand why she drew back and scrambled off him. She yanked her gown up as she backed away, but she did not turn in time to avoid him seeing the tears in her eyes.

Magnus rushed to get to his feet and stepped behind her. He placed his hands tentatively on her shoulders and tried to turn her to face him, but she refused.

"What has made ye so distraught?" Magnus knew she disliked that word and hoped it would distract her enough to prevent tears from falling.

"Ye ken I dinna get distraught. Dinna try to get a rise out of me."

"I would say the same to ye, but it's a little late, dinna ye think?" He slipped his arms around her waist and pulled her back against him. She could feel his cock pressing against her backside. "Deir, what is it? What did I say to upset ye? Ye ken I wouldnae do that on purpose."

"Ye think I am 'wee.' So, I do have the body of a lass and nae a woman. What mon wants a girl when he can have a proper woman?"

"I dinna ken what ye mean by a proper woman, but I ken vera well I want the woman who is in ma arms. Mo chridhe, ye are wee only because I amnae a proper size maself. Do ye really want a mon who doesnae fit in most chairs, who can barely fit through a doorway without either banging ma head or ma shoulders, or that most people assume is dimwitted?"

"Who says that? Who? I would ken right now." Magnus felt her stomp her foot on the ground.

"Mo eun beag, ye are quite quick to defend me when I tell ye that I am too large, and yet ye dinna believe I love ye just as ye are."

He nuzzled her nape and kissed the place where her shoulder and neck met, knowing it was a spot that aroused her more than anywhere else on her body.

"Vera fierce, too. I must say I rather like having ye as ma defender."

Deirdre spun in his arms.

"Now ye're just teasing me."

"Aye, but I prefer to see ye laugh or even angry rather than sad. I dinna like to think of ye as distraught." He ducked as she swatted at him. "Deir, ye and I will never be the same size. We dinna need to be, but ken that I crave ye just as ye are. There is nay one else who makes me hard just thinking of them. There is nay one else that I picture when I pleasure maself. There is nay one else who could ever taste as good as ye. In fact, I am famished, and there is only one thing that will satisfy ma hunger."

Deirdre looked into his smoky brown eyes and saw desire and mischief swirling through them. He led them back to the plaid and eased them to the ground. He slipped her arms from her kirtle and peppered kisses across her breasts, taking time to suck each nipple while his hands pulled her skirts to her waist. He pressed three fingers into her as the other hand pushed one leg up. He slid down and rested her leg over his shoulder as his tongue licked the scorching folds that glistened from her dew and then from his tongue.

Deirdre's head shot off the ground, and she struggled to sit up. A hand landed on her belly and tried to press her back down.

"Nay, Magnus. I want to see. I want to watch ye," she whispered.

Magnus's heart sped up at the sound of her erotic request. He knew she did not know how her words made him long to thrust into her. He wanted nothing more than to watch his own cock plunge in and out of her. He removed his hand from her belly and pushed her skirts up further. He scooped her backside into his hands and lifted her hips, bringing her sheath closer to his mouth. He breathed in her scent of crisp apples and woman. He would know her scent of apples anywhere, but now he knew something that no other man did or ever would.

His tongue lapped through her folds and flicked her pleasure button. She whimpered as her head fell back and she propped herself on her elbows.

Momentarily distracted, Magnus forgot what he was about as he took in the scene she presented. She did not look like a girl now. She looked every inch a woman who was being pleasured and enjoying it. He thrust his tongue into her as deeply as he could and sucked on her sensitive nub. Her hips jumped in his hands, and her moans had him returning his fingers to her. He worked her blazing skin with a purpose that had Deirdre crying out her release much faster than he expected. He wished he had drawn out her pleasure for longer.

"Magnus." He heard her panting.

"Aye, Deir?" He shifted onto his forearms and kissed her nose.

"I had nae idea that ye planned to make a meal out of me."

"Ye are the finest main course I have ever been served."

Deirdre lifted her head and stared a moment before pushing his shoulders as hard as she could and raising her body to follow. She flipped Magnus onto his back, but she knew it was only because he let her.

"Then I intend to have dessert."

Before Magnus understood what she meant, his plaid flipped back and hit him in the face. He pushed the material aside in time to see Deirdre examining his rod. He knew he was large and bigger than the last time they were together. He worried he would scare her, but there was no hint of fear when she looked up at him. Her eyes locked on his as she trailed the tip of her tongue from stem to stern. Her tongue followed the ridge until she reached the tip. She swirled her tongue around the hole that leaked and then sucked the head into her mouth.

Magnus thought he died and went to heaven.

"Deir, ye dinna have to do this."

But dear God, dinna stop. Fuck! How does she ken to take me in her mouth like that? How can she even take that much of me into her? Before her, when I wasnae yet this big, I couldnae find a lass willing to even try.

Magnus shook his head. The last thing he wanted at that moment was to think of another woman. He could not even picture a single face from his past.

Christ on the cross, now she's using her hand too. Breathe or this will be over right now. Ye canna come in her mouth. Whatever ye do, dinna do that.

Magnus groaned again when Deirdre used her free hand to explore his bollocks. She weighed them in her hands and shifted them around. When she rubbed the spot just behind them, Magnus's hips jerked off the ground, and his cock twitched. He knew he had to get her to let go immediately. He would not last any longer.

"Deir, ye must let go. Stop, mo ghaol, I dinna want to finish in yer mouth. I canna do that."

She swatted his hand away and sucked harder. Magnus was lost. His hands fisted in her hair and while he did not press her head, he could not stop his hips from rocking upwards. He felt his release crash over him as streams of his seed hit the back of Deirdre's throat. He felt her swallowing it down, and when she hummed, his release began all over again. He could not believe how rung dry he felt when his body settled again on the plaid at last. He slid his hands beneath her arms and lifted her up onto his chest.

Deirdre wiped her lips with her fingertips and considered what she had just done. She had no clue what she was doing, but when Magnus's mouth pressed against her mound and then his tongue entered her, she remembered how curious she was to taste him the last time they were together. She decided this was the perfect opportunity to not only reciprocate but satisfy her curiosity.

"It's salty."

"What?" Magnus choked. He knew what she was talking about, he just had not expected her to say anything. Then again, he most definitely had not expected her to take him in her mouth and suck him bone dry.

"Yer seed. It's salty. I dinna ken what I expected, but I didna ken it would taste like that."

"Deir, ye didna have to do any of that. I didna plan to come in yer mouth. Please forgive me for that."

"Forgive ye for what? Didna I come with yer tongue in me. I came in your mouth. That's different?" She watched him nod his head. "Why? Because more came out of ye than me. I dinna think it's different at all. Besides, I've been wondering what ye taste like ever since the woods at the MacKinnons'."

"Ye have?"

"Aye, thought aboot it quite a bit too. I wondered if I would ever get to try. Ye're a wee more than I planned for, but I think it worked out well enough."

"Well enough? Planned for? St Columbo's bones, I dinna even ken what to say to all of that. I didna even ken I would take ye with ma mouth, and here ye were planning yer strategy well in advance."

Deirdre smiled innocently and nodded her head.

"Did ye like it?"

"Do ye really need to ask?"

When Magnus saw doubt flash across her face, he realized that she did. She might have just given him more pleasure than he thought possible, but she was still inexperienced and nervous that she would not meet his expectations. He rolled them onto their sides and tucked her into his embrace.

"Mo chridhe, when ye stroked me in the woods, I thought that was the strongest and best release I ever had, and it was until today. What ye just gave me, what ye did for me, I canna even begin to put into words just how great it felt. Satisfying wouldnae even come close. Magnificent might be the closest I can think of."

She nodded her head slowly.

"Did ye enjoy what I did for ye, mo leannan?"

"How can ye even wonder, mo ghràidh?"

Deirdre realized that even though Magnus had called her his sweetheart, his love, and his heart, this was one of the few times she used a term of endearment. *My love.* It was not missed on Magnus either. He said nothing, but his smile told her he had longed to hear such things from her. She felt guilty she had not thought about it more. He held her tightly, and they stayed in one another's embrace until the sun shifted enough for them to feel an evening chill begin.

They had not even touched their lunch. They straightened their clothes, tossed the bread to the fish in the loch and the tarts to the ducks. They each chewed a hunk of cheese as they walked back to the keep. Before they were in view of the wall walk, Magnus stopped and pulled her in for the last swift kiss.

"I love ye, Deir."

"And I love ye, too, Magnus. Always."

"And forever."

~~~

"Did you see the beastly man last night? Did you see how he did not bother to dress properly for supper?" Mary Kerr was once again complaining about Magnus.

Mary Kerr's jeering voice yanked Deirdre back into the present. She ground her teeth to keep from interjecting. She did not like Mary, to begin with, but her insults about the Sinclairs endeared her even less, and now that Magnus was at court, her snide comments were putting Deirdre on edge.

"I thought him rather handsome. Braw. Isn't that what you Highlanders say, Deirdre?" asked Allyson Elliot.

"Yes, we say that." Deirdre's ire was rising from the baiting and discussion of her husband.

"You know what they say about their plaids," Isabella Dunbar said in a practiced whisper that was anything but. "They wear nothing under them!"

This elicited several gasps from the younger ladies and knowing looks from the older ones.

"He is a rather large man," added Allyson.

"Have you heard what they say about a man with large hands and feet?" jumped in Arabella Johnstone, "*Everything* about them is large. Even what's hidden under that plaid."

This drew more shocked gasps and outright laughter.

"I have a mind to find out if that is true," Allyson claimed.

"Not if I have already," snickered Cairren Kennedy. "There are many a dark alcove to disappear into, or better yet be found in. Highlanders crow on about their honor, well, he'd be honor bound to keep me."

Deirdre shot Elizabeth a warning look. Her temper was boiling, and waves of jealousy surged from the tip of her toes to the crown of her head. She could not be the one to say anything.

"Ladies, what if the queen hears you. You mustn't be so brazen, or we will all suffer for it in the chapel." Elizabeth intervened.

Before anything else could be said, Archibald Hay appeared from around a hedge. The ladies stopped speaking and stared between the newly arrived man and Deirdre. It was common knowledge that a betrothal was in the works, and many of the ladies fluttered about in excitement for better gossip.

"My lady, would you care to join me for a stroll through the garden?"

"Thank you for the invitation, Lord Archibald. However, I do not see the queen presently, and I cannot leave unchaperoned."

"I am sure the queen trusts me as we have an understanding, you and I." Deirdre did not miss the tinge of malice even if no one else seemed to notice.

"I would not have my reputation sullied, my lord." Deirdre countered but could do little more once she found her arm in a vicelike grip and Hay maneuvered her towards a section with thicker hedges than most other parts. He gripped her nape and dug his fingers into the side of her neck.

"Do not think for one moment you will ever be able to turn me down. For anything. You will do as I tell you the first time I tell you. Is that understood?" Hay squeezed her arm and neck mercilessly, and Deirdre could only nod.

"I am willing to forgive last night's little incident. You are not in control of that beast, and I am sure he misunderstood the situation. Such a large man usually is not particularly astute. But any further trouble will result in your punishment since there is little I can do to him."

Deirdre bit her tongue almost to the point of blood to keep from defending Magnus.

"Our betrothal will be announced soon, and I will have no one, especially that lumbering brute, interfere. I suggest you prepare yourself because our betrothal will not be a long one. Prepare your trousseau and say your goodbyes."

Hay released her arm and nudged her back to the main section where everyone gathered. Deirdre could hear peals of laughter that were even higher pitched than normal.

I wonder which poor sod they trapped now.

Deirdre almost stumbled when Magnus came into view with three women fawning over him with their hands on him and several more lingering to stare. She felt as though talons were growing from her fingernails, and she had an overwhelming desire to scratch all of their faces. *Mine, mine, mine* reverberated in her ears. She never thought a scene with other women paying attention to Magnus would elicit such visceral feelings, but she could not control the jealousy.

Magnus looked up when he noticed movement coming from near a large hedge. He was doing his best not to lose his patience with the women hovering around him. He already pulled his arms free at least five times and resorted to crossing them. When Magnus recognized Hay and Deirdre coming from the secluded area, his heart raced. He barely suppressed a primal need to snatch her and carry her away. His hands fisted as they itched to land on Hay's face all over again. He no longer heard or saw the other women, buzzing about like gnats. The approaching couple had his undivided attention. *Mine, mine, mine* echoed throughout his entire body.

Anger sparked in both Deirdre's and Magnus's eyes when they connected. Deirdre sensed that Magnus was barely keeping his emotions tethered and only did so for her sake. Magnus sensed that Deirdre wanted to run to the group and scatter the women like pigeons. Neither could extract the other, but a silent agreement passed between them.

"You would do well to stop looking at that uncouth behemoth. My wife will not ogle other men. Do not think for a moment you will have the freedom to take a lover. Not after you have given me my two sons and absolutely not before. Am I understood? I would not want there to be any misunderstanding between us as that is how unfortunate accidents come about."

Deirdre blanched at his threats because she could believe he spoke the truth. Magnus saw Deirdre pale even from where he stood. He cocked his head and ran his eyes over her. He squinted when he thought he saw red marks on her neck, and when he considered that they might be finger marks, everything he saw turned red. He stepped forward with no thought to the women around him who scurried to step out of his way.

"Excuse me," he managed to mumble before his long strides carried him to Deirdre and Hay.

Magnus tenderly grasped Deirdre's chin and turned her head. He thought his might combust with the rage that filled him. There were four clear marks that were already starting to darken into bruises. He leaned back and scrutinized every part of her he could see. He turned her head and found the matching thumbprint. She had a shawl draped around her arms to cover her bare skin. The day was cooler but still warm enough for capped sleeves. He pulled the shawl away and saw the finger marks that were a vivid red on her arms. He looked into her eyes and saw her fear. He knew the fear she felt now was for what he might do rather than what Hay had done.

"Did he threaten ye? Even a wee bit?" He whispered. Magnus watched her throat work, but she would not speak. Her silence was answer enough.

Magnus turned towards Hay and stretched to his full height. He breathed in, so his chest puffed out and his shoulders broadened. He towered over Hay who was already a tall but thin man. He visibly outweighed him by four or five stones. His hand rested on the handle of the dirk that was just barely visible in its sheath upon his belt.

"Ye touched her."

"I—" could not say anymore as Magnus's shadow fell over him.

"I warned ye nae to touch her again. Ye threatened her too. She isnae yer wife nor even yer betrothed. Ye havenae any right to touch her."

"And who are you to gainsay me? She is as good as betrothed to me, and once betrothed, she is as good as my wife. She is mine to do with as I see fit. Your meddling will not help her cause, Highlander." Hay kept his voice low but did not hide the menace.

Magnus leaned forward and looked down at Hay. Magnus craved the opportunity to pummel his fists into the shorter man's hawkish nose and cold eyes.

"Do ye plan to live long enough to make it to yer betrothal or wedding? Touch her again, and ye willna." Magnus straightened and crossed his arms. "I think it is time ye found somewhere other than here to be. Unless ye would like yer nose bloodied again. Mayhap a blackened eye?"

The ladies gawked at the scene and Magnus knew they were inching closer to snatch the latest *en dite* they could spread throughout the court. No one had heard the exchange, but Magnus's posture left no doubt to anyone he was intimidating Lord Archibald. All he wanted was to have a moment alone with Deirdre to reassure her and to hold her. He needed, for his own wellbeing, to be sure the odious man had not harmed her any more than he could see.

"Are ye well, ma lady?" He asked as the ladies-in-waiting surrounded them.

"Yes, thank you."

"You seem to have quite an interesting conversation here. We are wondering what could be so engaging. May we join you?" Allyson inquired.

"It was nothing important," Deirdre demurred, but that did not deter the ladies.

"Why would Lord Sinclair rush to you if nothing happened?" Mary Kerr spoke up for the first time. Her question had a bite to it as she glared at Magnus. She looked between Magnus and Hay, measuring the situation. "He seemed to be in quite a rush to help you when we all know you are betrothed to Lord Archibald."

"I amnae Lord Sinclair. *Laird* Sinclair is ma father." Magnus tried to steer the conversation away. "I am Magnus Sinclair."

"Are you all ready acquainted with Lady Deirdre?" Mary purred. "You seemed intent upon interrupting her walk with her betrothed."

"We have met before," Deirdre was unwilling to concede more.

"Then you can formally introduce us," Isabella angled herself closer to Magnus.

"I, too, have known Lord Magnus for several years," intervened Elizabeth. "The Sinclairs live in the most northern part of the Highlands upon the coast of the North Sea."

Magnus nodded but did not look away from Deirdre even though she would no longer meet his eye.

"You seem to know about the Sinclairs, but you have spent most of your life at court, Lady Elizabeth," Arabella observed.

"I have not always lived here. Remember, I, too, was born and raised in the Highlands. Besides, Lady Deirdre told me of her times at the gatherings and royal hunts. They took place throughout the Highlands. That is how she and Lord Magnus met."

Deirdre looked at her cousin and gave her head a minute shake, but Elizabeth was not looking at her.

"Lady Deirdre has been at court for seven summers now. How could she know Lord Magnus that well?" Mary pressed on, "Lady Deirdre, were you and Lord Magnus childhood sweethearts? He seems rather protective of you. When was the last time you saw each other?"

The world pressed in on Deirdre and black dots bounced before her eyes. She forced herself to breathe before answering.

"It has been seven summers since I saw Lord Magnus. We have not seen one another since just before I came to court."

"Him!" Lord Archibald had been silent throughout the questioning but now roared. "He's the bastard you gave yourself to? Seven years ago is when your parents said you committed your indiscretion. Your father has not paid me nearly enough to make up for it being some bloody Highlander you gave your maidenhead too. Had I known you'd whored yourself to a heathen, I never would have agreed to wed you."

Hay leaned into Deirdre so even Magnus could not hear what he whispered.

"You will pay for this. I hope you know what to do with that mouth of yours. A whore you were and a whore you will be."

Deirdre once again saw black dots dance at the corner of her eyes, and she felt the blood drain from her face. Magnus stepped forward, afraid that she would collapse, but her look stopped him. Archibald leered at her, and Magnus wanted to leave marks on his neck, except they would be evidence of him strangling Hay.

"Do not think this is over, Highlander. You have yet to resolve all your claims here at court. Tread carefully or you could see your clan impoverished and your arse in the dungeon."

Hay stepped around Magnus and stalked off, leaving Deirdre and Magnus staring at each other while the other ladies rushed to spread all that had come to light. Magnus caught Deirdre as she slumped against him, and Elizabeth's repeated apologies filled the background.

Chapter Seven

The Great Hall was filled to the brim with people as more families arrived for the royal hunt that would begin in the morning. Magnus entered the gathering hall and stifled a groan as he saw that most of the tables were already full. He scanned the crowd and found Deirdre sitting at the end of a table with her cousin beside her. The atmosphere around the table was visible even from the entrance. The other ladies-in-waiting were casting glances in Deirdre's direction but whispering among themselves. Deirdre sat mutely while Elizabeth talked to her. Magnus started towards the ladies' table but spotted Laird Fraser making his way to his daughter. Magnus circled around and approached from behind. He would give Deirdre her privacy and not make another scene, but he would be close enough to hear if her father threatened her too. Laird Fraser almost reached his daughter, but a courtier waylaid who led him to a group of other men.

Magnus looked around again and was about to take a seat at a table near the breeze coming through the windows, but he, too, was waylaid. This time a page came to him and stood before him.

"Aye, lad?"

"His Majesty has instructed me to inform you that your seat awaits you at the high table just below the dais. If you will please follow me, my lord."

At the appointed table sat some of the most well-known courtiers present. It was the table just below the salt, and so many of the wealthiest lords routinely sat there. This included Archibald Hay.

Magnus looked at the man, and his heartbeat jumped. He longed for the security and familiarity of having his broadsword strapped to his back, but once again, he faced the viper pit with his claymore locked in his chamber. His fingers itched to touch the hilt of one of his many dirks, but that would only draw more attention. There was only one seat left, and luckily for Magnus, it was on the opposite end and the same side as where Hay sat. He would not have to look at the man for the entire meal.

"I did not know they were giving away spare seats to just anyone." Hay's voice floated down to Magnus just as he lowered himself to the bench.

So much for nae having to deal with him. He is just looking for an excuse to insult me and humiliate me if he can. I willna be baited for Deir's sake. I canna do aught more to draw attention to her, or me for that matter. Nae until I conclude matters with the king.

Magnus picked up the tankard of ale and took a long draw before placing it back on the table. The men surrounding him continued their conversation with no interest or intention of including him. This suited Magnus as he held no desire to speak with these men who spent their time talking about war and defenses but rarely engaged in the dangerous business of battle.

"Tell us, Lord Sinclair, is there such a shortage of attractive women in the Highlands that you must come all the way to court to search for a beddable woman? I can only imagine how you men keep yourselves warm then?" The other men snickered at Archibald's implied insults.

Magnus took another drink of ale and broke off a piece of bread.

"*Laird* Sinclair is ma father."

He turned his attention to the serving boy who placed a trencher in front of him. The bishop blessed the meal as Magnus walked in, so he pulled out his eating knife and took his first bite of meat. However, Hay had no intention of being ignored.

"Magnus isn't it? Yes, Magnus, your mother's lessons in manners did not prepare you for court, or perhaps Highlanders do not care for manners. It is not polite to meddle in other's business. Such behavior tends to be poor for one's health."

Magnus let out a hearty laugh and leaned on one elbow, so he could see past the other men to Hay. He flexed his arm and chest which made his leine strain even more.

"Other than ma elbow on the table, ma mother would be proud to ken I have the manners to protect those who canna protect themselves. She always taught ma brothers and me that size doesnae make a mon strong or honorable. A mon who uses his size and strength to threaten those who canna defend themselves is naught more than a coward. He is either nae smart enough," he tapped his head and then his heart, "or brave enough to find a better way to overcome a challenge. A mon who must take by force does so because nay one offers him aught by choice."

The entire table sat silently. Some were shocked by how much Magnus said since most underestimated his intelligence. The others found their mouth agog when they digested what he said.

"By the by, I'm healthier than a bull and just as stubborn." Magnus dropped a piece of meat into his mouth and looked straight ahead while he chewed.

"A pity that not everyone we know has a healthy constitution. After all, a woman's constitution is so much frailer than a man's. They come to harm so much more easily, especially the thin ones like Lady Deirdre."

Magnus looked back at Hay as he spoke, and when Hay uttered Deirdre's name, Magnus pulled a dirk from his belt and laid it on the table.

"Using women to fight a mon's battle." Magnus tsked and wrapped his hand around the dirk, lifting it, he jammed its point into the table and let go. Everyone watched as the blade vibrated and the table shook. "Is a dishonorable strategy."

Magnus stood from the table and looked around. The men at the table watched him nod to several other Highlanders who caught his eye.

"Nay Highlander tolerates dishonorable men. Tread carefully. It seems there is something in our water or mayhap it's the fresh air, but ye may notice there isnae a wee mon here who wears plaid."

Magnus pulled the dirk from the table but did not resheath it. He stared at Hay until one of them would have to look away. Magnus refused to be that man. When Hay blinked, Magnus stepped away from the bench and prepared to leave the Great Hall if he could pull Deirdre away. He looked at her and saw misery written across her face as the other women cast conspicuous glances at her before laughing into their hands. Magnus's heart broke for her. He never intended for their choices to become common knowledge.

I speak of protecting those who canna protect themselves, yet I havenae done well protecting the one lass I've sworn to spend ma life defending. Would that I could whisk her away from here, but that would only draw more attention. Let there be a better scandal soon, so those vultures move on.

"Lord Magnus," boomed a loud voice that had many staring between him and the king. "Approach. I would speak to you of the hunt tomorrow."

Magnus walked to stand before the dais and bowed low.

"Making friends again, are you?" The king whispered over his chalice.

"Ye could say something of the sort, Yer Grace."

"Hmm, I think you would do well with something or somewhere to spend your energy. Join us on the hunt tomorrow."

Magnus did not miss the command. He bowed again before answering.

"As ye wish, Yer Majesty."

"There will be many fine horsemen and even a few fine horsewomen joining us on the hunt. I am sure you will recognize some." When Magnus looked up at the king, he knew to whom the king referred as the royal was looking at Deirdre.

"You've always been the best tracker of all the brothers. Only Mairghread comes close," the king chuckled as he remembered the five Sinclair siblings as children, especially the only sister who had been wilder than any of her brothers. "I would not put it past you to find the mark or bag the prey you choose."

Magnus did not miss the double meaning, but he was not sure if he was being granted permission to do away with Hay or abscond with Deirdre.

"Be in the yard at sunrise. We leave promptly." The king turned to the man sitting to his right, and Magnus knew he was dismissed. He backed away before moving to the side of the large Great Hall. He looked at Deirdre once more and decided that he would not abandon her simply to seek his own reprieve from the crowds. He found a wall to lean against in the back where he could see all the doors but was not as obvious to everyone else.

I will finally be able to wear ma sword again. Aboot ruddy time, too. And I am glad I brought ma bow. I wasna planning to be here long enough to stay for the hunt, but it looks like I dinna have much choice. I wonder if Deirdre still shoots as well as she did the first time we rode together on the hunt.

~ ~ ~

The air was crisp as everyone gathered in the Menzies's bailey. Horses snorted and stomped in the autumn air. Their saddles jangled as the stable boys attempted to wrangle the enormous warhorses and geldings that the sturdy Highland warriors favored. In among the crowd was an entirely black mare whose rider was arguing with her father about riding astride instead of sidesaddle.

"Father, we will ride far too fast and far too close for me to ride sidesaddle. I need to be able to use both knees to control Freya if I am to use my bow."

"If ye canna ride properly and appropriately, then ye dinna ride at all."

"But Father—"

"Nay more! I have given ye ma answer. Choose."

Deirdre slid from her horse and walked to the stables. She brought Freya inside and rushed to unsaddle her. She struggled to lift the large saddle from her horse, so she was unprepared for the weight to suddenly disappear from her hands. She knew immediately who stood behind her.

"Thank ye," she whispered.

"Deir, I dinna agree with yer father. I dinna like ye riding sidesaddle in the midst of such a large hunting party. The men arenae going to be paying attention to how unstable sidesaddle will be for ye. Dinna ride far from me. I will bring ye straight back here and turn ye over ma lap if ye drift." Magnus whispered as he quickly resaddled Freya with a sidesaddle. He grunted as he double checked the girth. He hated sidesaddles after his sister was thrown as a young girl. After that, their father banned his daughter from ever riding one again. He insisted that she only ride astride. Now that he was helping Deirdre mount, he wished he could insist upon her riding astride too.

"Deir, I am throwing that ruddy sidesaddle out when we marry. Dinna even bother bringing it with ye. I dinna want to see ye on it again," he growled quietly as he brought her out of the stables.

Deirdre knew the story of Mairghread's fall from when they spoke about their love for horses and riding during one of their earliest meetings. She knew he spoke out of fear, and while she knew he most likely would never spank her, a small part of her enjoyed knowing he was that protective of her.

"Magnus, dinna fash. I will stay close. Sidesaddle or nae." She flashed him a smile before maneuvering Freya closer to the Fraser party until they left the keep. She looked over her shoulder and winked. Magnus returned her grin as the hunting party moved through the portcullis.

The riders crowded together as they made their way to the woods. As they entered the treeline, they fanned out. The Frasers and Sinclairs rode together. Deirdre scanned the underbrush and caught sight of an unsettled leaf pile and a small bush close by that appeared to wiggle. She drew an arrow and shot. She was rewarded with red blooming through the leaves.

"Well done, Deirdre," her father boomed.

She smiled and dismounted to retrieve her rabbit. She pulled the arrow from it, wiped the tip, and brought the rabbit to the leather satchel attached to her saddle. Remounting, she looked over at Magnus, and her heart raced to see his look of pride. He grinned as she nudged her horse forward.

The morning carried on with Magnus and Deirdre taking turns bagging their prey. Magnus slid quiet compliments to her while she marveled at his strength to bring down several fowl within the trees.

Just after the morning, the Sinclairs broke off from the Frasers. Magnus tried to convince his father to remain with the other clan, but the king called them to join his group. Magnus rode at the back of the pack and slowed to a trot then a walk. When his family and the king were far enough ahead, he turned his horse and raced back to find Deirdre. He disliked the idea of her riding side saddle and refused to break his promise to be by her side.

As he approached, he saw her to the left of her clan members and father. She was aiming for a stag and did not see the boar emerging from the undergrowth. Magnus spurred his horse as he shot one arrow after another and finally threw a dirk at the beast.

The boar's movement and squeals of pain spooked Deirdre's horse. Magnus pulled alongside her horse and reached for the bridle as it reared. Despite his strength, he was no match atop his own horse to keep Deirdre's from rearing twice more and throwing her when she could not use both legs or free herself from the stirrup. For one terrifying moment, Magnus thought Freya might drag her, but Deirdre twisted her foot free just before her head and shoulders hit the ground.

Magnus stood in his stirrups and pulled on the bridle with all his strength, guiding Freya forward and away from Deirdre's unmoving body.

Magnus leaped from his horse and ran to Deirdre's side. He slid into the ground next to her and ran his fingers over her head finding a large knot on the left side. He ran his hands over her arms and legs without hesitation before running them over her front then sliding them underneath her to check her backbone.

"Sinclair, what the devil do ye think ye're doing touching ma daughter?"

Magnus did not spare him a glance as he continued to examine Deirdre.

"I'm making sure ye didna kill yer daughter by making her use that bluidy sidesaddle. Ye did this as much as the boar."

He did not wait for a response or the opportunity for the Fraser to check his daughter. Magnus scooped her into his arms as carefully as he could and lifted her to his saddle. Using the power of his legs alone, he mounted his horse. Cradling her and wrapping his body around her to protect her from the jarring of his horse's gallop, he raced back to the keep.

While the keep was not that great a distance, the ride back reminded Magnus of trying to walk through a bog. He could not reach the keep quickly enough as time seemed to slow. He kept looking down at Deirdre but except to unconsciously burrow closer to him, she had not moved nor had her eyelashes even fluttered.

Magnus was in a near panic as he rode into the bailey.

"I need the healer! Lady Deirdre has been injured. Someone find Lady Fraser."

Magnus dismounted as a stable boy took his reins. He lifted Deirdre down and strode to the keep's massive doors. One guardsman in the bailey rushed behind him and reached to open the door. Magnus barely nodded to him.

It took his eyes a moment to adjust to the light, but he saw Lady Fraser moving towards him. He snarled softly when he saw the lack of concern, instead almost disinterest, on Deirdre's mother's face.

"She was thrown while hunting."

"I told her she shouldn't go out gallivanting with men. Not proper at all."

Magnus stared at her agog for a moment before stepping around her and heading to the stairwell.

"On which floor is her chamber?"

"Ye can't go up there!"

"Can ye carry her? Nay? I didna think so. She's a nasty knot on the back of her head and needs the healer. I imagine she's badly bruised, but I didna feel any broken bones."

Magnus finished calling over his shoulder and he started up the stairs.

"That ye felt? How dare ye!"

Magnus paused midway up the stairs.

"Lady Fraser, ye can scold me later, but ye should tend to yer daughter. Ye're right lucky she didna break her neck."

Magnus left Lady Fraser standing in a huff and found a chambermaid to give him directions.

He reached her door when hell broke loose below stairs.

"Where'd that lad take ma daughter? What did ye do to her?" Bellowed Laird Fraser.

"He's carried her upstairs. He said he's touched her."

The Fraser barely spared his wife a look.

"Dinna fash. He didna touch her in any way I wouldnae. I want to ken why he thought he could."

"Fraser, mayhap ye should be thankful the lad was nearby and had the wherewithal to check her and bring her back here." Laird Sinclair spoke up. "Ma son has her best interest at heart. He wasna compromising her. He was trying to be sure she lives. Mayhap worrying aboot yer daughter would be better than harping aboot ma son."

Laird Fraser's face turned a shade of plum that had more than one person wondering if he would have apoplexy. He turned and stormed up the stairs with his wife closely in tow.

Magnus opened the door to Deirdre's chamber and laid her on the bed. He used pillows to prop her on her side to avoid more pressure on her head injury. Once he made her as comfortable as he could, he covered her with a plaid, stocked the fire, and closed the window dressing enough to dim the light. Magnus paced waiting for the healer. He nearly jumped out of his skin when the chamber door slammed open.

"What are ye doing in here alone with ma daughter?"

Magnus looked at Laird Fraser with a mixture of surprise and anger.

"Do ye really think I'm here to molest yer unconscious daughter?" Magnus felt the heat rising in his neck and into his face. "Dinna ye dare insinuate I did aught wrong. The door was partially open, and I amnae touching her. I am fed up with being accused. What is wrong with ye that ye arenae more worried aboot the lass?"

"Dinna tell me what I should or shouldnae be doing, ye upstart."

"Fraser, I am fed up with yer blaming ma son when all he has done is care for yer daughter. It was that damn side saddle that harmed her and yer lack of concern for her."

Laird Sinclair came to stand by his son and wrapped his arm around Magnus's shoulder. He looked into the young face that so closely resembled his own nearly two score years ago. Magnus looked at his father and saw only pride and support. He breathed a silent sigh of relief.

The healer walked in and looked at the giant angry men and the dour-faced woman. She bustled in and immediately began to run her hands over Deirdre just as Magnus had.

"Who propped the lass with the pillows?"

All eyes turned to Magnus.

"Ma laird and lady, be grateful that he did. He kept the pressure off her injury. Other than the knot on her head, she is unharmed as far as her bones. I will need to examine her further." She looked pointedly at the men.

Laird Sinclair squeezed his son's shoulder and nodded towards the door. Once in the passageway, his siblings came towards them. All four, Callum, Alexander, Tavish, and Mairghread, had been on the hunt and heard the hue and cry go up. They saw Magnus tearing across the open expanse between the woods and the keep. They, along with their father, had hurried to catch up.

"How does she fair?" asked an anxious Mairghread.

"She seems better than expected. A goose egg on the back of her head, but naught more serious."

"It was good that ye were with her, but I thought ye rode out with us."

"Aye, as did I," Laird Sinclair interjected.

"Da, I promised Deir, I mean Deirdre, that I would ride with her since neither of us was pleased aboot her using that shite saddle."

"Sidesaddle," Tavish piped in.

Magnus scowled and gave him a pointed look that had his older brother taking a step back.

"She's lucky she doesnae have a broken back or worse, dead," Callum stated the obvious. Alexander elbowed his brother as Magnus's face went white as a sheet then red as a cherry and then back to ghostly white all in a matter of seconds.

Magnus turned and walked back to Deirdre's door where he leaned against the adjacent wall.

"Son, ye canna stand there. It isnae proper. Come to the Great Hall and have a rest. I'm sure they will let us ken how the lass fairs."

Magnus adopted the stance that all four brothers learned from their father, feet planted apart and arms crossed. At eight and ten, he was already the largest of the giants that were the male Sinclairs. While he was only ever so slightly taller than Tavish, a hairsbreadth really, he was the same height as Callum and Alexander; however, he outweighed them each by two stones. He had the broadest torso and the widest arms and legs. He was a veritable mountain who made his unusually large older brothers look like hills.

Mairghread, who was slim and barely came to the center of any of their chests, walked to Magnus and rested her hands on his arms.

"I'll stay with ye, Maggie," she whispered, using her childhood nickname for him. She and Magnus were the closest in age and shared a bond that had changed over the past couple of years but was still unbreakable. Magnus nodded his head relieved that his sister, who knew him better than anyone, who knew the true nature of his relationship with Deirdre, would stay with him.

Laird Sinclair gave Mairghread and Magnus a long look before herding his other three children to the stairs and down to the Great Hall.

Once they were alone, Mairghread wrapped her arms around her brother, and he sank into her embrace. Since their mother died a few years prior, the brothers and sister relied heavily on one another and their father for emotional support, but Magnus and Mairghread always sought each other first.

"What if she dies, Mair? What if she lives but isnae the same? Canna be as she was before?"

"Wheesht. We will cross that bridge only *if* we must come to it."

"But neither Father nor Laird Fraser would ever let me marry her if she is permanently hurt."

"Ye would marry her even if she wasnae able to do things for herself or if she wasnae quite right in the head?"

Magnus ground his teeth so hard they could both hear it.

"All the more reason. Ye didna see or hear how her parents reacted to her injuries. I will take better care of her than either of them."

"But ye're awfully young to take on such a burden. What if ye decide ye--"

"Dinna," barked Magnus. "Dinna ye even dare call her a burden or tell me I amnae old enough to ken ma own mind. That lass will be ma wife one day, and God help whoever stands in the way."

Mairghread simply nodded and once again held her brother. She felt the shudders pass through him as she stroked her hand on his head and back over and over and hummed the tune their mother had used whenever they needed soothing as young children.

"Wheest, Magnus. It'll all come right," Mairghread whispered as Magnus composed himself. She looked into his red-rimmed eyes and took his hand. She guided him to sit on the floor and kept his massive hand in her tiny one until the chamber door opened.

Both Magnus and Mairghread clearly heard Deirdre calling Magnus's name, but the door shut tightly behind Lady Fraser and the healer. Magnus scrambled to his feet and attempted to reach for the door.

"Just what do ye think ye are doing?" Lady Fraser snapped.

"She's awake and calling for me. Ye've left her alone in there." He could hear crying from where he stood.

"Ye think that matters? Ye are mistaken if ye think ye will see her. Ye Sinclairs believe ye can always get what ye want. Ye're naught more than overreaching upstarts ever since yer father married that Sutherland chit."

Mairghread gasped and stepped between her brother and the woman standing before them. She wanted to do her bodily harm too, but she knew Magnus would do nothing with her in the way because he would not risk his sister's safety.

"Lady Fraser, I can see ye are overwrought with all that's happened. It's been a trying afternoon. I would be happy to stay with Lady Deirdre while everyone else settles in the Great Hall."

"Overwrought. That's what ye think."

Mairghread pressed her shoulders back and lifted her chin as she looked the older woman in the eye.

"What I think is that the king is partial to both me and Lady Deirdre, and I'm sure he would nae want to hear either or both of us are distressed."

Magnus bit his top lip to keep from smiling. He nodded and made his way to the stairs wondering what Lady Fraser could have against both the Sinclairs and the Sutherlands.

The night sky was black when Magnus crept from the chamber he shared with Tavish. He made his way down a flight of stairs and along the passageway to Deirdre's chamber. When he arrived, he pressed his ear against the door and heard nothing coming from the other side. He tested the handle and, discovering it was unlocked, pressed it open. There was a lit fire and a lone candle burning beside her bed. He pushed the door closed and walked to her bedside. He stroked hair back from her forehead and swallowed the lump forming in the back of his throat.

"Och mo chridhe, I failed ye. I swore to keep ye safe, and I didna. I dinna ken what I will do if I lose ye," he whispered.

"Am I going somewhere," came a raspy reply. Deirdre's eyes fluttered open.

Magnus felt like Atlas finally putting down his burden. His heart ached with relief.

"Magnus, are ye well? Ye dinna look it."

"It frightened me that ye wouldnae wake, then I heard ye calling for me and yer mother wouldnae let me see ye, then ye were sleeping so peacefully just now," he shrugged. "I was afraid for ye."

"Ye afraid of aught? I doubt that."

"Of course, I was afraid. I love ye. I canna imagine ever seeing aught worse than ye falling from that horse. Ye didna move once while I raced back here."

"Ye love me?" she said with a mischievous smile.

"Aye," he perched on the edge of the bed. "Ye ken these arenae words I just say, Deir. I mean them nae matter what happens to either of us. I wouldnae ever say them to a woman without meaning them. I wouldnae cheapen them."

"I love ye, too, Magnus. Always and forever."

Magnus leaned forward and breathed in her apple scent.

"Always and forever," he whispered before their lips met in a brief albeit tender kiss.

"I ken I shouldnae be in here, but I couldnae stand ye being alone."

Deirdre patted the open space next to her, and Magnus looked between the spot and Deirdre several times before moving around the bed. He had not worn his boots to soften his steps, so he only had to remove the top belt that held all his dirks and sporran. He would not risk being found in anything less. He laid down, and Deirdre angled herself, so he could spoon her. She looked back over her shoulder.

"I wish it could be like this every night, mo chridhe."

"One day soon, mo ghaol."

Magnus stroked her head until they both drifted off.

The early rays of morning were about to peek over the horizon when Magnus came awake to the sound of the door handle moving. He rolled from the bed and grabbed his belt before moving behind the door. It opened, and the healer walked in. As if sensing Magnus, she paused then peered around the door. She said nothing but gave him a knowing look and a nod of the head before standing aside. Magnus slipped from the room.

Magnus attempted to see Deirdre again each day for the next two but was always turned away. He sneaked to her room each night but was careful not to sleep so soundly, leaving before the healer came in. Frustrated with his limited time, he could only catch Deirdre's eyes briefly as both families left for their own lands.

~ ~ ~

Magnus realized that while he was scanning the room and watching Deirdre his mind wondered for far longer than he suspected. Servants cleared the meal and the tables were being pushed aside. He had been daydreaming through at least five courses. His heart ached from the memories of that hunting trip, and he looked for Deirdre once more needing a moment's confirmation that she was hale and hearty.

He saw her standing with her cousin, but none of the other ladies would come close. Instead, they spoke behind their hands and gave none too subtle glances in her direction. Magnus looked around and noticed many lascivious stares from the young men. He felt his heart speed up and the blood pound in his temples not only from possessiveness but indignation on Deirdre's part.

The music began to play, and Magnus pushed himself from the wall. He tried to make his way to Deirdre before any other man could, but despite his size, the now moving throng made it impossible before someone else asked her to dance. Magnus watched in silent irritation as a man whose hands were far too low on her back and held her far too close whisked Deirdre into a dance. He suffered through two more dances with different brazen partners before he and Deirdre managed, through mutual effort, to maneuver themselves together.

"I didna want to dance with them," Deirdre said anxiously.

Magnus held her just as close as the other men had though, he longed to hold his wife fully against his body. He drew small circles on her back with his thumb.

"Wheest, eun beag. I ken. I dinna like it but I ken. It isnae yer fault. If aught, the fault lies with me now and back then."

Deirdre squeezed his arm and hand as hard as she could.

"Dinna ever say that, mo fhuamhaire. Ye always gave me a choice, and I chose ye. I wish I had been strong enough to defy ma parents."

Magnus sighed. He had time to think about the past a great deal while waiting for the king.

"Deir, I dinna ken if it would have made a difference back then. I ken now ma da would have supported me, but I dinna think I would have believed that back then. I would have had us on the run. Ye've had a better, safer life with yer parents."

"Safer mayhap, but better definitely nae. How can ye say we were better off apart? That was seven years of pining and missing ye. Of thinking ye'd moved on, and I hadnae any desire to do the same. Magnus, we could have had a family by now. Ma parents stole that from me. From ye. From us. And why? For political gain. They didna think a marriage to ye and living in the north was advantageous enough. I didna understand another reason until only a year ago when I overheard ma mother speaking to ma aunt. Yer uncle Hamish spurned ma mother. She never got over the perceived slight, and since he's a Sutherland, her hate extended to the Sinclairs because of yer mother being a Sutherland originally. It is all so twisted and convoluted, but they didna think ye were good enough."

Deirdre was nearly in tears by the time she explained or rather confirmed, what Magnus already suspected.

"Deir, I never wanted us apart. That isnae what I meant. I was too young, too, to stand up for us. I didna ken how, and then time went by, and I couldna find ye. I thought ye were rejecting me though I kept sending the missives. Part of me felt there wasna any hope and another refused to give up."

Magnus gave her waist a squeeze as the song drew to an end.

"Ye are mine, and I am now in a position to see that through. Ken that I willna be sent away again. I will do *aught* I have to to keep ye."

Magnus's heated look made Deirdre's insides turn to gravy. She could only nod before one reel after another forced them apart. They partnered only as the dances dictated. They forced Magnus to watch her dance with three other men before she could disentangle herself from the dancers. Magnus noticed none of the women that worked their way in front of him, requiring him to dance or otherwise cause a scene. He nodded and murmured periodically as conversation required, but his eyes never left Deirdre, and each woman left with a harrumph.

Magnus was just about to attempt getting Deirdre's attention to slip out, but he heard the grating sound of Lord Archibald's voice.

"I understand we have several Highlanders at court. We should be more welcoming of our northern brothers. Perhaps they could show us the sword dance."

Magnus wanted to grumble. He did not want to linger in the overheated gathering hall or put on a spectacle for Lowlanders who only wanted to laugh at men they thought were barbaric.

As other Highlanders begrudgingly moved to the center of the chamber, eyes began to shift to him. There was no blending into the crowd. He scanned the group and found Uncle Hamish. The men looked around since none could wear their swords so close to the king in such a confined space.

Hay signaled, and a troop of men brought in old and rusted swords clearly left to rot in the armory. They were several grunts and angry glares turned to Hay. There were several heads shaken, and some even began to move away until the queen clapped and encouraged the audience to join in. Forced to comply, the Highlanders arranged the provided swords.

Magnus and Uncle Hamish partnered first, and family rivalry got the better of them. Only the fact that the other sets of partners finished their round forced them to stop. Magnus leaped and kicked his way through six more energetic rounds until he was dripping with sweat, and his knees and feet ached. The final round came down to Magnus and a Mackay who he knew was serving as a spy within the MacDonnell household. The two men began the complicated and intricate steps. Magnus quickly saw that the man was as skilled as he, and if it were not for Hay, the Frasers, and Deirdre being in the crowd, he might have been willing to concede. He pushed the speed and forced his body to jump higher. He knew his opponent was flagging just like him, but he pushed until the side of his opponent's boot glanced the blade of one sword. The sword vibrated only slightly but enough for the Mackay's honor to demand he concede.

Magnus grasped the other man's forearm and shook as he wiped his soaked forehead and hair on the sleeve of his leine. He caught the look of hate and malice on Hay's face before seeing Laird Fraser's look of surprise and disgruntlement as the laird marched over to Hay. Magnus watched a heated exchange between the men that had Fraser shaking his head then looking in Magnus's direction. Both men glared at him before others joined them and ended their tete-a-tete.

He scanned over the tops of most heads and spotted Deirdre, but before he could catch her eye, he was called to the king and queen's table. Several rounds of congratulations and a reminder of the hunt made Magnus long to escape. When he was finally free, he searched the area but could not spot Deirdre's blond spiral curls. He looked around and saw that Hay and Fraser were still engaged in conversation, but Lady Fraser was also not in sight.

Magnus eased his way to the wall and circled the room until he came to the exit he needed to reach the ladies'-in-waiting chambers. Despite his size, he moved silently and gracefully, as his dancing prowess just demonstrated. He was also the best tracker in his clan. He quickly caught up to Lady Fraser and Deirdre. As he followed at a safe distance, he overheard their conversation.

"Do not think we did not see the two of you dancing or how you kept looking at one another? Lord Hay was fit to be tied as you continued to humiliate him. You are as good as his bride and carrying on with the very man who caused your disgrace. The entire castle is buzzing about you being a fallen woman. You'll be lucky if they do not remove you from the queen's household. You are acting like a common trollop. You will remain in your chamber until your father or I summon you. You will not be attending the hunt. You may work on the stitching for your wedding kirtle. You will be in need of it soon."

The women reached Deirdre's door. She opened it only to receive a small shove from her mother who locked and pocketed the key. Magnus slunk back into the shadows as Lady Fraser looked both ways before walking away.

Magnus counted his customary twenty before stepping out. He rushed to the chamber next to Deirdre's. He tested the door and found it unlocked, so he slipped in and sprinted to the window. He opened it and stepped onto the ledge. Refusing to look down, he slid along until he could tap his fingers on the glass of Deirdre's window. It flew open, and he was tugged inside as he stooped to pass through. Once on his feet, Deirdre flung herself into his arms. She wildly scattered kisses over his face before clenching her fingers in his hair and biting his lower lip as they devoured one another. Magnus wrapped his arms around her waist and lifted her toes off the ground. He walked them to the side of the bed, and her feet were barely back on the floor before he was ripping the laces from her gown. Her hands slid down his back to grasp his buttocks. Her nails dug into his hard flesh.

Even his arse is made of steel.

They came together in a frenzy of combustible need then slowed their pace. Their time together was always at a premium, but with no immediate fear of interruption, this night was more drawn out. When they laid catching their breath, Deirdre smiled before rolling onto her side.

Deirdre's lips fastened onto his shoulder as she gave him a love bite. She repeated it on the other shoulder before leaving one in the center of his chest.

"Marking me?" Magnus gasped.

She could only nod once. She could feel her release building within her core.

"Mine," he growled before leaving several of his own love bites on her breasts.

Deirdre felt a tingle course throughout her body as her toes curled and fingers clenched. It was like a comet passing through her with a ball of fire followed by a long tail of sensations.

She paused and leveled him with a thoughtful look.

"Do ye think it was enough to get me with child?"

Magnus froze. He was not sure if she was worried or hopeful.

"Ye ken even the smallest amount could get ye with child." He watched her as he hesitated to ask, "Should I have pulled out?"

"Nay!" she exclaimed before settling for a quieter tone. "I didna mean that. I've dreamt so many nights of us having a family together. It's always been so clear. Ye would lead me and our children down to the beach at Dunbeath. We would picnic there and teach our children to swim. Other times, ye were teaching our daughter to ride or teaching our son to carry a wooden sword. We were a family in my dreams. Do ye ken what it was like to awake in the morn alone?"

"Aye," Magnus rasped. He tried to clear his throat, but his chest and throat felt too tight. "Do ye ken what it was like to dream of coming into the keep every eve after training to find ye waiting. To dream of ye growing round with our bairns. To walk the orchard picking apples with ye for yer soaps. I awake alone, too. It wasna just ye who dreamed. Not just ye who was cheated."

Deirdre rested her cheek on his shoulder and absentmindedly ran her hand up and down his chest.

"I'm scared, Magnus. Ma mother said I had to work on ma wedding gown tomorrow and that I would need it soon."

"I ken. I heard almost all of yer conversation after ye left the Great Hall."

"Ye did? She made me leave and accused me of making a fool of maself, standing around mooning over ye. She claimed I was looking cow-eyed at ye."

"Were ye?" Deirdre felt a soft rumble of laughter under her.

"Well, mayhap. But Magnus, that isnae the point."

"Dinna fash. I ken what ye mean," he ran his fingers along her spine then rested his large hand over one side of her bottom. He once again reveled at how it fit as though it was designed for his palm.

A small pinch of his nipple made him realize that she was still talking.

"I dinna ken how much longer we have. I think ma parents will push the betrothal to before the sennight is through and the wedding before the next moon."

Magnus felt the weight of the world settle back onto his shoulders after basking in a brief reprieve.

"I ken. The king has already told me he approves the match. I must ride out on the hunt tomorrow. The only thing that makes me willing to go is kenning both yer father and Hay will be there which means they canna force ye to say any vows."

"Magnus, I willna say any vows that arenae to ye. I'll go to a convent first. I'll even take a king's wrath and punishment, but I willna marry Hay or anyone else."

Magnus ran his hand along her spine again, and she calmed.

"Sew yer gown and ken it is for me and not for bald Archie."

Deirdre laughed at Magnus's joke and relaxed. She felt her heart slow after the excitement then fear.

"It willna be long now. I will be sure to get the king's decision and his approval, but if I canna, I will take ye away. I told ye before, I dinna want to do it, but I amnae above bride stealing."

Chapter Eight

*D*awn approached all too soon for Magnus. He slid from Deirdre's bed and found his clothing as quietly as he could. He attempted not to wake her, but he felt her soft hands on his back as she handed him his leine and belts.

"I wish ye didna have to go, but I ken that ye must. I dinna ken which window ye've used these past two times, but if ye can manage it, go two windows down. At least two of those lasses willna slept in their beds last night." She gave him a pointed look.

"At least two? How many sleep in that chamber?"

"Three, but that's Elizabeth's chamber. Ma cousin wouldnae tell anyone aught."

Magnus finished dressing, and before he climbed through the window, he pulled Deirdre into a tight embrace and kissed her with a passion that took her breath away. She returned it and wished they could walk back to the bed to resume what they had spent the night doing instead of watching him leave. They made love four more times, dozing in between while entwined in one another's arms and legs. Magnus did not pull out, and they both longed for his seed to take. Both knew it would solidify his claim on her, but even more, they both wanted the family they spoke of and missed.

When they pulled apart, Magnus brushed his knuckles along her cheek. He spent a lingering moment looking into her eyes. They were the vibrant color of the North Sea on a summer day after a storm. The blues and greens blended together and shimmered in the dim candlelight and weak sunlight beginning to enter her chamber.

"I love ye, Deir."

"I love ye too, Magnus."

And like that, he was climbing through the window embrasure.

Magnus slid his feet along the ledge and held his breath, once again refusing to look down. He came to the first window, the one he used the last two times. He paused and tried to peer into it, but the chamber was too dark to see anything. He prayed that since he could not see in, that no one would look out to see him. He hurried past the glass onto the second window. His fingers reached down to the latch, and once again prayed, this time in thanksgiving. He pushed the window open and waited. When no screams sounded, he lowered himself through. He scanned the chamber and saw that Deirdre was correct. Two of the beds were empty as were the trundles reserved for maids. Only one bed was occupied, and Elizabeth seemed to sleep soundly. He wasted no time to learn whether she really slept or only pretended. He strode across the room, opened the door a sliver, and peeked through, looking both directions. He slipped from the room as silently as he slipped in. He made his way to his chamber just in time to refresh himself and change his clothing. He breathed a sigh of relief when he returned his claymore to its rightful position strapped to his back. Since he was going on a hunt and leaving the castle, it would be permissible for him to carry it. Other than when he was with Deirdre, he only felt whole when he carried it. A Highlander's best friend and constant companion was his sword.

Magnus exited his chamber and made his way to the yard where the stable boys were saddling horses. His was among those already waiting. He did not like it, but he was not rude enough to say anything to the frazzled young men trying to ready and corral dozens of agitated and high-strung warhorses and stallions. Magnus quickly checked all the fastenings and the girth before leading his horse to an opening where his uncle stood with several other Sutherland men he had not seen before.

"Magnus, I'm glad ye came over. These are a few of ma clansmen who arrived last night. Ma wife and the bairns are remaining at the keep, and I've asked several of the men to stay behind and guard them."

"Guard them? Do ye think them in danger?" His mind whipped to Deirdre, and fear coursed through him that he had abandoned her to some impending doom.

"Nae necessarily, but ye ken it isnae ever a good time to be a Highlander at court. Besides, Lady Fraser had some less than flattering or kind words to say to and aboot yer aunt last eve. I dinna trust that viper."

Magnus gave his uncle a pointed look before replying.

"Neither do I, Uncle. Neither do I."

Hamish made the round of introductions, and five of the men walked away to assume their post outside the Sutherland chambers. The other five mounted with Magnus and Hamish.

It was not much longer before the king appeared and mounted his bedecked steed that wore an embroidered blanket and hood. Bells jangled from the harness, and just as Magnus wondered how they would ever approach their prey without giving themselves away miles in advance, the king called out to a stable hand.

"Who put these ridiculous bells on him? I'm going on a hunt, not a parade. Get these blasted things off my horse."

It took only moments before the bells were gone, the horn blew, and dogs raced out of the courtyard.

Magnus and the Sutherlands joined the fray as the men set off. He looked at those who gathered and saw that the Highlanders were banding together as they shifted to encircle the other riders. They rode the periphery and seemed to herd the others. The large men on their sturdy warhorses appeared to be adults riding among children. The courtiers were outsized and outpaced by the men who spent more time outdoors than in. Mangus spotted the MacDonnells and was sure to keep his distance, but he also saw Grahams, MacKinnons, MacLeods, and Grants. He watched in veiled amusement as a couple of courtiers tried to pull ahead of the MacLeods. Their horses received several nips and neighs from the warriors' horses who did not like being crowded. Easily controlled by their owners, the horses were allowed their head instead. Magnus could see the amusement on the other men's faces, too. On his side, he rode close to the king who preferred to ride on the outskirts rather than the center. Once upon a time, a Highlander himself, the king may have altered his speech and clothes, but his heart still beat for the hunt and chase.

The party rode for nearly an hour before coming to a woodland that promised various prey. Magnus spent the time bending the king's ear about the ongoing feuds with the MacDonnells, who remained on the far side of the hunting party, the de Soules, the Kerrs, and the Gunns.

"Yer Majesty, ye ken we didna start aught but only defended our women. I dinna ken how anyone could find fault in doing all and aught needed to bring ma sister and sisters by marriage home. Ye have heard from ma uncle Hamish. I am certain ye have heard testimony and evidence from others. There is naught for us to hide. We did, in fact, kill the Mackay's stepbrother, Alan MacDonnell. We also killed James and Laird Gunn, along with Laird Kerr, and Randulph de Soules. We canna change that, but neither can those clans change or deny what their men did to our clan and the laird's family. If aught, the Sinclairs should claim damages for the attacks on Mairghread and Siùsan along with the attempt on Brighde's life."

"Calm yourself, young Sinclair. I have heard all the evidence and testimonies from all parties concerned. And more besides, and I have come to my decision. It may not be a popular one, but I do find in your favor. You are Highlanders and live by a different code than those at court, but nothing anywhere should change your right to defend your families and your land. I shall set out a royal decree that clears all charges or claims made by the other clans. They will cease their complaints and the feuds or face my royal sanctions." The king nodded his head and turned to talk to the man who rode on his other side.

Magnus knew his audience had ended, and while he was more than satisfied with the outcome on behalf of his family, he was irritated that he was not afforded the opportunity to discuss Deirdre. He suspected the king purposely ended the conversation to avoid moving to that topic. He may have sided with the Sinclairs over the feuds, but Laird Fraser was a clear favorite.

The men began to form smaller groups and moved off in different directions. Magnus and the Sutherlands, along with the Grahams, kept close to the king. The other Highlanders made their own groups based upon well-established alliances and rivalries.

Magnus entered the treeline and slowed his horse. He looked around and took in the tree's trunks, looking for where a boar or stag might have sharpened tusks or antlers. He spotted a couple and nudged his horse forward.

"What see you, Sinclair?" The king called out.

"These trees have fresh scratches. From the height, both deer and boar have been nearby."

He nudged his horse again and felt the saddle shift slightly. He had already reached the trees, so he dismounted and tightened the girth. Then he ran his hand over the tree trunk and looked at the ground for any disturbed leaves. He let the reins of his horse go since he knew the steed would not move until summoned. He took several steps away from the king and his followers. He eased aside a pile of leaves and found what he suspected, paw prints formed by a small deer. When whistled to, his horse came to his side, and he remounted.

Signaling to the king to move on, the king shook his head.

"I shall ride with the others in search of a boar. Bag us a buck, I am in the mood for venison." The king rode off with a group that included a gloating Hay.

Magnus led the men in the direction he believed the deer traveled. It was not long before the woods opened to a small glade, and in the distance stood a herd. Each of the men drew their bows, and several knocked arrows, but all awaited to take the first shot. Finally, the Grant took aim and released his arrow. His arrow came close to the mark but slid just below a doe's chin. The men took their aim, and several arrows flew towards the grazing animals. Magnus knew the animals would scatter, and while a moving target was harder to hit, he also knew he had a better chance of his arrow flying free of the others to find its solitary mark. His eyes locked onto the largest stag as he rose in his saddle, digging his knees and heels into his horse to steady him. He drew back the arrow and relying on his exceptional height and strength, released his arrow. It soared over all the others, arching over the does and fawns to land unimpeded into the center of the stag's broad chest. The animal took several staggering steps before it collapsed.

"Well done, nephew," his uncle boomed.

Magnus nodded his head and waited as the men who bagged deer moved forward. Following closely, he guided his horse to claim his own catch. He arrived at the fallen stag and dismounted. He barely made it to the deer before an arrow whizzed past his ear. He fell to his stomach and pulled himself around the laying body in front of him. He lifted his head just high enough to look at where the arrow came from. Another whizzed past him, this time brushing his hair. He ducked back down and tried to calm his breathing. He had no idea who was shooting at him, but he could venture a guess who may have sent the would-be assassins. He checked over his shoulder and spotted the arrow but did not recognize the fletching. He rolled onto his belly and looked towards the riders whose hoofbeats he felt before heard. His uncle was charging forward with his sword drawn, the Sutherland battle cry ringing across the glen. Magnus was about to slide along the ground further away from where the two arrows flew from when another grazed his shoulder from an entirely different direction. He spotted a shape fading into the dark of the trees. He whistled for his horse which was unharmed and nearby. He barely noticed his shoulder as he mounted and galloped after the perpetrator. As his horse's body vibrated from the increased speed, Magnus felt his saddle shift yet again, so he pressed his heels down to keep his balance. That only made the leather move further to one side. He gripped the reins and pulled hard to slow his horse. He transferred his weight back, and his normally unflappable horse reared and then bucked, sending Magnus flying over its head to land hard on the grassy ground. The wind knocked from him, Magnus could only lay there staring up at the sky. His head and back throbbed with pain. He just needed to close his eyes for a moment to catch his breath.

"Magnus. Magnus, wake up. *Magnus!*" He felt water pour onto his face.

He spluttered and opened his eyes. His uncle knelt over him, blocking out the sun for which Magnus's pounding head was grateful.

"Are ye hurt?"

"All of me ruddy well hurts. Dinna shout." Magnus ground out.

"Magnus, let me look at ye. Yer arm is bleeding, and I need to check yer head."

"Bah, haud yer wheesht. Let me be or help me up." Magnus tried to sit up on his own but rolled onto his side to retch. When he finished emptying the little contents that were in his stomach after skipping breaking his fast, he wiped his mouth and took the waterskin from his uncle. He was pleased to find Sinclair whisky in it rather than water.

Uisge-beatha, the water of life, I ruddy well need this. Thank God for Uncle Hamish. Why the hell does everything hurt so damn much? Och, ye eejit, ye were thrown from a horse that stands nearly seventeen hands tall.

"Magnus, are ye listening to me? Where have ye gone now?" Hamish shook his shoulder.

Magnus tried to shake his head but thought he would cast up his accounts again. He rolled to his other side and gradually made his way to his knees and then feet. He swayed but remained upright. He ran his hand over the back of his head and found a cut and blood that was already drying into a tangled clump. He raised his other arm and saw the blood on his sleeve.

"Someone dinna like me vera much."

Hamish grunted, "Ye could certainly say so. I would venture to say a certain Lowland lord isnae too keen on ye swooping up his bride to be."

Magnus growled, and then groaned as his whole body throbbed.

"Can ye ride?"

"Do I really have a choice?"

"Nae really."

"Where is *Sealgair?*" Neither Magnus nor his uncle missed the irony that the horse that threw him was name Hunter. His uncle smile but it looked more like a grimace.

"Magnus, he is fine."

"That isnae what I asked." Magnus turned to look around but could barely see as black dots danced before his eyes.

"He took an arrow in the rear flank. When ye fell, the saddle also came off. Magnus, ye need to ken that the girth was nearly severed. It was done at the top where it isnae easy to see but would come free when ye either galloped too long or in this case when *Sealgair* reared and then bucked. It was the saddle that caused ye to be thrown. They also shot him after he threw ye. We found three small burs were on the underside of the saddle. The shifting saddle must have pressed them in, and then yer speed only made it more painful."

Magnus shook his head to clear the dots and took several deep breaths. The more his anger grew, the clearer his mind became. He spotted his horse and walked purposefully to the enormous animal that had never thrown him before. They saw each other through countless battles with no incident such as this. Magnus cooed to the animal as it shied away from him. He held out his hand until *Sealgair* knickered and came to but his head against Magnus's chest. Magnus hugged the animal and whispered in its ear before moving his hands along the animal's flanks on one side and then the other until he came to the wound. It was not serious, for which Magnus felt immense relief, but it was there nonetheless. Someone had not only shot him but shot his horse too. Nearly as important as his sword, a horse to a Highlander was his lifeblood in battle. Trained since he was a colt, only Magnus ever rode him, and most could not handle him. His horse stomped his foot and let out a soft whinny before looking back at him.

Magnus walked back to his head.

"Can ye carry me home, ma lad?"

The horse seemed to understand and nodded his massive head.

Magnus looked around but did not spot his saddle. He gathered the reins and struggled to pull himself up onto his steed's bare back.

"The king insisted that the saddle be taken back to the castle for further examination. He sent guardsmen into the woods to look, but I doubt they will find anyone. The mon or men were stealthy, except they used a rather distinct fletching. They didna plan well. It willna take long to deduce whose they are." Hamish rode alongside Magnus as he could only manage a walk and then barely a trot without feeling like he would drop under his horse's hooves.

"So, the king kens of what happened?"

"Aye, and that bastard Hay was beside the king the entire time. Bagged a boar of his own."

"Convenient."

Magnus thought about the arrows that flew past him and the one that hit his arm. He never saw those markings before, but he recognized the type of bird from which they came. While it was quite a common bird, the distinct red of the kestrel's feathers was not common on arrows because they were easily spotted among trees. Magnus would discover the responsible party and who fired the arrows. He would settle the issue, one way or another.

Magnus, Hamish, and the other Sutherlands and Grahams approached where the king waited. Hay was to his left, and a dead boar lay at his feet.

"Magnus, I heard you took a spill. How fare you?"

"Well enough sire," Magnus spoke faintly but with steel laced in his voice that no one missed. The king raised a brow.

"I understand the fall injured you. Perhaps you should return to the keep and have the healer attend you."

Magnus knew the prudent thing would be to agree and leave the hunt, but there was no chance, short of being ordered by the king, that he would leave now that Hay stood once again gloating before him.

Magnus looked at the scrawny boar before looking up and grinning broadly.

"Nae able to find this wee one's mother or father? They usually arenae far from their bairns."

Hay grasped the hilt of his sword but did not draw it.

"I do not see you with a catch. I do not see you even with a saddle. Not much for a horseman."

"Now, now, Lord Archibald. You know just as I do that Sinclair was thrown from a tampered saddle, and you also saw him maneuver that monstrous beast without one." The king paused and looked over Magnus's shoulder. "Ah, here comes his catch. I do believe that is the largest buck I have ever seen in these parts. Well done, Magnus. We heard how you were strong enough to shoot over all the others to reach this buck. I would say, that was an impossible shot, however, it does not surprise me that only one of you Sinclairs could accomplish such a feat."

Magnus turned to look over his shoulder as a couple of Sutherlands he had not noticed earlier carried his stag on two logs between them. When they arrived, they lowered the deer carcass next to the boar. The difference in size was ridiculous, and Lord Archibald was no longer gloating.

"Shall we mount up? I see no need to continue after such success. We shall have to discover what the others bagged."

Magnus returned to his horse, and despite his injuries, found it easier to mount this time. He pulled the whisky filled wineskin from his uncle's saddlebag and took several long draws from it.

"Sinclair, ride with me."

It did not escape Magnus that the king used his given name only when he allowed his true concern to show. When he attempted indifference, he resorted to Magnus's clan name. It did not bother Magnus one way or another, but he had seen how it nettled Hay.

"Did you, per chance, get a glimpse of the man who shot at you?"

"I believe there to have been more than one, Sire, as the arrows came from different directions. Whoever it was, used rather unusual feathers. It should not be too challenging to determine who did it or their employer."

Magnus kept his eyes straight ahead but knew he was getting under Hay's skin.

"It could very well have been poachers. They are always a problem on the king's land when there is so much to hunt."

"Dinna be daft, mon," Hamish interjected. "Ye really believe that anyone would be barmy enough to poach while the king rides out to hunt? Ye ken that isnae close to the truth."

"Who do you think it might be, Laird Sutherland?"

Hamish looked at Magnus before addressing the king.

"I would venture to say someone isnae happy that Magnus has arrived at court."

Hay snorted before saying, "There are plenty of people who are not pleased he is here. He brings the shame of the Sinclairs to court, trying to beg their way out of just desserts. Just like a Highlander."

"Enough! You go too far this time, Lord Archibald. I have already found in their favor, and perhaps you are not aware, but each of the Sinclairs is my godchild. I was at each of their christenings." The king glared at Hay until he ducked his head.

"You were saying, Sutherland."

"Och aye, I would say it was someone who feels threatened by Magnus's presence. Perhaps someone who worries he will be on the losing end." Hamish could not have been more obvious had he spelled out Archibald Hay's name.

"That very well may be, but everyone who rode out is accounted for. I know who I rode with." The king gave Magnus and Hamish a pointed look before an almost imperceptible tilt of his head towards Hay.

"Yer Majesty, do ye think someone trying to do away with me would do so himself? I would think he might try to keep his hands clean."

The king only looked at Magnus before they all picked up their speed to a gallop. Magnus held on and gritted his teeth, hoping he would neither vomit nor fall.

Chapter Nine

The hunters returned to the castle and entered the royal gardens to reach their chambers. Magnus and his extended family followed at a distance. Despite their enmity, the MacDonnells walked with Magnus. Everyone had heard of his accident, and while they might be far from allies at home, they were at court. The MacKinnons, Grahams, Grants, Sutherlands, and MacDonnells let the larger group drift ahead of them before turning into the hedge maze.

"Let us nae clishmaclaver," said Laird MacDonnell who kept a healthy distance from Magnus. The memory of Magnus and his brothers' retaliation for his unwitting part in their sister's abduction a couple years earlier was still fresh.

"We all ken someone tried to kill ye. I would venture to say it was Hay or Fraser. We all remember that ye and the Fraser lass were sweet on one another, and they have seen ye speaking and dancing with her. I would put ma last penny on them if nae one then both."

There were several nodding heads. As the men looked around.

"Are ye sure it wasna ye, MacDonnell. Ye dinna seem to be winning the king's favor. I hear the king has already found in the Sinclairs' favor," Laird Edward Grant spoke up. "It wouldnae be beyond the stretch of the imagination that ye're responsible."

"Thank ye for having such faith in ma intelligence, Edward," the MacDonnell snapped. "I came to court to resolve this feud nae bring the entire Highlands down on ma head or the king's wrath. If I wanted to kill him because of sour feelings, I would have done it before he even reached the court, or I would wait until we left. I wouldnae do it here with the king's dungeon so close."

There was more agreement and head nodding.

"We just wanted to be sure," added Laird Thomas Graham.

"So, does that mean we are all in agreement that the most likely culprits are Hay and Fraser?" piped in Adam MacKinnon, laird of his clan.

"I suppose we are," Magnus agreed. "That doesnae do us much good, though, if he manages to send someone else to finish the job."

"Is the lass the reason for all of this, lad?" Magnus felt Laird Graham's hand on his shoulder. He had known the man as long as he had the king, practically since birth.

"Aye. She was ma wife when her father took her from me, and she is ma wife still."

"But that must have been a handfast. It's over by now."

Magnus growled.

"It wasna ever over for either of us. Besides, she has wed me by consent since then. We've pledged ourselves to one another. I pity the mon who stands between us this time."

Hamish held his hands up in surrender.

"Easy, lad. Ye dinna need to convince any of us. We understand yer vow, and we ken yer honorable. We arenae questioning that. We must figure out how to get ye free of Hay, so ye can wed the lass in a kirk. Ye ken her father isnae going to let a handfast or even a marriage by consent stand. We are at court. He will have the king set it aside or petition the bishop to do it. The bishop willna say nay."

"Can I ask ye a delicate question, Magnus?" Laird Grant stepped forward.

Magnus looked up at the older man and knew what the laird would ask him.

"Aye, I have. We have. Then and now. And, aye, there is a chance." He would save everyone the embarrassment of hearing the questions.

"Then it shouldnae matter much what any of them want. She is yer wife," added Laird MacKinnon.

"Ye ken that, I ken that, we all ken that, but that is because we are Highlanders and respect our ways. The king conveniently forgets his roots," Magnus finished on a whisper as he looked around. "If it doesnae serve him, then he will conveniently forget what constitutes a marriage among our clans. Even the bluidy Frasers ken, but they have been at court long enough to pretend they arenae just like us."

"That may be. We canna change Donald or Maeve. They are two peas in a pod when it comes to their social climbing. We can only change how things stand for ye and the lass," the Graham stated.

"We are back to clishmaclavering. We have another day of hunting. Sinclair, will ye be able to join us?" MacDonnell was looking around as though the hedges might be listening.

"Ye can damn well count on it."

"Then we ride together. We dinna flank them like today. Let the eejit bastards ride as they want. It is us against them, just as it always has been. The time for civility came to an end when one of them tried to kill one of us." Laird MacDonnell looked Magnus in the eye. "Dinna think this means I like ye. And dinna think it pleases me the king has found in yer favor, but I will say Alan got just as he deserved. I count ma blessings daily that Beatris and that bitch, Sorcha, are here instead of aggravating me at ma keep, and I am sorry for what happened to yer sister."

Laird MacDonnell extended his arm to Magnus, and they shook. Neither offered implicit trust, but they were more alike than different. They would stand together against an outside foe. In this case, it was one Lord Archibald Hay.

The men nodded and silently exited the hedge maze only to find themselves within the buzzing swarm of ladies-in-waiting. Magnus's eyes saught Deirdre who sat with her mother.

That is why she was paroled. To do her duty to the queen, and her mother is her jailor.

Magnus tried to move through the garden without drawing much attention to himself, but Mary Kerr was having none of it.

"I heard someone tried to kill you. I see they failed. More's the pity," came her strident voice.

"Mary!" scolded the queen.

Deirdre's head whipped around at the sound of Mary's comments.

"It seems that I shall live to see another day. More's the pity that yer courtly nobles dinna ken how to do the job properly." Magnus stepped close to Mary and examined the feathers in a brooch pinned to her shoulder. "Ye seem partial to the kestrel's feathers. Perhaps a mon should have been sent instead of a lad. Then ye wouldnae be so disappointed."

Deirdre stood from her bench and took two steps forward before her mother grasped her wrist and squeezed. Her face went white when she saw the blood on his leine. She saw it on his sleeve and then his collar.

Bluidy witch's tits! Damn! Sorry, Holy Father. What the bluidy hell happened to him? Why does ma mother have to be here? Och that's right, she's nae letting me out of her sight. She is right to nae trust me because if I had ma druthers aboot me, Magnus and I would ride out this vera moment.

Deirdre glared at her mother, openly hostile for the first time in her life.

"Let go of me, Mother, or I shall make an almighty scene," Deirdre hissed.

Her mother held tight.

"It isnae like nay one kens he bedded me. I'm a soiled dove. What does it matter now? Ye've sold me to Hay, and he's paid. There arenae any returns for either party." She pulled her arm loose.

By the time she freed herself, Magnus was already walking past with his uncle and several other men she recognized but did not know. He looked at her, and his eyes softened even though he gave a tiny shake of his head.

"*Later*," he mouthed.

Her mother was behind her straight away.

"See, ye silly chit. He's had ye and is done with ye. He was done with ye the moment ye spread yer legs for him. Ye should count all the blessing God's given ye that yer father and I didna turn ye out." Deirdre's eyes opened wide, and her mother stepped back and looked around. In her anger, she slipped back into the burr she had covered up all those years ago when they arrived at court.

Deirdre spun and stalked from the garden. She no longer cared who saw her ungraceful exit or what her mother had to say.

Magnus opened the door to his chamber and a foul odor struck him like a wind gusting from the North Sea. His eyes swept the room before he entered with caution. It took but a moment for him to identify the cause of the rank smell. A dead blackbird with its neck snapped lay in a puddle of blood on the center of his bed. He looked around to see if any note was left or if anything else was disturbed in his chamber, but all was as he left it.

He spun around and pulled a dirk from his belt when he heard someone press on the outside handle of his door. Ready to launch himself at the intruder, it shocked him to see Deirdre enter. He hastily resheathed his dagger and pulled her into the room before checking the passageway.

"Lass, what are ye doing here? What if someone saw ye?"

"I dinna care anymore. What happened to ye?" Deirdre's tentative hand ran over his injured arm and then stepped around him to examine his head. "Dear God, Magnus, ye could have been killed. Yer head should have been stitched."

"It isnae bleeding anymore. I'll be just fine once it's cleaned. Ye shouldnae be here."

Deirdre froze. She looked around the chamber and then glared at him.

"Why would ye nae want me here?" Suspicion dripping from her voice.

Magnus looked down at her as if she sprouted a second head. He planted his feet and crossed his arms.

"Ye think after seven years of celibacy and having ye in ma arms every night, now is when I would stray? I canna believe ye could think that of me."

Magnus turned away and went to the washstand. Deirdre did not miss the look of anguish written across his face before he walked away. She went to stand beside him and dipped the linen into the bowl Magnus just filled with water. She lathered soap into it, and then pressed his shoulder down. She moved to the opposite side of the table and bowl. She tenderly washed the dirt and blood from Magnus's hair. She rinsed out the cloth and turned it over before lathering it again. They were silent as she methodically washed his hair and then the wound. When that was as clean as she could get it, she picked up another cloth, doused it, and lathered it. She pulled up his leine.

"Off," she said.

Magnus unpinned the extra length of plaid and then removed his leine.

This was the first time that Deirdre saw the entirety of Magnus in the full light of day. Her breath caught as she took in every rippling sinew of muscle that spread across and down his front. She walked around him and trailed her fingers over his back and then his good arm. She swallowed several times, and Magnus watched as her throat constricted. When she looked up at Magnus, there were tears in her eyes.

Magnus took the cloth from her and pulled her into his embrace.

"Why are ye crying, eun beag? I amnae that hurt."

"That isnae it though I ken if I'm going to cry for any reason that should be it."

"Then why?"

"Ye are even more braw than I realized, mo fhuamhaire. Women must have thrown themselves at ye over and over. I can see ye now, and I see now what plenty of other women have. I was suspicious a moment ago, and now I am thoroughly jealous of women I havenae even seen or ken."

"Do ye nay longer believe I've been true to ye?" Magnus whispered as his heart squeezed in his chest.

"I do believe ye. I just dinna ken how ye could have been. Ye must have had so many chances, so many options."

"There werenae any choices or any options because that would mean I even considered for a moment being unfaithful to ye. I told ye in the alcove the first night, I may have used women for information or used ma looks as a distraction, but never once did I stray from ma vows to ye. I never wanted to, and I never will."

"Then why did ye say straight away ye didna want me here?"

Magnus's squeeze tightened.

"I never said I didna want ye here. I've wanted ye here and in that bed since the moment I spotted ye. I said ye shouldnae be here because I fear what yer parents or Hay will do when they find out, which I'm certain they will." He wiped the tears from her cheeks and pressed his lips to hers for the one beat of their hearts. "I also didna want ye to see what someone left on ma bed. But ye are here, and ye should ken. I willna start keeping secrets from ye. There have been far too many around us for us to do the same."

He turned and allowed Deirdre to see past him to the bed. She gasped and covered her mouth with his arm. She peered around him and felt sick when she saw the dead bird.

"Hay did that. I'm sure, Magnus. It's his style, brutal and vindictive."

"I ken. That is all the more reason I dinna feel it's safe for ye here."

"Magnus, the safest place for me is wherever ye are. I ken ye willna let harm come to me."

She turned and reached back to pick up the lathered cloth. As Magnus continued to embrace her, she cleaned his arm and placed a tender kiss just below the shallow gash.

"Ye are fortunate that the arrow didna pierce yer skin nor did the fall do ye any real harm."

"I ken. It made me think again of yer accident."

"I dinna ever want to think of that again. Nae so much the accident, but how horrid ma parents were in nae letting me see ye. I wouldnae have lasted the two days confined in that chamber if ye hadnae visited me. I should have realized then that they never would have let us be together, but I was too naïve. I look back now and see it all written on the wall so clearly. Ma father may have loved me, but he loves his position more. I dinna ken if ma mother ever loved me. It matters vera little now. Either they are responsible for this or Hay, but they are one and the same as far as I am concerned."

"Deir, I dinna wish this for ye. Yer father does love ye, I believe, but he is trying to achieve his own goals, and I do think some of them are for yer clan's prosperity. I hate that ye are the sacrificial lamb to them. We will sort this out soon enough."

"It canna be soon enough. Magnus, ma mother told me that the negotiations are almost complete. Ma parents have already agreed to the bride price, and ma dowry is on its way from Fraser land. Canna we please go? Tonight? I dinna want to wait any longer. It scares me that we will miss our chance."

"Deir, if we run off before I have the writs from the king granting ma clan absolution of all claims, the king may change his mind. I made progress today, and the king agreed to side with the Sinclairs in all matters, but he hasnae signed any official decrees. Until that happens, ma clan and ye are at risk if I leave too early."

Deirdre bit back her tears and nodded her head but could not look at Magnus. His touch was soothing as he raised her chin and kissed her forehead, each cheek, the tip of her nose, and at last her mouth. She melted into him, and he held her close for what seemed like forever and only a moment at the same time. He stroked her hair as her hands ran over the muscles of his lower back.

A knock on the door had them separate. Magnus placed his finger over her lips, and he pointed towards the screen in the chamber's corner. She slipped out of sight, and Magnus waited until he was sure it completely hid her. He walked to the door and pulled a dirk before opening it.

"Uncle Hamish."

"Magnus, let me in. We need to talk."

"Can ye wait a moment, and I will join ye for a walk."

"Nay. This needs to be discussed in private." Magnus tried to block his uncle's entrance, but when the older man raised his eyebrow, Magnus had no choice but to let him in.

"For fuck's sake! What the bluidy hell is that mess on yer bed?" Hamish's bellow was loud enough that Magnus looked into the passageway before pushing the door closed and locking it.

"Someone left it as a gift but didna leave his name."

"Aye, the message is plenty clear though."

Magnus grimaced as he looked at the bed again. He walked over and pulled the cover back. The blood had already soaked through, and when he pulled back the sheet as well, he saw that the stain went all the way to the mattress.

"Ye canna sleep on that."

Magnus only nodded his head. He was not about to admit, even to his uncle, that he never planned to sleep in the bed. He only unmade it and creased the sheets to keep the chambermaids from gossiping. Otherwise, he was yet to sleep in his own bed. He was in Deirdre's instead. Hamish shot his nephew a speculative look.

"Ye ken, that I ken when ye and yer brothers are trying to hide something. Only yer sister has success bluffing. Ye and yer brothers all have a little something that gives ye away to those who ken ye. Yer mother, bless her soul, was the one who pointed it out to me and yer da. Did ye ken that? Och aye, yer mother kenned the lot of ye better than ye kenned yerselves."

Hamish wiped a hand over his misty eyes. Life had not been easy for him or for his sister when they were growing up. He regretted, even two score years later, that he had not better cared for his wee sister. He looked at his nephew and thanked God for at least the thousandth time that his sister married Liam Sinclair, but he cursed God in the same breath for taking her away too soon.

"Yer mother told me that ye will always wiggle the toes of yer left foot when ye are hiding something." Hamish pointed as Magnus stilled his foot from tapping. "Callum will look at yer ear rather than in the eye. Alex hooks his thumbs into his belt, and Tavish, well Tavish, has the most. He will laugh to distract or try to tell a joke, but mostly, he will turn his head a wee to the left. Only yer sister can completely school her features, but dinna tell her yer mother kenned her too. Kyla told me that Mairghread bites the inside of her cheek, so if one side looks thinner, then ye ken she isnae telling the entire truth."

"I hadnae kenned that aboot all of us. That is a fine piece of information to hold over ma brothers. Thank ye for sharing."

"Nice try, lad. I didna forget what we were talking aboot before that little family detour. Ye can also tell the lass she can come out."

Magnus went rigid.

"Dinna fash. I amnae judging nor am I going to tell anyone, but this involves her too."

Magnus walked to the screen and reached out his hand. Deirdre took it and stepped out in front of him. He guided her over to his uncle whom she curtsied before.

"Dinna bother with that, lass. We are family already," he pulled her into a warm hug that was more like being smothered by a bear than a cordial greeting. She could not help giving in and hugged the large warrior. It reminded her of the hugs her father gave her as a child but had long since withheld. She wrapped her arms around him and allowed herself to enjoy the moment of affection and kindness. She realized that before Magnus arrived, her parents starved her of affection and any signs of love. Elizabeth was full of smiles and quick embraces, but they were not the same. Stepping back, Deirdre experienced an immediate loss of security the older man's fatherly hug provided her. An arm snaked around her waist and pulled her back against the solid planes of Magnus's chest. He wrapped the other arm around her, and his broad shoulders wrapped around her, providing the security she craved as she prepared for whatever Hamish was about to share. She was sure she would not like what she heard.

"Lady Deirdre, I am rather glad ye are here because it will make relaying this information easier."

"Deirdre, please, ma laird."

"Uncle to ye, lass," Hamish smiled, and Deirdre could not resist smiling back. Magnus squeezed her, and she looked over her shoulder at him. He pecked her forehead.

"Now, I have just come from the Great Hall. There is a whirlwind of gossip going around aboot more than one thing, but it all involves the two of ye. Magnus, there is the obvious talk aboot the attempt on yer life, but many are putting two and two together. They are turning to Hay and Fraser, and both men claim the king as their alibi since they rode with him. Chatter aboot Deirdre is rather nasty. Women arenae kind, and until something more scandalous happens, she's the *en dite* on every woman's lips. There is nae doubt it will get back to the queen, and I doubt the gossip will please her—neither the content or the fact it's being spoken.

"What's worse is the king is threatening to withhold his writs until the matter of the threat is reconciled. He wants no one believing they have gotten away with aught with nae blame. He isnae conducting business with any of the Highlanders who came at his request. He also has his Privy Council sitting on tenterhooks awaiting his attention on matters that seem to be pressing. Essentially, he has the court in a tiswad over this, and it's only making ye both more conspicuous. Magnus, ye both must stay through the end of the hunt. Assuming nay more threats are made against ye, his majesty will scribble his mark across the writs, and we can all be gone from this dung pile."

Hamish looked into Deirdre's eyes, his smile sad and tired.

98

"I do believe they will announce yer betrothal within the sennight. Even if it is, they willnae plan the wedding for less than a month after Magnus leaves. There is plenty of speculation whether he is bedding ye again. Hay willna stand for questions aboot who sired yer progeny. It will be at least three days before ye will can leave. But, lass, ken that every Highlander within shouting distance is on yer side. We will see ye away safely."

Deirdre nodded before spinning in Magnus's arms and burying her face into his chest. Magnus could do little more than hold her and look at his uncle over the top of her head.

Chapter Ten

The next three days moved at a snail's pace for both Deirdre and Magnus. The expectation of riding out again with the king forced Magnus to leave Deirdre's warm arms each morning. However, the weather kept everyone indoors as buckets of rain poured from the heavens as thunder rattled the windows and lightning cracked across the grey sky. There was little for people to do besides gossip, and that is what most of the ladies-in-waiting did. Deirdre was growing more uncomfortable being in their presence, and she feared what might happen if the queen discovered the salacious talk that surrounded her. After Magnus left her chamber in the early morning, stepping onto the slick ledge, Deirdre wandered into the royal library to spend hours among the books. They had always been her refuge, and they continued to offer her solace when she and Magnus could not be together. Magnus spent most of his time with his uncle as the man was the only distraction that did not grate on his nerves but reminiscing about family and catching up on old news did not make the days pass any faster.

The morning of the fourth day shone brightly as Magnus made his way down to the royal stables. He borrowed a saddle from one of the Sutherland guardsmen who was staying behind. Magnus went over his horse from *Sealgair's* muzzle to whithers, along his flanks, and all the way down his fetlocks. He checked all four hooves and shoes to be sure they were in good condition. Magnus had been in two minds whether he should ride his warhorse after he took the arrow to his flank, but the stallion was stomping and neighing a greeting when Magnus walked into the stables. Magnus greeted his horse but moved on to look at another possible mount. *Sealgair* kicked the sides of his stall in jealousy, so Mangus brought him an apple, and with a chuckle, reassured his steed he would take him on the hunt. Magnus went over the borrowed saddle with a fine-toothed comb as well. He was not willing to take any chances of being thrown again. His body still ached, and his head throbbed on occasion from the abuse it took four days earlier, but nights spent in Deirdre's arms did much to restore him.

The king arrived, and the hunting party rode out taking a different route this morning as the approached the woodlands from another direction. As the men clustered together in various groups, the Highlanders maneuvered themselves into the center forcing all the other riders to the outskirts of the group. The number of enormous men on sturdy warhorses swelled from the day before as the lairds present brought more of their guardsmen with them. With close to three score men representing the northern clans, it was a veritable wave of plaid surging towards the forest as the horses pounded over the ground. They resembled Moses parting the Red Sea of courtiers. The increased numbers did not go unnoticed by the courtiers and other royal guests. Highlanders stood out not just from their clothing, but their hair was longer, their beards bushy, the muscles of their bare arms and calves glistened a much darker hue than their compatriots who spent most of their days inside. The height and breadth of each Highlander made the contrast even starker as it appeared as they rode with a passel of children alongside them rather than other adult men.

Magnus rode in the center surrounded by the lairds who offered their support the day before and encircled by the various clan members who served their lairds. Ostensibly, the Highlanders appeared to be guarding the king who rode in front of Magnus, but the men knew among themselves what the real purpose for the configuration was. The Sinclairs were an important clan in the far north, and Laird Liam Sinclair was well respected and admired by most. Magnus was well-liked, and there was no denying that he would be the best man to have on one's side in a battle. The attack on Magnus felt like an attack on them all. Even men who were not part of the clans that offered their support the previous day knew of the events and were silently banding together. The politics of Highland independence and self-rule felt at stake for many, and so it made for strange bedfellows that day. They set aside dislike and past grudges temporarily to unite against the common threat. Everyone realized, Highlander and Lowlander, Magnus's presence as a Highlander at least one person resented his presence, and the tale of his relationship with Deirdre Fraser, a Highlander herself, spread further each day. To allow his attack to go unnoticed without a unified front was an invitation for other attempts to subvert and manipulate the Highlanders. Their honor and freedom to continue their way of life felt in jeopardy, and they were responding in silent solidarity.

Magnus looked to the king's right, and the sight of Laird Fraser alongside him did not surprise him. Fraser tried to inconspicuously look back at the men who rode in tight formation, but his inability to disguise his actions made many of the men laugh out loud.

"Donald, ye've been here too long," called one man with a deep burr.

"His prey sees him coming before he sees them," rumbled another.

"Aye, every cock crows boldly in his own yard. Tis a shame, Donald, ye dinna remember where yers is," Laird Grant called out. No one misunderstood the double meaning of the well-known idiom, and the men howled with laughter.

The king rode further ahead to ignore the men's teasing as he was not sure he could keep a straight face, and he would not let them draw him into their squabbles.

Fraser cast them an angry glare before turning back to speak to Hay who now rode beside him.

"He does like to run his gob these days. I kenned him as a lad, and he never spoke that much. Must be because his wife isnae around. It's the only chance he has to get a word in edgewise," the Graham said none too subtly. "Ye ken, though, talk doesnae wear the clothes."

All eyes shifted to Fraser as they waited to see whether he would acknowledge the last insult. The insinuation he could do little more than talk implied that he was but a puppet. Someone else must do the work he could not. Hay turned a blank stare at Fraser not understanding the strange quips.

"And it's many a time a mon's mouth broke his nose," came Fraser's return jibe. The return of his burr made Hay gawk and the other men laugh. "I see what they say is true, everybody is good-natured until a cow goes in his garden."

"Och well, Donald, ye ken we, Highlanders, all like our gardens. The Highlands are like one vera large garden, ye ken." Hamish's warning was the last spoken as the men arrived at the wooded area. The silent reminder that the Highlanders would support one another rang in everyone's ears.

The day's hunt progressed without incident. Magnus was not sure if it was as simple as nothing was planned against him or if the personal guard of sixty men deterred further attempts. Either way, by the nooning, Magnus could relax enough to enjoy the hunt. He was not in as much pain as he had been that morning, and he bagged several quail and a doe.

The men stopped near a stream to water their horses and let them rest again. Magnus dismounted and checked *Sealgair's* wound to make sure it was not festering. When he was satisfied that his companion's side was still healing without further injury, he made his way to his uncle and the other Sutherlands. He immediately recognized Laird Fraser as the man speaking to his uncle.

"Your nephew oversteps his bounds yet again. It was bad enough he defiled my daughter all those years ago, but if he thinks there is even a remote chance he will get his hands on her again, he will find himself in the darkest and deepest oubliette this country has to offer. He will not destroy an arrangement that has been nearly three years in the making. I have paid a great deal of money to get where I am, and I will not have the upstart little pup getting in the way. I warn you, Hamish, only because you are a man I have known since we were lads, this is the only courtesy I will give you. Keep the bastard away from my daughter."

Fraser made to step around Hamish, but his uncle's arm shot out to block the other man.

"Or what?"

"What do you mean 'or what'? I just told you, he will find himself in a dungeon with no way out."

"Ye feel that threatened by the young mon that ye think a dungeon will solve yer problems. Ye're either daft or naïve if ye think ye can keep him anywhere for long. Do ye nae see all the men who have ridden by his side. If one more hair on ma nephew's head is disturbed, ye may find yerself in need of returning home to assess the damages."

"Are ye now threatening me? I didnae have aught to do with that bungled attack. I amnae desperate enough to risk the king's wrath nor give up all I have gained. That was someone else, but I canna say I'm disappointed it happened." Fraser's burr returned as his temper rose. He kept his voice low and modulated, but his anger was obvious to everyone nearby.

Hamish grabbed the front of his doublet and pulled him in close.

"We all ken ye are a but a puppet to Hay. And we all ken it was Hay who arranged the attack. Tread lightly, Donald or ye may lose yer balance."

Hamish shoved him away and only then noticed Magnus watching the scene. Fraser turned to see who Hamish was looking at and glowered when he saw Magnus standing there. For his part, Magnus stood with his feet planted apart and his arms crossed. He raised one eyebrow in silent challenge as he flexed his chest. Laird Fraser was still a man in his prime, and even though he did not acknowledge his Highland heritage, he trained in the lists regularly. But even as fit as he was, it was obvious he was no match for the younger man who stood a head and a half taller than him. Fraser chose to stalk away.

Once the Fraser was out of sight, Magnus relaxed. He walked over to his uncle and returned the hug offered to him.

"Dinna fash, Magnus."

"I amnae. And hearing ye speak reminded me of something I saw the last time we hunted. It was Mary Kerr who favors the kestrel. She has plumes from the bird in a brooch she wears. I think there may be quite a few who dinna appreciate ma presence. I wonder if the Kerr lass was behind ma attack, and mayhap Hay arranged the bird."

"That is possible. She has been making quite the stir for months now aboot yer family killing her father. She has not been subtle in her contempt since yer arrival either."

"How conveniently she forgets that it was her father who tried to have her half-sister killed for money. The apple didna fall far from the tree apparently."

"Och, we all ken there wasna any love lost between Brighde and her half-siblings. It doesnae surprise me in the least that Lady Mary would overlook her father's actions since she was probably hoping he would succeed."

Hamish's bluntness sent a shiver down Magnus's spine. He was fond of his sister by marriage and still despised her dead father for how he treated her, but his spine tingled knowing there was yet another person who might try to see him dead. He knew from his sister Mairghread's experiences with Lady Beatris and Sorcha that one should never underestimate a woman's vindictiveness. He resolved to keep the embittered lady-in-waiting in mind if anything else should befall him.

"True enough. Just another set of fangs to mind in this den of vipers."

The men remounted and headed back to the castle with their various hunting prizes.

Deirdre roamed about the royal library with no real purpose. Relieved to be paroled from her chamber again, she knew it was only because the men had ridden out on the hunt. As soon as Magnus returned, they would shut her away again. Her lack of freedom frustrated her, and even a place that usually brought her solace left her feeling isolated and alone. She scanned the shelves and spotted various books she had read over the years. She settled on a leatherbound edition of "The Letters of Abelard and Heloise." The notorious correspondence between the monk and nun turned lovers seemed somewhat apropos to her situation.

She took the book and found a seat near the hearth. She flipped through the pages until she found the letter that most stood out to her at that moment.

"I preferred love to wedlock, freedom to a bond."

I certainly prefer the notion of love with Magnus than wedlock to Archibald, the slimy bastard. Freedom is when I am in Magnus's arms. I feel more like maself when I am with him than I ever have in the seven years I've been here or the months that passed between gatherings and hunts. A marriage to anyone other than Magnus would be nothing else but bondage. A prison of ma person and ma mind, and nae least of all ma heart.

Deirdre felt the tears forming behind her eyes. She had cried enough over the years, and she resolved to not shed any more tears now she and Magnus were reunited. The only tears she would consider were ones of joy. She moved back to the shelves and returned the book that now made her feel like a stone rested between her breasts. She scanned the shelves again and nearly laughed at the next tomes her eyes alighted on. It was as though irony were flaunting itself at her. Trotula's *Book on the Conditions of Women* was sandwiched between the Italian author's other two books *On Treatments of Women* and *On Women's Cosmetics*. She was already familiar with the books that purported to understand and explain female physiology. Deirdre stumbled upon them when she arrived at court and curious about the explanations of the female body after her new found desires and pleasures Magnus taught her before they separated. Her naivety led her to think they would not be apart long and that any extra knowledge of her own body would increase their pleasure when they reunited. The memory of her last gathering spent with Magnus filled her heart, but her mind quickly shut those memories out with the breathtaking pain of remembering her parents ripping her from Magnus's arms just moments after they announced their handfast. She forced them aside and returned to the memories of Magnus becoming her husband.

~~~

"Sshh, come on, Deirdre." Magnus led Deirdre into the cave that stood at the edge of the shore where it met a rocky outcropping. This year's Highland Gathering was being held at the MacLeods on the Isle of Skye. The cold water from Hebrides swirled and crashed below the entrance to the cave. Magnus helped Deirdre scale the few feet of rocks needed to make their way into the secluded spot.

Magnus and Deirdre slipped away from the camp an hour after most of the women and children settled for the night. Dozens of men still gathered around fires sharing ale and whisky. Their noisy songs and banter carried on the wind. The young couple tiptoed their way to a cave Magnus spotted earlier in the day during the foot race. He and the other older lads charged past as they scaled the hills and trails that laced around the Isle of Skye. As his eyes began to adjust, Magnus pulled a candle that was barely more than a nub from his sporran and struck flint against the rock wall to light it. He held up the meager light and scanned the cave as far back as he could see.

"Wait here, a wee moment, Deir," Magnus stepped further into the cave and looked for any signs that it might be an animal's home. When he spotted nothing, he walked back to Deirdre. "I will gather some wood to build ye a fire. Dinna leave here, Deir. I dinna ken who or what might be near."

Magnus gave her a quick peck on the cheek before dashing out. He was not gone long, and Deirdre had already spread the plaid on the ground she smuggled out wrapped under her arisaid. The double layer of plaid had made her warm while they ran from her family's tent, but she appreciated having it now. She sat on it and was thankful for the buffer between her backside and the cold earthen floor. Magnus built a fire well back from the entrance. He thanked God and all the saints for a curve in the cave that allowed him to build a fire large enough to keep them warm without being seen from the outside. He brushed his hands off and looked back at Deirdre who had pulled the blanket closer. He sat beside her, and she immediately leaned into his side.

"I've missed ye, Magnus. The last six months have been the hardest yet. Ma parents have asked more questions aboot ma missives to ye. I think ma mother has even read them."

"I kenned as much before ye explained in Aramaic, which was a brilliant tactic."

"Aye, but that's what must have tipped them off that our letters are usually more than academic. I dinna ken which one she read first, but it must have been one of the more mundane ones because she didna confront me aboot it. When she saw the Aramaic warning ye nae to write aught personal, it must have made her suspicious. It's been miserable nae being able to share more than pleasantries with ye. Ma sisters are married now, and I only see them at these gatherings. They didna come to the last hunt as ye ken. Now that ma brother is older, he spends most of his time in the lists. I dinna have their company any more, and there is nae one to distract mother from me, so now she is watching me like a hawk."

Magnus heard the hitches in her voice and lifted her into his lap.

"Wheest, eun beag. We are here now." Deirdre melted into him at the use of his pet name for her.

"Mo fhuamhaire, I dinna want to be apart any longer. I dinna want to wait anymore."

Magnus paused as his cock twitched and his heart stuttered.

"Just what are ye saying, Deirdre?" She heard the seriousness in his voice and did not miss the use of her full name, something he almost never used anymore.

"I'm saying I dinna want aught but to be yer wife. Now. Nay some year in the future."

"Ye ken I havenae asked yer father yet." Magnus looked down at her and held his breath as his heart started to race.

"I dinna care."

"Are ye saying ye'll handfast with me right now? That ye are willing to become ma wife in truth? Here?"

"That is exactly what I am saying, Magnus. We talked aboot handfasting before our letters were being intercepted. I'm six and ten now. I am more than old enough to wed, and I refuse to consider anyone else."

"Ye would exchange vows with me and consummate our marriage now?"

"Magnus," she sighed in irritation, "are ye nae understanding me? I want to say our pledge, handfast, and then spend the rest of the night making love to ye."

Magnus could only nod as he took in her brazen statement, then he launched himself at her. He rolled her onto her back as he laid her onto the plaid. His mouth fell to hers as he licked the seam of her lips. She opened to him without reserve, and he sank his tongue in her warm, velvety depth just as he had over and over in the past, but this time, knowing she would be his wife before they left the cave, made it seem so much more significant. It felt spiritual as their souls blended together in that kiss. Her hands came into his hair as her tongue dueled with his, and when she latched onto the tip, she sucked it into his mouth. The rhythmic motion had him thrusting his hips against her mound. She raised her hips in a matching give and take of passion. One hand slid from his head to the groove on his hip that she loved. She dug her fingers into the taut flesh of his backside. His growl elicited a moan from her.

Magnus sat back on his haunches, pulling Deirdre up with him, refusing to break their kiss as he fumbled with her laces. In turn, she felt around for the brooch on his shoulder. She unpinned it and pulled back long enough to find the flap of his sporran and dropped it in. Once again pressing their lips together, she pulled the extra length of his breacan feile from his shoulder and unfastened the belt that held the exceptionally long length of plaid in place. Magnus raised up on his knees, so she could pull it loose. He pushed her gown down her arms and over her hips. They broke apart long enough for Magnus to rip his leine over his head, and Deirdre yanked her chemise over hers. They sat as he pulled off his boots and she her slippers, then they scrambled to take off their stockings.

Their bodies came back together with such force that Magnus wrapped his arms around Deirdre to keep from knocking her over. It was the first time they had ever been completely bare in front of each other. Their hands explored one another finding crests and valleys unknown to each other, previously hidden by clothing. When they finally had to catch their breath, they sat back on their haunches. Holding one another's hands, they sat silently looking into one another's eyes. Deirdre saw the amber in Magnus's eyes sparkle with the nearby flames' reflection. He sank into the depths of her hazel eyes as the blues and greens shone like the sun on the waves that broke just below the window of his chamber back home.

"Ye sure of this, Deirdre?"

"Ye keep asking me that. Aye, I'm sure, Magnus." She raised his hands and put his palms over her heart. "Ye have always given me choices and respected ma decisions. This is ma choice, and I've decided that I want to be yer wife now rather than wait any longer."

Magnus felt the steady beat of her heart as his raced. The regular rhythm calmed him, and he brought her hands to his chest before returning his hands to her.

"Deirdre Fraser, I love ye now and forever," Magnus began.

"Magnus Sinclair, I love ye now and forever," Deirdre answered.

"We swear by peace and love to stand," Magnus recited the ancient poem's beginning.

"Heart to heart and hand to hand" Deirdre followed.

"Mark, o' Spirit, and hear us now, confirming this our Sacred vow. To thee, I pledge ma troth." They swore together.

They leaned into one another and exchanged the most tender kiss they had ever shared. It was slow and lingering as they each poured forth all they wanted to share but did not have the words to say. A lifelong commitment was made not only in those words but in this kiss.

"Deirdre Sinclair," Magnus whispered.

"I rather like the sound of that, husband," Deirdre smiled softly.

"Wife," Magnus lowered them to the blanket again, and they lay on their sides looking at one another.

Slowly their hands began to trace one another's bodies as their fingers followed the shadows cast by the firelight. Hair had begun to grow on Magnus's chest since the last time Deirdre saw him, and she explored its feel against her fingertips. Magnus caressed her hipbones that were not quite as prominent as they had been. He had always been drawn to her body, but the softness that the past year brought to her body aroused him further.

"Do ye understand what we are aboot to do? What happens with our bodies?"

"Aye, I may never have done it, but I have heard enough of the maids talk to ken what happens."

"Ye ken it may hurt at first, and I wish I could prevent that from happening, but the pain will ease, and the pleasure will come."

"Magnus, ye dinna need to convince me. I ken ye wouldnae hurt me on purpose."

Magnus's hands roamed over her body as she rolled onto her back. She opened her arms to him, and he moved to prop himself up above her. Magnus watched as her pupils dilated and her fingertips brushed over his shoulders as they flexed and rippled from supporting his weight.

"Ye are so braw. I havenae ever seen a mon more handsome and strong than ye. I canna believe I can touch ye and feel ye."

"Everyday for the rest of our lives, mo chridhe. Everyday," Magnus smiled, and Deirdre swore her heart skipped a beat.

She felt his fingers rub along the folds of her damp flesh, and then his fingers slid into her. She arched her back as her head tilted. Magnus kissed along her throat. Her fingers gripped his upper arms as his fingers danced inside her. She craved the sensations of him stroking her core as his thumb worked the sensitive bud that emerged from the hood at the apex of her legs. She moaned as she felt herself moving towards climax. Deirdre reached between them and grasped Magnus's cock and worked her hand up and down his length. He gently clasped her wrist.

"If ye keep that up, this will end before it starts. It feels too good, and I am too eager."

"Eager?"

"Aye. I have dreamed aboot this endlessly for nearly three summers."

"I have, too. I've been growing more curious the more we share. But then we are apart for so long, I wondered if ye were as frustrated as I am."

"I have been, but do ye ken how I told yer that a mon can keep himself warm?"

Deirdre nodded.

"What ye're doing with yer hand is what I do to maself when I'm thinking aboot ye."

Deirdre glanced down at Magnus's sword in her hand and guided it towards her sheath as she opened her bent legs. Magnus settled between them and kept working her delicate flesh. As she felt the tide of pleasure building within, she arched her hips up to him. She positioned the tip of his rod at her opening. He worked his fingers faster and harder until the wave of release washed over her, and her body went rigid. As she began to relax, Magnus surged forward finally breaking her maidenhead and claiming her as his wife.

She winced at the pinch deep within, but her satisfying release was enough to dull the pain of his penetration.

"Are ye well, mo ghaol?"

"I think so. I had nay idea ye would be so big or so hard. I feel like ye are splitting me in two, but I crave more. Does that make any sense?"

"Aye. I didna imagine ye would be so vera tight that it's taking all I have nae to spill right now, but I want to feel ye milk me."

Magnus tentatively rocked his hips forward, and when Deirdre did not object, he pulled back before pressing in again. Her moan was one of pure femininity. Magnus thought he would spill right then and there. He forced himself to slow down, but as he took a deep breath, her apple scent flooded his nostrils and drove him to the brink. He caught himself thrusting far harder and faster than he intended. He slowed, but Deirdre's fingernails biting into his forearms had him looking down at her.

"Dinna ye dare stop now. Dinna slow either. Dear God above, Magnus, I couldnae imagine how good this would feel. I dinna ever want to stop. More. Please, more."

Magnus was happy to oblige. Ever mindful of his size compared to hers, he supported his weight on his forearms and knees as he sunk into her over and over. Her nails scored his back as she first wrapped her legs around his waist and then over his legs as she sought to find a position that allowed her to leverage her hips to meet each of his thrusts with ones of her own. She craved the friction on her pleasure button and found it as he ground himself into her.

"Aye. That's what I need. Magnus. Oh God. Oh!"

The sound of her voice and her warm breath against his ear was driving him to finish, but he refused to surrender until she was there with him.

"Come apart for me, Deir. I want to feel ye surrender as I find ma own release."

"So close. I'm so close. I can feel it," she panted.

Three more thrusts and Deirdre felt herself fly over the top as the strongest waves of pleasure wound their way around her and pulled her under. She felt as though she might drown from the intensity of her release.

"Magnus!" She screamed as she crested.

Magnus thrust once more and quickly pulled from her, roaring her name as his seed spilled across her belly.

"Deirdre!"

She pulled him down so most of his weight rested on top of her. She knew he still held much of it to protect her, but she needed the skin to skin contact for the full length of their bodies.

"I love ye, Deir."

"I love ye."

They held each other until Magnus could no longer support his shaking arms and worried that he would crush his tiny bride. He rolled them so she lay across his chest. He pulled the edge of the blanket over them and tucked her head into the crook of his neck. They lay there as their breathing quieted, and their hearts slowed. They ran their hands over one another in gentle caresses, enjoying the closeness they now shared. After simply basking in the afterglow, Deirdre could not help but wonder about how things finished.

"Magnus, why didna ye spill yer seed inside me? Dinna ye want to have children with me? Do ye want them at all?"

Magnus looked down at her as he swept back strands of hair still plastered to her forehead. He kissed her forehead and then rubbed his nose against hers.

"Of course, I want to have bairns with ye. I want a family we make together, but I wasna sure if ye were ready yet. I didna want to force ye into something ye didna want. I hadnae asked ye." Magnus shrugged his shoulders slightly.

"Ye're giving me a choice?"

"Absolutely. Ye're ma wife now. We are partners in everything including our family. If ye dinna want to have bairns yet or if ye want a score, ye have as much say as I do. More so, truth be told, since ye're the one who must bear them. I willna ever force maself on ye, and I willna ever force ye to bear a child if ye arenae willing."

Deirdre took all that Magnus said. It never dawned on her that she might have a say in whether or not she produced heirs for her husband. She never gave much thought on whether there was a means to control how many children she had.

"Ye're willing to wait?"

"Until ye are ready."

"And ye dinna want to have a bairn now?"

"I want a bairn whenever the Lord blesses us with one, but if it isnae what ye want now, then we will be careful to keep it from happening."

"I do want to have a family and soon, Magnus, but I think we need to tell our families before risking a pregnancy."

Magnus took a deep breath and blew it out slowly. He knew she was right, and he had prepared what he would say to her father long before he and his clan arrived for the games. He just was not sure how Laird Fraser would receive what he had to say. He regretted now not telling his father what he intended.

"Are ye regretting this?"

Magnus jerked his head down to see the look of concern etched on Deirdre's face.

"Dinna ever ask that again, Deir. I will never regret marrying ye. Nae now, nae when I'm a hundred. I married ye because there isnae aught I want more. I just am nae looking forward to telling yer father or mine. I wish we could skip past that and just return to Dunbeath to start our life together."

Deirdre nodded her head.

"Ma father willna be vera pleased, but there is naught he can do now. The deed is most certainly done."

Magnus's forefinger eased her chin up, and they came together in a tender kiss that rapidly fanned into a full blaze of passion. Magnus lifted Deirdre to straddle him and let her guide his iron shaft into her. He had no idea how he could be so aroused again after feeling like she had already extracted the last drop from him.

Years of self-denial. That is why I am so eager to go again. That and years of craving her. It never felt as good as this. What was I thinking all those years ago that tupping wenches was the perfect outlet? Making love to ma wife far exceeds tossing some barmaid's skirts or chasing a milkmaid. I havenae missed aught on that account, but sweet merciful Mary, I have been missing the greatest physical pleasure I have ever felt. Deirdre is so tight. Her flesh is so warm as I slide into her. I could spend every moment of the rest of ma life buried to the hilt in her and still crave more.

He guided her hips as she tried rocking and rising on his cock. She found that she most enjoyed the rise and fall as her body swallowed his cock over an over. She lay her hands over his chest to support her weight as he helped her lift her hips with each of his thrusts. She realized that she was pushing rather hard against him, so she moved her hands to rest beside his ears. This lowered her breasts to his mouth. He latched onto one nipple as he took the other into his hand. He alternated laving her nipples with kisses and nips and kneading the flesh of the other breast. He went back and forth between the two until her sounds of pleasure had his ballocks tightening, and he felt the telltale tingle at the base of his spine. He sucked hard on the nipple in his mouth as both hands gripped her hips to increase the speed of her gyrations, and he thrust harder into her until he felt her inner muscle clench his sword. He barely pulled from her sheath in time. He watched as the jet of milky seed shot from him, covering her breasts and his own chest. Deirdre stared down at him in awe before using the blanket to wipe them both clean. She scooted down his body but froze when she saw her virgin blood on his shaft. She looked up at Magnus but ducked her head in embarrassment.

"Deir, look at me, eun beag. Dinna be embarrassed aboot aught when it comes to our bodies. We shall share a bed now every night. We shall come to ken each other's bodies as well as we ken our own. There is naught for ye to ever hide. This is just a sign we are one now. Ye were a maid before tonight, and now ye are ma wife. It is proof of our commitment. It marks me as yers."

"Isnae it the other way around? That I am yers?"

"Mayhap, but I rather like it ma way." He winked at her, and he watched her relax. They wiped each other clean and settled back into their shared embrace.

As the night moved along, they lay snuggled together and talked about the future they planned. They spent several hours imagining what the future held, and the sky was just starting to lighten to the dark shade of blue that comes a few hours before dawn when they fell asleep entwined with one another.

The early rays of dawn were drifting into the cave when Magnus stirred. He woke to an empty spot next to him. He blinked his eyes open and saw Deirdre bending over the fire, stoking it back to life. The view of her bare backside pointing towards him had his already hard cock aching. He came to his feet and wrapped his arms around her waist. She squealed as he pulled her flush against him.

"Do ye feel what the sight of ye does? Do ye feel how much ma body craves yers?"

She spun in his arms, pressing her breasts against his chest and then skimming them along his hot skin. The heat that he seemed to perpetually give off mesmerized her. Magnus grasped her below her bottom and lifted her to his waist. She wrapped her legs around him and sank onto him. She gave a throaty moan as he filled her. The sounds from her spurred Magnus to walk to the cave wall. He pressed her back against the wall and slowly moved in and out of her.

"Magnus, I dinna want it slow. More."

"I want to, but ye must be tender this morning. I dinna want to hurt ye."

She grasped his ear and tugged.

"I will hurt ye if ye dither aboot. More, Magnus." She added on a whisper, "Please."

His control slipped, and he thrust harder as her pleas rattled around in his ears. Her moans only spurred him on more. She whispered words of encouragement, and he gave into their shared desire. She clung to him as tightly as she could, and while she could not move much on her own, she took every pounding surge of his shaft and squeezed her inner muscles around him. The harder he entered her the more she craved the mixture of pleasure and pain.

The blend of sensations was becoming too much, and she felt as though she could not catch her breath when her entire body seemed to spasm. Her nails bit into his back, and she would later discover that she broke the skin in more than one place, but it pushed him over the top too. He thrust as hard as he could twice more, and the scream of her climax echoed in his ears when he pulled out and yelled out his own release.

Magnus swung around and braced his back against the wall as he gasped. His legs shook as his kneecaps quivered. No longer able to stand, he slid down the wall until he sat on the dirt floor. Deirdre's limp body hung over his, and for a moment he was truly frightened that something was wrong because she felt so listless.

"Deir," he whispered.

She lifted her head when she heard the panic in his voice. She looked into his concerned eyes, and while exhausted, her smile reminded him of the cat that got into the cream. She looked thoroughly ravished, and now assured she was well, his pride swelled to know he put that look on her face and he exhausted her with their lovemaking.

They sat together until they both felt chilled. Finally, Magnus pulled himself out of his post-climax stupor and roused Deirdre, who must have drifted off. They looked at one another and came together in another fierce kiss. They would have started another round of lovemaking, but the shout of first her name and then his had them scrambling to put their clothes on. Magnus kicked dirt over the fire as Deirdre grabbed their blanket and rolled it up before tucking it into her arisaid. She did her best to run her fingers through her hair, but when Magnus shook his head, she knew it was a lost cause. If nothing else gave them away, it would be her riot of curls she knew must look like she had been dragged through a hedge backward.

~~~

Deirdre settled back into her chair after returning "The Letters of Abelard and Heloise" and pulling out a well-worn edition of Tristan and Isolde. The tale of the ill-fated lovers seemed appropriate.

"There ye are," came Mary Kerr's nasal voice.

Deirdre's head whipped around as she watched a group of ladies-in-waiting enter. She stifled a groan as she saw that among them were some of the most vicious gossips. The only young woman among them that Deirdre liked was Ceit Comyn, but she was quiet and not one to stand out among the pack of she-wolves.

"Yes, here I am." Deirdre simply looked as the women approached. She had never cared for Mary Kerr and the young woman's incessant complaints about Magnus's family had grated on Deirdre's nerves, but her recent vitriol of rumors about Deirdre's past with Magnus made her very wary. She refused to offer the courtesy of standing.

This slight did not go unnoticed, and Mary's eyes narrowed to little more than slits.

"Sitting here alone? Where is your betrothed? Has he, or should I say they, gone off and left you here by your lonesome?"

"Mary, you are tiresome. We all know the men have gone out to the hunt. We also know I am not betrothed to Lord Archibald yet, and you seem well-informed of my past."

"The queen's English again, I hear. Are you foreswearing your heathen lover to return to the world of civilized company? Are you sure that Lord Archibald will still have you?" There was a look of speculation and almost jealousy that flashed through Mary's eyes when she spoke of Archibald. It made Deirdre wonder if Mary was interested in Hay for herself.

If she wants him, she is welcome to him. They can drive each other barmy. One bampot for another. She is a right bitch, and since he's such a bastard, they suit each other well. If only I could convince Archibald that he would be better off with her than me. Christ on the cross, if Magnus's family hadnae killed her father, then she might have a dowry to woo Archibald away. I wonder if that's why she's so cold to everyone. She kens she hasnae aught to offer and rather than anyone discover she hasnae a dowry, she pushes everyone away. Bluidy hell! I bet that is exactly it. It isnae grief but resentment that drives her retaliation against the Sinclairs. She is bitter that they stole her chance to marry well. Nay dowry means nay wealthy husband. Nay mon would take her otherwise!

This newfound knowledge settled over Deirdre and made her better prepared for the inevitable onslaught she knew was coming. Mary did not disappoint.

Mary looked over her shoulder at the women who followed in her wake, women who learned that it was easier to allow her to be their self-appointed leader than to be on the receiving end of her vicious tongue.

"Did you know, ladies, that Lady Deirdre has known the Sinclair barbarian for years now. Since she was three and ten I believe. She spent quite a great deal of unsupervised time with him. I have heard tell that they used to disappear together for hours on end only to reappear looking disheveled."

Mary looked back at Deirdre and sneered before looking back at her disciples.

"Tale be told, she claimed herself wed through some ancient barbaric custom that excuses unchaste behavior. Her parents brought her here to atone for her wicked ways and to cleanse her of the filth she rolled around in."

Deirdre knew the wise course of action was to bite her tongue, but she knew her reputation was destroyed. There would be no salvaging it, and at this point, she had no desire to. Her future with Magnus was far more important to her than what anyone at court, even the queen, thought of her.

"You apparently know very little about the mechanics."

"I beg your pardon. What mechanics would I need to know?"

"Your ignorance simply confirms how little interest men have paid you. I could not roll around in *him*. But he certainly rolled around in me."

Deirdre sauntered past them on her way to the door. She caught Ceit Comyn's eye, and the girl smiled briefly at her before giving a slight nod of acknowledgment. Deirdre had almost made it to the door before she heard a voice she recognized from the passageway outside her chamber the night that Magnus first found her.

"The Sinclair men, all of them from what I have seen, are quite well endowed. I find it hard to believe such a braw and lusty mon as Magnus would have found much pleasure in such a spindle shanks as ye."

Deirdre turned back towards the women, but her grin was the last thing that anyone expected. She slowly walked back to Sorcha and stood before her. She looked her over while seeming to look down at her.

"There isnae a single Sinclair ye ever saw bare, and they banished ye to court with Lady Beatris after ye couldnae get past Laird Mackay throwing ye over for Magnus's sister. Ye werenae enough for Laird Mackay but seeing as Lady Mairghread is expecting her second bairn, I would say Laird Mackay has been enjoying her quite a lot."

Deirdre grinned as the other women gasped at both the return of her burr and her raunchy comments. As she pushed down on the door handle, she threw back over her shoulder, "and I saw ye in the passageway with Magnus. He jumped from ye like a scalded cat. Ye would think ye had the pox the way he pushed ye away."

Chapter Eleven

*A*fter her encounter with the other ladies-in-waiting, Deirdre found herself wandering and in need of a new place for solitude. It was not until she sat in a pew that she realized she made her way to the chapel. She looked around at the stained-glass windows, focusing on the Archangel Michael slaying the dragon. She stared as the light refracted through the lead paint and dust motes danced through the air. She tilted her head to the side as she looked at the holy image of a dark-haired man with a broadsword.

That is Magnus, but just which dragon is he slaying? Ma father? Archibald? The memories of our time apart? Will the dragon blow fire and take Magnus from me again? Does Magnus have the strength to defend himself, us, from such a powerful foe? I dinna doubt that he does, but at what cost? What will the king say if Magnus triumphs? What will Magnus's father say if he returns with a wife when he was sent to court as his representative? Why arenae there any clear answers to these questions?

Blessed Mary ask the Holy Father to forgive me ma sins and bless me with His grace. I havenae honored ma parents, and I dinna ken if I can. I ken that is a sin, but what of the sins they have committed? I dinna think I can bring maself to pray for their souls? Does that make me an even greater sinner? I dinna feel remorse because I choose Magnus over all else. I love him more than aught or anyone, Lord. I admit that ma love for him may well rival if nae surpass ma love for Ye and Yer blessed Son and Holy Spirit. If I must choose, it will always be Magnus. I willna be coerced into letting him go again.

St. Michael and all the angels guide me. Help me see what God has planned for me. I want to walk on the path He has in store for me, but I dinna ken if that includes Magnus. If it doesnae, I will forsake Ye, Lord, before I do him. Will I burn in Hell or will Ye lock me eternally in Purgatory? God, forgive me the heresy, but I just canna face going on without him. I love him. Why did Ye bring him into ma life just to take him away? Will Ye do it again? Nay! I ken it wasna Ye. Ye granted man free will, and it was the will of ma parents that did it. Please, God! Help me. What am I to do?

Deirdre looked at the cross that hung over the altar as she implored God for intercession. She had not even realized that she made her prayers directly to God until she finished. She wiped the tears from her cheeks and bowed her head once more.

"I ask this in Yer name, in the name of the Father, Son, and Holy Spirit. Amen." She crossed herself and looked up as she heard the whisper of the door open and close.

The last thing she wanted was company. She tried to slouch into the pew hoping whoever entered would either not see her or ignore her. She listened as the light footsteps approached, and she shut her eyes as they stopped alongside her.

"Deir?"

Deirdre's eyes flew open as she looked up at Magnus. He slid into the pew and clasped her hand against the seat before moving his plaid to cover them. Anyone who walked past would not see them touching, but they both sighed as the contact soothed them both.

"Deir, why are ye crying? What happened," Magnus whispered. He looked around to be sure they were alone.

"Naught really. I found maself in here, and I took the time to pray. I dinna ken what brought me, but I was looking at that window," she pointed to the one that pictured Saint Michael, "and it made me think of ye slaying our dragons. I wondered just which ones ye would have to lay asunder."

"Are ye worried that I will have to kill yer father?" Deirdre could barely hear Magnus's raspy question.

"Nay. At least nae much. I ken ye dinna want to do aught like that, but I also ken I willna let anyone stand between us again. I pray it doesnae come to that."

"Ken that that will always be the vera last resort. I dinna want to do that, but I told ye before that I willna let anyone take ye from me again. I will do aught I must."

Deirdre laid her head on Magnus's shoulder no longer caring if anyone saw them. He released her hand and encircled her shoulders with his arm. He drew her to his side and kissed the crown of her head. He breathed in her scent before kissing her once again.

"Let us worry aboot this only if we must. There is nay point in buying trouble where there is none."

He felt her head nod as her silky curls tickled his chin. She turned to look up at him, and he wiped the last of her tears from her spiky lashes.

"I want to show ye something, Magnus."

An idea occurred to her, and she stood from the pew. She held out her hand for him, and he clasped it. She led him to a door he believed led to the sacristy. He looked around, fearful they would be discovered entering the hallowed place meant only for the priests. Instead, the door led into the chapel's scriptorium. Magnus had not known the church within the castle had a monastic library. He looked around the spacious chamber lined with windows on both sides. Next, he looked at Deirdre and saw her comfort within the space. He realized she must have spent quite a lot of time here to know her way from within the chapel.

"Is this where ye work?"

"Nae as often as I would like. I used to slip into here for hours when I first arrived. It was the only thing that made court tolerable. The priests were skeptical at first aboot allowing me within these hallowed walls, but once they saw the vellums I'd transcribed, and I proved ma translation skills, they welcomed me any time I wanted. I could come daily until the previous bishop passed away. The current bishop isnae so keen on the notion of women reading and scribing. He has seen ma work but refuses to believe I did it on ma own. He insists that I must have had a mon instruct me. I dinna feel vera welcome here anymore even though the other priests are still kind. It's actually been many months since I was last here."

Deirdre walked along the bookshelves that lined the walls. She trailed her fingers over many of the books, and she craned her neck to look at the top shelves that came close to touching the ceiling. She looked over at Magnus who was intent upon watching her.

"Do ye remember how ye carried ma vellums back to the keep that day we met?"

"Of course, lass."

"Do ye ken I watched ye the next day while ye and yer brothers trained in the lists? I didna get vera far in ma work that next day because I couldnae concentrate."

Magnus approached her but did not touch her.

"Do ye ken I took the flat of a blade across ma ribs that day because I couldnae focus either?"

"We made quite the pair even then."

"Did ye ken I searched for ye at the next hunt for two days before I found out ye didna come? I thought mayhap ye hadnae wanted to come after all. I thought mayhap ye didna want to see me like ye said ye would."

"Ye thought I rejected ye?"

"I ken now that made nay sense, but at only six and ten, I doubted maself and whether I imagined our connection."

"Och Magnus, ye have felt the sting of rejection so many times, and yet, never once did I reject ye."

"I ken that now. I even understood it when ye explained yer mother's illness when we spoke in the Graham's solar, but before that, I thought ye didna want me."

"Is that why ye tried to forget me? Why ye tried to replace me?" Deirdre murmured.

Magnus lowered his gaze and shook his head. When he looked up, Deirdre's heart seized at the guilt that filled his eyes. She feared what she was about to hear.

Was there a part of his past he still kept from her, that he lied about? Had he truly not been faithful after all?

"Deir, I wish I could take back the women from before I met ye and from that year apart. I wish I could have come to ye a virgin just as ye came to me. I wish it had only ever been ye."

Deirdre felt the air rush from her lungs. That confession was not what she expected. As the air filled her chest again, she wrapped Magnus in her arms. He bent and lowered his head to her shoulders. It was awkward, but she stroked his back as he clung to her.

"Have ye felt guilty aboot that all this time?"

"Aye. I felt like I betrayed ye by being with the other women even though we had only met once. We didna have any kind of understanding, but I used those women. I didna want any of them like I did ye. I used them as a distraction and a replacement. I felt wretched aboot that, but I felt even more wretched that I coveted a child. Ye were barely three and ten when we met. I had already coupled with more than one woman before we met. I was closer to a mon than a boy, but I longed to touch ye as I kenned a mon touches a woman."

Deirdre stepped back from Magnus and held his shoulders.

"Have ye carried this guilt all this time? Ye never shared this before. I mean ye told me aboot the women," she grimaced, "but ye never told me that ye felt guilty aboot yer feelings for me. I was so enamored with ye, and the fact that ye were older just made ye seem like a greater forbidden temptation. I rather loved kenning that ye were older, but I didna think ye would remember me after a year."

"I could never forget ye," Magnus choked out. "I never did. That is why I could never move on. I dinna think I would have moved on even if we never found one another again."

"Why are ye telling me all of this now?" Deirdre asked.

Magnus looked around the room before looking at her again.

"If ma family hadnae needed me, and if I wasna so close to ma brothers and sister, I would have done as most youngest sons do. I would have taken vows and entered a monastery. I didna have any desire for any other life if it was without ye. I thought a life of service might absolve me of ma sins, of coveting ye when ye were far too young and for taking yer innocence without being properly wed to ye."

"Magnus, ye make it sound as if I was barely out of swaddling clothes." She smiled up at him. "Ye ken, as well as I, I wouldnae have been the first lass to be married at three and ten if ye had claimed me then. I was practically on the shelf by the time we did handfast. I honestly amnae sure how I've gotten to a score and three without ma parents forcing a marriage before now. But Magnus, I told ye before, I would go to a convent before marrying someone else. I petitioned the king and queen when I first arrived here, but they told ma parents. Two years later, I petitioned the queen to let me remove to a convent, but once again, they informed ma parents. If ye hadnae shown up when ye did, I would probably have snuck away the moment ma parents set the date for the betrothal."

"We are a right pair," Magnus kissed her forehead and then pulled her in for a kiss that inevitably escalated.

Deirdre tugged his leine as she backed up to a large table covered in scrolls. Magnus pushed them aside and lifted her onto the table. His hands slid under her skirts and pushed them back, as she lifted his plaid.

"Do ye ken that this has always been one of ma fantasies?"

"To make love in a scriptorium?"

"Nay, Deir, to push all of yer work aside and take ye on the vera table ye leaned over."

"Is this how ye imagined it?"

Magnus paused before shaking his head.

"Nae exactly."

She cocked an eyebrow.

"I pictured bending ye over the table and taking ye from behind."

Magnus did not blink until she slid from the table. She turned to face it and braced her hands wide. She looked at him and pressed her hips back. He growled as he pushed her skirts up and then lifted his plaid. He slid his fingers between her thighs and felt her dew drench them. He thrust into her and grunted as she moaned. Deirdre used one hand to hold her up as she reached back to grasp his thigh.

"Quickly, Magnus. I dinna ken how long we have before someone comes."

"I'm going to come," he growled close to her ear. He clenched a handful of her hair and pulled her head. She turned to look at him, accepting his savage kiss. This joining was quick and intense, as they both searched and received absolution from one another. Their consciences released guilt held needlessly for years.

"Magnus, I'm close too," she panted. "Now. I'm coming apart now."

Magnus felt his seed spurt from him as it hit her inner walls that contracted around him.

"Me too."

He collapsed over her, and they leaned heavily against the table. Magnus reluctantly pulled away and straightened her gown and his plaid. He was just in time as the door from the chapel swung open. The two priests who entered looked between them, shocked to find anyone, let alone a couple, in their sanctuary.

Deirdre curtseyed before taking Magnus by the hand and leading him through the door to the courtyard. Once outside, they exchanged a look and burst into laughter.

"Do ye think they would have absolved me if I wrinkled their parchment as I took ye over their table?"

"Sshh!" Deirdre giggled as they dashed across the courtyard holding hands. They were oblivious to anyone else until they heard several gasps coming from the gate into the queen's private gardens.

"Bluidy hell," Magnus whispered.

"Shite," Deirdre breathed.

Magnus looked down at her, but she only shrugged.

"Well, so much for being discreet or keeping this a secret."

They both held their breath as Mary Kerr once again led her group of followers towards them. Deirdre tried not to turn her nose up, but she was not sure how successful she was when Ceit Comyn gave her head a slight shake.

"What have we here, ladies? It seems we have interrupted a tryst." She pursed her thin lips and smirked.

She doesnae ken the half of it. Magnus and Deirdre exchanged a look, and they knew they thought the same thing.

"Lady Mary, are ye well, lass? Ye're looking a mite peaked."

Magnus leaned towards Mary who leaned back. Her chin pulled back into her neck, and her eyes widened. Her arms went wide to keep her balance. He placed his hand lightly below her arm and steadied her. She pulled her arm away and nearly knocked herself over. The other ladies giggled into their hands.

"I ken there are hard feelings between our clans, but I do wish ye the best, lass. Ye ken, for such a bonnie lass, it escapes me why ye arenae wed yet." Magnus looked at her innocently, but his eyes were trained on her like a hawk. He saw her nostrils flare before her eyes narrowed and her lips thinned.

"Get your paws off of me, you beastly man. How dare you touch me?" She tried to step away, but her skirts caught under her feet. She stumbled several steps before righting herself.

"Have ye been sneaking a tipple of whisky here and there?" Magnus winked at her as she spun around and flounced away.

This time the other ladies were not as quick to follow. Many looked between Mary's retreating back and the couple that stood before them. Ceit Comyn stepped forward.

"In for a penny, in for a pound, I suppose. You know you are making a dangerous enemy. She may seem like just an angry young woman, but you must remember that she's a very well-connected one. She has not been at court long, but she has made influential friends who give favors just as they take them."

Ceit stepped back and turned towards her friends before they moved away from Magnus and Deirdre and in the opposite direction from which Mary walked.

"Lord Fraser, I think you should know what your daughter has been up to." Mary Kerr barged into the chamber where the Fraser poured over documents with his scribe and several other members of the king's Privy Council. "Begging your pardon, my lords. I should have knocked before entering when you are clearly all busy at work."

Mary's cagey words evaded the truth that she knew who occupied the room with Laird Fraser and that she had every intention of interrupting. Fraser looked up from the documents he was examining and hurried to the young woman hoping to reach her before she could say more. He was not quite quick enough.

"The other ladies and I just stumbled upon that heathen Sinclair leaving the chapel with Lady Deirdre. I cannot imagine what unholy things they did in such a sacred place. Really, someone should teach Lady Deirdre how to do her own hair, so she can repair it before appearing in public. Quite disgraceful."

Laird Fraser gripped her arm above the elbow none too gently and steered her from the chamber.

"I don't know what game you think you are playing, lass, but you are dangerously close to holding enough rope to hang yourself. You may think humiliating my daughter will ingratiate yourself and support your claim against the Sinclairs, but you are too late. The king signed the writs this very afternoon. The decisions have been made, and not in your clan's favor. You may insult the Sinclairs to your heart's content, but continue to drag my daughter's name into it, and you may find your lover is not so enamored of you when you are through. After all, your lover is to be my daughter's husband. I'm sure he does not want to have the harpy he's bedding disparaging his own wife in public." Laird Fraser gave her a shake when she stared at him aghast. "Did you think your secret was any better kept than my daughter's? Do you think I would not know every little secret of the man who will marry into my family? Oh yes, I already know you promised him a romp between your thighs any time he wants if he helps you cause the Sinclairs' downfall. I also know you made that offer within days of arriving at court. It did not take you long to survey the scene, find your prey, and set your bait. I don't really care how many times the man tups you as long as you do not impede their marriage. Cross me, lass, and you will find yourself on a slow boat to Iona."

Mary stood staring, mouth agape, as Donald Fraser strode back into the chamber from which they exited together only moments earlier. Once she regained her composure, she set her jaw and pushed her shoulders back. She looked once more at the door through which Laird Fraser passed before she set off for the royal apartments.

Chapter Twelve

he next morning, Magnus left Deirdre near the passageway leading to the queen's chambers. She had excused herself the evening before claiming a headache. She could only imagine what was in store for her once she entered.

"Are ye sure that ye must go in there? Canna ye claim another megrim? Ye could retire to yer chamber and nae have to deal with those lasses. They all talk out of both sides of their mouth."

"Would that I could. I must admit to being surprised the Lady Ceit has been so outspoken. She says vera little from what I can tell. Many other ladies dinna think her too sharp. It seems to me that she is vera well aware of all that goes on around her."

"Still waters run deep."

"That would seem to be the right of it. Nay, I must go in there. I canna run from ma duties. That isnae fair to the queen, and it will only antagonize ma parents more. I am sure they have heard by now the other lasses spotted us leaving the chapel together."

Magnus gazed intently at her before finally nodding his head.

"I dinna like kenning ye are in there with those women without me."

"What would ye do? Glare at them? Mayhap growl? Och aye, stand there just like that." Deirdre giggled at Magnus as he unconsciously moved into what she now called his Odin stance, with his feet hip-width apart and arms crossed, because it made her think he guarded the entrance to Valhalla. He looked down and dropped his arms.

"Magnus, I dinna need ye to defend me from a group of gossiping magpies. They may be a bunch of clipmalabors, but that is all they have to do with their days. They sit and tell tales about others. I have heard it all before."

"But this is the first time someone is directing it at ye. It's one thing to ken the person being gossiped aboot and quite another to be that person."

Deirdre nodded, but there was little else that either of them could do. They both knew she did not have a choice; the queen expected her to join the others.

"I will be well. I will see ye at the evening meal."

Magnus watched as Deirdre pushed the door open just wide enough to slip in. He stood there for several minutes after she disappeared. He shook his head and went in search of his uncle.

Deirdre stepped into the chamber and looked around. The scene was one she witnessed countless times over the past seven years. The queen sat in a large, high backed chair stitching while one lady read to her. Scattered around the room were ladies-in-waiting who knattered with one another while they embroidered. Some read quietly or in whispered tones to one another. She stepped further into the chamber, but unlike every other time she joined the queen, everything came to a screeching halt at that moment. Deirdre heard a buzzing in her ears as all eyes turned towards her. She looked around and saw a mixture of pity and haughtiness in the eyes that stared back. Her gaze landed on the queen who continued to sew. She was ready to breathe easy and find her own basket of sewing when the queen's voice ricocheted around the silent chamber.

"Lady Deirdre, it has come to my attention that I have a soiled dove among my dule."

Deirdre felt the blood pound in her ears as it amplified the buzzing. She looked at the queen, shocked to see the disgust on the woman's face. This was the same woman to whom she confessed all when she arrived seven years ago. The very woman who had eased her transition into the royal household with kindness and patience. Deirdre could do little more than stare as she saw a different side to the queen, and she realized that as long as her dirty secret had remained just that, the queen had not cared just how soiled she was. However, she was no longer a girl of only six and ten. She did not consider herself soiled or damaged. She felt quite the opposite. A great burden was being lifted from her shoulders now that she no longer had to pretend to be something she was not.

She looked around the room and found her cousin Elizabeth sitting wide-eyed and horrified. Her gaze darted between Deirdre and the queen as tears filled her eyes. She covered her mouth with her hands and shrugged. Deirdre gave her a small, reassuring smile before looking back at the queen.

"A soiled dove, Your Grace? Mayhap a magpie or two as well." Deirdre looked unflinchingly at the queen. Her words came out softly, but there was no missing the steel in her voice.

"This does not concern you, Lady Deirdre? To be in the company of a young lady who has fallen from grace?"

"I suppose it is a matter of who has fallen." Deirdre lifted her chin almost defiantly.

"I believe you and I already know, and have known for some time, of whom we speak."

"Yes, Your Majesty. We have both known for quite some time, and it has been a topic best left alone this entire time. However, I see that is no longer the case," Deirdre paused before looking directly at Mary Kerr who sat gloating beside the queen's feet. "Is it a concern that such a damaged soul will lead others astray? Have not words spoken out of turn poisoned the water far more times than what takes place behind closed doors?"

"Mayhap, but mere words are not a mortal sin."

Deirdre sucked in air through her teeth and ground them together. This was going far worse than she could have imagined. She wished now she had listened to Magnus and stayed in her chamber with him. She looked down at Mary and something about the woman's spiteful look struck her as odd. She caught herself as she was about to squint. There was a level of enmity directed at her that could not have been just about her telling the queen about finding Magnus and Deirdre together. She might be fishing, but she wondered if her potential betrothal to Hay, Magnus's attack, Mary's vendetta, and her being exposed to the queen were not all related.

"Is coveting thy neighbor's wife, or mayhap future husband, not a sin?" Deirdre kept her eyes on the queen but used her peripheral vision to follow Mary's reaction. "Is not pride, envy, and greed among the mortal sins? Lest we forget anger. That has led to more than one murder plot."

It was very subtle, but Deirdre caught Mary's squirming. She looked down at the other young woman, temporarily forgetting about the queen.

"Lady Mary, it seems that Lord Magnus was correct when he observed your brooch with the kestrel feathers. How truly unique. The only other time I have heard of anything wearing kestrel feathers here at court were the arrows shot at Lord Magnus. Such an odd coincidence."

If I am to go down, I amnae going alone. Let that bitch figure her way out of this. She can scratch and claw all she wants, but I amnae a kitten any longer. I'm a wildcat with claws, and I scratch back.

Deirdre looked again at Mary and saw the unease creeping into her eyes.

"Lady Mary, I am sure the queen is grateful for your bringing this matter of my unchaste behavior to her attention. I wonder though, did you make your own confessions when you were recounting my sins? 'I tell you, on the day of judgment people will give account for every careless word they speak, for by your words you will be justified, and by your words, you will be condemned.' Did you mention you covet the man who is to marry me?"

Deirdre saw anger and fear flare in Mary's eyes, and she wondered if there was more that she had yet uncovered. She thought quickly for a way to fish more information.

"Do you carry a tendre for Lord Archibald?"

Nay embarrassment or even shame, but there is certainly a look of warning. So, she doesnae have any soft feeling for him, but there is something she wants to keep hidden. What could she be hiding if it isnae—Nay! It couldnae be, could it?

"Do you know, Lady Mary, that when you point a finger, there are still three more pointing back at you. How long has Lord Archibald been bedding you?"

The room was already hushed, but a pin could have dropped in the deathly silence. The queen rose from her chair and glared at Deirdre.

"That is enough, Lady Deirdre. You would besmirch another young lady's reputation to deflect attention from your own vices. You have committed the sin of lust, and for that, you shall be removed from your position as a lady-in-waiting. You are to return to your chamber until your family can make arrangements to have you removed."

Deirdre had expected as much, but it still came as a shock to have all that she did to serve the queen for the past seven years swept aside. She curtseyed and was about to take her leave, but Mary's look of triumph stopped her.

"Your majesty, I believe you speak of the sin of lust, but the church sanctions marital relations between a man and his wife, therefore, it was never a sin. I handfasted with Magnus Sinclair when I was six and ten. My parents may have separated us, but that did not undo what was already done. I was wed to Magnus, so we had the blessing of our union to sanction our actions. Lady Mary has not had such a blessing. Her carnal actions do not even carry a betrothal as a justification. Lest we forget Saint Matthew, 'Why do you look at the speck of sawdust in your brother's eye and pay no attention to the plank in your own eye?'"

Deirdre pulled the door open behind her and stepped out without taking her eyes from the queen or Mary. It was only once the door was closed that she rested her forehead against it and exhaled a shaky breath. After several steadying breaths, Deirdre straightened her spine and squared her shoulders. She turned to walk towards her chamber only to be greeted by her irate parents.

"Do nae speak," her father hissed. He took her arm and led her through the passageways to her chamber. When they arrived, her mother unlocked the door and then pocketed the key. Her father thrust her into the chamber, and her parents followed her in. Deirdre was unprepared for her father's hand to lash out, slapping her soundly across the cheek. She covered her stinging cheek with her hand as she looked in shock at her father. He had never raised his hand against her, not even when she was a young child.

"Yer whoring is buzzing aboot every nook and cranny of this castle. As though it wasnae bad enough all those years ago, but now ye're flaunting yerself for all to ken that ye let that bastard between yer thighs."

Deirdre gasped at his coarse language. She had never heard her father speak in such a way, and she had not heard his burr come out so strongly since before they moved to court.

"Father—"

"Silence!" His hand whipped across her other cheek. "Count yer bluidy blessings I dinna take a strap to ye. If ye think for even a moment that ye will build a future with that whelp, ye have lost the last bit of sense God gave ye. Ye will be a dutiful daughter and prostrate yerself at Lord Archibald's feet and beg him for forgiveness. Ye had best pray that he accepts ye because we have already paid yer dowry to him, and yer bride price is as good as spent to secure that stewardship. We will have that land, and I dinna care at this point if he beats ye every day till ye breathe yer last. Ye would deserve it for humiliating the mon, for humiliating yer family. Ye had best accept him as yer husband and do aught that ye can to keep him pleased. Ye clearly have already practiced being a slut, now ye can put those skills to good use. Keep him pleased long enough to get a couple sons on ye, and then he might be generous and let ye live out yer days at one of his keeps. Dinna please him, and it will be out of our hands how he deals with ye. Ye arenae more than chattel as a daughter, and ye willnae be more than chattel as a wife. Ye could have made a fair go of yer marriage, but ye insisted on being a willful and ungrateful bitch. Ye've made yer bed. Now lie in it."

Laird Fraser moved to the door but paused when his wife did not follow him. He looked back, and for a brief second, he worried that he had gone too far and worried what his wife might say, but one look at the defiance on Deirdre's face and his resolve returned.

"You have had the best that any young woman could hope for. Your father indulged you at every turn when I warned him not to spoil you. The only thing that was ever asked of you was to be dutiful and marry as you were instructed. You turned yourself into a strumpet who pined away for a boy who was never suitable for you. Not just because of his Sutherland blood, though that never helped. He would never have been good enough because you would have been holed up on that Godforsaken north coast and served us no purpose here at court. You were such an insipid child. You believed whatever anyone told you. You believed he loved you but in the same breath, you believed us when we told ye he did not want you. You were much easier to control and manipulate when you were younger and still served a purpose. It no longer matters that you have become unruly. Your husband will surely cure you of that, and if he does not, well that is, as your father said, easily cured by being sent to a remote keep while your husband enjoys his mistress here at court."

"Deirdre," She looked at her father, "the papers will be signed this vera afternoon and the betrothal announced before the king and queen this eve. Ye will be wed before the next moon."

Lady Fraser walked to the door and stood beside her husband.

"You were always such a disappointment."

Her mother pounded the last nail into the coffin that held their familial relationship. Her parents left, and Deirdre heard the lock turn. There were muffled voices outside her door. Deirdre moved to it and pressed her ear against it. The words were garbled, but she could make out enough to understand that her parents posted a guard at her door. She was now a prisoner of her parents and the royal court.

Chapter Thirteen

*M*agnus felt unease leaving Deirdre at the door to the queen's apartments, but he knew she was right. They had no other choice but for her to go in. He was on his way to find his uncle when a royal page stopped him and passed along a summons for him to meet with the king in the Privy Council chamber. Magnus prayed this meant he would receive the decrees that proved the king found in favor of the Sinclairs. He hurried to his audience with the king but stopped short when he saw Laird Fraser standing beside the king with his hands akimbo. He looked around and saw that there were only two scribes in the chamber and a couple of courtiers he did not know. Compared to usual, the chamber was virtually vacant. The hair on Magnus's arms stood on end as a powerful sense of foreboding crept over him and settled on his chest. He entered and made his way directly to the king.

"Yer Majesty," Magnus bowed deeply.

"Rise, Magnus. Enough of that. You've been here for days, and I've known you since you were in nappies. There is no one here that you need impress, and we are meeting in private."

I ken I dinna exactly need to impress the Fraser, a wee late for that, but forming any worse an impression certainly isnae going to do ma cause any good.

"I have your writs signed there on the table. The seal is drying, and they should be ready for you within moments. Despite many testimonies against your family," the king paused as Fraser's chest puffed wider, "I feel that this is the correct course of action. I suppose this means you will leave for home now." The king's comments left nothing to the imagination. Magnus was being dismissed from court without having a chance to discuss the matter of his marriage to Deirdre.

Magnus felt little choice, or he would never have the opportunity. He squared his shoulders and directed his gaze to Laird Fraser.

I dinna fear him now. I amnae a lad he can threaten any longer.

"There is one last matter, Sire."

"Oh?"

"Aye, there is the matter of ma wife."

"I did not realize you were planning to wed."

"Nae planning, Sire, I am wedd*ed*," he stressed the last syllable as he continued to look at the Fraser.

Laird Fraser took a menacing step forward but froze when the king cleared his throat.

"Your dalliance with Lady Deirdre has already been brought to my attention, Magnus. It has also been effectively put to an end. I have agreed to her betrothal and will sign the documents this evening when the announcement is made."

"It was never a dalliance, Yer Majesty, and I believe ye ken that." Magnus was treading dangerous waters, but he refused to be pushed about by either man.

"Listen here, *lad*. You dishonored and disgraced my daughter once, but I will not have it happen again. There was never any possibility of a match between you two. There was no way I would let my last daughter marry someone who would tuck her away in the wilds of the north never to serve her clan any good. There was no chance I would send my daughter to live among those who sided against her family."

"What are ye blathering aboot? Ma family never sided against yers in aught." Magnus paused, and his eyes grew wide. "Is this aboot Lovat and the Mackenzies?"

Laird Fraser glared at Magnus but refused to speak.

"Bluidy hell, mon! That wasnae even yer sept of the Frasers. They may be the larger branch, but they reside almost across the bluidy country from ye. When it the last time ye even visited them? I doubt any time within the last score. Ye didna even pitch yer camp near theirs at any hunt or gathering."

"We are still all Frasers."

Magnus shook his head as he scowled at the older man.

"How vera convenient for ye then and convenient for ye now. I dinna believe for a moment that that is the true reason for yer objection." Magnus cocked his head and then grinned when realization flooded him. He remembered something that both Deirdre and his uncle told him. "This hasnae aught to do with ma father supporting the Mackenzies. This has everything to do with yer wife squeezing yer bollocks. She may have married ye, but she never got over Uncle Hamish's rejection. If she couldnae marry into the Sutherlands, then she wouldnae let her daughter either, even if it was by a far stretch. She is a dog in the manger, and ye canna stop her."

Laird Fraser lurched forward with his fists clenched. He swung at Magnus, but the larger and younger man easily sidestepped him. Magnus spun around and kept his back to the wall.

"And ye didna want Deirdre to marry me because ye believed I wouldnae do ye any good politically. Ye threatened me by using ma father's good standing with the king. I will nae forget how yer threatened to tell the king I took advantage of Deirdre and that ma father would pay the price in coin and shame before the court. Ye may have been able to manipulate me at nine and ten, but ye neither scare me nor control me at a score and six."

Fraser rushed forward again and swung at Magnus. Magnus's arm swept out to block the incoming blow. The leather bracer on Magnus's forearm helped absorb some of the sting. Magnus bared his teeth and growled softly. Fraser's next swing resulted in the older man's wrist being pinned behind him thanks to Magnus's greater reach and strength.

"Cease, auld mon," Magnus whispered, "ye're making an arse of yerself before the king."

The reminder of the king's presence snapped Laird Fraser back into the present, and he jerked away from Magnus. The king sat watching the confrontation but waved his guards away when they moved to intervene. Now the king leaned forward.

"Magnus, I am aware that you handfasted with Laird Fraser's daughter, and while consummating the relationship was within your rights, you did not have the right to pledge your troth, to begin with. Fraser did nothing wrong in removing his daughter to court, whatever his reasons. You have no claim over her now just as you had none all those years ago. Leave be, Magnus. What is done is done."

The king looked at Magnus once more before pulling a nearby scroll onto his lap and read it.

Fraser gloated as Magnus bit his tongue to keep himself from admitting he and Deirdre had wed again, even if only by consent, and that they had consummated this marriage numerous times. Magnus backed from the chamber and would have kicked the wall if there had not been several other people in the passageway, many of whom seemed to have heard the scuffle coming from within the chamber only moments ago. Magnus nodded and moved to the passageway that would lead to his chamber.

Magnus was almost to his door when he heard a whispered voice call his name, a decidedly feminine voice. One that was most definitely not Deirdre's. He dreaded having to turn around as he was in no mood to evade a vapid husband hunting lady-in-waiting hoping to ensnare him into marriage. He decided to ignore the voice and continue to his chamber where he would lock the door from the inside.

"Magnus," the voice sounded more urgent, more desperate. "Magnus, wait. Please stop. You have to help Deirdre."

That made him halt. He turned to see an overwrought Elizabeth sliding along the way, tucked as far into the shadows as she could.

"What do ye mean?"

"Her parents have locked her into her chamber again, but this time it's much worse. They said horrid things to her, and I believe her father hit her at least once."

"What? How do ken this? Ye said they have locked her into her chamber. Did she say as much to ye through the door?"

Elizabeth blushed a dark shade of red against her fair skin but then took a deep breath and shook her head.

"I was with Dee when the queen summarily dismissed her from service. Her parents found her when she left the chamber, and I slipped out behind them. They led her to her chamber and all three of them went in." She looked around to be sure no one was within earshot. "Magnus, there is an entire network of secret passages in this castle. They run behind and between walls. Dee's chamber has a doorway to them," she whispered.

Secret passageways? Ye mean I didna need to risk ma neck on that ledge made for the fae?

"How do ye ken any of this?"

"I have been at court longer than Deirdre. I was practically raised here. I learned about them as a child, but I'm one of only a few ladies-in-waiting that are still here from that time. Some of the others use them to sneak away at night to tryst. I hadn't used them in years until recently. I followed Dee and her parents the last time they locked her into her chamber. With her removal from the queen's court, I knew this confrontation would be far worse than the first. I'm scared for her. I truly am. I do not know what her parents or Lord Archibald will do to her, or what she might do if she's that desperate to escape."

"Can ye take me through them," Magnus gestured to himself as he moved his hands up and down. He little faith he would fit in narrow corridors.

"Yes. The tunnels are as tall as some of the chamber's ceilings. They are a tight fit, but you should be able to make it if you turn sideways in some parts. The passageway from Deirdre's chamber leads past mine, and that one connects to two others before ending near the postern wall. It was always intended as an escape route but has been used to spy on the king and his councilors for scores of years. As I said, I used to play in them, too."

"Can ye take me there now?"

"Yes, but we must prepare a few things for your escape. You cannot take Deirdre away in one of her court gowns. It will be far too obvious the moment anyone sees even the hem. You need to find something that will allow her to blend in. You might consider a pair of breeches for yourself, at least until you are a safe distance from the castle and town."

Magnus scowled but knew Elizabeth was right. He had no desire to put on a pair of breeks, but if he could find a pair that belonged to a servant or even nearby farmer, he would blend in better than wearing his plaid. He doubted, though, that he could find any that would be long enough for him.

"How do you propose that we find these spare clothes?"

"Dee has always declined to have a lady's maid, but I have not. My maid has a small chest in my chamber which will have an extra set of clothes that Dee can wear. They aren't that far apart in size. As for you," she looked Magnus up and down before shrugging, "you may have to wait until you can pinch something from a local merchant or farmer. You definitely cannot wear anything from the royal household, and now that I think about it, I have seen none of the male servants are as big as you."

"I ken who I can find clothes from that will fit. Ye have a blacksmith within the bailey, aye? He will be aboot ma size, and I will have to fold ma plaid. I shall have to sling ma claymore to ma saddle."

"You won't be able to take your horse. There won't be time to go to the stables and then out the postern gate."

"Just how do ye think we will make our getaway if we are on foot? I amnae leaving ma horse. I've had *Sealgair* since he was a foal, and he's kept me alive more times than I can count. He may vera well be the difference between us getting away and getting caught."

Elizabeth thought for a moment before nodding her head as though she came to a decision.

"I think I know someone who can help us with that. He can get your horse and bring him around to meet us. We will have to go in the dead of night that way you are not noticeable."

Magnus raised an eyebrow and was about to ask who, but Elizabeth's sharp look and a small shake of the head kept him from speaking. Elizabeth looked around as though she could see through walls to whoever might be listening.

"We cannot stay out here much longer. Someone is bound to see us. I will lead the way, but you must follow at a distance that will make no one suspect you are coming with me. We need to go to the queen's music room. It will be empty at this time of day, so we can slip into the hidden passageways and go to my chamber for Dee's change of clothes. I will also show you the way to her chamber and then the way to the gate in case anything should happen, and I cannot guide you, but you must wait several hours before you can go to her. We cannot risk her parents coming back and finding you there or her gone too soon."

Magnus and Elizabeth spent the next two hours collecting her maid's clothes and then touring the passageways. Elizabeth led Magnus through each one with a lit torch and then insisted that he show her he could do it without one. She made the reasonable argument they could not guarantee they would be able to take a torch or that it would stay lit. Elizabeth reasoned that she could not even guarantee she could escort them to the postern wall. She insisted Magnus prove he could do it alone out of fear he and Deirdre would get lost or trapped within the walls.

Chapter Fourteen

*D*eirdre looked around her chamber after wiping her stinging cheeks with a cool compress. She moved to stand before the mirror and turned her head from side to side as she examined the splotchy red marks that remained from her father's hand.

Dinna still be red when Mangus comes. He will go berserk if he kens that ma father struck me. Twice. I dinna think I can talk him out of confronting ma father, and I dinna want him ending up in the dungeon. I need him now. Where is he? I'm sure he believes I am still with the queen.

Deirdre tried to blink and swallow away the tears that threatened. She had not cried from her father's mistreatment. She was well past tears over her parents. Instead, she longed for the comfort of Magnus's arms, for the chance to escape the castle, the royal court, and her parents.

I just want to leave here. I dinna care to ever return. I will happily miss every Highland Gathering or royal hunt until I breathe ma last if I could just leave now with Magnus.

The tears poured forth as she continued to look in the mirror. She thought back to the evening just over a sennight ago when Magnus led her to her chamber after the nasty confrontation with Hay. They had stood before this mirror, both staring into the reflection that showed how different their bodies were and how perfectly they fit together like the pieces of a mosaic. Deirdre tilted her head to the side and closed her eyes as she pictured them standing together.

Och, Magnus. Where are ye? I need ye right now. I dinna want to be alone anymore. I am scared of what is to come. What if ma parents really do announce ma betrothal? What if they send me away and ye canna find me again? St Columbo's bones, I willna survive that a second time. Nae now that I ken ye love me, that ye never ever stopped.

Deirdre opened her eyes and looked around her chamber again. She took in all her belongings she accumulated over the seven years of traveling with the royal court. While she had spent the most time in this castle, she routinely traveled with the royal couple. She had fond memories of some of the trinkets she collected, but for the most part, she felt no connection to the chamber or her belongings.

I can walk away right now and nae look back. I would be happy to do that. I need to ready maself for when Magnus comes, or if need be, when I make a run for it on ma own. I willna be trapped here.

Deirdre walked to the window embrasure and pulled the glass open. She looked out over the bailey wall to the town surrounding the castle then she looked at the narrow ledge that ran on both sides of her window.

By what grace of God did Magnus manage this? And more than once! His feet are at least twice the size of mine, and I dinna think even mine will fit.

Deirdre looked down and felt sick as she saw the distance to the ground.

Stop being a ninny. If ye must, then ye must. I would rather crash to the ground in a pile of broken bones than give in to ma parents. But I mustnae think it will come to that. Magnus has never let me down. It was ma parents, nae him, that have disappointed me. Repeatedly it seems. Magnus was always there. Always. He will be again. I'm sure.

She stepped back from the window and moved to the large armoire that held all her gowns. She pushed them aside and reached into the far back and found two plaids. One was her Fraser plaid and the other was a Sinclair plaid Magnus gave her during one of their brief encounters at a hunt. She had stowed it away when her parents brought her to court and kept it hidden all these years. She pulled it out often and imagined that she could still catch Magnus's scent on the wool. It was the only comfort she had during their seven years apart. Her parents burned all of Magnus's letters from before their handfast, and she now knew they rejected any correspondence once they separated the young couple. She pulled out the Fraser plaid first. She grimaced at it as she tossed it into the fireplace. She watched with satisfaction as the flames enveloped the yards of wool. She stopped considering herself a Fraser when she wed Magnus the first time but came back around to thinking of herself as one when she neither heard nor saw Magnus over the years. From the night Magnus appeared in the gathering hall on, she considered herself a Sinclair.

Deirdre laid the folded plaid on her bed and moved to one of her chests that stood in the corner. Everyone believed it held her most favored books and old scrolls, which was true, but it held other remnants of her past, of her years growing up in the Highlands. She carefully lifted away the scrolls that rested at the top. Sandwiched between her scrolls and leather-bound tomes were the proof she was still a Highlander at heart. She lifted an oilcloth from the chest and moved back to the bed setting it beside her plaid. She could not help herself and ran her fingers over the plaid once more before turning her attention back to her hidden treasures.

With care, she unwrapped the oilskin to reveal a set of gleaming daggers. There were three dirks and one sharp sgian dubh. Beneath them sat a set of bracers Magnus gave her for her fifteenth saint's day. The sgian dubh had also been a gift from him just before the fateful hunt where she was thrown. She pulled back the sleeves of her kirtle and tied a bracer to each wrist. She adjusted them so that the narrow sheath was on the underside of her wrist and then tucked a dirk into each one like Magnus had taught her. She found the thick leather thong she used for the sgian dubh. Magnus had insisted on teaching her not only how to throw the knives but to use them in close quarters in case someone snuck up on her. She thought it silly at the time, but Magnus foresaw a time when her attractiveness would be a temptation to men other than him. He insisted that she be able to protect herself. Before pulling up her skirts, she checked both hidden pockets of her kirtle to ensure her other dirks were there. She had become complacent over the years and did not always carry them, but after the incident with Hay in the alcove, she wore them again; however, she kept them in her pockets now, making them easier to reach. She tied the thick leather strap around her thigh and tucked the deadly thin blade into it. Looking back to the armoire, she spotted her riding boots which she pulled on. She tucked her last dirk into one boot and pulled one of her pocket daggers out to shove into the other.

After double checking each of her knives, she unwrapped the last two hidden items. She lifted a metal sword that Magnus had custom made by his clan's blacksmith. He gave it to her as her sixteenth saint's day gift only the day before their separation. She only had one training session with him, but she had taken to it immediately. At a quarter the length, if that, of Magnus's broadsword, it was customized for her height and strength. It was a small miracle she smuggled it into her chest. She lifted it now and marveled at how it gleamed in the firelight. The oilcloth kept it from tarnishing, and she spotted the entwined D and M on the hilt. She ran her fingers over it and closed her eyes for a moment to remember Magnus's pride and excitement when he gave her the gift.

Setting the sword on top of the plaid, she turned to the larger chest that sat at the foot of her bed. She lifted out scrolls, quills, and inkpots and set them aside. Next, she lifted out the small bow and quiver of arrows. This had been a gift from her father. Seeing it created a sour taste in her mouth, but she was practical enough to know she might need it if they ended up on the run, or worse, if she ended up running on her own. It was a short bow made of yarrow and had her given name carved into the wood, so no one would confuse with her sisters' bows. She had used it countless times over the years, and despite the now bitter memory of how she came to own it, she felt like it was holding an extension of herself. The feel was natural and easy. She pulled back on the string and made sure it was still in good condition before checking the arrows in her quiver.

Finally, she moved to the table that held her jewelry. She opened the drawstring pouch that kept her earbobs, necklaces, and rings. She had a veritable treasure in gems and gold she received as gifts from the king and queen on her saint's day and various holidays. Her parents also ensured that she was well bedecked. She understood better than ever before that making her look like a peacock was more about their ostentation than her fashion.

Once she had done that, she had little else to fill her time, so she resorted to her most frequent pastime. She pulled out a book and read.

Magnus and Elizabeth emerged from the hidden tunnels into the queen's music room. They closed the door in the wall firmly and crept across the floor. Just as they reached the door, they heard voices on the other side approach. Elizabeth's eyes went wide as Magnus pulled a dirk from his waist. He gestured for her to remain quiet as he slipped behind the chamber door. Elizabeth stepped back and darted to a shelf that held various pieces of sheet music. She picked up a set just as the door opened.

"Make her go to the chapel this very eve is what I heard," came a soft feminine voice.

"Her parents will forego the official announcement now word has spread about her dismissal from the queen's service. Lord Archibald is said to be infuriated. She has cuckolded the man one too many times in the past fortnight. He will bed her and ship her off by morning is what he told Roger," a male voice explained.

"She —oh Lady Elizabeth, I did not realize anyone occupied this chamber," said Lady Arabella who stood next to her surprised brother.

"Excuse us for bothering you," Arabella shot her brother a hasty glance before she nudged him to retreat from the room. They went as quickly as they appeared.

Elizabeth did not dare move as she was shaking so fiercely. She took three deep breaths before she could respond to Magnus's gestures to come closer.

"*Shite!* We canna afford to wait until tonight. It'll be too late by then. We have to get her now."

"No, no. Before she can leave, you must be seen leaving the castle. It cannot be too obvious that you left together. Let it be known you heard the gossip and are leaving in disgust. Take your horse and meet us in town. You must get clothes once you're away from Stirling."

Magnus nodded his head. He knew she was right, but he detested taking even one step out of the castle without Deirdre. A lead weight settled on his chest, and the fears and anger of their last parting resurfaced.

"Go, Magnus. Make a scene of leaving. I will get her and meet you at the far side of the city." Magnus nodded, opened the door, waited his customary slow count to twenty, and then went in search of his uncle who he suspected would be with several other noisy and talkative Highlanders. Sheer willpower kept him from checking over his shoulder, but he knew Elizabeth would take the secret passageways rather than step out of the music room.

137

Magnus wound his way through the castle ensuring as many people as possible saw his scowl and foul temper. He found his uncle just as he expected. The older man sat at a table with the Grant, the MacKinnon, the Graham along with men from clans Campbell, Drummond, Menzies, and Ramsey. He nodded to each man, most of whom he had known since childhood. He called Hamish over and began a conversation he regretted having to have. Telling his uncle only half-truths did not settle well with him, but there was no time nor a safe place to explain everything. The less his uncle knew, the less he would have to lie about when questioned.

"Did ya hear? Did ye? That bastard Fraser has moved up the wedding. They aren't even going to announce the betrothal. They're marrying her off this eve."

"Are ye sure, lad? That seems rather hasty of the king to agree to that."

"The queen dismissed her after word spread that I compromised her. Compromised ma own wife! The king wants her gone."

"Have ye seen the lass? Spoken to her?"

"I havenae, and she hasnae tried to speak to me. I canna believe there's a wedding planned for her tonight."

"Surely, ye dinna believe she is agreeing to this."

"What am I to believe? They canna say the vows for her, so she must be willing. She hasnae tried to seek an audience with the king." Magnus shook his head. He forced himself to say the next words even though the mere idea, even if not true, tore him apart. "She doesnae want me after all. She will let her parents pull us apart all over again. Just as they did seven years ago."

"What are ye going to do?"

"What is there for me to do? Speak out against the king? I canna vera well do that if I want ma clan to weather the storm. I will be left behind once again if I dinna leave first."

"Leave? Ye're nae going to fight for her?" Hamish looked at his nephew shrewdly. He had already deduced the pretext that Magnus was creating, but this stunned him.

"Fight for someone who doesnae want me. Someone who is playing me for a fool. Cuckholding me? Nae. This is too painful," he finished on a loud whisper. Magnus looked out of the corner of his eye and saw that the other lairds were not trying very hard to disguise their eavesdropping.

Good. Let them gossip like fish wives. The sooner it goes around that I left in a fit of temper, the greater chances they willnae think I nabbed her and made off with her. At least nae right away.

"Uncle Hamish, I wanted to let ye ken I'm leaving. I didna want to just take off without saying thank ye for yer support of our claims and for yer help while ye've been here."

"Och lad, ye ken I love ye and yer family. We are kin." Hamish pulled Magnus in for a bone-cracking embrace and pounded him on the back. The noise hid his whisper.

"Dinna go straight home. Weave as much as ye can to confuse them. Go to Sutherland if ye must but nae home until I can get word to yer da. Ye ken every mon in here kens what ye're doing, but they willna have to lie on yer behalf. They will stand behind ye if even from a distance. God keep ye."

"And God protect any mon who tries to stop me. Thank ye, Uncle."

They stepped apart, and Magnus once again bowed to the other lairds. He did not dally in leaving as he was not in the mood to linger long enough for questions. He made his way to his chamber and gathered his few belongings which were only his saddlebag and sword.

He made his way to the stables and readied *Sealgair*. There had been enough time to have his saddle repaired, and he double checked it now to be sure it was safe enough to ride with Deirdre mounted too.

He did not look back when he rode through the portcullis or the path that led down to the town below.

Dinna dilly dally, eun beag. Fly soon before the bells for vespers ring.

Magnus rode through town not attempting to hide. He wanted as many people as possible to say he rode out alone. When he reached the outskirts. He circled back around, and it did not take long to locate the blacksmith. The smithy was set away from the other shops because of the noise and constant heat. Magnus gave thanks when he saw that the man's home was attached to his workshop and hung on a line were a pair of very long breeks. Magnus dismounted and left his horse a fair distance away before creeping to the hanging laundry. He strained to hear any voices coming from a direction where anyone might see him. When nothing came, he darted out, grabbed the breeches, and made a beeline back to his horse, mounting within only minutes of leaving *Sealgair*.

Magnus rode towards the treeline and once he entered the dark arbor, he hopped down and pulled the breeches on before unwrapping his plaid. He folded it and tucked it into his saddlebag.

I may as well be standing here with ma arse hanging out. These damn breeks may be the right length, but the mon must have legs like spindly twigs. They are so tight they dinna leave much to the imagination. Magnus adjusted himself uncomfortably. *And they call our plaids indiscreet and improper. How will I hide the cockstand I'm sure to get the moment I touch, bah who am I kidding, see Deirdre. She'll be with Elizabeth too.*

Magnus groaned, and it sounded nothing like pleasure.

He emerged from the trees and walked *Sealgair* to a discreet spot where he could watch anyone coming from the town. He settled in to wait and tried not to tap his feet.

Deirdre heard a soft scraping sound coming from behind the tapestry by her bed. There was a creak and then a blast of stale air wafted in. She pulled a dirk from her boot before rolling onto her side. With nothing else to do but wait for Magnus or nightfall, she laid down on the bed. Normally the thought of shoes on the bed would disgust her, but she refused to waste a moment when the time came to make her getaway. Now she lay still as she saw the tapestry sway. She changed her grip, so she could easily throw the dirk if needed or could stab. Her heart lurched when she saw Elizabeth's head peek out from around the wall hanging. Deirdre scrambled off the bed and rushed to her cousin.

"How did ye get here?" Deirdre strained to see around Elizabeth. "Passages? Ye never told me!"

"Other than now, they are only used by a few of the ladies-in-waiting and their lovers."

Deirdre stared blankly before shaking her head. Elizabeth tossed her the pile of servants clothing, and Deirdre immediately knew what she needed to do. She turned her back to Elizabeth who yanked her laces free. She pulled her kirtle off and began pulling the plain clothes on.

"That explains much. But what're ye doing using them? Where's Magnus?"

Elizabeth quickly stuffed the gown onto a hook in the armoire before once again returning to Deirdre's side.

"I will explain everything on the way, but we must go. *Now.*"

Elizabeth reached for her, but Deirdre turned back to the bed. She scooped up the sword, bow, and quiver which she had wrapped in the plaid. It made it easier to carry. When she saw her cousin's surprised face, she shrugged.

"Ye didna think I would just stay here to do ma parents' bidding. But why are we leaving in broad daylight? It's too risky."

Elizabeth grabbed her arm and pulled her into the tunnel. After ensuring the tapestry hung flat and the door was closed, she took Deirdre's hand to lead her.

"Magnus and I were already planning to sneak you out through these hidden passageways, but we overheard Lady Arabella and her brother discussing your wedding that's planned for tonight."

Deirdre gasped and stumbled nearly dropping her bundle.

"Exactly. Your parents are forgoing an official betrothal announcement and arranging for you to be wedded and bedded this eve, so Archibald can send you away as soon as tomorrow morning."

"How convenient for them all. My father gets the stewardship, Hay gets ma dowry and a broodmare in me, my parents' hands are clean of me once I'm gone, and Hay can continue his affair with Mary. I don't see the queen dismissing the little bitch anytime soon."

Deirdre surprised herself with both her language and how calm she felt discussing her plight.

All the sooner I can be with Magnus. I need out of this castle.

"Where is Magnus? He hasnae confronted ma parents, has he?"

"No, he's already left to make it appear as if you've pushed him away. He's waiting outside the town for you. We will exit the postern gate. I made sure there is someone there who can get through town without too much notice."

It did not take long for the two young women to make their way to the outer wall of the castle. Elizabeth pressed Deirdre behind her as she eased open the door. It creaked and groaned from not being used often. There were small bushes that grew around the base, and vines strangled the hinges making it hard to open the door wide. Both women could squeeze through, but it was tight. Deirdre looked back into the tunnel one last time before pushing the door closed. Elizabeth was talking to a young man who gestured for them to hurry. There was something that seemed familiar about him, but it was not until Deirdre was standing next to him that she noticed a certain resemblance to Elizabeth. She looked questioningly at her cousin.

"Dee, this is my brother Thomas."

"Brother?"

"Aye, ma lady. But Beth means half-brother. I'm her father's bastard."

"I am not getting into this with you again Thomas, but that is absolutely ridiculous. Neither you nor I are a half a person, so you cannot be half my brother." Elizabeth gave him a quelling look. "Thomas will get us through the city to meet Magnus."

"Beth, ye canna come. Ye will stick out with yer finery."

Deirdre saw a willfulness she rarely witnessed in her cousin when Elizabeth set her jaw and put her hands on her hips.

"For all anyone knows, you are both my servants following me as I shop. If more attention is drawn to me, then less will be on Dee."

Thomas gave her a skeptical look but nodded. Elizabeth had found a bob cap in among her maid's belongings, and Deirdre was grateful for it as she tucked her telltale blond curls underneath. She could never go unnoticed if her hair was visible. For the umpteenth time in her life, she cursed her unruly hair.

They weaved and wandered through the town, appearing to be in no hurry, but each of them was surveilling everyone who passed them or seemed to notice their little trio. Deirdre was chomping at the bit to move faster and reach Magnus, but she understood the necessity of being inconspicuous. She did her best to remain patient, but when they walked past the last row of buildings and she could see Magnus move away from a rock, all she wanted was to sprint to him. Thomas grasped her arm and held her back with frown. He angled his chin to point over his shoulder. A group of women had just emerged and headed to the nearby stream. Deirdre nodded and walked as sedately as she could manage until she reached Magnus.

Magnus, on the other hand, had no compunction about being overt. He pulled Deirdre into his arms and lowered his mouth to hers. He intended only a taste at first as they took in the feel of each other's body pressed together. When her lips parted for him, he swept his tongue within her velvety mouth. Deirdre gave a quick, sharp tug on his tongue before they both stepped back.

Deirdre turned back to face her cousins and embraced Elizabeth.

"Ye have been much like a sister all these years. Ye made ma arrival at court bearable. I dinna ken what I would have done without ye. Thank ye." Deirdre could not say more around the lump in her throat.

The two women hugged, an implicit understanding that this might be the last time they ever see each other. Even though Deirdre knew she had kept things from Elizabeth over the years and had been more reserved in sharing than Elizabeth had been with her, she felt her cousin was her best friend. The knowledge that they may never again laugh or speak with one another was painful.

"You are doing the right thing, Dee. Don't ever let anyone tell you otherwise. I will be sure to keep your parents guessing for as long as I can. I wish you both Godspeed."

Magnus lifted Deirdre into the saddle and climbed on behind her. He spurred *Sealgair* as he wrapped his arms snuggly around her and the plaid bundle she carried.

"I'm sorry we couldnae bring Freya. Mayhap we can have her sent to us."

Deirdre just nodded. She loved her horse, but she knew it was unrealistic to think her horse would ever join her in the northern Highlands. She squeezed Magnus's arm and settled back against his chest.

They rode in silence for over an hour, but Deirdre could feel the tension radiating from Magnus as he kept his head on a swivel, alert to any threats or danger. He stopped them periodically to cover their tracks or to lead *Sealgair* of the main path onto ground covered with leaves that would better hide his hoofprints. They were two hours into their ride before Magnus relaxed enough to tickle her ribs.

"Is that ma plaid ye have all knotted up?"

"Aye, it is."

"The one from the Campbell gathering?"

"When could I have gotten another? Are ye wanting it back of a sudden? Do ye need some real clothing to wear?"

Magnus's chest rumbled as he guffawed.

"That plaid wouldnae fit me now anyway. Ma arse would catch a chill. I'd rather see it wrapped around ye," he nuzzled her temple, "but it seems to carry yer spare clothes."

"It isnae. I didna pack any other clothes."

Magnus slowed his horse as Deirdre unraveled the plaid, and she felt Magnus's breath catch when he caught sight of her sword and then the bow.

"Ye were able to keep that?" he whispered.

"Just barely. I smuggled it with me. Yer plaid was easier to hide, but there was nae chance I would leave this behind. Nae then and nae now."

"It looks to be in excellent condition after so long."

"I had it wrapped in an oilcloth within ma chest. I admit it hasnae seen the light of day in seven summers, but it's still as sharp as when ye gave it to me."

"And ye brought yer bow?" Deirdre heard Magnus's skepticism since he knew who had given it to her.

"Only for practical reasons. I was not sure if you would have yours, and we will need to eat. Once we are home, I will happily to toss it in the fire."

Home.

Chapter Fifteen

*M*agnus and Deirdre traveled several more hours the first day, well past the sun setting. She fell asleep in Magnus's arms more than once, and he luxuriated in holding her as he breathed in the scent of her hair. He coiled it around his finger as he teased her and gave it a gentle yank until she was laughing at his jokes. He did everything he could think of to ease her fears during that first long day and evening.

They made camp below the stars that night. It was too clear for them to have a fire since Magnus worried that the smoke would be visible even at a great distance. They were silent while they ate the dried beef that was ever present in his saddlebag. Deirdre laid out the extra plaid from Magnus's bag and wore his old one as an arisaid. Magnus propped his head against his saddle and opened his arms in invitation. She snuggled next to him as he wrapped the extra length of material from over his shoulder around them.

"Deir, we canna go straight to Sinclair land. We will surely be followed if the trackers arenae already on our heels. I do believe we can be home in ten days, but it will be a windy route we travel. We canna risk staying at any inns either, mo ghaol. I am sorry that I canna provide ye more comfort, but we must be as invisible as possible."

Deirdre stroked her hand over his chest and then down his hip while he ran his hand up and down her back. She lifted her chin and gave him a tender kiss that heated.

"I would say I am comfy now, but I can think of one thing that would make me even more comfortable." She flipped his plaid up and rolled on top to straddle him. "Ye make a vera fine pillow indeed. And I'm glad ye took those ridiculous breeks off. Dinna get me wrong. I quite liked seeing that ye were pleased to have me near, but I dinna like anyone else getting such a view of ye. That is for ma eyes only." She deepened her voice in an attempt to sound manly.

"It is all yers. Do what ye will but be merciful." He pulled her down for a searing kiss that moved them both to fumble, pushing clothing out of the way. The fear and panic of the day still weighed heavily upon both of them, and neither was in the mood to go slowly.

When they both relaxed, Magnus wrapped Deirdre in his arms and rolled them back over. He tucked her into his side and kissed her forehead.

"I love ye, Deir."

"I love ye," she yawned, "too."

"Rest, mo leannan. I will hold ye."

"Will ye sleep, too? Do ye," she yawned again, "want me to take watch for a while? After I sleep mite."

"Sshh. All is well. Sleep, mo eun beag." Magnus looked down to see she was already deeply asleep. He lay looking up at the stars as his hand drew lazy circles on her shoulder and his other hand kept her pressed against his side.

Keep her safe, Lord. Nay matter what, just keep her safe.

Magnus did not sleep more than a few minutes at a time as his mind would not quiet, and his senses were on alert for any hint of danger. He was exhausted when Deirdre awoke, but he refused to let her know he had not slept.

After two more days of travel and sleepless nights, Magnus knew he could not continue as they were. He had to admit to Deirdre that he needed sleep, so he suggested that they sleep during the day and travel at night. The possibility of encountering highwaymen did not thrill him, but he knew if he and Deirdre did not find them, there was always the possibility that the lawless men would find them. He would rather be on his horse than flat on his back with Deirdre less protected.

"If we travel at night, we can make camp in the early morning and build a fire that willna be visible. We eat and sleep, then just before dusk, we eat again. I dinna like suggesting it, but there may be times when climbing into a tree will be the safest place to rest. I ken of numerous caves all over this area, but I worry that the king's men or yer father's men will ken of them too."

Deirdre looked around at where they stopped to water the horse.

"I have traveled a great deal, but I ken I have never been to this area before. Where are we? I dinna think ma father's men would ken this area either."

"Buchannan territory. We rode straight east and should be close to the border with the MacFarlanes. I'm hoping we can make it to the coast and the MacDougalls. If we do, then we go to Ardchattan Priory and pray that the abbot will marry us."

"East? That is the opposite direction we need to go. Hopefully, that will keep them from guessing where we've gone, but Magnus, what then? Do ye think they've found our trail?"

"I dinna ken. We havenae heard aught in two days, but that doesnae mean they willna. As long as we can keep a few steps ahead. After Ardchattan, we make for the coast and try to catch a boat up to the MacLeods of Lewis. Callum's wife is a

MacLeod, and mayhap we can rest there before sailing for the MacLeods on the Minch. That's Siùsan's grandfather. He would see us the rest of the way to Dunbeath."

"Ye think any sailor would take me on board as a woman?"

"For the right price, many a captain will overlook superstition."

Deirdre drew out a small drawstring pouch from a slit on the side of her kirtle. She was thankful to have had the forethought to grab the collection. She opened the sack wide enough for Magnus to look in.

"I dinna think ye've noticed this at night, but I gathered these when I was preparing to leave. I wasna entirely sure if I would have to set out on ma own, and I kenned at the vera least we would need them."

Magnus looked from the bag to Deirdre and back again.

"There must be a king's ransom in here, lass."

"There is since much of it came from the king and queen. This should book us passage on any number of boats then."

"Aye. Ye were wise to wear it below ye gown." Magnus bit his lip before continuing with his morbid assessment. "If highwaymen attack, they are more likely to search ma sporran and saddlebags than to think ye might have something hidden."

What Magnus did not add was if a man attacked Deirdre, the folds of her kirtle would keep it hidden just as he had not noticed either night when they made love. The only way it would get to that was if he was dead. Then she would have to make her own way. If she survived too.

Magnus pulled her in for a tight embrace. The thought of any harm coming to Deirdre gave him the overwhelming need to touch her, to hold her, and reassure himself that she was safe with him.

Deirdre did not know how to respond to Magnus's sudden silent embrace, but she knew some thought was plaguing him. She returned his hug and squeezed before tilting her head back in invitation. He barely caressed her lips before she reached for his head and pulled him closer. She initiated the kiss, and he let her control it. It did not take long before it grew in intensity.

"I need ye, Deir."

"Aye," she moaned.

"We canna linger long. This will be quick and hard."

Deirdre looked around and turned to an outcropping of rocks a few steps away. She moved to them and leaned forward. Magnus was there in an instant, understanding her unspoken invitation.

"Like in the cave," Deirdre whispered as she looked over her shoulder and bunched her skirts around her waist. Magnus was instantly reminded of how the made love once during their only night together after their handfast.

Magnus thought he would spill his seed right there and then at the view she presented. He could see the dew between her thighs glistening in the sunlight. He intended to thrust into her, so they could finish quickly. However, the temptation to taste her was too great. He kneeled behind her and slid his finger between her folds before tapping her apex. He entered her with one finger and stroked the smooth skin of her sheath. She parted her legs wider and pressed her hips back. He drew his finger out and looked up to see her watching him. He licked it before popping it into his mouth.

"More intoxicating than the strongest whisky," he murmured before pressing two then three fingers into her. Her moisture helped his fingers glide in and out as he thrust them harder. He leaned forward for his first taste and groaned as he took in an aroma that was uniquely hers, fruit mixed with musk. He felt it go to his head as his tongue brushed against her. He lapped along her sensitive skin before sucking the hidden nub.

Deirdre writhed against the rock feeling pressure growing within her as Magnus laved her core and teased her.

"Now, Magnus. I canna wait. I ache." Her desire burned through her flesh and made her whimper.

Magnus rose to his feet and threw the length of his breacan feile over his shoulder. He grabbed her hips roughly, lining himself up with her entrance. The tip of his cock brushed up and down as he coated himself with her essence.

"Please," she begged, and he surged forward as he leaned his body over hers. He reached for her outstretched hands and entwined their fingers.

They rocked their hips in tandem as their need grew. He brought one hand down to her mound and rubbed where she most needed the contact. She came apart in his arms as she moaned, and he growled in her ear.

"Yers. Always yers."

He thrust once more before he felt his own pleasure surge. His hips kept pressing forward as he drained the last of him into her. Magnus once again entwined both of their hands, and they stayed joined until *Sealgair* nickered. Magnus was alert, but they both laughed when a bunny hopped out from under a bush, took one look at the horse's massive hooves and darted away.

They settled their clothes, refilled their own waterskins, and remounted. It relieved Deirdre to discover Magnus traveled well prepared with a couple of waterskins in his saddlebag along with the dried beef and extra plaid.

They did not ride for much more than an hour before Magnus pulled his horse to a stop. Deirdre swept her eyes across the landscape but saw little more than a hill nearby. She looked questioningly at Magnus. He dismounted and led his horse around to the other side of the hill where Deirdre saw a large gathering of stones that reached at least thirty feet into the sky.

"It'll be a tight fit with *Sealgair*, but he will keep us warm while we sleep. It will be much cooler in the shade there."

Deirdre's brow furrowed until she saw the gap between the rocks that was just barely wide enough to let the warhorse through.

"How do ye even ken this is here?"

"We played hide and seek near here once on the way to court when ma brothers and sister and I were barely more than weans. Mairghread snuck into here and we couldnae find her. Ma brothers and I searched everywhere that we could. We looked in the trees and behind trunks. Da was speaking with his guardsmen, and Mama was helping prepare our evening meal. The sun was close to setting, and we panicked when we couldnae find her. Alex made us look up and down the stream, in case she'd fallen in. As ye saw, it wasnae vera deep, but she couldnae have been more than five summers at the time. We were so frightened at this point that Callum insisted we tell our parents. It was Tavish who was brave enough to go to our mama. We were all in tears by the time Tavish was done telling both Da, who had walked over when he saw us all shifting and looking around, and Mama. Da was ready to skin us alive until Mama put her hand on his arm. He went silent, and Mama calmly walked over to this outcropping and said, 'Mair, enough terrorizing yer brothers. Ye must come out now.'"

Magnus shook his head and smiled fondly at the memory.

"She hid there the entire time despite hearing us call to her. We even passed right by but didna notice the opening. She climbed out and walked over to us. There wasnae even a hint of remorse on her face. She pulled Alex's arm until he picked her up. All she said was, 'I won.'" Magnus chuckled, "It was at that point we realized she was the most patient of us all and the best strategist to boot."

They were within what Deirdre now realized were standing stones. There were etchings on them from generations long past. She ran her fingers over them and tilted her head back, intrigued by how high the drawings reached. Magnus unsaddled his horse and placed it between the animal's legs. It was not ideal, but it was the only place for it.

"I will let him out to graze in a little while, but for now, we should try to sleep."

Magnus was right that the temperature was much cooler among the boulders. They huddled together with the extra plaid wrapped around them both. It did not take long for sleepiness to get the better of Deirdre as she rested her head against Magnus's chest. The steady beat below her ear lulled her. It took Magnus a while longer to relax enough to let slumber overtake him, and while he woke several times on the alert for any sounds or changes in their environment, he slept long enough to wake in the evening refreshed.

The sun was already dropping when Magnus nudged Deirdre awake. She rubbed her eyes and looked around as she regained her bearing.

"Do we ride now?"

"Soon. I must let *Sealgair* graze for a while, then we go."

Deirdre nodded and walked a short distance away to have some privacy. When she finished, she walked a little further to the stream. Kneeling, she splashed water onto her neck before scrubbing her face. She was rising when she heard voices carrying on the wind. Freezing, she strained to hear.

"—moving this way. They must be a day ahead of us. That heathen was smart to head east first. We will have to push hard since we are the smaller search party even though I am sure we are on the right path."

Deirdre knew in an instant that they referred to Magnus. She backed away until she could no longer hear the voices and was confident they would not hear her steps.

"Magnus," she whispered urgently as she approached.

When he looked up, she pointed behind her and mouthed 'men.' He nodded and reached out his hand. The horse was already saddled, so Magnus lifted her onto *Sealgair* and mounted behind her. He walked his steed in a wide arc to avoid being seen. They both were silent for the first half an hour.

Confident they were far enough past the search party to risk a whisper, Magnus asked, "what did you see."

Deirdre shook her head.

"I didna see aught, but I heard them. They said it was smart of the heathen," she grunted in indignation, "to travel east first. They think they are a day behind us and must keep pressing on because they are the smallest of the search parties. I did not wait around to hear anything else."

Magnus nodded but said no more. He tightened his hold on her middle and pulled her back to his chest. He rounded his shoulders, and Deirdre relaxed into the shelter he made for her.

"We must ride straight to Inveraray. We dinna have the luxury of stopping to sleep during the day if they are that close. We will only rest when *Sealgair* absolutely must. He's stout but has the endurance of a much leaner horse. I dinna want to push him to the point he goes lame, but we will have to keep moving."

For the next two and a half days, Magnus kept them away from any roads, paths, or trails where they risked encountering other travelers or worse, the search party. During one of the brief stops, Magnus spotted a large fir tree that had massive branches towards its base. There were vines climbing up an oak next to the conifer. Magnus instructed Deirdre to cut the vine from as high as she could reach while he sawed a branch free at his own tree. He was about to pull the branch over to his horse when he looked around and did not spot Deirdre. He panicked.

Where did she go? She was beside me only moments ago. I ducked to get to the trunk, but surely, she wouldnae wander off. I would have heard anyone approach.

He opened his mouth to call to her when a large chunk of vine landed on his head and shoulders. A soft giggle met his ears as he rubbed his shoulder.

"Ye didna realize I was up here?"

Magnus heard rustling before he spotted two small booted feet working their way down the trunk.

"The vines made it even easier to climb, and I wasna sure how much ye needed. I figured better too much and nae need it than need it and nae have enough." She shrugged.

Looking first at the long coil of thick, sturdy vine at his feet and then the woman he had climbed so many trees within their youth, he could not help but match her grin.

"Come on then and bring yer prize with ye."

They each dragged their load behind them. Deirdre watched as Magnus wrapped the vine through the needles of his branch and then along the actual branch. He pulled the extra length at each end and brought it to the back of his horse's saddle. He tied it to the rear rigging rings. Testing the knot by tugging hard enough on each side to make his steed take a step back, Magnus was satisfied that his makeshift brush would not easily come loose.

"This will have to do. Hopefully, it doesnae fall apart too soon at a gallop."

Magnus's ingenuity impressed Deidre. He assembled a large broom to sweep their trail clear. She waggled her finger for him to bend closer and gave him a peck on the cheek.

"Mo ghaisgeach." *My hero.*

Mangus's chest swelled, and he helped up.

They rode like that well into the evening and arrived at Ardchatton as the monks finished compline. Magnus lifted the brass knocker and was just about to let it drop when the wooden slat slid open. A pair of suspicious eyes stared back at him.

"You're too late," a refined voice stated. "We've locked the gate. Come back in the morn."

"I am Magnus Sinclair. I would see the abbot, please."

"You're too late. We've locked the gate. Come back in the morn," the voice repeated.

"I amnae alone. I travel with ma wife. Ye ken there isnae anywhere close by to make a proper camp for her."

"Is she increasing?"

Magnus's head jerked back. He had not thought of that possibility since the first couple of days at the castle.

"Possibly."

"Come back in the morn. She isnae that in need."

Magnus's temper flared, and he opened his mouth to insist when a small hand rested on his forearm. He looked down to see Deirdre slipping between him and the gate.

"Father, we seek sanctuary within your walls. We have had to escape an attack, and we have nowhere else to go. We beg the mercy of the church. I'm sure your abbot would not want us to remain in danger."

Magnus bit his tongue to contain his surprise, and pride when he heard the return of her cultured tones and the tact she used.

The eyes darted between Magnus and Deirdre, and then a put-upon sigh came through before they heard the key turn. The gate swung open, and it allowed them admittance.

"This way," the aggrieved priest motioned.

He was much younger than either Mangus or Deirdre expected. His tonsure reflected the moonlight as he led them past several groups of monks who silently made their way to the dormitory. Magnus wrapped his arm around Deirdre, but she shook her head once. She linked her arm through his as though they were back at court. Magnus looked straight ahead but nodded.

"Wait here." The monk barked before knocking on a wide wooden door that held a large metal cross in the center.

"Enter," was all that was said before the monk slipped in. He did not open the door wide enough for them to see the chamber beyond.

It was not long before the door opened again, and the young monk walked past them.

"Thank you, Brother Adam," an older, warmer voice spoke.

A sun-worn face with bright blue eyes and rosy cheeks greeted the couple as they stepped forward. Deirdre felt a sense of peace as the priest greeted them.

Mayhap this will all work out after all. If we can just be wed, then there is naught that Father or Archibald can do.

"I understand you and your wife are in need of sanctuary this night. Before I offer you the protection of this abbey, I would know with whom I speak."

"I am Magnus Sinclair, and this is ma wife, Deirdre."

The abbot looked at both, assessing their travel-worn clothes, dirty hands, and tired faces.

"You look as though you have been through quite a travail. Why do you seek the church's protection?"

Magnus looked behind him but could see no one. That did not mean there were not ears in the walls.

"Might we speak in private, Father?" Magnus looked back again. Unease was creeping up his spine. He did not feel like the three of them were alone. He sensed a presence and wondered where Brother Adam disappeared to.

"As you wish, my children." The older man ushered them, seating himself before his desk. There were no other chairs in the chamber, so Magnus and Deirdre were left to stand. "Once again, what brings you here as night approaches?"

"It is a bit of a tale to tell, and I confess to not being entirely honest with yer monk. We werenae exactly attacked, but we are seeking shelter to avoid that. I am Magnus Sinclair, and this is Deirdre Sinclair, née Fraser. We seek yer aid nae only for shelter, but we would have ye marry us."

"Just a moment," the priest held up his hand. "You just introduced this woman as your wife and now you ask me to marry you. It cannot be both."

"But it is, Father. Deirdre and I handfasted and consummated our union seven years ago. We were both young, and her father refused to acknowledge the marriage. Since then, we have been separated, but recently found one another. We have exchanged handfast vows again, and Deirdre has stated her consent three times. More than thrice. We have lived as a married couple ever since. We ask for the church's blessing and an official record of our marriage."

Magnus held his breath as he awaited the abbot's decision. He felt Deirdre tremble beside him. He straightened his arm and slipped her hand into his. Their familiarity did not go unnoticed by the priest.

"I am afraid it is not that simple. Does the lass's father still disagree to the match? If you do not have his consent, which it would appear you do not, then I cannot marry you. You're not married to anyone else are you, my lady?" This last question he directed at Deirdre.

Neither Magnus nor Deirdre missed the use of her honorific. Deirdre squeezed Magnus's hand. They knew he was now fishing. She shook her head.

"Seven years is an awfully long time to be apart. Lord Sinclair, are you married to anyone else, betrothed even?"

"Neither of us has ever wed anyone other than each other."

The abbot looked at them shrewdly and scratched his chin.

"As far as I am aware, the Sinclairs do not regularly have business this far south unless it is at court, and last I heard, the Frasers were members of the royal court. How do you come to be here?"

"A betrothal to another man was being negotiated by *ma wife's* father. While her father may not recognize our vows, our second handfast and our marriage by consent do still stand. We were not willing to risk Deirdre's eternal soul with the sin of bigamy. Father, she is well past the age of majority. The law does not require her father's consent."

Deirdre bit her tongue to keep from making any visible reaction. Magnus was not wrong, but she had not expected him to use this approach.

"The man she was set to marry has mistreated her and threatened her more than once. I fear for her safety, and I am unwilling to repudiate her."

"Is that so? I would hear the young lady tell me of these events." He looked at Deirdre, and while he appeared to have a kind face, she started wondering if avarice was at work. While the two men spoke, she observed the riches present in the abbot's solar. There were several gold crosses hung from the wall or standing on shelves. There was a sideboard with a silver goblet and plate. There was meat on the plate which the abbot must have been eating when they disturbed him.

Meat? This mon doesnae live like an abbot is supposed to. I pray we havenae made a mistake in coming here.

"Your Grace, my father intended to sell me to Lord Archibald Hay in return for the stewardship of a small parcel of land adjacent to ours on the coast of the North Sea. It would give the Frasers more land for farming and fishing, allow both the Frasers and Hay to control the area against the Keiths, and offer my parents more influence at court. Lord Archibald would receive my sizable dowry and a wife of childbearing age favored by the king and queen."

"What of this mistreatment?"

Deirdre's face drained of color as she thought back to the evening when Archibald tried to accost her in the alcove. Her tremors increased, and Magnus scowled before wrapping his arm around her shoulders. He angled them, so his body protected her.

"It's all right, Magnus," she murmured. He relented and turned back.

"Lord Archibald followed me out of the Great Hall the evening I saw Magnus for the first time. He grabbed my arm and pushed me down the passageway to an alcove. He shoved me in and threatened that if I did not cooperate, he would make our marriage miserable. He would send me to his land and visit only when he decided he wanted to beget an heir and then a spare. He manhandled me and was about to--," Deirdre choked as the words refused to come out.

She shuddered once more before continuing, "he was about to—to—enter," she could not finish. She buried her head in Magnus's side as she began to shake.

"Do ye need to hear aught more?"

"Were they in fact betrothed? If they were, he was within his rights to engage in conjugal activities."

Magnus saw red.

"Ye would condone a mon forcing a lass who is half his size. That any mon molest a woman. Nay. They were never betrothed. He had nay rights. He never would have had the right to assault her. Marriage doesnae mean a mon can violate his own wife."

"Young man, you know as well as I do that there is no such thing as violation in a marriage. A woman's duty is to submit."

"They werenae betrothed. He had nay right to touch her. He had nay right to threaten her. Ever."

"There were other threats?" he directed his question to Deirdre.

She nodded her head.

"That is not enough. You will have to tell me in your own words, lass."

Deirdre hiccupped as she tried to catch her breath.

"I was a lady-in-waiting to the queen. On one occasion, we were in the gardens when Lord Archibald approached. He forced me into a secluded area where he put his hand around my neck, squeezed it, and warned me I would be his soon enough, and he would do whatever he wanted."

"The fingerprints were visible on her neck and her arm when she returned to the group."

"You were there and did not intervene," the priest skepticism was obvious.

"Clearly, I wasnae there when he dragged her away. I arrived in the garden unaware they stepped away. When she returned, I could see the red marks from a goodly distance away."

"Your Grace, there was also an attack on Magnus's life. An arrow hit him while someone shot several others at him on the royal hunt. Someone tampered with his saddle, and his horse threw him as he tried to escape. A dead raven was left on his bed in a puddle of blood. These are not the normal course of things at court. We are undoubtedly in danger and in need of sanctuary."

Not convinced yet, the priest cocked his head and looked at them from the corner of his eye.

"What made you decide to run? It is obvious you have been on the run for some time. How many days has it been?"

"We departed when word reached us that the betrothal contract signing and wedding were to be held at the same time. That night. We have been traveling for five days."

"Five days from Sterling to here? Inveraray is not that far that it should take you that long."

"As ye may imagine, we didnae exactly travel the main roads. We had to stay off the paths and trails which meant take a less direct path. I double backed and weaved to try to keep our trail less obvious. That took time."

"And during this little misadventure, you have traveled alone?" The disapproval dripped from his voice at this point.

"Why would I nae travel alone with ma wife. We arenae in need of chaperones since we are wed. As I told ye at the beginning, our union was consummated seven years ago." Magnus's voice was quiet but there was no missing the determination.

"That may be so, but until a church blesses your union, and you would do well to remember you are not in the true Highlands yet, your handfast is not a guarantee to your claim."

Deirdre could see the two men were only to go around in circles, and it was their safety in jeopardy if the abbot would not concede.

"Father, while you consider our situation and *pray for guidance*, I would like to make a contribution to the abbey. It is the least we can do if we might at least stay the night."

"A contribution? Of what type?"

"I have only a single piece of jewelry, but I think the abbey could find a means to benefit from it. If you'll pardon me for a moment."

She turned from the two men and made sure that her skirts rustled to prove her need for privacy. She slid her hand into the pouch and fished around for a string of pearls. It was a valuable piece but far from the most precious of her kitty. She brushed down her skirts and turned back around.

"I beg you forgive for the impropriety, but as you can imagine, I had to keep it safe."

She handed the necklace to the priest whose eyes lit up before he remembered his self-control.

"You may go to the well to refresh yourselves, and then make your way to the commissary. You may eat, and by the time you finish I should have a decision for you."

Magnus knew he was in no position to demand anything, but he trusted the priest far less by the time the interview concluded than when they entered his solar. He had a very distinct feeling he and Deirdre would need to leave before the sun rose. As long as they were wedded by the church before their departure, he would deal with the consequences when he must.

Chapter Sixteen

*D*eirdre and Magnus were finishing their meager meal of dried figs, bannocks, and watered ale when they were summoned back to the abbot's office. This time he was not alone. An even older and more distinguished man was there too. It was obvious that this was the bishop. Magnus stood behind Deirdre with his hands on the outside of her shoulders. He did not like being positioned behind her, but the cramped room and his size did not allow for many options.

"I understand you would like to receive an official church blessing to make your handfast permanent, is that correct, my children?" There was a lilting burr to the bishop's words that gave him away as a Highlander. From the real Highlands as opposed to the abbot's observation that Magnus and Deirdre were barely out of the Lowlands.

"Aye, Yer Grace."

"You're a Sinclair, and you're a Fraser. I believe your families had a falling out some years ago. Is that correct?"

"Aye, over the Mackenzies."

"Yes, I remember now. Magnus is it not, your father sided with the Mackenzies."

Magnus was not sure if this would be in their favor.

"Aye, Yer Grace."

"My nephew is the current Mackenzie laird. I believe he is the father by marriage to your oldest brother."

"That is right."

"Then we are family. I suppose that means we should move this wedding along." The bishop indicated the door, and the four of them moved through the silent halls to the chapel.

The bishop entered the sacristy followed by the abbot. It was not long before both returned fully vested in their clerical robes.

156

"I do not believe a full Mass is in order at this time. I think a brief exchange of vows and a blessing shall suffice." Mangus and Deirdre nodded. "Very well, face one another and join hands."

Magnus paused before removing his brooch and pulled forward the extra length of plaid. He took Deirdre's hand and wrapped the plaid around their hands and forearms. There was far more fabric than needed, but the custom was preserved. The bishop smiled, and Magnus did not feel the same unease that returned the moment he looked at the abbot.

"Magnus Sinclair, do you pledge yourself to this woman, Deirdre Fraser, so you may both be joined as one? That you shall live out the holy sacrament of marriage, forsaking all others, giving Deirdre the first bite of your bread and the first sip of your wine? In this lifetime and the next?"

"Aye, by the grace of God, I pledge ma troth to Deirdre Sinclair, that we may be one in the eyes of God and His holy church. All that I have is all that I give, that we may share in it as one."

"Deirdre Fra—Sinclair," the bishop conceded, "do you pledge yourself to this man, Magnus Sinclair, giving yourself freely to be wed? Forsaking all others? That you shall provide him comfort and succor, that you shall obey and cherish? In this lifetime and the next?"

"Aye, by the grace of God, I pledge ma troth to Magnus Sinclair, that we may be one in the eyes of God and His holy church. All that I have is all that I give, that we may share in it as one."

"Then let this marriage be blessed by the Father, Son, and Holy Spirit. What God has joined, let no man put asunder. Amen." Bishop Mackenzie made the sign of the cross and nodded.

Magnus pulled Deirdre to him, ignoring the bishop and abbot, and kissed her soundly on the lips. Throat clearing and a cough were not enough to dissuade the couple from sealing their vows with a tender, drawn-out kiss.

"Mo bhean." *My wife.*

"An duine agam." *My husband.*

They rubbed noses together as had been their own show of affection since their first kiss.

"I love ye," they said together.

"If you are through," the abbot stepped forward, "I believe we have chambers prepared for you."

"Chambers?" both Magnus and Deirdre asked.

"This is a monastery, not a brothel."

Magnus stepped in front of Deirdre as best he could with their hands still bound.

"Dinna speak that way aboot ma wife, Father. It willna turn out well for anyone," he warned. The abbot's marked change indemeanor made Magnus nervous, but he would not allow anyone to insult Deirdre.

The bishop raised his hands, and Magnus relaxed.

"The abbot is correct in that customarily, men and women would be separated, but since you are a newlywed couple and extended family of mine, I offer you my chamber for the night."

"Thank you, Your Grace." Deirdre murmured before tugging Magnus's hand below the plaid. He unwrapped the wool and put it back in place.

"Bishop Mackenzie, if we could ask one more favor of ye. I would ask that we are given two copies of the marriage decree signed and sealed by ye."

"A written marriage decree, and two at that?"

"I have reason to believe we shall be in need of proof we have been wed before a priest, a bishop no less."

Bishop Mackenzie studied them both before nodding his head.

"One moment please," and the priest disappeared into the sacristy only to emerge minutes later with two pieces of parchment. He stepped near two candles and held the parchment close enough for the heat to dry the ink and his seal. Once he was sure the documents would not smear, he folded them and pressed his seal to the outside.

They followed the bishop to a well-appointed chamber that had a window and large fireplace with a roaring blaze. The bed was larger than most in an abbey but would be a tight fit for Magnus even without Deirdre. He was not sure how they would fit when they slept.

Once left alone, Magnus and Deirdre looked at one another and then burst into gales of laughter. The pent-up fear, frustration, and anger found its release through laughter. Magnus tucked a few curls behind her ear.

"Finally, mo eun beag."

"Finally, mo fhuamhaire."

They kissed briefly before both pulled back, suddenly feeling awkward.

"Does it seem wrong to ye to make love on a bishop's bed? That seems to be sacrilege. Is it considered hallowed ground?" Magnus cocked one eyebrow.

Deirdre knew he was joking, at least partially, but she felt much the same.

"He must ken what he was offering, but it doesnae seem right to me either."

They looked at each other for a long moment.

"So, we willna consummate our wedding on the night of." Magnus shook his head.

"I dinna think so," Deirdre's disappointment was clear, and that made Magnus chuckle again.

"We have every night for the rest of our lives." He lightly gripped her chin between his thumb and forefinger before giving her a swift peck. "Let us sleep while we can. We still have many days ahead of us."

Magnus pulled the spare plaid from his saddlebag and walked to the fireplace.

"What are ye doing?" Deirdre asked. She knew what he intended, and she was not pleased.

"Ye see the bed. There isnae enough room for me alone, and I would squash ye if we tried to share."

"Nay," she barked. She crossed her arms and planted her feet imitating his Odin stance. "I forbid it."

"Ye forbid it?" Magnus stalked back to his tiny wife as though he were a lion after his prey. "Forbid what exactly?"

"Ye sleeping on the floor. On our wedding night. I willna have it."

Deirdre squealed as Magnus grabbed her around the waist and twirled her around.

"Ye've become demanding now we're officially wed."

"Ye dinna ken the half of it. But seriously, Magnus, ye are nae sleeping on the hard floor when there is a bed available."

"If I lie next to ye, there will be nay other option than to be pressed together. If I'm pressed together with ye, ma already screaming cock will burst. I thought we werenae going to make love on a priest's bed."

"Ye will just have to learn some control." Deirdre pulled away and stripped off the filthy kirtle for the first time in days. She stood in only the now grey chemise. She had abandoned stockings days ago and taken off her boots as they entered the chamber. Magnus could not look away as she turned down the bed. He unpinned his breacan feile and unfastened his belt before pulling off his stockings. He placed them on the only chair in the chamber and walked slowly to the bed.

He pulled back the other side of the blanket, not that it had far to go.

"Ye dinna sleep like that." Deirdre jutted her chin at his leine.

"Neither do ye," he dipped his chin towards her chemise.

They both knew if they were naked, they would not stay apart. By mutual silent agreement, they crawled into bed. Magnus shifted onto his back as best he could and drew Deirdre over most of the top of him. He was surprisingly comfortable with her stretched out along him with one leg draped over both of his and her head in the crook of his neck. Exhaustion was stronger than desire for once. They were both soundly sleeping before either had a chance to regret their lack of opportunity.

Magnus awoke to the sound of voices in the corridor. He glanced at the window and saw it was still night, and the fire burned down. He was about to relax believing it was the priests heading to chapel. Unsure of how long he slept, he assumed it was matins or lauds. His eyes were drifting shut when a realization had him climbing out of bed. If it were the monks on their way to prayer, there would not have been any voices. He crept to the door and pressed his ear against it. He could still hear voices, but they were muffled. He did not want to open the door, but his intuition said he needed to know what was being said. He pressed the handle, and when it made no noise, he pulled. He only opened the door wide enough for him to feel the cool air seep through. He pressed his ear to the gap and listened.

"I would venture to say that pearl necklace is not her only piece of jewelry. I am sure she had others, and he probably has coin in his sporran. Even if they do not, there is bound to be a reward for them both."

"Go now. You will have to take the ass since you will need to travel farther and faster than you could on foot. They said they were attacked on the road but clarified that they were avoiding a search party. There must be one in this area. Ask in all the villages and hamlets you pass. Spread word that the king's fugitives are here. Move quickly while the others are at matins."

Magnus recognized the voices of the abbot and Brother Adam. He jumped when he felt Deirdre's hand at his waist. She looked at him silently as she strained to hear too, but the men moved away before she could hear anything. Magnus pressed the door closed and locked it this time.

"Get dressed."

"What's happening?" her whisper could barely be heard.

"Sshh. I'll explain once we are away. Just hurry."

Whatever Magnus heard was making him dress faster than she had ever seen. He did not even properly pleat his plaid. She pulled her clothes on as he moved around the room to make sure there was no evidence except for the wrinkled sheets, and he built up the fire, so it would seem like they were there longer. He walked to the window and tested the glass. It opened outward to the courtyard they passed through when they arrived. He watched a single figure dart across to the stables. It was not long before the lone figure was trying to hush and lead an unwilling mule. Magnus's hand held Deirdre back from the window, but she ducked under his elbow. They watched as Brother Adam opened the gate and passed through. There was no way for him to relock it, and Magnus breathed a sigh of relief since the bolt had been loud. Magnus pointed to himself and then out the window, then he pointed to Deirdre.

He threw one leg over the sill and dropped to the ground. It was not far but jarring. Deirdre was quick to follow, and Magnus caught her before her feet touched the ground. Grabbing her hand and staying in the shadows, they sprinted to the stables. Once inside, Magnus did not wait to saddle *Sealgair*. Deirdre offered the horse a carrot and then an apple to keep him occupied. Magnus nearly yanked her away when he saw his horse's teeth move towards Deirdre's hand, but this normally cantankerous warhorse was a lamb in her hands. He shook his head.

I truly dinna understand the women of this family. Mairghread then Siùsan, and now Brighde and Deirdre all turn our beasts into pets. Magnus shook his head as he watched and saddled at the same time. *I suppose they have plenty of practice on their husbands. We are a sad lot. The only one who hasnae fallen is Tavish. He has the furthest to go, and I would bet ma last farthing he falls the hardest. Some lass will have him by the bollocks.*

Magnus finished preparing his horse. He led Deirdre and his steed to the stables' entrance. Before emerging, he lifted her into the saddle. He led them to the gate, and marveled not for the first time, at how sure and light-footed his enormous horse was. Once they were through the gate, he swung up behind Deirdre, and they cantered to the treeline that was not far from the abbey. Magnus dismounted and quickly reattached his pine bough to the saddle. He pointed *Sealgair* northwest and spurred him to a gallop.

Once again, they rode in silence for nearly an hour before Magnus felt comfortable speaking.

"The abbot and Brother Adam conspired to get more of yer jewels and to turn us over to the scouts. It was Brother Adam we saw leaving. He was off to find any of the search party. They assumed, probably accurately, there would be a ransom for us. If we can reach Kilchurn before nightfall, we can cross Loch Awe there. We would have to turn south to find a place to ford. I dinna want to do that. We may be able to reach Dunstaffnage by tomorrow eve. If we can make it that far, then I'm confident we can catch a birlinn that will take us through the Sound of Mull and hopefully out to sea. We sail towards Glen Gary and try to avoid the MacDonnells. I may have made peace with their laird, but I doubt they will ken that yet. The MacLeods arenae that much farther past."

Deirdre nodded as she took in the information about the two priests. She was disappointed but not surprised that they would be deceived. She sincerely hoped that the bishop was not part of the conspiracy against them.

"Did ye hear me?"

"Huh? Nay. I was thinking aboot the priests."

"I said we will have to travel closer to the main roads to make better time. I will keep us out of sight, but there is a greater chance we will be seen. I may have to cut the brush loose since it's vera conspicuous."

Deirdre just nodded, and they settled back into companionable silence.

Chapter Seventeen

he sky was changing as the sun set. The pinks and purples were mixing with the grey of thunderclouds. Deirdre and Magnus felt the odd drop now and again, but the heavens appeared ready to open. They were in a glen with little options for cover when the rain fell. Magnus spurred his horse to a gallop as he tried to reach the next set of woods before they were soaked. Eager to run, Magnus gave *Sealgair* his head, and the animal shot forward. Even with the charging horse moving them closer to the trees by the minutes, there were drenched by the time they reached cover. Magnus's well crafted sweeper was torn to shreds, too.

Deirdre began to shiver the moment they dismounted and lost Magnus's heat.

"Ye canna stay like that. Even stripping down and wrapping a plaid around ye willna be enough. I must get ye warmer. Stay near Sealgair, and I will fetch firewood."

"Ye canna build a fire. Too visible," her teeth chattered between each word.

"And I canna afford ye catching the ague." Magnus's voice was resolute, so Deirdre chose to save her flagging energy for foraging some berries and acorns. The animals were well under cover by now, so hunting would be futile. Supper was going to be sparse that night. They were nearly out of Magnus's dried beef even though they were rationing it.

It did not take Magnus long to return with an armful of logs and branches, nor did it take him long to build a fire. He helped Deirdre out of her gown and pulled his spare leine from his bag.

"I didna even realize ye had this. Ye could have changed ages ago."

"And make anyone who crossed us wonder why I was clean and ye were scruffy? Nay. What type of husband would I be?" he chuckled. "The quality of ma horse makes it obvious we arenae tenant farmers from somewhere, nor do we look quite rough enough to be horse thieves. People may believe we simply fell upon hard times, which means a sad tale that nay one wants to hear. It should keep people away.

Deirdre slipped into the clean shirt and felt better than she had in days. She wished she was not so dirty underneath, but beggars could not be choosers. Magnus took off his own leine and laid it on the ground near the fire and next to Deirdre's. It was not long before they were both feeling warm and once again comfortable. The sky remained covered in angry clouds, and it looked much later than it was. They shared their meager supper, and Magnus promised to hunt once the weather cleared.

"I need to gather more wood. Will ye be all right for a wee bit?"

"Of course. Do ye want ma help?"

"Nay. Stay bundled up."

Magnus walked into the trees, and it was only seconds before he was completely out of view. Deirdre let her mind wander as she daydreamed about life for her and Magnus once they reached Dunbeath. She thought Laird Sinclair would welcome her, but she was not sure what her brothers by marriage would think or their wives. She was nervous to join such a close-knit family. She knew Magnus's brothers were aware of his history with her, but she was mostly sure that only Mairghread knew the full extent of their relationship or the hardship of being separated.

The leaves rustled over Deirdre's right shoulder. That was not the direction Magnus walked unless he circled around. The forest quieted, and Deirdre relaxed. A moment later she was fully alert. The forest was too quiet. She no longer heard any of the birds cawing about the rain or squirrels jabbering as they got wet. Slowly, Deirdre reached below her skirts to pull the sgian dubh from its sheath and flicked a wrist making another dirk appear. All the hair on her arms stood on end.

Without warning, three large, filthy men sprang from the trees.

"*Magnus! Magnus!*" Deirdre screamed as loudly as she could before one man lunged at her.

She swiped her small blade across the palm of his hand and recoiled in pain.

"The bluidy bitch cut me." The man said as if mesmerized that such a thing might happen, that a woman might defend herself.

Deirdre tried to keep all three in her line of sight while edging to place the fire between them.

"Dinna come closer. Ma husband is nearby. He willna forgive ye if ye touch me."

Deirdre felt an arm encircle her waist, and a hand clasp over her mouth. She tried to kick her feet back but she had no room. She bit at the man's palm, but she could not gain any purchase. It came out more like a lick, and the man chuckled in her ear as he pressed his hard groin against her backside. Deirdre's eyes flared as she felt his arousal rubbing against her. She flicked her wrist backward and stabbed as hard as she could with her upper arms pinned to her sides. The arm around her waist slackened until a fist jammed into her belly. The air rushed from her lungs but with her mouth closed and the man's thumb now covering her nose, she could not gasp even one breath.

"I planned have some fun with ye before I killed ye. Now I think I will just kill ye." The man sneered.

"That isnae what we agreed on! Ye promised us each a tup with her after we killed her mon and before we killed her."

"Colin is right. Ye promised—"

The man did not finish as a dirk lodged in his throat. Deirdre tried to turn her head away from the sight of blood squirting from the severed jugular.

"Get yer filthy hands off ma wife, or yer life is forfeit just as yer friend's was."

"Ye won't do aught as long as the bitch is in front of me."

The man holding Deirdre backed away from the fire and edged towards the darkness. As he maneuvered, the other three looked at each other and charged Magnus. Magnus whipped another dirk from his hand, and this one found its home in one of the highwaymen's eyes. He howled before dropping to his knees, and Deirdre thought she would retch as she saw the man pull the dirk free. Magnus drew his sword as the last man inched forward. He already had his drawn, and in the light from the fire, his short and thinner swords looked more like a toy compared to the two-handed broadsword that Magnus easily brandished in one.

"This is yer last warning, and it is a fair one. Let go of ma wife and leave, or I will kill every one of ye and sleep like a bairn."

With a roar, the man leaped at Magnus. Magnus sidestepped and brought his blade down on the man's hand. It severed it from his wrist, and as he staggered backward, he stumbled through the fire. His clothes ignited as he tried to run away. The air filled with the stench of burning flesh. Deirdre's stomach heaved, and the man must have felt it because he yanked his hand from her mouth in fear of being vomited on.

With her mouth free, she could move her head. She slammed it backward and heard the crunch of her skull hitting his nose. The man holding her spun her around and drove his fist into her stomach before reaching back to swing towards her face. She thrust her sgian dubh into his gut and twisted. She knew the short blade would not be lethal at that angle, but she prayed it slowed him enough for Magnus to finish him. The fist that had been raised, yanked the blade free. He looked stunned at Deirdre as she kicked out at his leg. She managed to break free and ran towards Magnus.

Magnus watched in horror as the lawless man's fist contacted with Deirdre's belly. Everything around him, even Deirdre, faded from his vision as it tunneled upon the man who dared touch his wife. Magnus stalked forward as the other man backed away, drawing his own sword from his hip. Magnus kept walking straight towards the man, and with a bellow that shook the leaves, Magnus thrust his sword forward, catching the man's ribs. He would kill the bastard slowly and make him suffer for putting his hands anywhere near Deirdre. With another roar, Magnus swung his sword through the air. Deirdre heard the swish before it struck the man's arm, cutting a deep tear into his bicep. The attacker thrust and parry against Magnus.

Deirdre heard several horses whinny as they drew closer. She searched, but it was far too dark now for her to determine who approached. She knew it was no friend, she wanted to know which foe. Behind Magnus emerged a man who held the reins to five horses. When this new man saw his comrade battling the mountain that was Magnus, he drew his sword and entered the fray. Magnus was now battling two men. The new arrival was the better swordsman of the two outlaws. He slashed and swung with speed and agility unexpected for a man who made his life robbing others. These were the maneuvers of a trained warrior. Magnus fended off the two men as he reached to his waist for another dirk. He pulled it loose in time to stab the neck of the man who held Deirdre, but this opened him to a deep incision into his thigh from the warrior.

Magnus was fed up of finding men trying to do him and his wife harm. He felt a twinge of annoyance that he killed the man who held Deirdre captive too quickly, but the new man, clearly a former warrior, was requiring too much of his attention for him to continue to toy with the other. As he pulled his dirk from the man's neck, he felt a searing pain cut through his thigh. He roared as he twisted and swung his sword as hard as he could. The last man standing might have been well trained, but he was no match for Magnus's savagery. Magnus's blow landed exactly as he intended and cleaved the man's head from his neck and almost sliced his shoulder off.

The moment that the last man fell, Magnus dropped his weapons and ran to Deirdre. He pulled her into his arms and pressed her head to his chest. He felt her shuddering breath against him, but he could feel his own tremors just as strongly. His entire body shook as fear and bloodlust drained from him. He staggered as he drew Deirdre back with him and sunk down against a trunk. He brought her down to his lap, and his hands skimmed her face, head, shoulders, and all that he could reach before rising to do it again. Deirdre captured his hands and kissed his palms.

"I am well. They didna harm me. Ye were there in time."

Magnus did not realize that tears flowed from his eyes until Deirdre's fingers feathered across his cheeks and wiped them away. He pulled her back against him and tucked her head under his chin. They sat that way with Deirdre quietly humming and stroking his arm for a long time. He could not flush from his eyes the image of Deirdre being held captive or receiving such a punch to her belly. He squeezed them shut as more tears broke free. He had not cried since his mother passed away. He had controlled his emotions when he and his brothers found their

165

sister being assaulted after being abducted. He controlled his emotions when Siùsan was held captive and attacked. He controlled his emotions when Alex fell ill after his battle for Brighde. He always controlled his emotions. The heartbreak of losing Deirdre when he was still young taught him to keep his thoughts private and his emotions secret. Now though, he could not seem to regain it.

"Magnus," Deirdre shook his shoulder. "I'm well, I promise. Magnus, please look at me. Ye saved me, and we are together now."

"I failed ye. I never should have left ye alone. What if I hadnae heard yer screams? What if I'd wandered too far?"

"Ye didna and wouldnae fail me. Magnus, ye have never failed me. Nae from the beginning till now. Do ye remember how ye punched the lad in the face and the other in the stomach the night we met? Ye didna like their comments aboot me, so ye made them shut up with yer fists. And then ye chased me down to be sure I was all right." She kissed his chin. "Ye're been protecting me since day one. I love ye today just as I loved ye back then. When ye climbed the tree because I wouldnae come down, ye made me fall head over heels for ye."

Deirdre shifted her position and reached behind her to brace herself. Magnus groaned as she pulled her hand back. She felt something wet and sticky with a metallic scent. She saw the blade hit his leg but did not realize how bad the injury was. She scrambled from his lap and threw back his plaid.

"Oh ma God, Magnus. Oh ma God." The wound was gushing blood and so deep that she could see through to the muscle. "I have to tend to this but I dinna have anything to sew it up with. I must clean it."

"Later," he breathed heavily as he pushed himself up and tried not to flinch in front of her. "We canna stay here. We need to move on. At our next stop, ye can tend it."

"Nay. We arenae going anywhere until ye let me rinse it clean and bandage it."

Magnus wanted to argue, but his head was fuzzy, and his stomach roiled making him queasy. He nodded his head.

Deirdre ran to his saddlebag and pulled the wineskin she knew held whisky. When she returned, she pulled Magnus towards the fire and pressed him down to sit. She examined his leine she was wearing. Finding a clean patch, she yanked it over her head and used the dirk still in her boot to cut a swatch from it and then several strips.

"That was ma good leine."

"And we'll be saying that *was* yer good leg."

She looked around and found a twig for him to bite down on, but he shook his head. He took a deep breath and nodded when she asked if he was ready. She poured the whisky directly into and over the wound. The air hissed through Magnus's teeth, but he made no other sound. Deirdre watched as Magnus's face strained and the blood vessel in his temple and the one in his forehead pulsated. She hated causing him such pain, but she knew his wound would surely fester without being cleaned. She placed the clean swatch over the wound and then bound it tightly with the strips of his destroyed leine. She dressed and then quickly helped him. She kicked dirt over the fire to put it out before saddling *Sealgair*. She led the enormous horse over to a rock where she whispered to it as she prepared to help Magnus mount.

"Such a braw laddie, ye are. Mo fhuamhaire, ye'll behave now. I ken it."

"I thought only I was yer giant."

"Jealous?"

"Aye."

Deirdre looked back and saw Magnus try to smile, but it was much more of a grimace.

"If I hold his bridle, and ye use the rock, can ye mount?"

"I dinna have much choice."

"I'll ride pillion if it would be more comfortable."

Magus shook his head but then looked like he would cast up his accounts.

"Nay. I need ye in front. If I canna hold the reins ye must be able to control him. I hate admitting this, but I may need to lean against ye from time to time."

Deirdre walked over to him and took both hands.

"Ye can always lean on me." Magnus understood her meaning.

She helped him mount and then slid with care onto the saddle before him. He tried to grip the horse with both legs, but his thigh screamed in protest.

"Just let me," Deirdre said as she took the reins in one hand and pulled each of his snuggly around her middle.

Chapter Eighteen

When they stopped to water the horse, Deirdre checked Magnus's injury again. It was still raw and angry, but she saw no signs of pus or red lines streaking from it. She held her breath and prayed that it would remain like that until she could stitch it closed. They had ridden throughout the night and only stopped when Deirdre could not wait any longer to relieve herself. She helped Magnus off the horse and assisted him even though he demanded privacy.

"If ye want to be stubborn and believe ye can do this all on yer own, then I shall leave ye to it." Magnus had sighed thinking he could relieve himself in private, but when he heard the creak of leather and saw Deirdre nudging his steed forward, he conceded and begged her for help.

That had been hours ago, and Deirdre knew Magnus was tiring faster than he wanted to admit. She kept the horse at a walk because she did not trust that she or Magnus could keep him in the saddle if they rode any faster. Magnus was leaning against her more as the time ticked by. The sun made an appearance early in the day and stayed fairly strong through midday, but as afternoon approached, a chill picked up. Deirdre was warm, but she first assumed it was from the sun and then from Magnus pressing against her. When sweat rolled between her shoulder blades, she wondered if she was becoming ill. She shifted slightly to wipe her brow, and Magnus sagged to the right. Deirdre reached for him and felt the skin of his neck. It was on fire. She pulled the horse to a stop and twisted in the saddle. Magnus's face was pale and clammy, his lips were chapped, and his eyes were closed. She placed the back of her hand against his forehead. She knew before she made contact that she would feel a fever. She brushed her fingers next to his temples, feeling the heat radiate from him.

"Magnus, wake up."

She tried squeezing his hand, but it was lifeless.

"*Magnus.*"

She gained no response. Deirdre was not sure what to do. She looked around but saw nowhere that would offer them cover or camouflage. If they stayed on the horse, Magnus might fall off. If she could get him off the horse, she had no guarantee he could get back on. She most assuredly could not do it herself.

"Magnus, just hold on, mo chridhe. I'll find us somewhere we can stop."

Deirdre saw no hint of where they were or how close to Loch Awe they were. She looked toward the sun and oriented herself. This was another thing Magnus taught her during a summer gathering. She felt the sun against her face and looked towards the horizon. She was not so concerned about the time as she was whether she could find due west. If she could get them to the loch, she could either find them a boat or continue along the shoreline.

Knowing midday passed, she pointed the horse in the direction of the sun and spurred him forward. She held tight to Magnus's arms as he bounced about behind her. They rode for what Deirdre believed to be another two hours. *Sealgair* needed a rest and so did she. She wanted to push on because she was sure they must finally be close, but she would not risk laming Magnus's horse, and she was exhausted from the physical and emotional strain of holding her giant of a husband on the back of the horse. She let *Sealgair* amble over to some higher grass. He nibbled and shifted his weight as if to tell her they needed to get off. She was considering whether she could dismount without knocking Magnus from his steed when he decided for her. He moaned loudly, the first sound he made all day, and then lurched to his side, toppling off the horse. He landed with a sickening thud. Deirdre scrambled to dismount and rushed to him. She was frightened to roll him over, remembering he had a head injury less than a fortnight ago. It seemed a lifetime ago after the past days of fleeing first the castle then the abbey.

"Deir," Magnus moaned. "Water."

She brought the water skin to his lips and as much dribbled down his chin as went in his mouth. His eyes fluttered open, and she had never been more relieved to see their dark amber as she was now.

"Magnus, ye're vera ill. I need to see yer leg again."

"Wheest," he tried to flap his hand at her, but he couldn't lift it higher than his knee. "Dinna fash. It'll all come right."

His head lolled to the side.

Unconscious or just asleep, Deirdre did not know, but she wasted no time pushing back his plaid. The bandage was soaked through. She chastised herself for not checking it sooner. She pulled it away and moaned when she saw the state of his wound. It was festering with angry red lines shooting out from it like a spider's web of infection. It smelled sour and rotting. Deirdre went back to the saddlebag and found the wineskin of whisky. There was not much left but enough for everything

169

she needed to do. She took a small swig and then poured a healthy dose over his thigh. He jerked awake with a curse.

"Magnus, it's going putrid. I need to clean it, but I also need to tend to it properly. I canna do that without building a fire. I must get ye back on *Sealgair*, but I canna do that alone. Ye must help me."

Magnus looked blankly at her through fever hazed eyes. He appeared to be considering what she said, but he did not seem to be able to make sense of it.

What is she talking aboot me being ill? Why is it so bluidy hot all a sudden? This is Scotland. I need only wait a moment and the next season will come. Then this heat will end. Why does ma leg hurt so damn badly? Shite! That fucking hurts. What is wrong with ma leg? Och, that's right. I remember now. That bastard thought he could take ma Deirdre and still live. Who was that welp who joined him? He cut ma damn thigh. Fuck! That hurts.

"Magnus, I ken it hurts, but I need yer help getting ye back onto yer horse. We canna stay here."

I dinna want to ride a horse. I'd much rather ride ma wife. She is mighty bonnie. I am the luckiest mon in Scotland. I love her, she loves me, and now I can tup her morn, noon, and night. Bluidy lucky.

"Ye can most definitely '*tup*'me any time ye like. Once ye are well. Magnus. Ye are beginning to really frustrate me. I dinna think ye understand that ye're speaking most of yer thoughts. They arenae staying in just yer head."

"Beginning," he chuckled, "I'm only now frustrating. Then I amnae doing ma job correctly in bed."

"*Magnus!*" Deirdre pulled the stopper from the other waterskin and poured the contents onto his face. He spluttered, but his eyes seemed to focus more. "Magnus, I need yer help getting ye onto yer horse. Now!"

Magnus shook his head and looked around. He had no memory of how he came to be on the ground or even where they were. He rolled to his good side and forced his legs under him. He wobbled, and Deirdre rushed to support him. They staggered together until he stepped onto the rock. He used the last dregs of his strength to pull himself onto *Sealgair*. He was drenched once more in sweat, and his eyes had lead pinning them shut. Deirdre grasped the reins and pulled herself onto the saddle to ride pillion. She had no way of moving Magnus further back nor did she think she could get on in front of him without knocking him off. She did her best to hold the reins and see where they were going, but Magnus's broad body was impossible to see around. As the horse moved from a trot to a canter, she felt Magnus slipping again. She reined in and hopped down. Digging in the saddlebag, she found the hobbling ropes.

This is perfect! This will keep him on the horse, and I'll be able to see where the hell we are going. Why didna I think of this before? Hell, why is the sea salty? I dinna ken the answer to either, but let's get on with this.

Deirdre pulled at Magnus's shoulders and managed to drape him over the saddle pummel to lay across the horse's withers. She pulled his arms onto each side of the horse's neck. She used the hobble ropes to tie Magnus's arms together. She cinched them as tight as she dared without cutting off his circulation. She was glad for his bracers that protected his skin. She turned his cheek, so he could breathe. After adjusting the stirrups to her height, she swung back into the saddle and pushed the horse into a canter. When he did not move an inch, she pushed the horse to a gallop.

The feel of the wind rushing past her, pushing her hair off her face and free of her neck was liberating. She pushed her heels down and squeezed with her thighs. It had been ages since she could gallop across a wide and open expanse. She rode Freya whenever she could, but she was limited in how far she could go if she wanted to ride astride, and it was never deemed ladylike to ride at a gallop. She leaned over Magnus's prone body and urged the horse to keep going faster. Despite the weight of two riders, *Sealgair* leaped at the opportunity to run free, so she gave him his head, and they ate up the landscape. When the warhorse's pace slipped, she slowed him to a trot, and they both caught their breath. Deirdre scanned the horizon as they crested a hill. She caught sight of the loch and wanted to whoop as they descended to the shore. She led *Sealgair* all the way to the edge where it lapped against the shoal that met the bank. She did not worry about him drinking his fill since this was a fresh-water loch. She splashed water onto her face before cupping her hands and bringing the cool liquid to her mouth. The chilly water soothed her dry throat and slid an icy trail down her chest to her empty stomach. She craned her neck to catch sight of any fish that might be close enough to spear. She slipped her boots off, rolled down her stockings, and then hitched up her skirts. She pulled the dirk from her thigh band and slowly shuffled her feet into the water. The chill took her breath away, but her movement disturbed a school of fish that darted by and between her legs. She jabbed and pulled a wiggly fish up with her knife. It was larger than she anticipated. This would be enough to feed both her and Magnus until something better could be snared or shot.

Returning to Magnus's side, she untied his wrists and tried to help him slowly dismount, but as soon as she shifted his weight, gravity did the rest, and she found herself pinned under her husband.

Beastly mon! He is a giant. I'm stuck, and he's out cold. Now how do I get free? I canna even wiggle ma little toe.

Deirdre lay there and looked up at the blue sky as she caught her breath. With a bit of energy restored, she dug her heels into the ground and propelled her body up to tip him off her. She rolled free. Magnus groaned as his eyes fluttered open.

"Deir? Where are we, lass?"

"We've made it to Loch Awe, but where on the loch I dinna ken. We just arrived."

"How did I end up on the ground again? I remember climbing onto *Sealgair* but naught after."

"Ye rolled off the horse and rolled onto me. I wriggled free." At Magnus's horrified and then guilt-stricken face, Deirdre felt bad but not soon enough to prevent a giggle from slipping out.

"Ye're laughing? I could have crushed ye! I amnae doing well at being a husband. Mayhap yer father was right." Magnus trailed off.

"What? Nay!" Deirdre dropped to her knees beside him. "Dinna *ever* say that again. It must be the fever speaking."

Magnus shook his head.

"I ken I'm nae well, but I amnae dead yet. I should be caring for ye, nae the other way around."

"That is the most ridiculous clishmaclaver I've heard in yonks. Did ye forget our vow already? Or were ye nae paying attention when I spoke? Too busy thinking aboot tupping me morn, noon, and night?"

Magnus winced. He could not remember saying that last bit, but he must have from the look on Deirdre's face.

"I pledged to offer ye comfort and succor, and that is precisely what I am doing. Now haud yer wheesht. Ye are going to wish for a different type of comfort by the time I am done. Can ye get to yer feet? We need to move back a bit."

She grabbed his outstretched hand with both of his. She pulled as hard as she could as he leveraged himself up. She almost flew backward when he was upright, and she was still pulling. Magnus's other arm shot out and caught her.

"See. Even in yer state, ye're still protecting me."

Magnus muttered under his breath at the saucy smile she offered him. Deirdre was relieved that he could move about on his own and he was coherent again. She wanted to giggle again as the weight she did not realize rested on her shoulders lifted. She gathered loose twigs and branches that scattered the bank. She brought them back to near where Magnus had settled away from the waterline. She looked around and picked a handful of leaves to use as tinder. Magnus gave her the flint from his sporran, and she soon had a strong blaze going even if she kept it small.

She set about cutting more strips from Magnus's spare leine. She soaked a few in water and a couple in the last of the whisky.

"Did ye really just pour the last of ma whisky on that scrap?"

"I had to."

Magnus huffed, but she refused to apologize when she intended to do all she could to save his leg and to save him.

When the fire was burning blue at the base, she knew it was hot enough for what she needed to do. She pulled a dirk from Magnus's waist. It was longer than hers.

He was curious butsaid nothing. She used one of the whisky soaked clothes to wipe the blade thoroughly.

"Magnus, I dinna want to do this, but I must. I have to cut away the putrid flesh. If I dinna, it will only fester more. It'll never heal properly."

Magnus nodded.

"I ken it has to be done. Give me the knife, mo eun beag. Ye dinna have to do this."

Deirdre shook her head, took a deep breath, and flipped his plaid back. She unwrapped his injury and was not sure if she wanted to cry, vomit, or both when she saw the condition of his leg. She sucked in air through her nose as she forced her hand to steady before she lifted it to his leg. Magnus grasped her wrist and pulled the knife from her hand.

"Deir, go see to that fish I saw on the shore before ma horse eats our supper. Take yer bow and see if ye can find something else to eat. I am ravenous, and since I canna ravish ye, I will settle for a warm meal." Deirdre shook her head and did not move even though she let him take the dagger. "Deir, go. Dinna do this, please. Let me deal with it."

The tears leaked from her eyes. She was torn. She knew she should tend to his leg for him, but she also knew she might be ill if she stayed. She understood he wanted to maintain some of his dignity. She backed away and fetched her bow, but she could not bring herself to leave their makeshift camp. She knew he was aware that she was still there, but she remained out of his sight. She heard his grunts of pain and retched. When she no longer heard him moving about or groaning, she ran back to his side terrified that something went wrong.

"It'll come right, Deir."

He tried to cover his leg before she saw the fresh damage done. She steeled herself to what she would see and moved next to him. She picked up the whisky drenched cloth and moved his plaid from his leg.

"Ye canna keep putting this filthy thing over yer wound. It'll never come right if ye do."

She straddled his calf and pressed her weight down as her hand braced against his thigh. The hand with the cloth pressed over the wound. Magnus howled in pain. His leg shook and bucked, but she would not let up. Eventually, she pulled the cloth back, folded it once, and wiped the edge of the wound. Seeing the flesh was now pink and healthy relieved her. She did not want to imagine the pain Magnus must have endured to cut away at his own leg. Biting her lip, she knew what she had to do next. There was no way she would allow Magnus to do this to himself. She moved off his leg and took his dirk to the water. She rinsed the blood from it and brought it to the fire. She pushed the blade into the hottest part of the flame. She watched as the metal heated and the fire popped. When the blade was glowing with blue waves shimmering across it, she knew it was as hot as it was safe to make it. She turned back to Magnus who was watching her. He nodded once.

Deirdre found herself in the same position as before. She straddled his calf, but this time she used her free hand to pinch the wound as tightly closed as she could. She looked into Magnus's eyes before lining the blade up with his wound.

"Look at me, Deir." Her eyes shifted up, and before she realized what he intended, he pressed her hand holding the blade down to his skin. The smell of burning skin and hair filled the air around them. Magnus did little more than flinch as he held her stare.

"Dinna look away, Deir. Look at me," he ground out.

She nodded and swallowed. When they were both sure that the wound had been cauterized, they lifted the blade. Deirdre threw it to the side, and Magnus pulled her into his arms. She twisted to stay away from his wound. She curled into a ball. Guilt for not being stronger for him, shame at her weakness, exhaustion, and fear churned into a conflagration of emotions as it scorched through her.

"Mo ghaol, I am all right. I swear to ye. Ye did so well tending yer cranky patient. I am proud of ye, lass." He kissed the top of her head and lifted her chin with his thumb. "Dinna fash. It takes more than a little scratch to do me in. Deir, I ken ye've seen and felt the other scars. This isnae ma first battle wound and I am certain it willna be ma last. Dinna work yerself into a puddle of tears. I would much rather be kissing ye than wiping yer neb."

Magnus smiled as her hand flew to her nose to check if it was running.

"Ye're a cruel, cruel mon." She swatted at him playfully.

"Much better," he kissed her with a tenderness that made her sigh.

Magnus leaned back against the hillock he had found to rest by. His eyelids grew heavy. Deirdre ran her finger between his brows, and the furrow relaxed. She slid her fingers to his temples. There was still more heat than normal radiating from his head, but it was not as bad as before. She slipped from his slumbering body. She moved about refilling the waterskins. She scaled and deboned the fish and cooked it over the flames. She woke Magnus to feed him the fish and water. It was not long before he was drifting back to sleep.

There was still quite a bit of daylight left, so she gathered her bow and quiver. She moved parallel to the shore, keeping Magnus's position in sight if she looked back over her shoulder. She meandered towards a clump of scrub brush. She found a small stone and threw it as if she were skipping rocks. A fluffle of rabbits scattered as she picked off one after another until she had three dead rabbits to take back to the fire. She freed her arrows from her quarry and turned to look at the sky.

Odd! There isnae a cloud in the sky now, and I hear thunder.

She gazed across the loch and saw no clouds there either. *Sealgair's* angry whinny drew her attention. She could see the tall horse from where she stood. His ears were twitching, and his body swayed with unease. The roll of thunder sounded again, and this time she felt the ground rumble.

Shite! That isnae thunder! Horses!

Deirdre looked to the distance on the far side of the beach where Magnus rested. She could see a cloud of dirt billowing in the hazy sunlight. She dropped the rabbits and took off running, pulling her bow and quiver over her head and shoulder as she ran.

"MAGNUS! MAGNUS!"

She waved her arms over her head trying to gain his attention, but he did not seem to rouse. She pushed herself to run as fast as she could, ignoring the stitch in her side, the tightness in her chest, or the pain in her legs that were sore from riding longer than she was used to.

"MAGNUS! RIDERS, MAGNUS! *WAKE UP!*"

Deirdre saw his head pop up at last. She was close enough to see his face when he caught sight of the approaching party. He scrambled to get to his feet but fell backward. Deirdre pushed herself again as she felt herself slowing.

They will kill him if they catch him. And I will kill them.

Deirdre slid into the sand next to him as the faces of the men came into focus. Her father led the search party, and Hay rode to his right. Deirdre could not believe her eyes when she saw several Highlanders riding with them. Her anger flared at the betrayal. She pulled at Mangus and got him to his feet. They shuffled to the horse. Magnus lifted her into the saddle and was about to mount behind her when they heard her father's voice.

"Stop now, or I will kill him, Deirdre."

Magnus glanced up and saw that Deirdre had hold of the reins. He slapped *Sealgair's* rump as hard as he could.

"Ride! Go, Deir! Dinna stop! Go!"

The horse shot forward, lurching up the sandy bank to firmer land. Magnus turned to the search party and raised his hands in surrender. He was prepared to give himself up now that Deirdre was on her way. He knew his warhorse could outrun any of the other mounts that raced along the beach to reach them.

"On yer knees, traitor!" Hay spurred his horse past Laird Fraser as he drew his sword. Magnus dropped to his knees, but Hay did not stop. He kept charging with his sword pointing at Magnus's chest. He was mere feet from Magnus when an arrow whizzed past Magnus and embedded itself into Hay's shoulder.

"Dinna think I missed. Kill him, and ye will find yerself buried next to him."

Another arrow landed beside Hay's mount's hoof. The horse shied away and nearly unseated the livid noble.

Magnus struggled to turn around. He wanted to groan. He did not know if he should be proud of his wife's stubbornness. She looked glorious mounted on his enormous horse, arrow nocked, curls blowing in the breeze. She looked like an ancient Greek goddess of the hunt or war. Or if he should be furious that she did not ride away and was risking her life.

"Come down from there, Deirdre. It's time to stop playing; your games are over."

Deirdre turned her arrow towards her father, his patronizing tone grating on her frazzled nerves.

"Dinna make me choose, or ye willna like ma choice."

She pulled back further on the bowstring. Father and daughter stared each other down. Laird Fraser must have seen something in his daughter he recognized because he nodded. Deirdre lowered her bow but did not take the arrow away. Instead, she rested it on her lap.

"He rides with me." She jerked her chin towards Magnus.

"Absolutely not! You have whored yourself long enough. It is time to behave yourself and end this nonsense."

Hay howled with pain as a dirk settled into the hand that rested on his pommel.

"Dinna think I missed," Magnus echoed his wife's words. "Insult her again, and ye'll find yerself buried under ma horse's shite."

"*Enough!*"

Mangus recognized his uncle's bellowing voice. The man pushed between Hay and Fraser.

"Lass, ye ride with me. Give the wee beastie a break after working him into a lather. Graham, get ma nephew on a ruddy horse and tie him on. He looks as if he'll keel over in a strong wind. What the bluidy hell happened to ye anyway?" He finished by looking at his nephew again.

Magnus shook his head and gritted his teeth. He would ride without assistance. He would not show a single sign of weakness in front of these men. A horse was brought forward, and Magnus ground his teeth together as he forced himself onto the horse in a fluid movement. His plaid gathered over his wound and rubbed painfully. He tried to arrange the wool without being noticed. His luck was surely gone. His uncle dismounted and walked to him. He pushed Magnus's hand aside and pushed up the plaid.

"Holy fucking shite!" He let out a string of other curses that Deirdre never heard before. She tucked them away to ask Magnus about later as they seemed highly effective. "What the fucking hell happened to yer leg? How are ye even awake? Do ye have the fever?"

Hamish studied Magnus's face more closely. He saw the cracked lips, the grey pallor around Magnus's mouth and eyes, and the glassiness that had not left Magnus's eyes. He let out another string of curses

"What happened?" he asked again, more calmly this time.

"Someone thought to touch Deir and take her for me. They're now dead."

Hamish looked between Magnus and Deirdre.

"How many?"

"Five."

"When?"

Magnus looked to Deirdre and shrugged.

"Night before last."

Hamish walked to Deirdre and rested his hand on the horse's neck.

"Did ye close his wound?" Deirdre saw the older man's throat tighten as he forced out the words.

"We both did," she murmured.

"Thank ye," he whispered.

Hamish walked back to Magnus.

"Yer da will kill *ye* and string *me* up by the bollocks," he ground out.

Hamish remounted his horse and edged it next to Deirdre. He looked over his shoulder, but Magnus could not see to whom. He knew when he found himself surrounded by lairds Graham, MacDonnell, MacKinnon, Campbell, and Menzies. Magnus understood now why the Highlanders rode after him. It was not to run him to ground but to protect him once he was found.

Chapter Nineteen

The search turned recovery party took the direct path back to Stirling. No one spoke much during the days on the road. Magnus and Deirdre were never allowed to be near one another. They could only communicate silently. Their looks were easily readable by each other but seemed to baffle the others. Magnus rode with the lairds throughout the day and then slept encircled by them. There was a Highlander, be it a laird or one of their guardsmen, on watch throughout the night. Magnus was sure that this was as much to protect the camp from intruders as it was to be sure none of Hay's or Fraser's men murdered him in his sleep. His fever broke at some point during the second day of travel back to court. Now, his leg throbbed with a fierceness that stole his breath at times. He hid his discomfort as much as he could, but he saw Deirdre watching him every time he could look over. She slept with her father's men surrounding her. Hay silently seethed, drinking far too much whisky every night.

More than once Hay spouted off after having a few too many swigs. His insults were generally directed to Magnus, but a few times, his loose tongue turned on Deirdre. More than one Highlander had to be held back as they stood to her defense. Fraser tried to keep Hay separate when he behaved like this, but even his fist being driven into the man's nose one night was not enough to convince the Lowland lord that the less said, the better.

They rode into Stirling court just as the sun began its final descent. The entire party was exhausted and filthy. Magnus was sure he had ground some of his teeth down to the gums from the nagging and ever-present pain the radiated throughout his entire body. Each jarring step nearly knocking him from his seat. Deirdre was beside herself with worry over what would happen to Magnus once they arrived. She had even thought of ways to try to delay their arrival, but Magnus finally shook his head, and she gave up.

Magnus was pulled from his horse and pushed through the castle passageways until he found himself standing before the king in an empty Great Hall. The king did not appear as welcoming as he had the last time Magnus arrived at court. Magnus heard Deirdre's scream as her mother and three of her father's men dragged her away. Magnus tried to rush to her but found a set of swords crossed before him and two grim royal guards staring at him. He spun back around.

"Sire, where is ma wife being taken?"

"Yer wife?" mocked Hay. "She cannot be your wife when she is already contracted to be mine. You abducted my betrothed and defiled her. I would not worry so much about where *my* betrothed is as to where you will be going."

The king sat in silence, looking bored.

"I will consider this issue, but I am not inclined to do so now. I have other more pressing matters."

The king nodded to his guardsmen who led him away. Magnus assumed he would be put under house arrest in his chamber or even a smaller one. Instead, he found himself being led in a direction he knew led to only one place. When the dank air hit his face, and the sound of dripping water greeted his ears, he knew his luck ran dry. He was shoved into a cell that stunk of human waste. He heard the scurrying taps of paws across the stone floor. It was too dark for him to see, so he used his hands to feel about. He stepped on a pile of hay, but the movement released a stench that made him heave. He stepped away and slid his hand along the wall until he found a somewhat dry spot. He lowered himself to the ground and massaged his aching thigh. There was nothing he could do but wait. He was still confident that the king would not put him to death, not with so many Highlanders still present. Nor would the king risk his father leading an uprising with the potential to spread throughout the Highlands. Instead, he knew he would be left here to rot indefinitely. In the meantime, he had no way of knowing how Deirdre faired. He tilted his head back and closed his eyes.

Shite.

"Uncle Hamish! Uncle Hamish, slow down."

Hamish spun around wondering how Magnus could be calling his name, but he was relieved and shocked to see his nephew Tavish jogging towards him.

"Uncle Hamish, what the devil is going on? I arrived at court three days ago. The king is refusing me an audience, and no one will tell me where Magnus is. I asked for ye, but I was told ye were away. I havenae seen anyone I ken."

Hamish looked around and pulled Tavish into a chamber he scanned to be sure was empty.

"Ye brother has found himself in the king's dungeon."

Tavish's eyebrows flew to his hairline.

"Aye. Do ye remember Deirdre Fraser?"

Tavish's eyes narrowed, his feet spread apart, and his arms crossed.

"How could I nae? The lass broke Magnus's heart. He's nae been the same since she left him. Dinna tell me she got him thrown in there. The bitch." Tavish unfolded his arms and turned to the door.

"I wouldnae let yer brother hear ye speak like that aboot his wife. The last mon to insult her is having his hand seen to by a healer after having a dirk stuck in it."

Tavish froze then turned back to his uncle.

"Wife? Auld mon, I think ye have a tale to tell and dinna dither aboot. Ye best explain this sharpish."

Hamish sighed and rubbed his brow. He motioned to the bench near the window. The two men sat on the ridiculously small piece of furniture. It protest as they settled onto it.

"Ye brother found her soon after his arrival. He had nay idea she was at court. It seems he's been sending her missives that are always returned to him. He never kenned where she was as she's been, or was, a lady-in-waiting and traveled with the court. Her father intercepted the missives and never told her aboot them.

"Magnus saw her leave the Great Hall pursued by a mon. He witnessed the mon push her through the door, so he followed. He prevented this mon, Lord Archibald Hay, from raping her. This is the mon her father arranged for her to marry. I dinna ken all the details, but somewhere between rescuing her and their running away together, they reconciled. Word of their previous relationship," at this Hamish raised an eyebrow and gave Tavish a pointed look, "began flying aboot like snow in a blizzard. Deirdre was disgraced and dismissed from the queen's court. Her parents and Hay decided to move everything along, so they could remove her from court and presumably hide her at one of his keeps. She and Magnus fled. Their disappearance was not noticed until that evening when her mother went to fetch her for the wedding. Needless to say, holy hell broke loose as her father and Hay began organizing search parties. The other lairds and I rode out to make sure Magnus came back alive. We just arrived nae an hour past. Tavish, they took yer brother to the dungeon."

Tavish took in all that his uncle told him. He was not the least surprised by any of the tale. He knew neither he nor any of his brothers would overlook a woman being mistreated. He also knew Magnus still considered himself married to the lass. He refused to look at any other woman no matter how many times Tavish tried to tempt him or thrust women at him. Tavish just did not know about the unanswered letters. His jaw ticked to discover his brother kept such a secret from him. While Magnus and Mairghread were the closest in age, with Callum and Alex only being a few months further apart, he and Magnus always paired together. They had since they were both old enough to enter the lists. They shared a chamber whenever they traveled and trained first with one another before moving to any other partner. Tavish realized that he was hurt to learn his brother had not entrusted him.

180

He didna think I could be trusted. He thought I would tease him or tell others. That ruddy well hurts to realize. Am I that great a disappointment? Do others think I canna be mature enough to be told something in confidence?

Tavish pushed his focus back to his uncle and tucked those questions away for further consideration at another time.

"I assume that their reconciliation involved them considering themselves still married?"

"Ye would have the right of that."

"Then I dinna ken how the king doesnae see that there couldnae be a betrothal with another mon. Does the king ken aboot their handfast all those years ago?"

"Aye, but he doesnae take it seriously."

The door to the chamber opened and a page summoned them to the king's Privy Council chamber.

"Tavish, it is good to see ye at court. What brings ye here?"

Tavish looked about the room filled with courtiers. He tried to disguise his disdain and focus on the king, but the mutual dislike that flowed between the Highlanders and Lowlanders was nearly palpable.

"Sire, thank ye for the welcome. Ma father sent me to check on Magnus. He has been gone longer than expected. We didna ken he found his wife after all this time."

The chamber came to a screeching halt as all eyes swung to him. The intrigue was well known to everyone within the castle, noble or servant. The king frowned at Tavish.

"I am not sure I understand your meaning."

"Magnus's wife. Deirdre. Yer Majesty, do ye nae remember that Magnus and Deirdre handfasted when the MacLeods hosted the Gathering? They slipped off, seems to be a habit I see now, and handfasted. The entire keep was in an uproar when neither were found. They came back into the bailey like two cats that had gotten into the cream. Well, at least one cat in the cream." Tavish chuckled at his own humor, but when no one else even cracked a smile, he sobered. "Before Magnus and Deirdre could find ma father to tell him, Laird Fraser found them and yanked her from Magnus's arms. He yelled for his family and clan to pack because they were leaving. Magnus sought me and ma brothers out at the mead tent. We were, uh, being entertained. By the time he could pull us away, word was already swirling around the camp that the Frasers had left. Magnus was beside himself. He didna say over six words at a time for over a year. Apparently, he kept sending missives to the lass, but someone sent them back. From what I understand, he wasna able to find her for the entire seven years they were apart."

Tavish turned to stare at Laird Fraser as he continued.

"It would seem Deirdre's father purposely kept her location a secret from Magnus to force their handfast to run out. Except they already consummated their handfast. She has always been his wife since neither repudiated the other. Laird Fraser stole ma brother's wife and kept her a veritable prisoner within yer court, Sire."

Tavish watched Laird Fraser's face turn scarlet, but all he did, in turn, was smirk.

"Tavish, ye lay quite a heavy claim at my feet. There seems to be more to this tale of woe than I ever realized. When Lady Deirdre petitioned both myself and the queen to return to your brother, we thought her to just be a lovestruck lass who would outgrow her infatuation. It was at her parents' insistence that her whereabouts were kept from your family. They believed if they had no correspondence, she would move on. When she stopped speaking of the matter, the queen and I thought she no longer held a tendre for Magnus."

"By yer leave, Yer Grace, ye seriously underestimated the value of faithfulness among the Sinclair men. If ma brother pledged himself to the lass in any way, it was never for just a year and a day. It was always meant to be a lifetime. Ye ken we dinna stand for infidelity, and Magnus wouldnae ever betray a lass like that. I can vouch that he has been a monk for the past seven years."

"Be he a monk or not, that does not change the fact that he had no right to handfast with her in the first place. It was not a marriage. He was older and defiled her. Since arriving at court, he has disrupted her honest and legitimate betrothal and impending marriage."

"Ye would have yer daughter be a bigamist?" Tavish infused shock into his voice, but the scorn was just as obvious. "Ye are a Highlander nay matter what pretentions ye may put on. Ye ken just as well as any other, including the king, a fellow Highlander himself, that a handfast is a marriage if it's chosen by the couple. It is only a trial when arranged by clan leaders. Ma brother married yer daughter, and ye would risk her soul and excommunication, so ye can, what, gain land, a new title, mayhap gloat to the other lordlings. I shall pray for yer soul and that ye beg the Lord's forgiveness."

Tavish glared at the older man and did not move when his uncle's hand came to rest on his shoulder.

"Sire, ye have heard a great deal from ma nephew. He hasnae been here long enough to ken all that has transpired. He hasnae even seen his brother yet. What he tells ye, he does so because it is the truth he has always kenned."

The king nodded and looked at Laird Fraser, but before he could speak, Tavish cleared his throat.

"Sire, nae to state the obvious, but ma brother and sister by marriage have been traveling throughout the Scottish countryside for how many days? Alone? Do ye honestly believe there is a chance they didna claim their marital rights? At the least, they would have handfasted again, and surely they consummated this union."

Tavish cleared his throat. "It's a mite late to even claim she's been compromised. I'd say it's gone a far sight beyond just compromise."

Laird Fraser lunged towards Tavish.

"Ye bluidy Sinclairs think ye have the answer to everything. Ye're all alike. Ye're nay better than yer brother, the bastard."

"Dinna speak of ma mother like that, or ye may fall asleep but nae wake up." Tavish ground out. "Considering me as good as any of ma brothers is an honor. They're the finest men I ken."

"Cease, Fraser. Sinclair has given me much to think about. Tavish, retire to a chamber. I will summon you when I am ready to decide."

Tavish looked at the king and then bowed. He and Hamish backed towards the door, but just before leaving, he turned to Laird Fraser once more.

"By the by, yer burr is showing again. Ye can hide here, but ye're a Highlander, and ye ken exactly what that means. Find ye honor before ye lose yer soul."

Chapter Twenty

eirdre fought against the men dragging her through the passageways. She struggled to free her arms as she twisted and scratched. She let her body go limp and forced the men to change their hold on her to accommodate her dead weight. When they eased their grasps, she struck out and kicked one in the bollocks and the other in the shin. She broke free and tried to run back to the Great Hall where she saw Magnus being taken. She felt hands grab hold of her, and this time she was lifted off her feet. She arched her back and thrashed until she felt a hand sink into her hair and wrench her head back. A sharp slap cracked across her face.

"You will gain control of yourself, or I will see you restrained. We have had enough of your self-involved, melodramatic performance. You will cease this rebellion, or I will have it ceased for you. You are one sideways glance away from being locked in a dungeon yourself," Lady Fraser threatened.

Deirdre froze at the mention of a dungeon.

"Oh yes, you should know that is where your lover ended up. I know you did not cease your tantrum because you fear being sent there. No, I know you did it to learn what became of the traitor."

"He is nae a traitor," Deirdre ground out.

"That is exactly what he is. He defied the king and went against the king's directive for you to marry Lord Archibald. That brands him a traitor, disloyal to the crown."

Deirdre began to laugh hysterically.

"Ye have lost yer mind if ye think anyone would believe a Sinclair is disloyal. Ye dinna ken that clan at all if ye think that will float higher than a turd."

Her mother's hand whipped across her face again.

"You will cease such crass speech. You will be done with that dreadful accent."

"Ye mean the same one ye had all yer life until seven years ago when ye became a pretentious social climber. Ye think I dinna remember what ye sounded like when

I was growing up. I was a woman wedded and bedded when ye brought me here. I remember it all."

"Cease!" her mother snapped.

They arrived at a chamber, but it was not hers. This one was dark and cold. She was pushed into it, alone, and the door slammed behind her. She heard the key turn in the lock and a bar drop across it. She could see nothing. She tried to move further into the room but stumbled into a crate. She felt around with her hands, but she encountered one crate after another. They had locked her into a storage closet. She sank to the floor and rest her head on her arms that she crossed over her knees.

Magnus, where are ye? I would ken if something serious happened to ye, wouldnae I? Ma mother said ye are in the dungeons. Is that so? Why? We didna do aught wrong. I love ye.

Deirdre let herself drift to sleep. There was nothing else she could do, and she needed the rest if she was to be prepared for whatever might happen next.

Deirdre awoke to the sound of the bar being lifted from her door and the key turning in the lock. Light poured in from the passageway, and she had to shield her eyes. Someone pulled her to her feet and dropped a sack over her head. Before she could fight back, she felt a rope being tied around her wrists. She was pulled into the passageway. The only noise was that of her captors moving about. She sniffed the air.

"Mother, Father, Archibald, ye should nae use such distinct fragrances. Yer expensive taste only makes ye easier to recognize. Father, this is what ye have come to? Mother convinced ye that ye should abduct yer own daughter from the king's keep. Magnus never had to force me to go with him. Consider that."

A hand wrapped around her throat and squeezed.

"You are mine now. Your father has signed the documents and the king sealed them. It no longer matters what your mother or father say or do. I make your decisions now, and if you would like to remain unharmed, I suggest you shut your mouth on your own," Hay leaned in to whisper in her ear, "or I will shut it with my cock."

He squeezed again before shoving her away. She stumbled but stayed silent. She was shuffled through the empty passageway until cold air hit her neck and shoulders. She still had her arisaid wrapped around her. No one had removed her Sinclair plaid. Not yet.

She heard several horses stomping impatiently. Before she could get her bearings properly, she felt herself flying. She landed belly down, hard, onto a saddle. Someone, Hay she realized, mounted behind her. A firm hand pressed against the small of her back.

"If you want to survive and not fall to your death below galloping hooves, I suggest you remain still."

With that, the horse lurched into a canter and then a gallop as the sounds of the hoofbeats changed from echoing on cobblestones to dirt. Several other horses clattered out after the one on which she lay. She was not sure if being hooded helped or not. Her head spun, and her stomach lurched, but not being able to see the shifting ground kept her from passing out.

They rode through the night and only stopped a handful of times the next day before continuing throughout the second night. Deirdre felt the horse flag under her when they eventually came to a stop. She was jerked from atop the horse and pushed up steps into a Great Hall. The hood was hauled over her head and blood rushed back into her arms and legs. She shook her head to focus on her surroundings as her limbs burned and tingled.

The Great Hall was dark with a small fire burning in one of the massive fireplaces. There were only a few people spread throughout the gathering area. They slept, unaware of the arrival of their lord and his guest. She refused to consider this as permanent.

Hay grasped her upper arm and a blade pressed against her throat.

"Speak, and I shall cut it."

He led her, none too gently, up the wide stairwell to the second floor. He pushed a door open and practically threw her into the room. She heard the all too familiar sound of a lock turning and bar dropping into place. She looked around and realized she was in the lord's chamber.

She moved to stand before the fire, chilled from traveling night and day with little food for close to a fortnight. She raised her hands to the fire and inspected the rope. No one thought to check her for weapons, so no one found any of the dirks on her body or in her boots. She would bide her time until she could make her escape.

She was not alone for long. The door opened, and Hay entered. Deirdre did not move, not even flinched, when he came to stand before her. He reached out and grabbed the front of her kirtle. He pulled her close and then palmed her breast.

"Small but perky. They will do." He ran his thumb over her breast until he found her nipple. He circled it and then squeezed. Deirdre bit her tongue, refusing to give him any response.

"I see. You still plan to be obstinate. I have plenty of ideas on how to cure you of that." He slipped his hand into the neckline of her kirtle, but before he could reach her nipple again, she stepped back.

"I am nae yer wife. I canna be. I have a marriage decree signed by Bishop Mackenzie from Ardchatton." She fumbled to pull the sealed vellum from the pocket she had found sewn into the kirtle. She freed the document and held it before her. "This proves I am another man's wife. Ye have nay claim over me."

"I have every claim I want. I am the one here. Your northern barbarian is not, now is he? I believe he is keeping company with the rats of the king's dungeon."

Hay plucked the parchment from her fingers. Curiosity got the better of him, and he ripped open the seal. He scanned the writ's contents and then tossed it in the fire. Deirdre did not flinch, and Hay's sneer slipped.

"Whether ye believe me married to ye or another mon, I am sure ye dinna want anyone questioning if the bairn I bear is yers or someone else's. Ye ken there is every likelihood I am already carrying Magnus's child. Bed me now, and ye will never be sure if yer heir is yers or if yer giving everything to a Sinclair."

Hay moved to stand so close to her that the toe of his boot tapped hers. He leaned so that his hot breath wafted across the bridge of her nose. She wanted to retreat, but she made herself hold her ground.

"There is more than one way to ensure you are not carrying that man's bastard. Since I need you to live long enough to bear me an heir, I suppose killing you will not work. The village healer can prepare you a tincture that will cleanse your womb of any unholy seed that may have planted itself there."

"Ye may as well kill me now."

"Such dramatics."

"Nay, ye really may as well kill me now. Ma parents gave me such a tincture when we arrived at court once they knew Magnus and I made love. It vera nearly killed me. I was violently ill for three days. I bled so much that the healer feared I would bleed to death. I vomited blood for a fortnight and could not keep anything down. By all means, if ye dinna intend to free me, then kill me and have done."

Hay gave her a long, hard look before stepping back.

"I am not usually a patient man, but I can wait a fortnight. I have other ways to entertain myself. I believe you know her. Mary Kerr has not defiled herself with some illiterate peasant."

When no look of surprise or dismay passed Deirdre's face, Hay stormed out and slammed the door shut.

I kenned he'd bedding the witch! It explains how Archibald could hunt near the king while someone tried to shoot Magnus. They conspired together. I wonder if they planned this all along or if greed makes strange bedfellows.

Deirdre heard horses below the chamber window. The sun was just rising, and she saw Hay mounting a horse.

Where is he going now? Is he leaving me here?

Deirdre ran back to the door, but she already knew it was locked. She rushed back to the window in time to see Hay ride out with his entourage following. Deirdre stared in disbelief as they faded over the rise. She remembered seeing people sleeping in the Great Hall, but she had no idea if anyone even knew she was locked in here. She forced herself to calm as she puzzled through the situation.

This isnae the first time ye've been locked away while others wait to see if ye are increasing.

~ ~ ~

"I willnae drink that! Ye canna make me. I warn ye, I will only spit it out."

Deirdre thrashed her head from side to side, her hair coming loose. Her sisters held her in the chair, one pinning her arms behind her while the other pulled her hair back. Her mother pried her jaw open and poured the bitter tincture into her mouth. Deirdre had already taken a deep breath through her nose, so when she felt the liquid pool in her mouth, she blew hard from deep within her throat. The foul brew spewed from her and splattered across her mother's face. Her mother stared at her in disbelief before slapping her.

"I dinna ken who ye have turned into since meeting that beast, but ye arenae the daughter I raised."

"Ye raised?" Deirdre laughed raucously.

"Ye ungrateful wretch. Ye would squander yer family's opportunities all because some behemoth lad turned yer head. Are ye that desperate for attention since ye dinna inherit the good looks yer sisters did?"

Deirdre sensed her sisters shrink away from their mother's vitriol. Deirdre was used to her mother's caustic comments about her insufficiency. They still hurt, but they no longer created the desperation they once did.

"Magnus chose me. This time around ye didna have to buy a husband for yer daughter." Deirdre heard her sisters' gasps. She regretted being unkind to them until she remembered who had her pinned to the chair.

Lady Fraser once again stepped to her daughter's side. This time, she pinched Deirdre's nose close. She waited until Deirdre had no choice but to open her mouth and suck in air. She quickly poured the brew down Deirdre's throat not pausing despite her daughter's coughing and spluttering. When the last drop dripped from the cup, her mother stepped back.

"It doesnae matter what either of ye chose. Ye willnae be carrying a bastard by morn."

Deirdre looked defiantly at her mother. At that moment, she had never hated anyone as much as she did her mother.

Her mother took a deep breath and patted her hair back into place. She straightened her gown before looking back at Deirdre. Deirdre recognized her mother's court persona had slipped back into place.

"Daughter, you would do well to remember that this lad you claim to love did not even wait until you left the keep before he was in the mead tent with a woman splayed across him, her bosom heaving before him. You may think you love him, but

188

clearly, the feelings are not mutual." Maeve Fraser stared down at her daughter's crestfallen face and smiled. She nodded to her two older daughters, and the three women left the room. Not an ounce of remorse passed through the older woman. Not for her rough treatment of her daughter or the lie she told.

Deirdre woke to an excruciating pain gripping her midsection. She could not tell if it was her stomach or her back that was causing her such agony. She tried to roll over, but the cramps seized her and stole her breath. She moved her legs and a flood was unleashed from between her thighs. She pulled herself up to look at what drenched her. The entire bedding around her was soaked crimson.

Dear merciful heavens. That is blood!

Deirdre let forth a bloodcurdling scream that bounced around the walls of the chamber, slid under the door, and echoed through the passageway. Her screams continued as pain ripped through every inch of her as her body hemorrhaged. Her mother and father burst into her chamber. Laird Fraser took one look at the bloody sheets and blanched. The battle-tested warrior thought he might collapse at the sight of his youngest daughter surrounded by blood. Lady Fraser merely grinned and clapped once.

"Donald, we have naught to worry about now."

Laird Fraser looked blankly at his wife.

"How can ye say that? Our daughter is dying."

"Don't be foolish. She is not dying, but her body is purging her of the bastard she must have carried."

Deirdre released another scream that sent shivers along everyone's spine who heard it. It was a mixture of pure pain and heartbreaking agony. Her sisters huddled in the corner, wide-eyed and shocked to see what was happening to her. Deirdre's cries continued as she curled into a ball, feeling as though a flame burned through her middle and that every inch of her insides was being torn from her.

A crowd was beginning to form in the passageway when the queen stepped into the chamber. Her gasp brought all eyes swinging from Deirdre's to the royal. Bows and curtseys were made and ignored as the queen rushed to Deirdre's side.

"Child what has happened to you?" The queen looked around and summoned the healer.

Deirdre could do nothing, but sob as black dots danced around the corners of her eyes. She tried to move past the pain, but it consumed every cell of her being. She wished for death at that moment if it meant a release from the pain. She moaned as she prayed that Magnus could find her and rescue her once more.

"Magnus. Magnus. Where is Magnus?" she whispered.

"What is that, my child? Who are you asking for?" the queen leaned forward. "Who is this Magnus?"

"Ma husband," was the last thing that Deirdre whispered for a sennight.

She floated between darkness and lucidity. She thought she heard Magnus's voice but when she reached for him, there was no one to touch. No one came near her except for one pair of cool and soft hands. Someone tended to her but never said more than a few calming words. Escaping to the blackness was easier than the pain in her body or of knowing Magnus was not there.

"She's rousing, ma lady. Her fever broke in the night."

"Very well. Thank you. You may go."

"But, my lady, she is still very ill. She still needs constant care."

Deirdre heard her mother's beleaguered sigh. Her refined tones were once again in place, gone was the Highlander and back was the courtier.

"Fine, but she is not to know there was never any child. She is not to know there was no reason for this to happen. Is that understood? If she learns of it, I will know it came from you, and I will have you sent away with no coin and no references."

"Aye, ma lady."

Deirdre kept her eyes closed as she took in all that she heard. She was never pregnant. She and Magnus had not made a child together. There was never a baby to lose. She curled into a ball. The pain of losing what might have been, what could have been, was as excruciating as experiencing the purge all over again. Tears leaked from her clenched eyes. She buried her sobs in her pillow.

"It's all right, lass. She is gone now. Ye dinna have to cower. Let it out, lass." The gentle hands Deirdre recognized soothed her and brushed back her curls. "I ken ye heard me speak to yer mother. I dinna agree in the least. Ye should ken that ye were never carrying. There was nae evidence of a bairn. Yer life was at risk for nay reason than fear and pride. Ye had a vera serious reaction to what ye mother gave ye. Lass, listen and hear me well. Ye canna ever have one of these purging tinctures again. Ye body doesnae tolerate it. Ye vera nearly died. If it's given to ye again and there isnae a skilled healer nearby, ye will die."

Deirdre could only look at the woman and nod. She rolled back onto her side and sobbed until sleep swept her away again.

~ ~ ~

Deirdre placed her hands protectively over her belly. She was certain she was carrying this time. She felt different after she and Magnus made love at the rocks. She knew that instant she had conceived. Something within her told her, and she believed the silent voice.

190

With Hay gone, she no longer feared being molested. She sat down on the bed and then laid down. She would not cut her bindings yet, not until she knew who her jailor was or if Hay would return, but she would rest.

Chapter Twenty-One

Magnus massaged the area around his aching wound. He was sure that infection was setting in despite having the gaping incision seared close. His head felt hot again, and his skin was clammy. Or it could have all been from his days spent below ground in the rat-infested dungeon he now called home for his indefinite future. The first couple of days were easy compared to now. He was left in virtual solitude. His only visitor was the guard who brought him water and gruel once a day. If it was possible for water to be stale, then what he was served would qualify. He was not convinced that water was all he was receiving. The gruel consisted of fatty putrifying meat and some other substance with a runny consistency. He ate and drank only enough to keep himself alive. They searched him and removed most of his daggers before they threw him into his cell. There were a few left on him in places the guards had not thought to look. This made him grin. Not for the last time did he marvel at the differences in culture between the northern and southern halves of his country. Anyone from his region would have known where to look for his extra blades.

His cell was swallowed in darkness, so he did not fear pulling one of these extra dirks loose from within his stocking. He kept it gripped in his hand while he dozed. When he felt the razor incisors of a four-legged intruder, he stabbed the rodent and flung it across the cell. He attempted to estimate the size of his cell without moving. He determined how wide it was by how long it took for the flying carcass to hit the far wall. His cell was tiny.

Magnus spent as much time as he could asleep those first few days. His body resigned to not leaving the dank underworld, his mind released him to restorative sleep. He never would have bedded down there voluntarily, but it was better than being dead, he decided. However, not even sleep was a reprieve from the ever-present fear for Deirdre. His gut churned with the need to know where she was and how she fared. He was beside himself that Hay or her parents might mistreat her.

The sound of Hay's voice was a double-edged sword to Magnus when the man's jeering tones roused him on the fourth day. Hay's presence meant he was not terrorizing Deirdre, but his presence meant that Magnus's reprieve came to an end.

"How low the mighty have fallen. You seem to be quite at home within this squalor. Mayhap it reminds you of home? The king contends you should be moved to a chamber rather than keep you here, but I argue against casting pearls before swine. What need do you have in the niceties of a chamber? After all, you are being branded a traitor for defying our king."

Hay turned to speak to someone that Magnus could not see. The door to his cell scraped open and Magnus hurried to slip his dirk back into the sheath on his hip before the light from the torch landed on him. He raised his arms to block out the offensively bright light and succeeded only in offering something for the guard to grab onto. They hauled him to his feet and drawn out of the chamber. Magnus waited for his eyes to adjust before lifting his head to stare at Hay. He knew there was not much he could do, but he had not lost his ability to intimidate most men with his sheer size and singular focus. The guard pulled him along by his bound wrists, but Magnus continued to stare at Hay without speaking. They led him into a large chamber with a high wooden table in the center. Magnus did not need any hints to understand where he currently stood. Rather than look around at the instruments of his upcoming torment, he continued to stare down Hay.

Magnus would not look away, and his stare finally drew Hay in. Their eyes locked, and Magnus saw something flash through them. There was malice and cruelty, but there was also a moment of uncertainty. It was gone before he could be sure.

"My wife sends her regards," Hay taunted.

"I hadnae heard ye wed the Kerr bitch. My felicitations."

"I may fuck her, but I would never marry her. No. no. Deirdre was asking about you. She wondered what became of you."

"So, it is my name she calls out?" Magnus's gut clenched at the thought that this vile man may have violated Deirdre. He would fish for information if he had to.

"She screamed, but it was never your name." Hay threw back.

Magnus ground his teeth together as he waited for the next volley of words. Instead, Hay nodded, and a second guard appeared. Between the two, they led Magnus to the table. One man kicked the back of Magnus's knees, forcing him to the table. They tugged him onto the wooden platform and stretched his arms and legs to the shackles that hung from the sides. The weight on his injury was more excruciating than the torment that began immediately. A cat o' nine tails swished through the air, cracking seconds before it landed across his back. Magnus arched in pain but refused to make a sound. The whip landed twice more before Hay paused to hurl more insults.

"Thank you for breaking her in for me. She is skilled in servicing a man. I must credit you for a job well done. And despite being a bit overused, her sheath is still tighter than my fist."

Magnus sucked in air through his nose and tried to ignore the grating sounds of his tormentor's voice. Hay walked to him and leaned in close.

"I had no idea that all of her tasted like apples. Quite a tasty morsel. I rather enjoyed my apple tart."

Magnus growled, and Hay laughed.

"With four siblings, I would think you're used to sharing."

The whip hissed as it cut the silence before splaying Magnus's back open again. His leine was in tatters, and he could feel the threads sticking to his newest wounds. The pain in his back distracted him from the pain in his leg. He was sure it was not a mercy. Hay nodded once again to a guard who ripped the back of Magnus's shirt clear of his back. The chill breeze that came from somewhere Magnus could not identify eased some of the sting in his exposed skin. No one ever lashed him before, but he had survived his share of beatings in the lists and in battle.

The leather throngs continued to bite into his back, lash after lash, but Magnus no longer listened to the droning taunts that Hay doled out. His mind drifted to various memories he collected over the three years of his courtship with Deirdre. He thought of the conversations they shared about her studies, most often held among the leaves of her favorite climbing trees. His mind jumped to the numerous jokes they shared in their missives. He remembered their first kiss in the Graham library. He remembered how she tasted the first time he brought her to climax. He let his mind wander to the first time they made love. He lingered there as he pictured them in the cave. That memory morphed into the one at the boulders. He forced himself to keep his mind on Deirdre and not the torture he endured. It was only when Hay's voice flagged, and frustration filled it that Magnus brought himself back to the present.

"I suppose you never knew she carried your child all those years ago." Magnus's head jerked up as his reverie, born out of mental necessity, came to a screeching halt. "Oh, so you did not know. Such a pity you could not enjoy that child or the one she just lost."

Magnus howled as a pain slashed through him far more potent than anything physical.

"You did not think I would allow her to bear me a bastard. I thought I was being kind ridding her of the parasite rather than drowning it at birth."

Magnus felt a violent need to punish the man course through every muscle, bone, and synapse of his body. He funneled all his strength into ripping one then the other arm cuff loose. He strained to free his legs and rocked the table until it almost overturned. The guardsmen who had been silent witnesses rushed to seize him and subdue him, but Magnus was beyond the point of any self-control. He reached to his stocking and pulled a dirk free. He reared onto his knees and swung. His wide wingspan allowed him to slash closer to one guard than any of his captors expected. The guard jumped back and would have landed against the door if it had not swung open.

"*Hay!* I will kill ye!" Magnus's head whipped around at the sound of his brother's voice. "The king didna authorize ye to torture ma brother. Ye dinna want to obey? Neither do I."

Magnus watched as Tavish stormed into the chamber with his sword drawn. Hay circled the whip in the air before attempting to lash out at Tavish. Hay wasted the time spent building the whip's momentum because Tavish thrust his sword into his side.

"Magnus, would ye like the honor of killing this pile of dung, or can I just be done?"

"Neither." Tavish glanced at Magnus.

"Neither? Why the hell nae?"

"I have just the perfect place for him to visit."

"Purgatory?"

"It shall feel more like hell."

"Then it willna be a visit. More like a new home."

"That's aboot the right of it."

Throughout their banter, Hay pressed his hand to his side. His knees weakened as the torture device fell to the floor beside him. He slowly sank to the ground and then keeled over.

"Tav, did ye kill him? I told ye nae to do that." Magnus could see Hay's back still rising and falling, but it was his turn to be tormentor rather than tormented.

Tavish looked for the guards, but both men fled some time during the confrontation. Tavish rushed to unfasten Magnus's legs and helped him from the table.

"Och, Magnus. Ye're in a right state. I dinna ken what to say."

"That's a first," Magnus's quip lost its bite as he groaned in pain.

"We need to get ye to the healer sharpish. Ye dinna look well."

"Ye must be pleased aboot that. Ye might finally be the handsome brother if never the tall one."

Tavish barked out a laugh. The four brothers were all a similar height and build. It was obvious that Magnus was the broadest of them all, his frame larger and bulkier, but Tavish was barely a hair's breadth shorter than the other three. It was an endless source of teasing among the men, despite Tavish bearing the closest resemblance to their father, who was a veritable bear with a barrel chest and thick limbs. There was nothing to underestimate about Tavish when it came to him compared to his brothers. They were all deadly with their charm and their weapons.

"Ye canna be that close to dead if ye still have yer sense of humor." Tavish supported Magnus as they moved to the door.

"Are ye sure ye didna kill him?"

"Bah, the wee mon just canna handle a little twinge. It isnae like I ran him through. Naught but a scratch to the ribs. Probably just canna stomach the sight of his own blood." Tavish used his boot to roll Hay over. Blood was visible on the man's doublet, but Tavish was correct. The wound did not look that serious. "Someone will find him here soon enough."

They walked from the chamber only to encounter the two guards who seemed to find their courage.

"Where do ye think ye're going? This mon's a prisoner of the king."

Tavish moved to walk past them as Magnus leaned heavily on him, but the men stepped in front. Magnus and Tavish looked at one another. Magnus was in no condition to fight. The strength used to free himself from his bindings had been for nothing once his brother showed up. Exhausted, he simply wanted to lie down, even if it was in his cell. He shook his head slightly, and despite his disbelief, Tavish relented.

"Vera well. I will go to the king directly. When I return for his release, ma brother will have been given real fresh water nae the pish ye give prisoners." Tavish's words echoed throughout the catacomb of cells. "Do ye understand? I dinna need to be clearer, do I?"

The guards saw Magnus rip free of the restraints and how Tavish fought Hay. They did not need further convincing. They nodded and led the way back to Magnus's cell.

"I will be back as soon as I can, little brother. Dinna fash. Ye'll nae even have time to miss me." Tavish grinned as the guard shut and locked the door between them.

"Tav, what aboot Deir?" Magnus asked as Tavish turned away.

Tavish paused and looked back at him.

"I dinna ken. Nay one has seen her in days. Her parents insist that she is unwell and confined to her chamber. I have heard otherwise. I believe she isnae here anymore, but I dinna ken where she is either."

Magnus swallowed as he took this in. Perhaps Hay had not molested her, but perhaps she was ill too.

"Tavish, wait. I need ye to give something to the king." Magnus dug into his sporran and pulled the sealed vellum out. "It's our marriage decree."

Tavish nodded once and rushed from the dungeon.

Did she really lose our bairn? Did she survive? Deir, where are ye? I will find ye, and once I do, I willna ever leave yer side again. I dinna care aboot aught else but being with ye. Da can keep me training the men and overseeing the armory, or I will become a farmer, but I amnae leaving ye again.

Magnus felt the blackness creeping around the corner of his eyes, and it was not the lack of light in his chamber. His head floated above him, and his body felt lighter than it should have. He rolled to his side, trying to keep his weight off his thigh and his back. He moaned once before surrendering to the abyss.

"Uncle Hamish, I saw Magnus," Tavish confided as he took a seat next to his uncle in the Great Hall.

"Aye," Hamish said under his breath as he brought his mug of ale to his mouth.

"Hay got to him."

Hamish lowered the mug and looked at his nephew.

"Cat o' nine tails."

Hamish swore loudly. He pushed the bench back so hard that it wobbled even with Tavish's weight to hold it in place. He stepped over it and walked purposefully to the dais. Tavish was not far behind.

"Laird Sutherland, I see you found your other nephew. Quite the family reunion here at court," the king smiled but it did not reach his eyes.

"I would like to reunite with ma other nephew. It seems ye saw fit to see him tortured. I would like to ensure he will survive."

"What?" The king slammed his hand on the table as his goblet crashed down. "You are accusing me of torture. On what grounds?"

"On the grounds that Tavish just came from the dungeons where he found Magnus beaten and lashed by a cat o' nine tails."

"I did not authorize that." The king looked around and frowned. "Hay. Where is Lord Hay?"

The king's face turned purple with rage when a page leaned in to whisper in his ear.

"That man oversteps for the final time. Fraser, you have a fair amount to explain when this is said and done," the king looked at Deirdre's father who sat a few men down. Looking back at Hamish and Tavish, the king looked slightly embarrassed.

"It seems Lord Hay took matters into his own hands. No one was given instructions or permission to abuse Magnus. Tavish, it seems you have handled the matter of Lord Hay." The king turned his head in dismissal.

"Yer Majesty, I amnae even nearly done with the matter of Lord Hay. I amnae content to leave ma brother to fester and die, either. He is badly beaten and in need of a healer. This never should have happened. Ma brother and his *wife* are legally wed. I have the proof here." Tavish pulled the parchment from his sporran and stepped forward.

The king frowned at his uninvited approach but nodded when a page took it from Tavish.

"Bishop Mackenzie?" The king muttered as he examined the scroll. He pulled the wax seal loose and unfolded the document. He scanned through, but then reread it with more care. When he had read it three times, he lowered it and looked around. Everyone at the dais knew of the situation, and silent faces stared between the king and Tavish and Hamish.

"There is more here than just the formal statement of a marriage. Tavish, it would seem all you stated upon your arrival is accurate. Bishop Mackenzie has provided multiple dates to corroborate your accounting of Magnus and Lady Deirdre's relationship. In the eyes of the church, the couple has been married for the past seven years. Their exchange of vows before the bishop was a reaffirmation of their union not the initiation of a new one." The king stroked his chin before leaning forward to look at the Fraser again. "I cannot set aside, nor do I want to, a union blessed by God. There is sanctity in marriage, and this marriage has weathered enough storms. That said, Tavish, your father will pay a bride price to the Frasers that is well past due. You shall give the same amount to the court as recompense for the time spent providing for Magnus's wife as she served the queen."

The statement was outlandish and unreasonable but a small price to pay for freedom.

"Name the price, Sire. I believe I can have it arranged before morn."

"How can you be so sure you can afford such terms?"

Tavish looked at the king, his patience was not his virtue.

"When Magnus didna return when expected, we feared something happened to him. Our fears are justified. Ma father sent me with a ransom chest in case I should need to buy his freedom." Tavish looked at Laird Fraser and then back to the king. "I came well prepared."

"Very well. Retrieve your coin, and I will have Magnus sent to his chamber. He is free from the dungeon, but until you settle the bride price, he remains in royal custody."

"Vera well, Sire. Will ye send his wife to him now? I understand she has been poorly, but I am sure they would prefer to recover together." Tavish's pointed questions had many people looking around to see if Deirdre was present.

"I will have her sent to him forthwith."

"Your Grace," Fraser cleared his throat, "that will not be possible. At least not immediately."

The king raised one eyebrow.

"Your Grace, Lady Deirdre is not at court right now. She resides where we believed she would live with her husband. Or rather Lord Archibald," he amended.

"Where exactly is she?"

"Crichton, Sire."

"That is the other side of Edinburgh!" The king slammed his hand on the table again. "Fraser, you are testing my patience."

The king waved a man over from the far end of the dais.

"Have Magnus freed. Give him food, clothing, whatever aid he needs. See his horse is ready whenever he decides to ride out." The king looked haggard when he glanced over at Hamish and Tavish. "This wrong will be righted."

Chapter Twenty-Two

Magnus stank. He could smell himself, and he wanted to heave. All he wanted was to find his brother, arrange for a bath, and have his wounds covered in a salve. He wished he could sleep for a sennight, but despite his pain and flagging strength, his need to reach Deirdre surpassed all else. The last thing he wanted was to face Deirdre's cousin Elizabeth. He tried to be polite but between his injuries and his hygiene, he simply wanted to make it to his chamber alone. Elizabeth seemed to be of another mind.

"Lord Magnus, please will you wait just a moment? I know this is a most inopportune time, but there is something you must know. Dee could be dangerously ill. As in life-threateningly ill."

Magnus halted and spun around to look at the young woman's distraught face. He realized she was not exaggerating. She was out of breath, and her eyes darted about as she scanned to see if they were alone.

"When Deirdre arrived here seven years ago, her parents worried that she might be carrying your child. My aunt found some woman in town who gave her a tincture intended to rid Deirdre of a child. She fought against it, but her mother got it down her, and she became violently ill. She bled for days and days then had a raging fever. The healer at the time cared for her, but it was nearly too late. Deirdre was never carrying, but the healer said she had a horrible reaction to the medicinal anyway. The healer warned her parents she was never to have anything like it again, or she might die. I fear what her parents or Hay may give her since they took her."

"How do ye ken all of this? And what do ye mean taken?"

"I was excited when my cousin arrived at court, but she was mysteriously kept out of sight and then became ill, my curiosity got the better of me. I hid behind the wall of her chamber. I opened the door just a crevice and heard everything the day the healer gave her warning. Deirdre was awake and heard too, but I do not think her mother ever found out what Deirdre, or I, discovered."

Magnus listened in disbelief to what happened to Deirdre all those years ago, what she endured. His heart ached for her all over again. The separation altered his personality in many ways, but his life was never in danger. Guilt flooded him as once again he struggled to overcome his failures.

"And taken? What did ye mean by taken?"

Elizabeth's face was ghostly and drawn while she recounted the tale of Deirdre's near-poisoning, but now it grew cherry red with anger.

"Once again, my aunt and uncle locked her into a chamber, except it wasn't hers. It was a storage room. When they and Hay were ready for her to leave, they put a sack over her head, so she would not know where they took her. I saw Hay toss her over his saddle onto her stomach and ride away. I did not know where he took her, but, as you learned, she is now at Crichton. If Hay is here, I can only imagine who is caring for her."

"I dinna ken if that is a blessing in disguise."

"Magnus!" He turned to see his brother approaching with a woman he had met once or twice before. He could not remember for sure. The woman carried a basket over her arm and looked dour compared to how she appeared in the past.

"Magnus, this is Ceit," Tavish said when they stopped before Magnus and Elizabeth. "She has knowledge of the healing arts. I asked her to take a look at yer wounds, and she agreed."

Magnus tried to smile but grunted instead.

"I amnae ready yet for ye to tend them." He looked down at his soiled clothes and filthy skin.

"I ken. I've already had a bath sent to yer chamber. Once ye are presentable, Ceit has a salve for yer back and yer leg."

"I dinna mean to be unappreciative, but canna ye just give the salve to ma brother?"

"Lord Magnus, I need to look to see the extent of the damage. Ye could have an infection starting. If that's the case, then I must treat it differently than I would just a deep cut. As for yer leg, I need to be sure ye sealed it thoroughly. If it wasna, then I may have to reopen it and cut away the putrid skin."

"That was already done before Deirdre branded it shut."

"That doesnae mean it is healing."

The woman was soft-spoken, and someone could easily mistake her for timid, but the resolve in her eyes made Magnus wonder who she was. She had a burr when she spoke to them, but he was positive he had not heard it previously.

"Ye're wondering aboot ma speech. I havenae been at court that vera long. If I concentrate, then I can hide ma accent, but I dinna see a need with ye." She nodded to Tavish, Magnus, and Elizabeth.

"Vera well." Magnus sighed.

He knew when he was outnumbered, and this was one of those times. The trio followed Magnus to his chambers. At his door, Elizabeth paused.

201

"I will fetch some of her belongings. She will need at least fresh clothing."

"Thank ye, Elizabeth."

"Beth. Dee calls me Beth in private. We are family now." She hurried away to complete her errand.

Magnus entered his chamber but blocked the doorway. He turned to look over Ceit's head at Tavish. He frowned before looking down.

"I amnae coming in, so dinna fash. I amnae interested in watching a mon bathe." Tavish's scowl did not go unnoticed by Magnus, but he was not interested in his brother's latest conquest. "There is a special soap in there that I would have ye use to clean yer back."

She turned to look over her shoulder at Tavish and raised an eyebrow when she saw his scowl. He was looking at his brother, so she did not realize what caused an expression that did not match his usual charm.

"Ye have to help him."

"What?" Both men responded.

"I havenae needed anyone to bathe me since I was just out of short pants."

Ceit looked between them in disbelief.

"Ye're brothers. It's nae like either of ye havenae seen the other in the buff. Ye have the same parts. There is nay way, Magnus, that ye will be able to scrub yer own back. Tavish, help yer brother. Dinna be selfish."

Tavish glared down at her, but she was already looking back at Magnus.

"Unless ye would prefer I summon a maid."

"Nay." Magnus shook his head. He had never enjoyed the notion of someone else bathing him like he was a bairn or feeble.

On second thought. If it were Deir, I think I could quite enjoy a bath. Especially, if she's in it with me. And I can use ma tongue to clean her off.

"Magnus. Stop fantasizing aboot yer wife. Ye can do that on yer horse on the way to fetch her."

"Right."

Magnus took the basket from Ceit and stepped into the room. Tavish moved around her but paused at Ceit's soft hand on his arm.

"Dinna be afraid to be a bit rough. I can see already that his leine has dried into some of the cuts. Ye must get them completely clean. There canna be even a single thread left in one if ye want to prevent infection."

Tavish saw the seriousness in her eyes and nodded.

By the time Magnus finished bathing, Elizabeth returned allowing Ceit to enter the chamber accompanied. The healer made short work of examining Magnus's wounds and slathered gobs of salve onto his back before wrapping him from armpit to waist in fresh bandages.

"Magnus, I heard Hay departed the castle half an hour ago. No one knows where he headed, but I would venture a guess. Be careful and hurry." Elizabeth warned as Ceit worked.

They exited Magnus's chambers, and the men turned to leave.

"Magnus, don't forget Dee's things. And Ceit, here are yours. I gathered clothes for you too."

"Nay. Absolutely nae. Lass, ye canna come with us. I dinna ken what we are riding into." Tavish took Ceit by the arm and pulled her away.

Magnus watched as a heated debate ensued. Despite employing his own Odin stance, Magnus knew his brother's goose was cooked. He did not oppose to Ceit coming since he feared the condition in which he might find Deirdre, but Tavish seemed adamant she not. It did not take long before Magnus recognized Tavish's capitulation. He dropped his arms and growled. The young woman tapped him on the chest twice and turned to Magnus and Elizabeth. From her blush, she clearly forgot there were others about who saw their familiarity. She set her shoulders and walked over, taking the bundle from Elizabeth.

"We ride," Magnus announced.

Chapter Twenty-Three

The three riders pushed their horses as hard as they dared, stopping only when the horses were lathered and panting too hard to continue. Ceit surprised Magnus by how well she held her own. She was a strong woman despite her courtly appearance. She had not stopped to change and rode astride in her ornate gown. She seemed unconcerned and disinterested about its condition. As long as she kept up, Magnus did not care what she wore or how she rode. They picked up Hay's trail but were never able to catch him despite gaining on him. They arrived at the Hay keep midafternoon of the second day.

"State yer business," came the call from the wall walk.

"I am Magnus Sinclair, and I am here to claim my wife," he boomed.

"For the last time, savage. She is not your wife," came the irate voice of Archibald Hay from the battlement.

Magnus looked up and saw the man gripping the stones in front of him and wrapping an arm around his middle. Magnus would swear that he could see the man's knuckles turn white.

"She is ma wife. Ye ken it, I ken it, the king and God ken it. Ye will release her, or I will kill ye. We arenae at court anymore. I willnae be so compliant for the sake of the king. Return her to me now, or I will take her back by force."

Deirdre heard a commotion coming from the bailey below her chamber window. She was shut away for days and was wondering if Hay forgot about her. She prayed he had. She was alone the entire time with a young servant girl bringing her two small meals a day. She saw no one else, not even men training in the lists or servants moving about the bailey. On occasion, she heard voices from outside, but the window angle precluded her from seeing anything.

"Return her to me now, or I will take her back by force." Deirdre heard from below.

Magnus! He's come. He's found me, but how? That doesnae even matter. How am I going to get to him? I ken they lock the door as I couldnae open it the last time I tried. Mayhap I should have tried to push past the lass, but where would I have gone then. How would I have gotten away without being spotted? Magnus!

Deirdre's mind swirled like a tropical storm as her thoughts jumped from place to place. She went to the window and pulled the glass open. She had cut her bindings within an hour of Hay's last departure. When the serving girl came, she did not say anything about Deirdre being untied, so Deirdre did not bring it up. She leaned as far forward as she could and craned her neck. She could just barely see an angry man gesturing from atop the battlements. She tried to see the other side, but it was impossible; however, she recognized Magnus's voice.

"Come down and fight like a mon. I challenge ye to single combat as is ma right. Dinna be chicken shite, face me like a mon. Or can ye nay do it without the assistance of a guardsman? Nae prepared for a fair fight? Only when ye are sure of an advantage. Ye're naught more than a coward. Nay wonder the king makes ye stay behind when the real men ride out with his standard."

Magnus continued to taunt and lob insults at Hay who swore and paced. Deirdre could see Hay's agitation and wanted to laugh if she was not so focused on how to escape her chamber. She looked around and saw nothing that would open a door locked from the outside. She ran to the armoire and said a prayer of thanksgiving when she found extra linens stacked at the bottom. She pulled the sheets out and looked between the bed and window. She did not relish her plan, but she could not see any other option. She divested the bed of all its covers and tied the sheets together. She wrapped one end around the bedpost twice before knotting it. She tied the other end around her waist and stepped to the sill. She looked behind her once more before swinging her leg out. As she pivoted to pull her other leg out, she had a moment of doubt, but she scooted off the ledge until she was ready to hang.

What am I doing? I shouldnae tied the end around me. I thought it would catch me if I fell, but now I dinna have aught to climb down. Shite! I canna pull maself back up, and I dinna feel much for ma feet to stand on. Now what?

Get yerself together, lass. Magnus walked the ledge outside yer window how many times? Dinna be a ninny.

Deirdre forced herself to stop and think. She realized that if she held onto the sheet and leaned back a little, she could walk down the wall rather than shimmy or slide down the sheet. She took a deep breath and began her descent.

Magnus caught sight of movement from the corner of his eye. He tried to ignore it, but a flash of yellow had his sliding his eyes over to the left. He did not move his head as he had a sneaking suspicion about what he would see, and he did not want

Hay to notice. His heart lurched so high he was sure it hit the back of his teeth. He watched as Deirdre wiggled out of a window and paused. He thought he would expire right there and then. Then his heart kicked into a rapid staccato as he watched her work her way down what he realized were sheets.

Deir! What the bluidy hell are ye doing? Ye waited this long. Ye couldnae give me a moment more? If ye break yer ruddy neck, I'll thrash ye.

Magnus waved to his brother whose horse sat just behind him to the right.

"Tav, to the left. Up."

"Fuck!" came his brother's uncouth response.

"Shite," came a feminine whisper that was enough to have both brothers looking at Ceit. She shrugged, and Magnus pulled his focus back to Hay.

"Hay, ye're stalling. What's it to be? Are ye willing to accept ma challenge of single combat or nay?"

"I could just have ye shot from here."

"Ye could, but ye willna."

"How can ye be so sure?"

"Do ye think I traveled with only ma one brother and a lass? How quickly ye forget the three scores of men who rode out with me on the hunt after yer little stunt with the arrows."

"You and I both know I was not responsible for that, though I wish I could take the credit for it."

"They may have been Lady Mary's men, but I am sure as it rains in Scotland, that ye had a hand in it. Ye arranged for the dead bird on ma bed."

"I cannot entirely take credit for that either. Mary's idea but I did make the arrangements."

"Ye're quite the pair."

Magnus kept Hay talking as Tavish maneuvered his horse to the left to better keep an eye on Deirdre's progress. As long as Hay did not see the movement, then Magnus was confident that Deirdre would have enough time to make it to the ground.

"Enough dithering aboot, Hay. Be a mon or admit ye arenae brave enough to fight me one on one. Mayhap Lady Mary kept yer bollocks that last time ye tupped her. Are yer twig and berries really just that?"

"You are rather arrogant for a man who just took a lashing from me."

"I am also the same mon who's ridden here in record time and has been ready to fight since I arrived. I amnae the one being evasive. Have done already, mon."

"Lord Archibald," Magnus shot an angry glare at Ceit, but that did not stop her. "I would think with Lady Mary in residence, you would want to prove to her that you can vanquish her nemesis. Her hatred of the Sinclairs may very well be stronger than your hatred of just Magnus. I am surprised she is not here insisting you accept the challenge. Or do you want her to see you passed up the opportunity she so craves for herself but will never be granted?"

"She's here?" Magnus whispered.

Ceit shrugged and whispered back.

"She wasna seen at court the last few days, we all ken they are lovers, and Hay's run off too. Where else would she be? She kens if they have Deirdre, ye will come. I would bet a pound to a penny she orchestrated this entire ordeal to punish ye and to rid herself of competition."

"Birds of a feather. They can have each other."

"If all goes well, there will only be one left."

"I'm sure Mary will be chomping at the bit to forgive me then."

"Very well," Hay called down.

Magnus heard the gate crank open. He looked through the portcullis and saw Lady Mary standing in the courtyard. Magnus led Tavish and Ceit into the bailey as Hay descended the stairs. Magnus's eyes darted to the left as once again motion attracted his peripheral vision. Deirdre was creeping along the side of the building with a dirk in each hand. She caught Magnus's eye and flashed a smile before gesturing with her head for him to look ahead.

He dismounted *Sealgair* and dropped the reins. He knew his horse would go nowhere until summoned. He drew his sword as Hay circled him. He allowed the other man to position himself before Magnus began his own circle. He made sure that when he made the initial contact, Hay could not see past him to Deirdre. They danced about one another; Magnus always ensuring that Hay could not see Deirdre.

Hay's impatience got the better of him, and he was the first to lunge. His thinner sword, only half the width of Magnus's, would have been formidable against most opponents as it was quicker and easier to yield. However, Magnus, just like his brothers, handled a sword as though he were born to it. It was no longer merely a weapon but a part of him that was indivisible from him. Magnus parried each of Hay's thrusts and allowed the man to tire and grow impatient. They both suffered from their injuries.

"You were the one who wanted this, and now you dance around like a rag doll avoiding the fight you asked for," Hay panted.

"I amnae avoiding aught." Magnus used Hay's tactical error of speaking, making his breathing more difficult. He released his left hand from the hilt and thrust his sword forward as he flicked his wrist to release the dirk from his bracer. Now, not only did he fight two-handed again, but he fought with two weapons. Magnus attacked with a flurry of sword swings and dagger thrusts. He hit home in more than one place. He stabbed into Hay's sword arm as his claymore cleaved through Hay's ribs. He pulled his sword back, and as Hay's arm went limp and he looked down to his side, Magnus thrust his sword through his opponent's chest.

207

"I warned ye in the alcove to never touch her again. Ye should have listened." He pulled his sword free as Hay crumpled to the ground dead.

A horrible, high pitched screech traveled across the bailey as Mary Kerr ran towards him with her arm raised and a nasty dagger clasped in her hand.

"You've taken everything! Everything! I will kill you for this. Mark my—"

She did not finish as Deirdre stepped from the shade and moved in front of her. Mary impaled herself as Deirdre thrust the dagger into her belly. As Deirdre felt the blade sink through the skin, she twisted and pulled up, ensuring as much damage as she could. She stepped back and saw Mary's horrified expression as the other woman looked down at the dirk embedded in her abdomen.

"You," blood bubbled from her mouth. She tried to pry the blade free and howled in pain. The moment she succeeded, blood poured forth and the life appeared to evaporate from her. She collapsed in a heap and convulsed before going still.

Magnus dropped his sword and dirk and sprinted to Deirdre. He pulled her into his arms and tucked her head under his chin. Lifting her off her feet, he walked them through the portcullis until they could no longer see the bailey.

Placing her back on the ground, Magnus dropped to his knees in supplication as his arms wound around her hips and his head rested on her belly. Deirdre ran her hands through Magnus's hair as she stared at a man who was a replica of him and then at Ceit Comyn.

"Magnus, I'm well. Please get up. I canna hug ye like this." When he did not respond, she tugged on his hair.

Rather than stand, he pulled her down to his lap and encircled her in his arms. He buried his head into the crook of her neck, and Deirdre felt dampness trickle along her collarbone. Magnus did not speak instead rocking them slightly. Deirdre ran her hand over his back but felt the bandages. She pulled the collar of his leine away from his neck and gasped to see the bandages dotted with fresh blood in some places.

"Magnus?"

He still did not answer. Rather, his embrace tightened almost painfully.

"Magnus? What is it? Ye're scaring me." At the tremble in her voice, Magnus gave in and lifted his head.

His eyes were dry, but Deirdre was sure she detected moisture in the corners.

"Are ye—did they—are ye still—were ye?" Magnus shuddered each incomplete phrase as his hand rested on her middle.

"Elizabeth told ye aboot last time ma parents kenned we coupled."

Magnus nodded his head. Deirdre blew out a puff of air that made one of her curls bounce off her forehead.

"I wish she hadnae done that. I wanted to spare ye that story but seeing Ceit means Beth must have been frightened enough to reveal it." She bent her head and rubbed her nose to his. "Nay one gave me a tincture of any kind. I dinna ken if I'm carrying. I told Hay what happened the last time and warned him that my death would be vera inconvenient for him. He relented and agreed to wait to see if I was pregnant before he would touch me. I reminded him that if he rushed and there was a bairn, he would never ken if yer bairn would inherit all he had."

"He didna—" Once again, Magnus could not finish his thought.

"Nay. He didnae poison me nor did he molest me." Deirdre saw no need to tell Magnus of Hay fondling her. The man was already dead, and Magnus battled enough guilt. "Mo fhuamhaire, can we go home now?"

Magnus pulled back and cupped her face in his hands. They melded together as their mouth opened to one another. Their tongues battled much as Magnus just had but with a much more satisfying purpose. Magnus swept his tongue throughout her warm cavern and slid it against hers. Deidre responded by sucking on his tongue until his cock ached for release.

"Tonight," Deirdre whispered as he feathered kisses along her cheek to her jaw and down to her shoulder. She tilted her head to grant him more access as her fingers scrunched the material of his leine into her palm.

"Tonight," he breathed. "I am home." He covered her mouth with his once more.

Chapter Twenty-Four

hey arrived back at the royal court after two hard days of travel. They rode at a slower pace even though they were all eager to put distance between them and Crichton. Deirdre had not understood why Ceit traveled with the men until the first evening, and Magnus removed his leine. Ceit unwrapped his bandages and insisted that he allow the cool night air onto his broken skin. Deirdre felt a rage unlike any she had known before surge from her toes to her scalp. She had to walk away from the fire and took a moment to collect herself. Magnus followed her, and they stood in silence staring at one another before they reached for each other. They found solace in each other's arms, both pouring out their guilt and remorse silently. They held each other until they knew Ceit and Tavish would begin to wonder. They returned to camp holding hands. Little was said for the rest of the night beside a small argument between Ceit and Tavish about the placement of their bedrolls. Magnus and Deirdre were too occupied with each other to pay attention.

Their arrival was heralded, and Deirdre saw her parents in the bailey as they crossed under the portcullis. She was riding in front of Magnus, and his arms cinched tighter as he felt her go rigid.

"Ye dinna owe them aught anymore. If ye dinna want to speak to them, ye dinna have to. I willna allow them to badger ye any longer. Ye arenae theirs to control. Ye are mine to protect."

Deirdre nodded and patted the forearm that held her in place.

"Daughter," Lady Fraser's expression was anything but welcoming. She looked past Deirdre to Magnus. Scorn and distaste oozed from her gaze. She appeared as if she looked down her nose at Magnus while she looked up to see them.

"Mother."

"Dee, what're you doing back here? With him? Again?" Laird Fraser's halting speech belied his anxiety. He looked up to Magnus and shot him a look of warning.

"Enough, Father. I amnae here to be a part of yer political machinations."

Magnus pulled *Sealgair* to a halt and assisted Deirdre to the ground. He pressed her behind him and placed his hands on the hilts of his dirks. The message louder than if he had screamed his warning. He glared at the older couple, daring them to challenge him.

Lady Fraser huffed and turned towards the castle's entrance.

"We cannot stay out here all day. People will talk."

Deirdre rolled her eyes before pressing her hands to Magnus's hips, nudging him forward. He looked back at her and shook his head. He crossed his arms and stood like an immovable oak tree.

"Let's get it over with, aye?"

Deirdre feared for a moment that Magnus would be awkward, but he relented when he saw wariness enter her eyes.

"Vera well." He took her hand and walked with her to the Great Hall. Tavish and Ceit followed close behind.

They passed through the doorway when a squeal of excitement greeted them. Elizabeth launched herself at Deirdre and they embraced.

"I've been so afraid for you. I could not stop your parents even if I had tried. I'm so sorry."

"Wheest, Beth," it felt good to use the pet name again after so much time holding herself in reserve. "I ken it must have been ye who told Magnus what happened all those years ago and that ye were desperate to protect me now. Thank ye for the clean clothes. I kenned ye thought of that."

"What is this talk of protection and what incident all those years ago," the queen had silently entered the gathering hall, and all conversation halted at her question.

While Beth's excitement raised a few brows within the crowded chamber, the queen's question brought all eyes to the disheveled travelers and Deirdre's family.

"Lady Deirdre, perhaps you care to answer my question?"

I dinna care to at all but I dinna have much choice, now do I?

Deirdre inhaled, but before she could reply, her mother spoke up.

"Your Majesty, the ladies refer to Deirdre's previous indiscretion and the righteous wrath it brought upon her."

Elizabeth looked at her aunt before scanning the room for her own parents. She spied them as they gave her a look of warning. She chose to ignore them.

"That is not the entire truth. It barely touches the truth."

There were numerous gasps, and whispers buzzed about like a shaken hive of angry Hornets.

"Pray tell, Lady Elizabeth. That is quite an accusation."

"Your Majesty, it is not an accusation when it is the truth. By now, everyone has heard the tale of Magnus's and Deirdre's handfast those many years ago. What most do not know is that her parents lied, telling her that Magnus was unfaithful before she even left. When they brought her here, Lady Fraser forced Deirdre to take a tincture to end a pregnancy my aunt feared would be the result of Deidre's night with Magnus. You may recall how poorly Dee was shortly after she arrived but before anyone could meet her. Her mother poisoned her, and Dee nearly bled to death over a babe that never existed."

"Sire," Laird Fraser interjected as he directed his plea to the monarch who sat mute through this all. "That is a gross exaggeration of the events. Lady Maeve did not poison our daughter. It was an unfortunate and unpredictable side effect."

The king ignored the Fraser and signaled for Elizabeth to continue, but she shook her head. She looked to Deirdre who stepped forward. Magnus stood cupping her shoulders, a pillar of support that kept her upright and from fleeing.

"Your Majesties, once I was recovered, ma parents engineered ma placement into the queen's household. Ye may recall I was always the first volunteer to travel with the queen. I have since learned this was done so Magnus could not find me. He was never informed that I became a lady-in-waiting." She paused to collect herself. "Ma husband has seven years of unopened, returned missives he sent me and that I was denied access to."

"She could not be allowed to conspire against her own best interests. The lad took advantage of her and manipulated her into allowing him to bed her. Someone had to guide her and rein in her impetuousness."

"The only manipulators were ye," Deirdre said quietly before looking over at her parents. "Ye swore that he forsook me. Ye said his infidelity was his repudiation of me. He has never once been unfaithful. Nae once in half a score of years. Aye," she swept her glance around the room, "ma husband made his first vow of fidelity to me ten summers ago when he asked me to consider him. When I accepted, he pledged to be with nae one else. He held to that promise until we handfasted and consummated our union. He made the same pledge again as he spoke his vows. He kept his oath. He cared for me more from a distance than ye ever did and ye were with me. Ye even had ma sisters lie and pin me to the chair as ye tried to kill any life that grew within. Count yerself lucky that there hadnae been a bairn or I would have named ye murderers years ago."

Deirdre could not go on. Her anger and bitterness consumed her. She spun around and gripped Magnus as her fury caused her to tremble. He enveloped her in his embrace, sheltering her from the memories and horrors of the past.

"Laird and Lady Fraser wanted whatever stewardship it was they would receive if Deirdre married Hay. They kenned of the mon's mistreatment and threats to her, but they refused to reconsider a marriage. They pushed her towards a man who openly threatened to kill her and tried to force her on more than one occasion. What's more, they locked her in a chamber more than once, most recently in a storage one, and took her against her will this last time with a sack over her head."

The king's cold eyes bore into the Frasers as he looked between husband and wife.

"Did this all occur as has been told here? And before you answer, consider that you have already lost your position here at court, would you also like to lose your position within your clan? I can arrange both."

"Your Grace, the events occurred as stated but not as they were described."

"And what exactly does that mean? Did Lady Deirdre receive a tincture that nearly killed her after she refused it? Did you refuse to allow her contact with her husband within the year and day of their handfast? Did you intercept his missives and send them back? Did you lie to her and swear her husband was unfaithful and repudiated her? Did you confine her to her chambers? Did you forcefully remove her from this court with a hood to keep her from knowing her captors or location? Did you turn her over to a man who molested and threatened her?" The king's voice rose with each question and was a bellow by the time he finished his interrogation.

Laird and Lady Fraser could only stand in place. Laird Fraser resigned to his downfall, while Lady Fraser remained proud and defiant.

"And what was wrong with my godson that he was not fit to wed your daughter?"

"Your godson?" Lady Fraser spluttered.

"Och aye, did ye nae ken? All the Sinclair bairns are ma godchildren, or did ye forget I'm one of those bluidy savages, barbaric heathens, what else did ye call us Maeve? Ye forget yerself, lass. Ye're Highlanders, too."

The king stressed the burr he hid at court. His scorn dripped from his voice as he looked with contempt at Lady Fraser.

"Did you believe the Sinclairs were not good enough for you? Was Magnus not considered an advantageous enough match? Would he have been if you knew his connections to me were closer than yours?"

Laird and Lady Fraser had the good graces to remain silent, but one person no longer cared to do the same.

"Maeve, dinna leave aught out." Hamish stepped forward. He tilted his head to the side and raised both eyebrows in invitation for her to speak for herself. She turned her nose up at him.

"Vera well. Dinna say I didna give ye yer chance to say yer piece." He looked at the king and queen. "Mayhap ye remember the first time I visited the court after becoming a laird. I was introduced to a young Lady Maeve Ross who was a lady-in-waiting to the king's mother. She ignored me the first eve even though we partnered together for several sets during the dancing. She took an interest, however, when she learned I was a Sutherland. She had a page carry a message to me saying that ma brother by marriage, Liam Sinclair, had arrived and was looking for me. When I went to the appointed meeting place, Liam wasna there, but she was. Conveniently,

213

a friend of hers walked in to find us alone in a chamber together. Nevermind we were at opposite ends of the room and hadnae said a word to one another. She tried to trap me into marriage, but Fraser wanted her for his own clan's alliance, and he seemed to hold a tendre for her," Hamish sounded puzzled by his last comment, "so Donald took her off ma hands." He finished with a nod in Laird Fraser's direction and a grateful smile.

Magnus was sure Lady Fraser bared her teeth at his uncle.

"Lady Fraser, you have a held a grudge for a score and half summers? But how does that affect Magnus? He was not even born yet."

"Her hatred of me and her perception of a slight extended to all Sutherlands, and since ma sister, Kyla, was married to the Sinclair, it extended to them too."

The king sat back in his chair and looked to his wife who had fallen silent as the great tale of woe unraveled before them. She looked out at the crowd that was now blatantly staring and listening as each salacious detail was exposed. She looked back at her husband and nodded.

"Very well," the king smiled to his wife and then turned his attention back to the assembled mass, "as things stand now, Fraser, you will return any of the bride price paid to you by the Sinclairs. I shall return half of the price paid to the court. Donald and Maeve, you will retire to your land and make an appearance only when summoned. Deirdre and Magnus, you have our sincerest apologies for the blind role the queen and I played in keeping you both apart. We did not realize the significance of Deirdre's requests when she asked all those years ago to return to you. We cannot give you back the years you lost, but we offer you our blessing along with God's grace that you may find happiness in your marriage just as your parents did, Magnus. You have our best wishes."

Deirdre looked up from Magnus's chest.

"It's over? Really?" she whispered.

"Aye. Let us retire, and we can leave before first light."

Magnus led Deirdre from the chamber followed by Elizabeth, Hamish, Tavish, and Ceit. When they arrived at Deirdre's chamber, she paused before the door.

"I dinna want to go back in there," she shared with Magnus.

Elizabeth stepped forward.

"Dee, I'll arrange for everything to be packed and readied for your departure tomorrow. Don't think twice about it. It will be taken care of."

Deirdre pulled her cousin in for a hug.

"Thank ye, Beth. Ye are the only one who made this place bearable."

"You're more like a sister than a cousin. It pleased me to have you here too."

"What will you do now that you spoke out against your family?"

"I do not know, to be honest, but it did not seem to displease the queen, so I should retain my position. As long as I have that, there is little they can do after the scene your parents made. Their disgrace may be my protection."

They hugged again before Elizabeth slipped into Deirdre's old chamber to begin the process of removing her cousin's belongings.

Deirdre and Magnus turned to walk to his chamber but found Tavish and Ceit in another heated argument.

"Tav, we are going to ma chamber. Our chamber. We ride out at first light. Be ready."

Tavish turned to listen to his brother, but when he looked back to Ceit when Magnus finished speaking, he saw the train of her kirtle swish around a corner. He scowled and shook his head.

"I amnae leaving yet. Da sent me to resolve another matter, and it isnae taken care of."

"Ye didna tell me aught of this." Magnus crossed his arms and gave his brother a hard look. "What matter is that?"

"The matter of ma betrothal." Tavish crossed his arms and returned his brother's stare.

"Betrothal?"

"Aye, and ma bonnie bride has just disappeared from me, again, after giving me a good ear chewing."

Magnus took in his usually charming brother's expression that was a mixture of disgust, longing, pride, and confusion. He could not contain his laughter. He wrapped his arm around Deirdre and led her to their chamber as his brother stalked away.

Chapter Twenty-Five

The pink hues of dawn were stretching across the horizon as Magnus kissed his wife awake. Their first full night together in a chamber of their own was spent making love off and on until they were both too spent to do more than cuddle against each other.

"Bhean, ye canna be a slugabed this morn. We must be on our way. We have a long journey ahead of us." He kissed her bare shoulder as he held her tucked against his front. She shifted her hips back and pressed her bottom against his prodding cock.

"I believe we are both up, an duine aice," Deirdre chuckled as she glanced over her shoulder. "I do like hearing you call me wife. I dinna think I will ever tire of that."

Magnus leaned in to nip her earlobe.

"And ye can call me husband all that ye want for I shall always answer."

Magnus pressed his hips forward again and was about to begin another round of lovemaking when a knock came at their door. Magnus groaned.

"What now," he muttered before calling out, "Go away."

Deirdre giggled as she climbed from the bed. Magnus reached for her but she danced away. His hand hit her now vacant spot then he rolled onto his stomach before pounding his pillow.

"So aggrieved, mo fhuamhaire," she laughed as she pulled her chemise on and threw Magnus's leine over it, "spoiled is more like it."

"Well I should be, mo eun beag," he grumbled playfully. She looked back and saw him propped up on one elbow.

Will I ever grow tired of looking at him? Will he ever seem less braw? I dinna think so. I will wake to that face, that body for the rest of ma life, and I canna think of aught I want more.

Magnus watched as his wife padded barefoot to the door and opened it a crack. Her hair was a golden riot of curls that fell down her back. He could see the shape of her backside through the fabric of his shirt.

There is something incredibly arousing aboot seeing her in ma leine. She doesnae even ken how beautiful she is. I am far luckier than I should be. I will wake to this sight for the rest of ma life.

Magnus rose from the bed and wrapped the sheet he pulled from the bed around his trim waist. A troop of servants brought in trays of food. An older woman oversaw the delivery before announcing that Deirdre's chests would be loaded onto a wagon that would follow behind once they departed.

Magnus sighed. It would seem that the feast he intended to indulge in would not happen. They ate and stuffed the extra packages of food into their saddlebags.

Deirdre squeaked when she saw Freya waiting for her in the stable yard. She turned to Magnus and threw her arms around his waist.

"Did ye do this?"

He nodded.

"I love ye!" She tugged his leine until he bent over far enough for her to kiss him.

He lifted her into the saddle.

"Aye, before ye even ask. I did have that bluidy sidesaddle thrown out. This is yer saddle, and ye shall ride properly from now on."

This time it was Deirdre who leaned over for a kiss. Magnus mounted *Sealgair*, and they rode out without looking back.

The journey lasted ten long days, but this time there was no fear of pursuit or discovery. They spent some nights under the stars, but they spent most tucked away warmly and safely in an inn. They stopped when they felt like it, often taking a dip in a stream or small loch. These rest stops stretched longer than necessary for their horses to eat and drink. The couple made the most of their time alone together. They knew privacy would be at a premium once they arrived at Dunbeath with a large clan and a full keep now with three of the four brothers married, and Mairghread and her family often visited.

"This was a much better journey than the last one. I dinna worry that ye will keel over and die on me either from a wound or breaking yer neck falling from yer wee beastie."

"Dinna speak that way aboot him. Ye will embarrass him in front of Freya. I dinna think he ever forgot her either."

"Keep yer randy stallion away from ma innocent mare." Deirdre's coy smile had Magnus chuckling.

"That isnae what ye've been saying this last sennight and a half. I'm pretty sure I've heard ye ask to be closer and for more." He grabbed her horse's bridle as he slowed them for a kiss.

"Losh! Is that ye Magnus?" Magnus pulled away to see his brothers riding towards him. Callum raised his arm and waved.

"Welcome home, Deir," Magnus grumbled. He was not ready to share his wife.

"Crivvens! Is that Deirdre Fraser?" Alex asked as they pulled their horses to a stop in front of Magnus and Deirdre.

"Deirdre Sinclair," Deirdre smiled.

Callum and Alex exchanged a look before grinning wildly at their brother.

"I think there is a tale here, and Siùsan will skelp me if I hear it before her."

"Ye think Brighde would be any more forgiving?"

"Hello?" Magnus grumbled again.

"Och aye, a hello to ye too, Magnus," Callum tossed over his shoulder. "Tell us, lass, did ye really shackle yerself to this giant?"

Deirdre looked at Magnus with a grin. She winked as she mouthed, "mo fhuamhaire."

They rode into the bailey with a clatter of hooves. Two women both round with child, one appearing ready to deliver at any moment, stepped from the garden. Alexander and Callum dismounted and walked to the women. Callum pulled the one with the larger belly in for a kiss as he rubbed it. Alex embraced the other woman and kissed her as he rubbed the small of her back.

"Ma braw brothers and their wee wives," Magnus said sarcastically. He dismounted and walked around to Deirdre. He plucked her from the saddle and held her as she wrapped her arms around his neck.

"Ye ken ye arenae any better."

"I amnae anywhere as bad as they are."

Deirdre looked over her shoulder at the two happy couples.

"We shall see what jig ye are dancing in aboot seven and a half moons."

Magnus stared at her as she wiggled. He was so stunned that he let her slither to the ground. She took his hand and tugged him after her.

"Magnus," boomed a loud voice that had Deirdre stopping midstep.

She had not seen Laird Sinclair in as many years as she had not seen Magnus. She looked at the three brothers and then their father. The resemblance was remarkable. She noted that Tavish truly did mirror their father the most with the same build, but the Sinclair men were clearly hewn from the same tree.

"Deirdre Fraser? Is that ye, lass?"

This time Magnus made the correction.

"Deirdre Sinclair."

Liam Sinclair stared at his son before smiling warmly at his newest daughter by marriage.

"I think there is much to be shared. Come inside."

The family gathered around one of the large fires as Hagatha, the housekeeper, bustled about bringing food and drinks from the kitchens.

Each husband sat and pulled his wife into his lap. Deirdre welcomed the comfort of being able to claim her husband and the sense of belonging that came from the other couples' displays of affection.

"Ye finally got yer wife back?" Alex asked.

"Finally?" Laird Sinclair asked. He had an uneasy feeling that there was something his children all knew and that he might not like discovering.

"Thank ye, Alex. If ye dinna mind, I'll tell ma own tale." Magnus thumped his brother on the shoulder but yanked his hand back when Alex scowled and held his wife tighter.

"Da, there is much to tell ye, but for now, I will tell ye the history that the others ken, but ye dinna." Magnus waited for his father. When the older man nodded, he continued. "I dinna ken if ye remember ma friendship with Deirdre. We corresponded for three summers, and I courted her during that time. The year the MacLeods hosted the games, Deirdre and I handfasted."

Laird Sinclair sat forward in his chair and looked between Magnus and Deirdre. She had retreated and looked nervously at the renowned warrior.

"Magnus, a moment," he held his hand out and looked at Deirdre, "lass, I believe I already ken where this story is going. Yer parents havenae been fond of us for some time, and I believe I understand why now. Ken this, ye arenae yer parents. Whatever has transpired to bring ye here doesnae matter to me as long as ye came by choice and both ye and Magnus are happy."

Deirdre caught herself staring open-mouthed at her father by marriage. She snapped her mouth shut and nodded.

"Lass, ye are family now. Ken that ye are welcome here." Laird Sinclair leaned back in his chair and nodded for Magnus to continue.

Magnus and Deirdre shared their story from start to finish as the afternoon rolled into evening and supper was served.

"Magnus, tell me, lad, do yer brothers and sister already ken this tale?"

Magnus looked sheepishly at his father and nodded.

"Why did ye nae tell me sooner? Why nae come to me while we were still at the MacLeods?"

"I wasna sure ye would support me," Magnus could barely speak louder than a whisper. He felt foolish now as an adult, but at the time, when he was only just becoming a man, he had not been so confident.

"Ah son, I will always support ye. I wish I made that clearer when ye were younger. I wish I could have saved ye both the heartache." Laird Sinclair shook his head.

Deirdre reached past Magnus and covered the Sinclair's hand with hers.

"We ken now. That is what matters. I ken I am home now."

The meal progressed with more cheerful conversation and laughter.

"Da, what's this aboot Tavish and a betrothal?"

Laird Sinclair smiled enigmatically. Deirdre liked the way that the lines creased around his eyes and mouth when he laughed. She felt more at home and a greater sense of belonging than she ever had at court or with the Frasers. She sat back and listened to the conversation flow around her. When she could no longer hide her yawns, Magnus excused them from the table. He scooped her into his arms and carried her to their chamber.

He pressed the door open and then kicked it shut.

"Welcome home, mo eun beag."

"Aboot bluidy time, mo fhuamhaire."

They looked at one another and then burst into laughter. They were in silent agreement that laughter was better than tears.

Epilogue

Seven months later

eirdre was going to commit bloody murder if her husband did not stop hovering. She swatted at him as she tried to hang the dried herbs over the large table in the croft's center. She nearly had it when enormous hands wrapped around her expanded midsection and lifted her from the table upon which she stood.

"Magnus put me down."

"Down is exactly where I am planning to put ye. And it ye werenae carrying our bairn, I would turn ye over ma knee for giving me such a fright."

"If I wasna carrying a bairn, ye wouldnae be carrying on like a bodach."

"I amnae a cantankerous auld mon!"

"And I amnae a wean in need of a scolding."

Husband and wife squared off against each other as they both stood like Odin. Except Magnus could not stay angry with his bonnie little wife whose arms rested on the crest of her rounded belly. He dropped his arms and pulled her to stand between his legs.

"Ye worry me, Deir. I dinna want aught to happen to ye. I dinna ken what I would do without ye or our bairn."

He reached between them to place his hand on her belly. When it jumped beneath his hand, his smile practically melted Deirdre into a puddle on the floor of their croft. She unfolded her arms and placed her hands over his heart.

"I ken, but Magnus, women have been having bairns since time began and life hasnae come to a screeching halt each time."

"Other women may have, but ye havenae. And I dinna give a fig aboot anyone else's wife or bairns. I care aboot ye and our bairn."

Deirdre sighed. Her husband's overbearing concern was suffocating at times, but she knew it came from love and not control. She leaned into his embrace and rested

221

her head over his heart. He rubbed his hands over the small of her back and eased the knots from between her shoulder blades. He drew her into the small bedroom of the croft they shared. They only stayed in the keep for three moons after they arrived home. It rapidly began to feel too snug with some many people and a constantly expanding family. The newlyweds requested their own croft and had enjoyed their privacy for nearly four moons. They knew one day it would come to an end, but they were in no rush for that.

Magnus slowly undressed his wife, marveling in the constant new discoveries of how her body changed with pregnancy. Deirdre unpinned his plaid and helped him draw his leine over his head. Magnus led her to the bed and helped her onto it. She turned and kneeled waiting for him to join her after shucking off his boots and stockings.

They kneeled facing one another, just as they had so many years before in what they considered their cave, and their hands roamed over one another's body. This time, it was not discovery and exploration as they came together. It was familiarity and belonging. It was the fulfillment of pledges made and kept.

"I love ye, eun beag."

"I love ye, mo fhuamhaire."

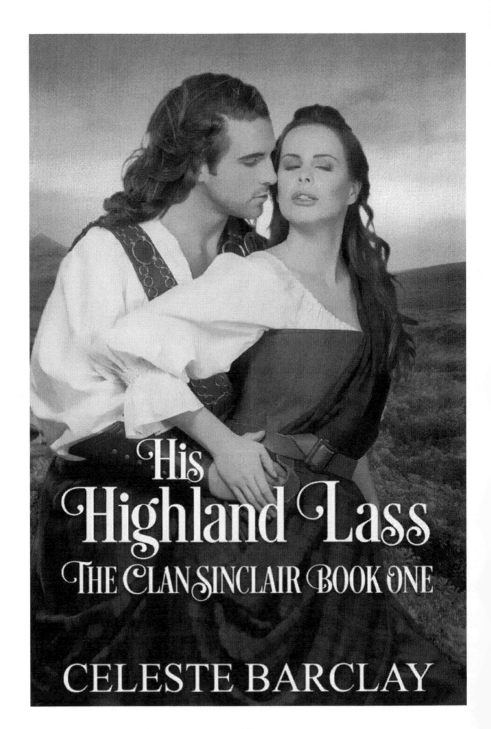

His
Highland Lass
THE CLAN SINCLAIR BOOK ONE

CELESTE BARCLAY

His Highland Lass
The Clan Sinclair, Book 1

An undeniable love... an unexpected match...

Faced with a feud with the Sinclairs that is growing deadly, Laird Tristan Mackay is bound by duty to his clan to make peace with the enemy. Tristan arranges a marriage for his stepbrother, Sir Alan, but never imagines that he would meet the woman he longs to marry. When things sour quickly between Tristan's stepbrother and Lady Mairghread Sinclair, Tristan is determined to make her his. A choice that promises to change his life forever.

Raised with four older warriors for brothers and as the only daughter of the Sinclair laird, Mairghread is independent resourceful, and loyal to her family. When her father arranges a marriage to a man she has never met for the sake and safety of her clan, Mairghread tries to accept her fate. Mairghread is betrothed to one man but it is the dark, handsome, and provocative laird who catches her eye. Arranged to marry Sir Alan, Mairghread finds herself drawn to Laird Tristan Mackay. After meeting her intended, Mairghread knows she cannot go through with the marriage, but she must find a way to end the feud that is tearing the two clans apart.

When the wedding is called off by Mairghread's father, Tristan and Mairghread see an opportunity to be together. Neither of them imagined that they would find the passion that grows between them. However, a spurned mistress and a jilted suitor stand between Tristan and Mairghread's happiness. Tristan and Mairghread must fight for the love they have found with one another.

Destined for another...

Mairghread Sinclair is not prepared for the danger that awaits her while visiting the Mackay clan. She must use her wits to keep herself alive when danger pulls her away from the man she loves.

Fated to be together...

Laird Tristan Mackay was not looking for a wife, but could Lady Mairghread Sinclair be the one to open his heart and bring peace to their clans, or will their passion tear the two clans apart?

Available purchase or download on Amazon

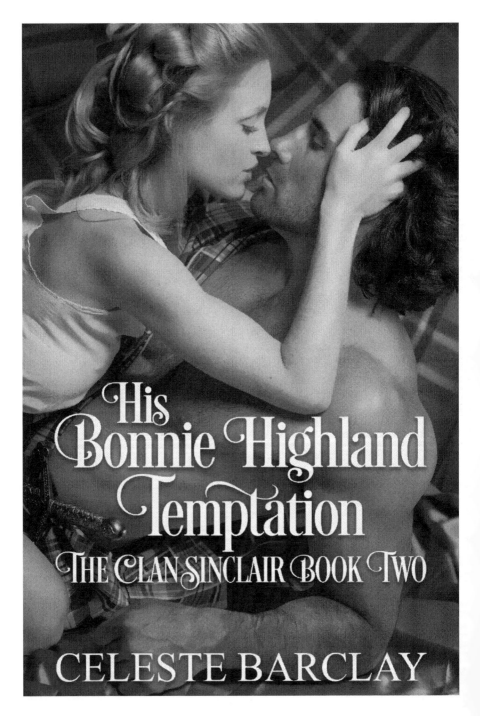

His
Bonnie Highland
Temptation
THE CLAN SINCLAIR BOOK TWO

CELESTE BARCLAY

His Bonnie Highland Temptation
The Clan Sinclair Book 2

Unwanted and unloved...

Siùsan Mackenzie has spent a lifetime feeling unwanted and unloved after her mother dies in childbirth and her father abandons her for a new wife and new family. Forced to start her life in her clan's village and then brought to the castle as no more than a servant, Siùsan longs for the chance to escape her clan and the hurt of being ignored. When her father, the Mackenzie chief, unexpectedly announces her betrothal, Siùsan is filled with fear that her father is sending her off to an ogre who will treat her no better or possibly even worse. When she discovers who her intended is, she seizes the chance to leave behind those who sought to punish her and manipulate her.

Could Siùsan's father finally have done right by her? Will Siùsan find happiness in her new home, or is her future only to repeat her past?

Unaware and unready...

Callum Sinclair, the heir to Clan Sinclair, knows that he will one day have to marry to carry on his clan's legacy. He just did not know that his bride-to-be would arrive less than a week after his father announced the betrothal. Enjoying the company of women has never been a struggle for Callum, but as are all the men of Clan Sinclair, he is committed to being a faithful husband. When Siùsan arrives, Callum is unprepared for the gift his father has given him in his soon-to-be wife. Callum is eager to get to know his fiery haired bride who barely comes up to his chest, and Siùsan is tempted by Callum's whisky brown eyes and gentle nature.

But if only it were that easy.

A tangled web of jealousy and deceit is woven when members of Siùsan's clan join forces with outsiders to keep them apart.

Will Callum be able to reach Siùsan to prove to her that she will never be unwanted or unloved again? Can Siùsan put her trust in a man she desires but barely knows?

Available purchase and download on Amazon

His
Highland Prize
THE CLAN SINCLAIR BOOK THREE

CELESTE BARCLAY

His Highland Prize
The Clan Sinclair Book 3

Lost and pursued, searching for protection...

When Brighde Kerr collapses in his arms at Castle Dunbeath in the middle of the night during a Highland thunderstorm, Alexander Sinclair does not hesitate to bring her inside to receive medical care and shelter. Hiding secrets that she is sure will only bring danger to the Sinclairs if revealed, Brighde struggles against her growing attraction and affection for Alex. She attempts to keep her identity a secret, but it does not take long before Brighde realizes that Alex could be the one person to save her.

Steadfast and determined, willing to protect...

Alex dedicates himself to nursing this mystery woman back to health and offers her the security of the Sinclair Clan. Alex's ongoing support and determination to protect Brighde fuels their growing passion but often puts them at odds when Brighde is not convinced they have a future together.

Both in need of love...

When the source of Brighde's fears shows up at their gates, Alex proves that he will not give up on Brighde no matter the risks or consequences. Now can she accept that Alex's pledge for protection or will she keep fighting the inevitable?

Available purchase and download on Amazon

Thank you for reading
His Highland Pledge

Celeste Barclay, a nom de plume, lives near the Southern California coast with her husband and sons. Growing up in the Midwest, Celeste enjoyed spending as much time in and on the water as she could. Now she lives near the beach. She's an avid swimmer, a hopeful future surfer, and a former rower. When she's not writing, she's working or being a mom.

Visit Celeste's website, www.celestebarclay.com, for regular updates on works in progress, new releases, and her blog where she features posts about her experiences as an author and recommendations of her favorite reads.

Are you an author who would like to guest blog or be featured in her recommendations? Visit her website for an opportunity to share your insights and experiences.

Have you read *Their Highland Beginning, The Clan Sinclair Prequel*? Learn how the saga begins! This FREE novella is available to all new subscribers to Celeste's monthly newsletter. Subscribe on her website.

www.celestebarclay.com

Made in the USA
Middletown, DE
28 February 2019